"KEITH, YOU MUST HELP ME...."

Mona slid into the tender comfort of his arms, and they clung together for wordless moments. It had been too long—much too long!

"We have to talk," she pleaded.

"Your 'talk' usually means another problem." His voice was harsh with frustration. "What is it this time?"

"The same one—me against my family, and I could use some moral support. You keep telling me to resolve things quickly so we can be together. How do I do it? I feel so alone."

Keith's eyes softened, but he looked tired...so tired. "There is another delay—isn't there, my love?"

"Y-yes," she admitted miserably. And as he kissed her with an aching passion, she feared it would soon be too late for them....

AND NOW…

SUPERROMANCES

Worldwide Library is proud to present a
sensational new series of modern love stories –
SUPERROMANCES

Written by masters of the genre, these longer,
sensuous and dramatic novels are truly in keeping
with today's changing life-styles. Full of intriguing
conflicts, the heartaches and delights of true love,
SUPERROMANCES are absorbing stories –
satisfying and sophisticated reading that lovers
of romance fiction have long been waiting for.

SUPERROMANCES
Contemporary love stories for the woman of today!

BARBARA KAYE

A HEART DIVIDED

A SUPERROMANCE FROM
WORLDWIDE
TORONTO · NEW YORK · LOS ANGELES · LONDON

Published January 1983

First printing November 1982

ISBN 0-373-70046-6

Printed in Canada

CHAPTER ONE

CANDLES FLICKERED, silver shone, crystal gleamed and talk flowed around the dinner table. The demolished remains of a leg of lamb rested on a platter in the center of the table. Goblets were refilled with burgundy liquid, and a tray of cheese and fruit was passed. Dinners at the Lowery home were always spectacular, and tonight's had been no exception. Kitty Lowery, mistress of the Highland Park mansion, considered it her appointed duty in life to live with style and elegance, and this was reflected in the superb cuisine, the faultless table setting and the serene charm of the dining room.

Mona Lowery watched over the rim of her wineglass as Keith Garrett leaned forward to speak to her sister, Claire. Keith was becoming a more and more familiar sight around the Lowerys' house, the latest in a long procession of the beauteous Claire's hopeful suitors.

Tonight all Mona's thoughts were centered on Keith. Poor man. So tall and darkly handsome, so charming, so completely masculine. By far the best of the lot, Mona thought. But she was afraid he was destined for the same fate as the others. Claire would toy with him until she tired of him, then would set about finding a new victim. She never had to wait long or look far for her next conquest. There were always a few hopefuls waiting in the wings.

Mona wondered for perhaps the hundredth time just what there was about Claire, just what that elusive mysterious quality was that made all men from seventeen to seventy fall madly in love with her. Beauty, of course, but surely there was more to it than that. Was it that fluttery clinging-vine pose, that whispery little-girl voice? Men were drawn to her like a moth to a flame, and she was such a fake!

Mona watched as Claire wove her magic spell around Keith Garrett, amazed that such a man would fall for all that feminine foolishness. Keith was an urbane, intelligent, good-looking, successful man; one would think he would have seen through Claire's false facade long ago. Yet he seemed as crazy about her as all the rest.

Mona sighed and stared at her own reflection in the mirror behind her mother's immaculately coiffed head. She was constantly being compared with Claire, and she thought this unfair. Although she and her sister shared certain family characteristics—dark hair, enormous dark eyes and flawless skin—the resemblance was not a remarkable one.

Mona's eyes were open and candid and inquisitive, while Claire's were secretive and seductive. Furthermore, Mona was taller and leggier than her petite sister, and her sleek hair fell to her shoulders in a cascade of lustrous dark silk. Claire, on the other hand, was a slave to Jesse's Hair Designs, and her hair was forever being cut and permed and styled to conform to whatever latest fad captured her fancy. Mona thought the short curly style Claire now wore was the most sensible and flattering yet. In all truth, she suspected Claire could shave her head and still look smashing.

Claire and "beauty" seemed to be synonymous, whereas when people commented on Mona's good looks they often used the word "arresting." She had strong features that few people ever forgot, while Claire's delicate bone structure made her seem vulnerable and brought out protective instincts in others.

And no two women could have been more dissimilar in temperament and personality. Claire was totally preoccupied with herself and the events and people that affected her directly. She had read nothing more intellectually stimulating than fashion magazines since leaving school, and her conversation was centered on her own activities and those of her small select social circle.

Mona, on the other hand, was vastly curious about everything and everyone. In school she had excelled both academically and socially. She was well-read and erudite and in many ways seemed far older than Claire, who was four years her senior.

Once Mona had overheard a conversation between her parents. She never had forgotten it. "Claire certainly got the beauty," her father had said, "but Mona got the brains and talent."

How well Mona remembered what her immediate reaction had been: *to hell with brains and talent!* She had been sixteen at the time and convinced that beauty was everything. She no longer felt that way, having since met some very beautiful but very vapid women, but in those young blossoming years she had thought her father might as well have said she had an incurable disease. For a time after that she had tried concealing her intellect behind a flippant exterior and had even gone so far as to try imitating Claire. But she felt foolish, and all that playacting was exhausting, so she quickly reverted to being herself, consoled by the hope that someday some perfectly splendid young man would come along who would see her for what she really was, would love her brains and talent, would appreciate her unique looks, as most men now did so easily with Claire.

Now Claire was laughing—a light, lovely, lilting laugh. When Mona wasn't preoccupied—despite her good intentions—with being jealous of her sister, she admitted there was a special enchantment about Claire. The older woman could be as hard and cold as ice on occasion, but she was at her beguiling best when in the company of a handsome man. Tonight she was turning on the charm full force, and adoration shone clearly from Keith's granite-gray eyes.

Such hungry eyes, Mona thought. *He's already in love with her, and I feel sorry for him.* Sorry for him? With his looks and money? *Yes, sorry for him because he could have half the women in Dallas and he wants the one he won't get. Claire is a fool, an imbecile! There aren't men like Keith Garrett standing on every street corner. Claire is such an idiot, and worse than that she's cruel and heartless. She enjoys playing with human feelings. Why don't men ever see that in her? Why do they only see that incredible beauty and follow like lambs to the slaughter?*

Oh, if I looked like Claire. . . .

Kitty Lowery was speaking. "We did so want Mona to come to Palm Springs with us this summer but she enrolled in summer school without telling anyone of her plans. All the child does is study. Work, work and no play."

Now all eyes traveled to Mona, who looked startled at the mention of her name. "Oh. . . well, it just seemed such a waste of time to laze around Palm Springs all summer when I could be accomplishing so much here. I'm only months away from my degree and I'm getting anxious. By going to summer school I can finish up in January instead of next June. Madeline Porter told me she wants me to redecorate her town house as soon as I've graduated, and Madeline knows everyone in Dallas. If she's pleased with my work she'll tell others. That should get me started.''

''Just what exactly are your plans after graduation, Mona?'' Keith inquired, flashing his charming smile.

It occurred to Mona that he had the whitest teeth she had ever seen. He was the only one of Claire's young men who had shown the slightest interest in anything Mona said or did. Keith had never been anything but pleasant and kind to her, and he expressed a real interest in her dream of becoming an interior decorator. Mona often wondered if perhaps he was merely trying to ingratiate himself into her favor, thinking she had some influence with her sister. If so, he was badly mistaken. She and Claire couldn't have had less in common if they had been born on different planets.

''I have my eye on a little shop dad has graciously consented to buy for me,'' Mona said, and her twinkling eyes met her father's. Benjamin Lowery was a man of the old school; he honestly saw no reason for a woman to ''do'' anything—just get married, run a home, raise a family. Yet he had been completely supportive of Mona's ambitions. Mona knew there weren't many fathers like Ben Lowery around, and she loved her male parent without reservation.

''I'm really pleased for you, Mona,'' Keith said seriously. ''To have set a goal early in life, then to have pursued it so persistently. Not many young people have that kind of tenacity. You'll do well. Determination and tenacity. You can't fail when you have those.''

Mona felt a warm glow of pleasure, her normal reaction to Keith's flattery. Keith was a gracious man, almost courtly—at least he was when he was a guest in the Lowery house. He passed out compliments with a lavish hand, but they always seemed genuine and heartfelt. Even if he did not mean them, he had the talent for making one feel he did. Mona's eyes moved to her sister, and she saw the grim pinched look on Claire's face.

Kitty Lowery basked in the admiration Mona was receiving, feeling it to be a reflection of her success as a mother. ''Oh, I'm sure Mona will do well,'' she said. ''She's never wanted to be anything but a decorator. When she was a child her father gave her a dollhouse one Christmas—a really grand one, as I recall—and she never stopped redecorating it. It was she who came up with the color scheme for this room.''

Several pairs of admiring eyes took in the cream-and-apricot dining room with its huge expanse of glass, tasteful watercolors on the walls, profusion of plants. Light and airy, like all of Mona's work.

Claire shifted restlessly in her chair, bored as always when the conversation strayed very far from her. She tossed her dark curls in a haughty manner and said, ''Well, I'm glad *I* don't have anything to keep *me* from going to Palm Springs. I adore the place. There's so much to do, so many exciting people, and Dallas can be so dreadful in the summer. I would be bored to tears.''

Keith had turned to Claire when she began speaking, and so Mona could see only the back of his head, but she wondered at his reaction to the callous remark. She suspected Keith Garrett was much too socially sophisticated to allow his expression to betray his emotions, but Claire's words would have to sting a bit. She could have cheerfully kicked her sister, for she knew Claire's motives. God knows, she had watched her sister at work often enough. Claire toyed with their feelings, tried their patience, stretched their devotion to the breaking point.

Why, Mona wondered, *don't any of them ever see that she can be absolutely malicious? Why do they view Claire's rejection only as some sort of failure on their part? If I had a dollar for every sad-faced young man with dashed hopes who has cried on my shoulder....*

Kitty stood up, signaling the dinner's end, and the others did the same. "Why don't we have our coffee on the veranda, Ben? It's a lovely evening. Would everyone like coffee?"

"Pardon me, Mrs. Lowery," Keith said politely, "but I thought I would ask Claire if she would like to go for a ride. And you, too, Mona, of course."

The afterthought. Mona the Afterthought. It was like a title. But at least Keith sometimes thought to include her; none of the others ever had. And how Mona would have loved to go with them! Keith had a 1965 Mustang convertible that he had restored to showroom condition—a true collector's item. He was extremely proud of it, and Mona didn't blame him, for the car was clearly a classic. What fun it would have been to go for a ride in it on this sparkling, clear spring night. She had been hoping for an opportunity to ride in that car since the first time she'd seen it.

"No, thank you, Keith. I have some studying to do," she said, catching the unmistakable warning in Claire's look.

Keith turned expectantly to Claire. A small pout crossed her pretty face. "Well, all right. But do put up the top on that thing, Keith. The wind just ruins my hair."

"Of course," he agreed quietly.

Mona watched them leave with a twinge of jealousy, then halfheartedly followed her parents out onto what Kitty referred to as "the veranda," what Mona thought of as a side porch. Lettie Powell, the housekeeper, appeared with coffee, which Mona declined.

"No thanks, Lettie, no coffee. But please tell Lucille that she outdid herself with the dinner tonight. It was scrumptious." Lucille Blake, the Lowerys' longtime cook and Lettie's sister, was a kitchen artist with an easily damaged ego. It irritated Mona that Kitty so seldom praised either of the women but if something went wrong the offender heard about it immediately!

Lettie scurried away, and for the next half hour or so Mona and her father listened politely while Kitty talked of mindless unimportant things. Mona genuinely loved her mother and she tried to understand her, knowing she was a woman who was completely satisfied with her lot in life. Kitty's days were spent in an endless round of coffees, teas, luncheons, cocktail parties and dinner parties with a never changing circle of friends. The chief activity at these affairs was the dissection of the actions and motives of all their mutual acquaintances. This, however, was not done out of malice; gossiping was simply the way the women whiled away their hours. It was a kind of sport, a form of entertainment.

Mona was quite certain her mother had never experienced even the tiniest desire to make a speech, write a poem, chair a committee, get a job. Kitty was the complete and perfect picture of an affluent society matron, a woman devoted to doing the "right" thing at all times. She would have preferred death to having someone think her improper or ungracious. She deferred to her husband in all matters, loved and cared for her children, ran her household with the precision of a well-coached football team and reveled in her position in the community. There were times when Mona almost envied her mother's complacency, but at no time had she ever wanted to emulate her.

Kitty's chatter droned on. So-and-so did this, so-and-so said that, and had they heard about so-and-so's alleged misconduct while in Las Vegas? This was the sort of thing she considered real conversation. Politics, economics, religion, literature, nuclear disarmament—such things only bored her.

While her mother carried on her monologue, Mona watched her father. He was so good and patient with Kitty. He treated her like a Dresden doll that required the most careful handling. Kitty could have anything on earth it was in his power to provide, and he spoiled her shamefully. Often it did not seem to Mona that her mother did much to warrant all this pampering, but Ben indulged his wife's every wish and whim.

Truthfully he was good and patient with all of them, for he was a man who strongly believed in family ties. Mona had heard it all her life—the family unit should be as solid as Gibraltar—and the Lowery clan came down to the four of them. Ben's older brother had died some years before and his family had moved to California. The only communication with them was the obligatory Christmas card with a short note enclosed. Kitty had a younger sister in the east somewhere, but Mona had never met her and she sensed some sort of estrangement.

It really was something of a pity: Ben Lowery was a man who would have liked a large family. Mona suspected he would have relished siring seven sons who in turn would each sire seven sons. She was certain of one thing—he would be appalled and horrified if he knew of the enmity she often felt for Claire. It was something Mona carefully concealed from all of them.

Presently Ben rose from his chair. "We're going in now, dear," he said to Mona. "Are you coming?"

"No, I don't think so, dad. Not just yet. I think I'll sit here and stargaze a bit. The night's too lovely to waste indoors."

Her parents departed, and Mona stretched full-length on the chaise lounge. The soft night breeze rumpled her hair. A thick stand of honeysuckle enclosed the porch, perfuming the air and creating a feeling of privacy. How she loved this side porch! It had been a sort of playhouse for her when she was a child and was still the place she escaped to for solitude. In fact, she loved every inch of this big old house where she had lived all her life.

Well, no, not all her life. Ben Lowery hadn't always had so much money, but when Mona was five he had inherited a small machine shop from his father. From those humble beginnings he had built

Lowery Industries, a multimillion-dollar concern. So Mona and Claire had coasted through life, having all that money could buy, with love and security thrown in for good measure.

Sometimes Mona felt guilty that she had so much through no effort on her part. Perhaps that was the source of her fierce determination to accomplish something on her own. But even then she had a crutch. Her father's money was paying for a very expensive education, and it would buy her the shop she wanted. Her mother's wealthy friends would be her first clients. But after that? After that she would succeed or fail through her own efforts—a challenging but sometimes frightening thought.

Mona stirred restlessly on the lounge. She should have been in her room studying, and normally it would not have occurred to her to do anything else in the evening. But tonight she seemed to be held in the grip of a lifeless languor, and this was something new to her. She was by nature a young woman of energy and stamina who despised inactivity. Her father often cautioned her against becoming a workaholic when she went into business, and Mona was quite aware that she was inclined that way.

Claire, on the other hand, was laziness personified. She could sleep until ten, spend an hour doing her hair and putting on her makeup, then idle away long hours lounging by the pool, killing time until some splendid man arrived to take her out for the evening.

Once Mona had ventured to speak to her mother about Claire's inactivity. "Mom, you really should encourage Claire to get a job or something. She's too old to sit around on her fanny and do absolutely nothing."

Kitty had made a helpless gesture with her hands. "In all honesty, Mona—and I certainly wouldn't want you to tell anyone I said this—I don't think Claire *can* do anything."

"That's ridiculous, mom! Everybody can do something."

"Not Claire," Kitty insisted. "Why, she can't even type! Even I can type!"

Claire apparently was not interested in anything but the latest fashions and her latest man—especially her latest man. And now that man was Keith Garrett, the heir apparent to Garrett Instruments, an electronics firm that did business all over the world. Tall handsome Keith, with that thick thatch of dark hair, those steel-gray eyes that a woman could fall into, that charming smile that showed all those perfect teeth, that lean hard body. He was so utterly and completely virile and the only one of Claire's men whom Mona would have categorized as exceptional. Normally she bent over backward to ignore Claire's men friends, but it had been impossible for her to ignore Keith. It seemed to Mona that the man literally filled up any room he entered. When Keith was around, she found herself casting surreptitious glances in his direction. Not that it did any good; once a man had fallen under Claire's spell, he acquired a good case of tunnel vision.

If I looked like Claire I'd hold on to Keith Garrett, that's for sure!

Mona had never been in love. She hadn't even come close to love, although a few times she had harbored brief hopes. And, adhering to a strict family rule, she always brought the more promising young men home to meet her family. Unfortunately, anyone appealing appealed to Claire, too, and once the man in question had got a look at her sister, Mona apparently was found wanting. On a few occasions it had hurt. . . a little bit, for a little while.

The jealousy and out-and-out anger she often felt toward her sister was the only disturbing facet of Mona's otherwise well-ordered and placid life. She would have given anything to develop a warmer, closer relationship with her only sibling, but she thought perhaps that would never be possible, given their disparate natures and the fact that Claire seemed to delight in wooing Mona's young men away from her.

So Mona ignored her sister when she could, accepted her when she could not, continued to formulate her own plans for her own life and made absolutely certain that her parents never, ever suspected her true feelings toward Claire. Not for anything would she be the one to cause dissent within the family.

Her reverie was interrupted by the sound of an automobile's approach. It stopped in the driveway just beyond the porch. Lights were switched off. Mona raised her head to peer over the honeysuckle bushes. The shiny yellow Mustang, its top up, was parked a few yards away. Mona lay back down and closed her eyes.

Within moments she heard the harsh sound of angry voices. Then a car door slammed. Another door slammed. There was the tapping of high heels across the porch, and Claire ran past Mona without seeing her and entered the house. Quick behind her came Keith, a grim and frantic look on his face. Mona raised herself on her elbows to watch him. He reached the door just in time to have it firmly closed in his face. He stood looking at the closed door for

several long disbelieving seconds, his chest heaving in
anger, his hands clenched into fists at his sides. Then
his body sagged and his shoulders slumped in a gesture of helpless impotence. He uttered an obscenity
that Mona heard all too clearly.

"Trouble?" she asked softly, and Keith turned,
startled.

"Oh, Mona...sorry. I—I didn't see you." Even
on the dark porch she could see the black fury raging
and boiling in his face.

"Obviously," she said with a wry smile. She sat
up, swinging her slender shapely legs off the lounge.
"Why don't you sit down?"

He looked back at the closed door, then again at
Mona. "Oh...it's getting late. I guess I'll be going.
I'm afraid I wouldn't be very good company...and
there's no sense in taking it out on you."

"It's not late at all," Mona insisted, "and I've got
a hide like an elephant's. Rail at me all you like. Sit
down and let's talk. It'll do you good to cool off
some before getting behind the wheel of that fabulous car. Can't have you crashing off embankments
or anything like that."

He looked back at the closed door, as though hoping it would open any moment and a contrite Claire
would appear. Then, resigned, he crossed the pourch
and took a chair near Mona. Broad of shoulder, lean
of waist and hip, he moved in a loose easy gait. His
dark slacks hung perfectly—custom-tailored, Mona
suspected. His short-sleeved cotton shirt was open at
the neck, revealing a tanned V of skin, a tuft of black
chest hair, tanned muscular arms. How did a business executive acquire a tan like that so early in the
season, Mona wondered.

She also wondered if he was aware of his striking masculine good looks. Did men think about their personal appearance the way women did? She knew so little about men, never having got close enough to one to get inside his head and heart.

She studied the angles and planes of Keith's face, the sensuous line of his mouth, the firm jut to his chin. Mona thought it was a good strong face, a face capable of great emotion, be it love or hate, pleasure or anger. But at that moment it was such a patently miserable face that her heart went out to him.

"You know," she began brightly, trying to lighten his dark mood, "it's suddenly crossed my mind that the Mustang might be too valuable to drive."

"What?"

"I mean, a dent or scrape on anything else is simply a dent or scrape that a body shop could fix, but on that car it would be a real tragedy."

"No doubt you're right, but what good is a car that can't be driven?"

"Good question," she said, smiling. "In another few years it will be worth a lot of money, won't it? I mean a *lot*?"

"Possibly. Not that I'd ever sell it."

"You did such a beautiful job on it, Keith. I wouldn't trust something like that to this horrendous Dallas traffic."

Keith gave her an appreciative look. "Instinct tells me you're not simply making small talk or complimenting my car because you know it will please me."

"You're right."

"It must be the decorator in you who can appreciate it, Mona. Claire refers to it as my 'old' car. She much prefers going around in my Cadillac. I've tried to explain that the Mustang is much more valuable, but I don't think she believes me.''

"Sounds like her," Mona said tartly, wrinkling her nose. A few moments of strained silence followed while she carefully tried to pick and choose the right words. Finally she asked softly, "Would you like to talk about it? Sometimes it helps. Sometimes getting it out in the open minimizes it.''

He frowned. ''Talk about what?''

"Come on, Keith, spare me the idiot treatment. You look like a June thunderstorm about to break. Are you really so much in love with Claire?''

Surprise softened his grim expression. ''What an audacious girl you are!'' he exclaimed.

Mona chuckled lightly. ''Audacious? Am I? I don't mean to be, but. . . yes, I suppose I am. Mom says I should learn to be more tactful. She says I step on toes when I don't know I'm doing it, but when mom talks about being tactful she means 'lie a little.' I guess most people don't like to hear the truth, but I do. I'd much rather have someone insult me than lie to me. Wouldn't you?''

Keith smiled, and Mona could see a relaxation taking place within him. ''I'd really never thought about it, but. . . yes, I guess I would. At least you have a clear idea what you're up against. You know, Mona, I take back what I said about your being audacious. Audacity somehow carries with it a connotation of impudence, and you aren't impudent at all. Rather, you're frank and forthright and maybe just a little bold. Whatever you are, you're refreshing.''

Feeling the first fragile beginnings of a friendship with this good-looking man, Mona was encouraged to continue. ''Keith, would you mind some well-meant advice?''

His gray eyes bore down on her, and they were mellow and kind and a little amused. "I have a feeling I'm going to get it whether I mind or not."

Mona curled the fingers of one hand and studied its nails. "Find someone else—another girl. You're going to get hurt."

"I'm a big boy—and not so easily hurt."

"Baloney! You should see your face right now. You're hurt, all right."

"No," he said thoughtfully. "More angry than anything."

"Want to talk about it?"

He looked at her for a time without speaking, and she knew she was being sized up. He was trying to decide if she was a trustworthy confidante.

"How old are you, Mona?" he asked at last.

"Twenty."

"Do you know what a tease is?"

Mona's eyes widened. "Ah, so that's it! I often wondered. I mean, the way Claire toys with her men, always dangling them on a string. I wondered if she did that, too." She made a face in disgust. She had always suspected that all really decent women despised a tease in much the same way that all really decent men despised a man who openly bragged about his sexual conquests. There truly wasn't much that was likable about Claire—which made this dynamic man's infatuation with her all the more difficult for Mona to understand.

Keith reached for his shirt pocket, then hesitated. "Do you mind if I smoke?"

"No. And I'll have one, too, please."

He arched an eyebrow. "I didn't know you smoked." He withdrew the package, lit a cigarette and handed it to Mona, then lit one for himself.

"How could you know?" she asked frankly. "You don't know anything about me. But I don't smoke very often because it upsets mom. Did you know Claire smokes?"

"Yes. . . yes, I did."

A wry smile crossed Mona's face. "My parents don't. When I want one, I want one, so I light up and suffer mom's displeasure. Claire smokes behind closed doors, usually in *my* room. When mom smells the smoke or finds cigarette butts in the ashtrays she assumes it's my doing. The story of my life!" She inhaled, exhaled and watched the smoke curl into the air above her head. "Now talk to me, Keith."

He twirled his cigarette in his long slender fingers. Something told him he could trust this frank young woman. His face hardened as he spoke. "One minute she was practically begging for it, and the next minute I was getting my face soundly slapped. Dammit! I don't understand her. Claire knows I'm not just on the make."

Mona was momentarily startled. What did that mean? Had Keith professed serious love to Claire? Was this splendidly virile man actually in love with her empty-headed sister? For a brief second she dwelled on the possibility that they might be lovers and was shocked to realize it bothered her tremendously. Why did she care?

"Keith, I don't know how to say what I want to say without sounding too critical of my own sister, but. . . I often wonder if Claire will ever be able to have a sound, lasting relationship with one man. She's so used to having men fall in love with her that it means nothing. It's sort of a game with her. You're just the latest in a long line of dreamy-eyed men who—"

"Dreamy-eyed!" Keith exclaimed in mock horror. "Good God! I am not, nor have I ever been, dreamy eyed!"

Mona cocked her head to one side and studied him. "Not now maybe, but at dinner tonight...."

"Good God!" he repeated.

"Keith, I don't pretend to understand Claire, and God knows I've tried. I suppose that incredible beauty of hers is something of a curse, almost a burden. When you've been stared at, admired, lusted after all your life...well, I guess you can't be expected to behave like an ordinary mortal. It has to mess up your sense of values a little."

Keith lapsed into silence, and Mona wondered if she had gone too far. She often did, as her mother had pointed out countless times. She watched Keith as he sat lost in contemplation. What if he were really in love with Claire? He might well resent the things Mona was saying about her.

Oh, it was so incredible to think that Keith Garrett could actually be in love with Claire. He was head and shoulders above any of Claire's other men. One would think a man like Keith would want a woman of more...well, of more substance.

Keith flicked his cigarette out onto the lawn. Mona ground hers under her heel and kicked it off the porch. His preoccupation was making her uncomfortable.

"Are you really so much in love with her?" she asked again, quietly but with the utmost interest.

"Love? I don't know, Mona. I swear I don't. Perhaps I'm simply enthralled or fascinated—call it what you will. I don't seem to be able to put her out of my mind, but I think that's because she's so...so elusive. One minute she's sweet and soft and responsive, then the next minute she's cold as ice."

"I know," Mona said sympathetically.

"And, too, I'm thirty years old, and it's high time I was thinking about settling down and getting on with the business of raising a family. Dad reminds me of that almost daily. So when I met Claire I was a prime candidate for romance. I waited a long time before she consented to go out with me."

"Ah, yes, she sent Joey Willis packing about then, as I recall," Mona said, more sarcastically than she intended. "Poor Joey. I thought he was going to have a nervous breakdown when they split up. Keith, did it ever occur to you that perhaps it was the necessity of pursuit that enthralled you?"

He frowned. "What?"

She gave him a gentle look of understanding. "I have a feeling you aren't a man who is accustomed to having to work so hard on your conquests."

"Conquests, Mona? I assure you, I've never thought of any of my lady friends as conquests."

"Then you are an unusual one!"

He stared at her then as though he were seeing her for the first time. The steady regard in those steely eyes was unnerving. "Mona," he said thoughtfully, "in some ways you seem so much older than Claire, so much wiser in the ways of life and love."

Mona laughed derisively. "*Me?* Hardly!"

"Tell me, if I'm not prying...have you ever been in love?"

"Nope. Never."

"Never? That seems incredible coming from a young woman who looks like you. Beauty runs in this family."

Again his compliment warmed her tremendously, and she was not a woman who doted on compliments. Most never seemed genuine, but Keith's flattery was something else again.

"To tell you the truth, Keith, Claire has never let me keep anyone long enough to fall in love. I've tried to stick up for myself, believe me, but it's never seemed to do any good once Claire has turned on her charm."

Keith laughed. "You are painfully honest, Mona, even with yourself."

"Especially with myself. Claire, on the other hand, has been in and out of love dozens of times. She's in love with the idea of being in love. I don't think she knows what she wants half the time. Don't brood about her, Keith, and above all don't let her make you miserable. I've listened to so many tales of woe from other men, but the others I didn't care about. You're different."

The corners of his mouth lifted, and he gave her a speculative look. "I am? In what way?"

She shrugged. "Just...different."

"I'm going to take that as a compliment," he said. Then he placed his hands on the chair's arms and pushed himself up. "Well, now it really is getting late. I'd better be going. Thanks for letting me talk to you."

Mona stood also, sorry that the interlude had ended. "I enjoyed it. Feel free to talk to me anytime. I have a sympathetic shoulder, and I'm a good listener. Lord knows I've had enough practice." She preceded him down the steps and walked beside him to his car.

"What do you intend doing with your summer?" he asked. "Not only studying, surely."

"Just about. I'm so close to my goal."

"I'm thinking maybe it's a good thing Claire is going away for a while. It might help me get my head sorted out." He opened the door to the driver's seat. "And there's always the chance she'll miss me."

Mona scarcely heard him. She was looking at the car's interior. "Oh, it's exquisite!" she exclaimed.

She could have said nothing that would have pleased him more. He rubbed the automobile as though he were caressing a woman. "It was a real mess when I got it, but two years and thousands of dollars later...."

"Fantastic!" Her hands began a sensitive journey over the upholstered seat. "Such leather!"

"I found a fellow in Fort Worth who is a real artist with leather. He did it all for me. Of course I paid through the nose for it." He thumped the car's door. "Drives like a dream, too. Solid as a rock. They still made real cars back in those days, not the aluminum-foil junk they turn out now. I'll take you for a ride in it one of these days if you'd like."

"Oh, I'd love it!" she enthused.

"I'll even let you drive it," he announced grandly, as though he were offering the ultimate favor.

Mona's big dark eyes widened. "I couldn't! Something might happen while I'm behind the wheel, and I'd never forgive myself. You don't have any idea what kind of driver I am."

He grinned down at her. "What kind of driver are you?"

"Superb!"

He laughed. "I thought so. I'll take you out in the country, maybe to my ranch. Would you like to see it?"

"You have a ranch?"

He nodded. "River View. It's been in our family for generations. Nine hundred acres fronting on the Brazos, a two-hour drive from here. And it's not just a hobby or a tax dodge. River View pays its way."

"Ah, so that's where the tan comes from. You must spend a lot of time there."

"As much as I can manage. When I was a kid I never wanted to leave it, and I guess in my heart I still don't. I'd like nothing better than to live there and work it all the time, not just on weekends or during vacations. Dad never really took to ranching, but I'm a pretty fair working cowhand, and I've got great plans for River View."

"I'd like to hear all about it," Mona told him truthfully. "It sounds wonderful. But what about Garrett Instruments?"

"Well, of course I have to keep my hand in the business, but dad's a vigorous man. He'll be active for years, and with any luck I'll have sons someday."

"Oh, of course," Mona said a trifle caustically. "Every man thinks he's going to have a son to take over someday. I suppose dad thought that at one time, but look what happened to him. Two daughters! What if that happens to you?"

"Then my daughters will take over someday," he said simply.

"Good for you!" Mona said, unabashed admiration for this man shining from her eyes. "It sounds perfectly splendid, Keith."

"Do you think so, Mona? Yes, I believe you really do. How different from your sister you are. Claire won't even go out to the ranch with me. She professes to hate the country. I haven't dared talk to her about my plans for the future. I'm afraid I know what her reaction would be."

Mona laid a hand on his arm. *Don't you see,* she wanted to say. *Can't you see that she simply isn't the right one for you?* But she said nothing. She feared she had already said too much.

Keith, however, was surprised to find he was experiencing an odd sense of communion with this lovely dark-haired girl. Ten years separated them, yet in many ways he felt closer in maturity and intelligence to her than to many people his own age.

"Mona, I hope I'll see you sometime this summer."

A curious, hopeful feeling swept through her. "I hope so, too, Keith," she said, striving to keep her voice casual.

He slid in behind the steering wheel and closed the door, then leaned his head out the window. "And, Mona—" incredibly, one hand reached for the nape of her neck and gently forced her head down "—thanks for being such a nice wailing wall." Then he placed a soft kiss on her cheek.

"My pleasure," she said lightly, but her heartbeat had increased dramatically.

She watched the disappearing set of taillights and touched the spot on her cheek where Keith had kissed her. *Oh, if I looked like Claire. . . .*

CHAPTER TWO

THE LOWERYS' ANNUAL EXODUS to the California desert was preceded by preparations only slightly less elaborate than those of a full-scale military operation. There was a flurry of shopping excursions, and the house was in a ferment of activity for days. Kitty issued a constant stream of orders, and poor Lettie and Lucille ran their legs off.

Watching from the sidelines, Mona was alternately amused and appalled. Her mother could get in such a snit over things. Why on earth, she wondered, didn't they just throw some things in a suitcase, hop on a plane and then buy whatever else they needed when they got to California? Kitty and Claire would spend half the summer shopping anyway, so it would be sensible to travel as lightly as possible. She was glad school occupied so much of her time. She could escape the worst of the hubbub.

Finally departure day arrived. A mountain of luggage was piled on the front porch, and Ben's chauffeur-driven Cadillac waited in the driveway to take them to the airport.

Claire swept out the front door, hesitated, then swept back in. "Oh, dear," she said. "I forgot to call Keith and tell him goodbye. There's simply no time now, and I know he's going to be disappointed.

Mona, will you please give him a call and tell him I was just so busy that I—''

"Yes, yes. I'll call him.''

Kitty's face was creased by one of her worried-mother looks. "Mona, you know I'm not going to rest easy knowing you're here. I wish I had insisted—''

"Good heavens, mom, why on earth would you worry about me? I'm not a child. This summer will fly by. It's just going to be one long bout with the books. I doubt I'll leave the house except to go to school, and come January I'll be awfully glad I stayed. I'll be fine, really.''

"Well, I wish you were coming with us, but the servants have their instructions, so you should have everything you'll need.''

Mona offered her cheek for her mother's cool kiss. "I know, mom. Everything will be smooth as glass. Lettie and Lucille will cluck over me like mother hens.''

Ben embraced his younger daughter enthusiastically. "If something comes up that needs immediate attention, call the office. One of the boys will be out here in nothing flat. I trust them completely—otherwise I wouldn't be taking the summer off.''

Mona responded to her father's embrace with a hug of her own. "Thank you, dad. But why would I call the office? If the fire department or police department or doctor have to be notified, I know how to use a telephone.''

Kitty's hand flew to her breast. "Oh, good heavens!''

"Mom, I was kidding!'' Mona cried. "Now go on and have a good time and don't worry about me.''

There was another last-minute round of hugs and

goodbyes, then Mona watched, almost relieved, as the Cadillac drove away. A summer to herself! Undreamed-of solitude. It sounded marvelous. Her parents staunchly believed in a lot of family togetherness, and while it was nice in one way, it could also get rather stifling at times.

Remembering Claire's request, she went into the library, looked up the number of Garrett Instruments in the directory and got Keith on the phone.

"Oh, it's you, Mona. When my secretary told me Miss Lowery was calling, I naturally assumed it was Claire."

"Sorry to disappoint you."

"You didn't disappoint me—not at all."

"I hate to disturb you at work, but I didn't know any other way of getting in touch with you. I have a message for you from Claire."

"Oh? What is it?"

"Goodbye."

There was a split second of silence, then his deep throaty laugh came over the line. "That's it?"

"That's it. She was so busy she forgot to call, and she said you would be heartbroken."

He laughed again, much to Mona's relief. "Well, I'll do my damnedest to get over it. How have you been doing, Mona?"

"Oh, I'm doing fine."

"Studying hard?"

"Always." Mona bit her lip, squelching a wild desire to invite him over to the house. She told herself she wanted to see him only because she enjoyed talking to him so much. Inviting him to drop by for a drink or a dip in the pool would be the most natural thing in the world, she argued inwardly. He wouldn't think a thing of it. But she couldn't do it.

"I sure appreciate your calling, Mona," Keith said.

"You're welcome, Keith. I'll see you around."

"Sure, Mona. Goodbye."

Mona's hand rested on the receiver for several minutes after she had hung up. Unconsciously she had harbored a vague hope that Keith would remember his promise to take her for a drive in that splendid convertible, to take her to see his ranch. But it no doubt had been nothing but an idle remark uttered to fit the moment. He probably had forgotten ever saying such a thing. Mona doubted she would see him again until fall, and that was just as well. She was reminded of a long-ago promise she had made to herself—to never, ever have anything to do with any man who was interested in Claire. It saved a lot of wear and tear on the old heartstrings.

THAT EVENING AT DINNER Mona stared at the plate of food Lettie placed before her. Roast beef, baked potato, green beans from the garden, homemade rolls and strawberry pie for dessert! "Good grief, Lettie! Please tell Lucille that there is no need to cook like this for me all summer. I'm perfectly capable of getting something for myself whenever I'm hungry. You two turn these three months into something of a vacation for yourselves, too."

Lettie looked perfectly aghast. "Oh, Mona, the missus wouldn't like it!"

"How will she know?" Mona asked with a mischievous smile. "I won't tell her."

Lettie shook her head, horrified at the mere suggestion of such a breach of household routine.

"Missus Lowery knows everything. She'd find out," the housekeeper said sagely and moved out of the dining room.

Mona stared after Lettie's retreating figure, as amazed as always at the power her mother wielded in the house. Kitty represented absolute authority even when she was twelve hundred miles away. There was an art to managing servants, and Kitty had mastered it long ago, having grown up in a wealthy household herself. Lettie and Lucille fairly quailed in her presence, and yet, to Mona's knowledge, her mother had never so much as raised her voice to either woman.

Mona ate as much of the huge meal as she could manage in order to spare Lucille's feelings. If an appreciable amount were returned to the kitchen the cook would be at her elbow in an instant, demanding to know what was wrong with the food. It had never got through to Lucille that there were times when normal, healthy human beings simply might not be very hungry.

After dinner Mona carried a cup of coffee upstairs to her bedroom, where she prepared for an evening's work at her drafting table. Armed with a copy of *Historic American Homes*, she was restoring a Victorian mansion to its former glory--on paper at least. She had been working steadily for over an hour when Lettie tapped lightly on the door.

"Mona, that nice Palmer boy is downstairs in the kitchen asking for you."

Mona smiled. The Palmer "boy" would be Alan Palmer, twenty-six years old and the Lowerys' next-door neighbor for all the years Ben had owned this house. "Tell him to come up, Lettie." In less than a minute Mona heard Alan's heavy tread on the stairs. Then his fair head was peering over her shoulder.

"Hey, how you doing?" he greeted her.

"Hey, yourself," Mona said, not looking up from her work. "Long time no see. What have you been up to?"

"Not much." Alan stood behind her chair for a few minutes, watching her work. "You're pretty good at that, aren't you?" He indicated her sketch pad with a jerk of his head.

"Fair." Mona laid down her pencil and turned around. "Sit down." He moved away, and she cried out when she saw where he intended sitting. "Yipes! Not on the bed!"

Alan jumped. "Why not?"

"That's a new bedspread, and sitting on the edge of a bed ruins the springs. Take the chair."

"Sorry!" Alan draped his tall lean frame into the wing chair that stood in the corner. His blue eyes twinkled and he lavished a grin on Mona, a grin that had sent more than one female heart racing on a runaway course. Alan Palmer was devilishly attractive; even Mona, who had known him most of her life and thought of him more as a brother than anything, had to admit that. He was wickedly charming and had a gift of gab that was second to none. Kitty thought him "darling," and Lettie and Lucille all but swooned when he tossed all that blatant flattery their way. And since Alan was only too aware of the devastating effect he had on most women, and since he was the only heir to an almost obscenely large fortune, Mona supposed it was inevitable that he had grown up to be one of the last of the great playboys of the Western world. His brief but passionate affairs had been numerous and well chronicled within the Lowerys' social circle, and a favorite pastime among their mutual friends was speculating on the young woman who would finally rope and tie Alan Palmer for good.

It often amazed Mona that she liked Alan. He could be arrogant, conceited and totally without scruples. He had never done a day's work in his life. He was the complete antithesis of the kind of man she admired. Yet they were friends and, at times, confidants. She supposed she felt sorry for him, as ridiculous as that was. She suspected Alan's frivolous rakehell ways were only a studied pose designed to hide some very real and restless longings. Not that Alan would ever admit such a thing, and she would certainly never pry.

"I guess the family got away all right," Alan commented.

"Oh, yes! Amid much fuss and flutter, I might add. All that was missing were trumpets and a police escort to the airport."

"How come you didn't go?"

She tapped the drafting table with her forefinger. "School."

"God! Is that all you ever do?"

"Just about," she admitted.

He groaned. "I remember my college days as among the unhappiest of my life."

Mona chuckled. "That's right, you went to the university in Austin, didn't you?"

"Briefly. Only briefly. It was a disaster. But dad had all these grandiose plans about my becoming a petroleum engineer. I guess he had the silly notion that the kid who was going to own the company someday should have some idea what the company did. But it no longer matters. When dad died, mother sold out, and now we're in 'investments,' whatever the hell that is.''

Alan stretched out lazily in the chair, filling it up and spilling over. He was already very tanned, the result of mornings on the tennis court and lazy afternoons around the swimming pool. His hair was the color of ripened wheat. His mouth, which could smile so charmingly, was usually curved into something of a leer, for Alan worked hard at fostering his image of a hedonistic scoundrel. Only in Mona's presence did he ever relax his guard and let something of a warm personality shine through.

Mona waited a moment, then asked, "Did you want to see me about something in particular, Alan?"

"No...not really. I was just bored out of my mind and thought I'd come over here and pester you awhile."

Mona laughed. "Thanks."

"Hey, I didn't mean that quite the way it came out."

"That must be one for the books—Alan Palmer so bored he's reduced to calling on the neighbors. No one would believe it, you know."

"God! You'd be surprised how many boring evenings I spend—and not all of those boring evenings are spent alone."

Mona stared at him thoughtfully. "Then why don't you settle down?"

"With *one* woman?" he cried incredulously.

"Is that all you ever think about? I didn't necessarily have a woman in mind. For instance, how are you planning to spend the summer?"

Alan shrugged. "The way I spent the spring and winter, I guess."

"Let me see if I can guess what that was. Tennis at the racket club, golf at the country club, lunch at the Petroleum Club, dinner who-knows-where with who-knows-who. Right?"

"Probably."

Mona grimaced. "No wonder you're bored. Alan, has it ever occurred to you to, pardon the expression, get a job?"

He clutched at his chest and feigned shock. "*Job?* You mean as in w-o-r-k?"

Mona nodded, perfectly serious. "Lots of people do it."

"Perish the thought! What would that do to my reputation? Actually, I've been considering a short fling in Las Vegas or maybe New Orleans. Someplace that's delightfully decadent." He winked at her. "Want to come along?"

"No, thanks. Unlike you, I have plenty to do. If I didn't I'd probably be in Palm Springs tonight."

"I'm surprised Claire went. I thought she and Keith Garrett were getting pretty serious."

"I...I don't know, Alan. Claire never discusses her men with me." She hoped not. If Claire was serious about Keith there was no doubt in Mona's mind that she would get him. It shouldn't matter to her one way or another, but it did. Keith simply seemed too extraordinary a man to be wasted on the likes of Claire.

Immediately Mona chastised herself. She simply had to stop all these snippy thoughts about Claire. The woman was her sister, for heaven's sakes!

"Well, it seems to me they've been seeing an awful lot of each other," Alan was saying.

"Yes, but Claire's going to be gone for three months. Anything can happen with Claire in three months. She always falls in love in Palm Springs." She looked at Alan with twinkling eyes. "You know, it's just occurred to me that you and Claire are a lot alike."

"I haven't been in love in months, Mona."

She made a clucking sound with her tongue. "So long? I'm surprised one of those beauties you squire around town hasn't lit a fire in you by now."

Alan uttered a sharp laugh. "Oh, a few have lit a fire, all right. But it's always quickly and permanently doused."

Mona shook her head in bewilderment. "Sometimes I think Claire and I are the only women in Dallas who haven't succumbed to your charms—and we don't count."

He snapped his fingers. "Hey, there's an idea! How about it, Mona? What say we have a passionate affair? That would be a great way to spend the summer."

"Oh, God!" she breathed. "Just thinking about it exhausts me."

He gave her an exaggerated leer. "You ought to give it a try. You might be wildly in love with me by September."

Mona laughed. "A fate worse than death! I can't think of anything more terrible than being madly in love with you, Alan. Right off the top of my head I can think of five or six young women who wish to God they'd never set eyes on you."

She had hit a nerve, not meaning to at all. Alan's manner changed abruptly. "I never lied to any of them, Mona. And I made damned sure every one of those lovely ladies went into our relationship with her eyes wide open.''

Chagrined, Mona leaned forward and spoke to him earnestly. ''Oh, Alan, I shouldn't have said that. It's none of my business. But as one friend to another, why don't you tone down that playboy image a bit? You ought to try being a little more serious about life. Someday you're apt to find a woman you really care for, and that bon-vivant routine might turn her off. She might wonder if a playboy could ever be a faithful husband.''

Alan looked at her levelly. ''That's an act, Mona. Most of it, anyway. And can I help it if I was born filthy rich? Am I supposed to live from hand to mouth, punch a time clock and live in a two-room walk-up to prove that I'm really a swell guy?''

''Oh, don't be tiresome! Of course not!'' Mona exclaimed with irritation. ''But you could at least go through the motions of doing something with your life. For instance, why do you still live at home?''

''Damned if you aren't an audacious one!''

There was that adjective again. Keith had called her audacious, too, but he had tempered it a bit later on. Well, if she was, she was. ''Since when do I have to mince words with you, Alan? And you didn't answer my question: why do you still live at home? A twenty-six-year-old man who still lives at home... well, some women might fear he's a mama's boy.''

Alan guffawed, completely nonplussed by Mona's candor. ''Then they don't know my mother! I see her all of twenty minutes a month! The house belongs to me, Mona. Mother moves in occasionally, when she's between husbands. She never stays long because she never stays unmarried long. Right now she and Jeff are talking about moving to Hawaii.''

Mona seized the opportunity to change the subject. ''Jeff? Oh, that's right, you have a new stepfather, don't you? What's he like?''

''Jeff? He looks and acts just like Paul, who looked and acted just like Harry, who was the living image of dad. I don't know why mother persists in getting married. I suppose she's still searching for dad. But you have to give her credit—four husbands and not a gold digger in the crowd. I sorta hated to see Paul get the heave-ho. I liked him.''

Mona's heart lurched, thinking of her own secure serene upbringing. ''Walk a mile in my shoes....'' Alan had so much...and so little. She vaguely wondered if perhaps loneliness could be the reason for all that frantic womanizing. He truly was the epitome of the poor little rich kid.

Alan pushed himself up and out of the chair. ''I came over here to get cheered up and damned if you haven't depressed me,'' he said, but there was amusement in his eyes. ''Besides, I'm keeping you from your work.''

''Oh, no, Alan, sit down. This—'' she waved her hand at the drafting table ''—can wait. There's no great hurry.''

''No, I think I'll just mosey on over to the house and curl up with a good book.''

Laughter bubbled up in Mona. ''Oh, I'd like to go along and get a picture of that! Alan Palmer, the dashing young man-about-town, curled up at home with a good book!''

''There you go again! I'm not quite the worthless bum everyone thinks I am ''

He had moved closer to Mona; she reached for his hand and gave it a little squeeze. "I know you're not, Alan. I was teasing. But you work so hard at being so devil-may-care. Do you know what I really wish for you? A lovely adoring wife and somebody to call you 'daddy.'"

"And—don't tell me—an ivy-covered cottage!" he cried in a horrified voice.

"Why not? And grandchildren to dandle on your knee someday."

Now a laugh escaped. "Somehow that picture of me as a hearth-hugging homebody won't form, Mona." He nudged her. "Listen, if you find yourself at loose ends this summer, give me a call. We'll see what kind of trouble we can get into."

"I'll do that, Alan."

She walked downstairs with him and watched from the back porch as he made his way down the path between their houses that they had worn over the years. Pictures came to mind: she, Alan and Claire, three little rich kids, playing cowboys and Indians around the grounds of their mansions. Claire had abandoned them rather early, as soon as she became more interested in ribbons, ruffles and patent-leather slippers, but tomboy Mona had dogged Alan's footsteps until he had reached late adolescence and regarded her as a nuisance. By the time she was old enough to realize just what he had abandoned her for, his reputation was firmly established. Dashing, debonair Alan Palmer. Sports car, cabin cruiser, private plane—a man who thought nothing of flying to the Gulf coast simply because someone knew of a great little place that served superb shrimp gumbo. Supreme seducer of women.

But Mona knew another Alan, and she thought she had seen a glimpse of him tonight. She vowed to stay in touch with him during the summer. In some mysterious way she thought he needed her.

THE FOLLOWING EVENING Mona was again working at the drafting table in her bedroom after dinner. Totally absorbed in her work, she was startled by the telephone's ring. She reached for it absently but instantly perked up at the sound of a familiar baritone voice.

"Mona? This is Keith."

"Yes, Keith. How are you?"

"Fine, thanks. Have you heard from your family?"

Mona made a face. From Claire, he meant. "Just a phone call telling me they had arrived safely and were looking forward to seeing old friends."

"That's good. Listen, I've had a brainstorm. I'm driving out to the ranch Friday afternoon. I plan to spend the weekend there. You seemed interested in it, so why don't you come with me—provided you have no other plans?"

She was so surprised and delighted by the invitation she was momentarily speechless. Keith misunderstood her hesitation.

"Mona, there are plenty of people at the ranch. My housekeeper and her husband live in the main house, so we won't be alone—in case you're thinking it wouldn't be proper."

Recovering, she said, "Oh, Keith, I wasn't thinking that."

"I realize that a young woman like you probably has big plans for the weekend, but—"

"I have nothing planned," she quickly said, "and

I would just love to go!'' Why was her heart pounding so?

He sounded genuinely pleased. "Great! Will four o'clock Friday be all right with you?"

"I'll be ready."

"We should arrive in time for a swim and a couple of drinks before dinner. Just bring a swimsuit and some jeans, casual things like that. No one dresses up at River View."

"It sounds absolutely wonderful!"

Indeed it did. Mona couldn't remember anticipating anything with such restless pleasure, and she knew Claire would have been livid had she known about it. Mona had no idea whether her sister was any more in love with Keith Garrett than she had been with any of the others, but knowing Mona was with him would have made her furious.

For several long minutes after she had hung up, Mona sat at the drafting table, drumming on it with her fingers and humming a little tune. This was more than she ever would have dared hope for, and she wasn't about to spoil it by dwelling on the wisdom of spending a weekend in the company of a man she already found disturbingly attractive—a man who was interested in Claire into the bargain.

Mona tried to focus her concentration on her work, but suddenly her drawings no longer held her attention. Normally she got so caught up in her work that nothing else mattered, but tonight her mind wandered and she made sloppy mistakes. Giving up, she put her work away, then bathed slowly and luxuriously before bed. Once the lights were out she snuggled under the covers and gave in to her desire to think about Keith Garrett.

He had been so different from the beginning. Claire's young men, even the ones Mona had unwittingly brought home to her sister's attention, had always seemed a faceless, ever changing mass of male humanity, none of them standing out from the crowd. Not Keith. Although he had plainly fallen under Claire's beguiling spell, he wasn't so foolishly besotted that he could see nothing else. He had expressed a real interest in Mona's work, in her ambitions, and had incurred Claire's displeasure in the doing.

Mona could clearly remember the first time he had ever spoken to her. She had been sitting on the side porch, sketching a room, giving full rein to her imagination. That was the fun side of interior decoration, just letting her creativity run rampant. It would be more difficult when she was in business and had her client's budget to contend with, she knew, but it would also be more challenging. She had been so engrossed in her sketching that she hadn't heard Keith approach, and she turned only when she had the distinct feeling she was being watched.

"Oh...hello," she said, her gaze raking over the very handsome stranger.

"Charming," he said, indicating her sketch pad. "You have real talent. I think I would enjoy living in that room."

"You think so? It's not too feminine?"

"No. That's what I like about it. You've managed to convey a feeling of soft restfulness without making the room too feminine. By the way, my name is Keith Garrett."

"Hi, Keith. I'm Mona Lowery. You're here for Claire, I suppose."

A flicker of amusement danced in his eyes. "Yes, I am. How did you know?"

She shrugged. "They almost always are."

Again he indicated her drawing. "I hope you're doing something serious about that."

"I've been studying it in college for almost three years, if that's what you mean."

He nodded. "Good. You've found your real calling in life, Mona. You'll do well."

"I'd better, or my father has wasted an awful lot of money."

He had laughed then, and now that she thought about it, it was that thoroughly masculine laugh rather than his thoroughly masculine good looks that had caused her to take more than casual notice of him. It was a deep, throaty, infectious laugh that made her want to laugh along with him. Mona remembered staring at that handsome angular face, at those deep gray eyes, startled to realize she was looking at a perfect stranger and assessing his sex appeal. Keith exuded an air of potent virility, with none of the mischievous sexiness that one found in so many strikingly handsome men. She had thought, *Claire's got herself a real man this time. He's too good for her.*

From that time on, whenever Keith was in their home he never failed to seek her out and inquire, "How's it going, Mona? What are you working on now? Would you let me see it?" And the fact that Claire plainly was displeased over his attentions to her little sister had not seemed to dissuade him a bit.

Oh, this weekend was going to be special. She just knew it! A time she would cherish and want to relive in her mind for a long while. And she didn't want any

of the family to know about it—for reasons that
weren't clear to her, but they went far beyond the
fact that Keith was one of Claire's men. Mona had
not had many really special moments in her life. This
was going to be one, and she wanted to keep it all to
herself.

She would give Lettie and Lucille a phone number
and a vague reference to some friend who lived in the
country. That would satisfy them, although Mona
felt sure she didn't really have to worry about the two
servants. They never volunteered information to Kitty. Time had taught them it was politic to say as little
as possible to their mistress.

And she would ask Keith not to mention this weekend to Claire in his letters, if indeed he did write to
her. Even though he might wonder why or think her
silly, somehow Mona knew he would do as she asked.

CHAPTER THREE

LATE FRIDAY AFTERNOON the yellow convertible, its top down, sped away from the megalopolitan proportions of the Dallas-Fort Worth Metroplex toward a region of lazy limestone hills, through which the Brazos and Paluxy rivers meandered. Ahead of them the cedar-covered hills rose to meet the oft heralded vastness of the blue Texas sky. The sun beat down relentlessly, so Mona wore a big floppy hat to shield her smooth skin from the worst of the burning rays.

"Too much wind?" Keith yelled over the rushing noise. "Do you want me to put up the top?"

Mona shook her head emphatically. "No! I love it!"

"Good girl!" he shouted and grinned.

With the top down the wind's noise made conversation next to impossible, so Mona occupied herself by studying the pastoral scene flashing by and casting surreptitious glances in the direction of her traveling companion. Keith, she decided, was even more handsome in tight-fitting jeans and scuffed boots than he was in his custom-tailored clothes. He had a superb physique, and the casual attire molded to his broad shoulders, muscular arms and lean hips accentuated it perfectly. It astonished her that she should be so aware of him, of his body and the way he looked, for she couldn't remember ever paying so much attention to a man's physical appearance. Most men did not interest her sufficiently to make her want to look beyond the general—height, color of hair, eyes and so forth. Yet she found herself studying Keith with an intensity that surprised her. For the first time she thought she knew the meaning of the term "heartthrob." He looked so good he actually made her heart throb—a most peculiar sensation.

In fact, today he looked younger, happier, more relaxed and more vital than usual. Unfettered, she thought; that was the word. Before today she had never seen him when Claire wasn't hovering close by, and she wondered if perhaps Claire had a sobering effect on him. Mona could certainly understand that; Claire had a sobering effect on her.

Abruptly Keith slowed the automobile, eased it to the side of the road and stopped. "Now you drive," he commanded.

"Sure you want me to?"

He slid out of the car and made a courtly half-bow. "Madam, your chariot awaits. Just follow this road for five more miles and we'll be there."

Keith hurried around to get into the passenger seat while Mona, with some difficulty, slid over the console separating the bucket seats and got behind the wheel. Smoothly she eased the Mustang back onto the road and continued their journey. Ben had often told her she drove an automobile "just like a man"— the ultimate compliment—and it was true she felt perfectly comfortable and competent behind the steering wheel. She thought she read admiration in Keith's eyes as he watched the expert way she handled his prized machine.

Within moments Mona was maneuvering the little

vehicle through the massive wooden gate that marked River View Ranch's easternmost boundary. Ahead she saw the sturdy, rambling ranch house. It was built on a rise and loomed high above a maze of outbuildings and corrals. Her first impression of the Garrett ranch was that it looked greener and more prosperous than most of the ranches they had passed on their journey. The rolling grasslands fanning out in all directions from the headquarters were studded with rust-colored dots, the cattle that Mona assumed were the reason for the ranch's existence. The homestead itself, constructed of native stone and cedar shingles, was shaded by great stands of oaks and surrounded by a meticulously cared-for Bermuda-grass lawn. Small riots of color from petunias, marigolds and salvia were beginning to peep from beneath shrubbery. A sprinkling system had been turned on, and every blade of grass, every leaf, every flower glistened in the late afternoon sun.

Peaceful, Mona thought. An untroubled little world free of ever demanding clocks. The ranch house and its surroundings seemed to be slumbering. "Oh, Keith, it's absolutely lovely!" she cried enthusiastically. "If I were a painter I think I'd want to bring along my brushes. Is there really a view of the river?"

"Sure is—over there and down. The Brazos can be downright hostile on occasion, so we built up and away from it."

The sweeping drive that led to the house rose ahead of her. Mona's eyes darted from side to side. "It has something of the air of a plantation," she commented.

"But here we have very little land under cultivation. It's the pastures that are important."

They had arrived at the house. Braking, Mona eased the Mustang to a halt at the front steps and switched off the engine, and she and Keith got out of the car. "You know, I can understand why you want to live here all the time," she said. "If I had something like this, this is where I'd want to be."

"I wish you'd talk to your sister."

Dammit! If he was going to spend the weekend thinking about and talking about *her* it would ruin everything. "I have no influence with my sister," she said rather icily. "And to tell you the truth, I can't see Claire here. The two don't go together." And he could make of that what he wished.

Keith apparently chose to ignore the remark. "Someone will see to our things," he said, and taking her by the arm he ushered her into the cool interior of the house.

Mona blinked to accustom her eyes to the dimmer light, then glanced around. The house was old and solidly built. The rooms that she could see—the living room on her left, the dining room on her right and a sun room opening off the living room—were all large and pin neat, but they lacked any real warmth or personality. Just rooms full of furniture, all sturdy and masculine and a bit on the somber side. *What I could do with this place,* was her inevitable thought.

"Come, Mona," Keith said. "I want you to meet Mamie. She and her husband take care of the house for us, and she's a wonder. If you want to be pampered, Mamie will do it in spectacular fashion, and if you want to be left alone, she'll see to it that you have all the privacy in the world. And wait until you taste her cooking!"

Mamie was a plump cheerful woman who had been working for the Garretts since Keith was a child. She assumed a motherly protective attitude toward him. "The city's bad for you, Keith," she scolded. "You look downright peaked, and you're too thin."

He laughed and hugged her. A great camaraderie existed between these two people, and it showed. Childless herself, Mamie had showered Keith with all her maternal love. "Well, I feel marvelous," Keith assured her. "Mamie, I want you to meet Miss Lowery."

Mamie's round dimpled face broke into a bright smile. Approval shone from her eyes. "Ah, the Miss Lowery I've heard so much about!"

Keith coughed lightly and looked uncomfortable.

"No," Mona interjected quickly, sparing him the trouble of having to do the explaining. "I'm Mona, the other one's sister."

"That's too bad," Mamie said bluntly. "I haven't seen the other one, but you I like. You're a pretty little thing."

"Why, thank you, Mamie."

Keith nudged Mona. "Get your swimsuit on. I'll meet you at the pool in fifteen minutes."

"Steak for dinner, I suppose," Mamie called after their retreating figures.

"Great!" Keith called back, then looked down at Mona. "You like steak, I hope."

"Love it," Mona assured him.

"We eat lots of steak here," he said, and Mona recalled all those roadside signs she had seen on the way to River View, the ones that urged everyone to Eat Texas Beef!

"And Keith's great with a barbecue grill," Mamie told Mona.

"Not tonight, Mamie," Keith said with a shake of his head. "You do them tonight."

"All right, but they won't be as good," Mamie said as she walked away. "But I don't blame you for wanting to spend all your time with your guest."

Keith turned to Mona. "She likes you."

"That's good, because I like her, too."

He slipped an arm around her waist. "Come on, let me show you to your room."

KEITH WAS NOT YET at the pool side when Mona arrived, so she dived in and crossed the pool twice with smooth expert strokes. Then as she lifted herself out of the water she saw Keith lying on his back on a lounge. His eyes were closed and he looked blissfully relaxed. She couldn't seem to take her eyes off him. It was a peculiar feeling, this apparent need to look at him. She studied the way his brief white swimsuit hugged his body. Her gaze traveled the length of him, taking in the long muscular legs, the fine mat of dark chest hair that tapered down to his stomach and disappeared into the swimsuit.

Then Keith opened his eyes and raised his head, and Mona quickly looked away, regretful that she had been unable to look at him long enough to satisfy her curiosity. She pretended to be preoccupied with retrieving a bottle of tanning lotion that had fallen on the ground, until she heard a strange sound coming from Keith. She raised her eyes and saw that the smile on his face had frozen, the pupils of his eyes had grown dark and he was giving her an unreadable look.

"Good God, Mona!" he exclaimed.

Startled, she looked around to see what had prompted his reaction. "Wh-what's wrong?"

"Wrong? Nothing. But there ought to be a law against that suit. Maybe there is."

Mona glanced down at the emerald green one-piece suit. Other than plunging to slightly below the waist in back and having molded cups that emphasized her full round breasts, the suit was quite modest, she thought. That was the reason she'd brought it. She was surprised at Keith's reaction to it. "This? I have bikinis at home that are far more revealing than this. The sales clerk said it was very conservative."

His eyes never left her. "Believe me, Mona, on you that suit is anything but conservative. Lord, what a body!"

He stared at her for another minute, then lay back down and closed his eyes. Mona took the lounge next to his and reclined, too, but she didn't close her eyes. Instead she turned her head in order to look again at the bronzed masculine length beside her.

A small smile tugged at the corners of her mouth. How odd it was to derive such pleasure merely from looking at a man, to be filled with delicious warmth simply because he had admired her body. Mona had never seen anything remarkable about her figure; Claire was far more abundantly endowed than she in that department. But Keith had admired *her* body, and he hadn't been faking it. No one was that good an actor. A ripple of pure delight raced up and down her spine. It seemed she was being constantly assaulted by unfamiliar sensations. She closed her eyes and tried to still the growing excitement inside her.

They had been lying side by side for perhaps ten

minutes when Mona had the distinct feeling there was someone watching them. She raised herself with a jerk and saw a tall man dressed in denims and a plaid shirt holding a Stetson in his hand. He was standing close to her lounge and grinning down at her, a young man, probably some years younger than Keith. He had a boyish face, sand-colored hair and a disarming smile.

"Oh!" she said, quickly sitting up. "Hello."

The man bowed his head to her and said, "Hello, ma'am," and his appreciative eyes made a thorough blatant sweep of her. Suddenly Mona wished she had some kind of cover-up to shield herself from this man's frank gaze.

At the sound of voices Keith had sat up. "Hi, Jim. How's it going?"

"Not too bad, Keith," the man said, reluctantly tearing his eyes away from Mona.

Keith smiled knowingly at the expression on the man's face. "Mona, I'd like you to meet Jim Browder. He's my foreman. Jim, this is my friend, Mona Lowery."

"A pleasure, ma'am," Jim Browder said with a grin. "How come none of *my* friends look like you?"

Mona squirmed under his open scrutiny. "How do you do, Jim. It's nice to meet you."

Now Jim gave Keith his full attention. "Are you gonna want to look at the new calves in the morning, Keith? I'll tell you, old Kingsley's worth every nickel you paid for him."

"I'll be out bright and early," Keith promised. "But don't expect too much work out of me this weekend. This is Mona's first visit, and I want to give her the grand tour."

Jim nodded. "Can't say as I blame you." He bowed again. "Nice meetin' you, Miss Lowery. Hope to see you again soon." He put the Stetson on his head and walked away, but not before another admiring inspection of the woman in the green swimsuit.

Keith watched the foreman depart, then turned to Mona with a wink. "There," he said, "is someone else who likes you."

THE WEEKEND TURNED INTO two glorious, relaxing, rejuvenating days. There was something to all that fresh-air-and-sunshine business after all, Mona decided. She felt as energetic as a puppy. But the most delightful aspect of her visit to the ranch was how much she enjoyed Keith's company. He seemed to need good talk and easy companionship as badly as she did, and after two days with him Mona felt as though she had known him all her life. It was a rare thing—two people coming together who were so finely attuned to each other. She wondered if Keith's feelings in any way mirrored her own.

After determining that Mona could indeed ride a horse, Keith saddled up on Saturday morning and took her on a tour of his ranch. A great deal of it was still timbered with pecan and oak, and cedar was everywhere, green black in its lushness. Deer, dove and quail abounded. It occurred to Mona that as a city girl she had grown used to looking at man-made things. This closeness to nature was a new and invigorating experience for her. At River View one was never far out of earshot of the rushing noise the Brazos made on its leisurely—sometimes—journey southeast to the Gulf of Mexico, and there was a pungent freshness to the air that caught in her throat.

"My God, Keith!" she exclaimed, twisting in her saddle and gawking. "We could be a thousand miles from the nearest city. It's...it's beautiful. Almost primitive."

"We're in sort of a transition zone here," Keith told her. "This is the western edge of the blackland prairie and the eastern beginning of the big ranching country of west Texas. River View straddles the ninety-eighth meridian."

"What does that mean?" Mona asked.

"Oh, a long time ago someone is supposed to have figured out that the ninety-eighth meridian is the cut-off point for twenty-six-inch rainfalls. I don't know how accurate that is, but I do know that some years we get our twenty-six inches and some years we have to make do with the twelve or so the west Texans are used to." He looked across at her with a smile. "If you spend much time around here, Mona, you'll hear an awful lot of weather talk. When a man starts ranching, rain suddenly becomes the most important thing in life."

"Do cows really need all that water?"

"Of course they need water, but that's not the point. I can truck water to the herd if I have to. What rain means is grass and crops. To a farmer or rancher rain is...life! It's as simple as that." He pushed the big hat farther on his head and scowled up at the crystal-clear sky. "And we're sure overdue. If we don't get some rain soon I'm going to have to cull the herd."

It crossed Mona's mind that what had seemed to her a perfectly splendid day might not seem so lovely to people desperately in need of rain. "How many cows do you own?'' she asked, gazing out over a grassy hill blanketed with creamy-faced Herefords.

Now Keith chuckled. ''Let me give you a lesson in country etiquette, Mona. Never ask a man how many cows he owns or how many acres he has.''

She frowned. ''Why?''

''Because it's like asking him how much money he has—and he'll probably lie to you anyway. Besides, acreage is relative. Nine hundred acres on the Brazos is far different from nine hundred out in west Texas or the Arizona Strip, where there are thirty or forty acres per cow unit.''

''I take it this means you don't want me to know how many cows you own.''

He laughed. ''I run a herd of three hundred or so, depending.''

''Depending on what?''

''Oh, weather conditions, market conditions, lots of things.'' Again he looked at her, squinting under his Stetson. ''You sure are full of questions.''

''How else am I going to learn? What do I know, stuck in my Highland Park mansion? The closest I ever get to nature is Sunday in the park or a trip to the zoo.''

They had made a wide sweep of Keith's property and were now heading back to the headquarters. Nearer the ranch house were the hay field and Mamie's vegetable garden, a barn and a smokehouse, the corrals and other working structures. One in particular aroused Mona's curiosity.

''What's that?''

''Kingsley's domain.''

''Who's Kingsley?''

"Our certified grand-champion bull. Would you like to meet him?"

She shrugged and laughed. "Of course."

Kingsley didn't look too friendly, but he was a magnificent specimen, and the ribbons and pictures festooning the walls of the barn attested to his superior status.

"Kingsley cost a small fortune, but he sires hundreds of calves a year for us," Keith told her proudly.

"Hundreds?"

"Sure. Artificial insemination. Kingsley is far too valuable to trust him to the random ways of bulls and cows left to roam the pastures at will."

Mona shot him a look of distaste. "Oh, I think that's terrible! Profit-minded cowboys tampering with nature."

Although Keith's expression remained perfectly serious, Mona sensed the amusement lurking beneath. "Kingsley doesn't mind," he said.

"Who cares what Kingsley minds? It's the poor cows I feel sorry for. They won't have a bit of romance in their lives, and they won't have the slightest idea how they came to be mothers."

Keith threw back his head and laughed lustily. "Oh, Mona, what a delightful girl you are!"

One thing became quickly evident to Mona: at River View Keith was in his rightful milieu. She had imagined him to be a corporate president who ranched as a hobby, but it was almost the other way around. Here he was the boss, and everyone knew it. Before the weekend was over Mona met most of the ranch hands—young and old, tall and short, lean and paunchy, taciturn and talkative—and if they shared a common denominator it was that they liked working with horses and cattle and respected Keith's knowledge of both.

What the men thought of her she didn't know but she could guess, and it bothered her. "Keith," she ventured tentatively, "do you suppose the men think it's improper for me to be here?"

His dark eyes narrowed. "It's not their place to think anything about us. Why, Mona? Has someone said something?"

"No, no. They're all very polite...almost too polite. They're always tipping their hats and calling me 'ma'am.' But I've noticed some speculative looks. Perhaps it's only my imagination. I can't be the first woman you've brought to this ranch."

"As a matter of fact, Mona, you are the first *person*, man or woman, I've brought to spend a weekend on this ranch. So that no doubt explains the speculative looks. They're probably wondering why you're so special. Above and beyond your obvious, er, physical attributes, I mean."

JUNE'S SOFT PURPLE TWILIGHT had descended. There was a certain magic enchantment to the country in the evening. Never would Mona have imagined night could be so absolutely dark and quiet. She and Keith were sitting on the patio under the stars, finishing their wine after another of Mamie's superb meals.

"You fit in here, Keith," she told him. "I can just picture you sitting around a campfire, swapping tales about stampedes, brush fires and cattle rustlers."

He pulled on his chin and smiled. "Yeah, sometimes I think I would have liked that life. Cowboying has changed a lot, although on some of the really big spreads out west they still do things the old way.''

"I noticed that the ranch hands, even the ones who are so much older than you, treat your word as though it were gospel.''

"That's because they know I'm a pretty fair cowhand myself. If I weren't, none of those men would give me the time of day. The *Morning News* ran an article on Garrett Instruments not long ago, and in it I was referred to as an 'electronics magnate.' I remember thinking, *who, me?* My dad's the electronics whiz, not me. I take after granddad. Now there was a cowboy! His greatest regret in life was not having been around for the big cattle drives. I'm more at home in faded jeans sitting astride a horse than I am in board meetings. The days I spend on this ranch are the happiest of my life, and that doesn't sit well with Claire, believe me.''

Mona sighed. She would have given anything to spend the two delightful days with no mention of Claire, but she supposed it was inevitable that her sister's name would come up. She sensed that Keith needed to talk about her, so she listened sympathetically. That seemed to be her lot in life—consoling her sister's lovesick men.

"How did you meet Claire?'' she asked him.

"Oh, it was some sort of party. She walked in, and every head in the room turned. I spent all evening trying to wrangle an introduction. She was dating Joey Willis at the time, but I couldn't get her out of my head. When she and Joey broke up I was first in line...and I don't think I've had a minute's peace since. She drives me mad, but she can be so charming and likable at times.''

A familiar story. Mona had heard it so many times

before. There had to be something about Claire, something that just hadn't got through to Mona yet. If this exceptional man could be interested in her, there had to be something. "I know," she said quietly. "You can't imagine what it was like growing up with her. Everyone would say, 'Oh, you're *Claire's* sister,' and the comparison would begin on the spot. I hate admitting it, but I suppose I've always been a little jealous of her."

Keith turned his head to look at her. When Mona had changed for dinner she had eschewed jeans and chosen to wear long green lounging pajamas that clung seductively to her young body. Keith studied her thick fluttering lashes, the tilt of her nose, the full sensuous bottom lip, the curve of her chin. "Not many young women would confess that so readily," he said in a warm voice. "But you shouldn't be jealous of her, Mona. You're quite a delectable girl yourself, you know."

A self-deprecatory laugh escaped Mona's lips. "Well, this 'delectable' girl has some pretty nasty memories of ugly thoughts about her sister—as if Claire can help it that she's so gorgeous. But I don't think I ever brought a fellow home who didn't just fall all over himself when he saw Claire. It was almost funny to watch them. They'd get all starry-eyed and tongue-tied. So I'd vow never to bring anyone home again. Trouble was, I wasn't allowed to date anyone my folks hadn't met, so I'd try to pick a time when I knew Claire wouldn't be home. It got to be a ridiculous game—and the most ridiculous part of it all was that I didn't care all that much about any of those fellows." She paused to gauge Keith's reaction to all this reminiscing. "Silly, huh?"

He gave her a sympathetic look. "It's easy to call it silly when you're looking at it from the vantage point of time. But adolescent emotions are very real and hurtful at the time you're experiencing them. And sibling rivalry is hardly unusual."

"No," she agreed, "but I think I carried it a little far at times. And yet in a way the jealousy was good for me."

"Good for you?"

She nodded. "It made me so determined to do something special with my own life, something separate and apart that couldn't be compared with anything Claire had done. I knew I would never be the raving beauty she was, so I decided to become the brains of the family. God, how I used to study! I carried that a little far, too. I think I would have died if I'd missed a year of making the National Honor Society. *There* was something Claire couldn't do!" She pursed her lips. "Keith, do you suppose I'm an extremist?"

He chuckled. "Just a determined young lady perhaps."

Mona shook her head ruefully. "All that competition with my sister! What a dreadful waste of time! And I wasn't upsetting anyone but myself, because Claire didn't even know I was competing with her. I used to think Claire was insecure because she needed compliments and adoration, but all the while *I* was the insecure one, letting my jealousy guide me. Thank God I got myself channeled in a worthwhile direction. When my interior-design shop is a success—and it will be—I'll move out of the house, get an apartment of my own and live a life very different from the one Claire is going to have."

"Oh? And what sort of life is Claire going to have?"

Careful, Mona, her inner voice warned. *This man is fond of Claire—perhaps fonder than you realize. And Claire brings out the worst in you. She always has. Best not say too much.*

"One like my mother's," she said obscurely, and let it go at that.

Keith reached out, took her hand and patted it, a surprisingly warm and affectionate gesture. "There's no reason for you ever to be jealous of anyone, Mona. You are a perfectly delightful person in your own right."

He did not release her hand, and Mona's fingers laced through his, seemingly of their own volition. How pleasant it was just to hold his hand. Such a simple thing, yet full of amiable rapport. "Thanks," she said gratefully, and deep down she really did believe in her own self-worth. But still she couldn't completely ignore the petty feelings that Claire aroused in her. Human nature was a multilayered, strange thing, she reflected.

"The worst part of all that jealousy," she suddenly decided to confide, "was knowing how upset my father would have been had he known about it. He wants nothing more than family harmony."

She settled against the back of the chaise, inhaled deeply, then exhaled, letting the soft night air wash over her. "What time do we have to go back tomorrow?" she asked.

"Not early. I usually try to get back around six, to get ready for another work week."

"You've given me a pretty thorough indoctrination into ranch life. Now tell me something about Garrett Instruments."

"What would you like to know?"

"Oh, how it got started, what you do. Things like that."

Keith reached in his shirt pocket and withdrew a cigarette. Thinking he might need another free hand, Mona loosened her grip, but Keith clutched her hand firmly. Clamping the cigarette between his lips he pulled out a lighter, flicked it, then replaced it in his pocket. "Want one?" he asked. She shook her head, content to sit beside him, hold his hand and listen to him talk.

"Dad was always a tinkerer and he was fascinated by electronics, so he went into the business of making talking educational toys. They were a huge commercial success, so dad branched out. The technology from the space program was beginning to be tapped by then, so we went into the predictable things— pocket calculators, data-control systems. Now we're working on a word-processing unit that we hope will be so simple to operate and economical to own that small businesses and individuals like free-lance writers can justify the cost of one."

"Sounds fascinating. But this is where your heart lies, right?"

He gave her a look of empathy. "Yeah, I guess so."

"I can't say I blame you. This has been so nice, Keith. I can't thank you enough for the weekend," she said, thinking how quickly it had ended.

"I'm glad you had a good time, Mona, because I enjoyed having you here with me."

Her heart leaped at the nice words. "Your ranch is beautiful—and that great old house! When was it built?"

His brow furrowed. "I'm not sure. My great-grandfather built it with money he made from cotton. It must have been in the 1920s, but it's been through major additions and renovations since then. I hope you noticed that we have indoor plumbing. The original didn't."

Mona laughed. "Oh, I noticed plenty about it. Whoever built it meant for it to be around a long time. The woodwork is really fantastic. I'd love to get my hands on a house like this."

"Would you? Well, Mamie has been after me for ages to do something with the place, but men never seem to have the time or inclination for that sort of thing." He paused in thought. "What do you mean by 'getting your hands on it'? Would you be interested in doing some sketches for me? I guess that's the way one starts. . . and I'd gladly pay you for your time."

"I'm not a professional yet, Keith. I'd do it strictly because I wanted to—and because it will be fun." A warm thought crossed Mona's mind then: if she did some sketches of the house he would have to see her again, if only briefly. It did no good to remind herself that the less she saw of Keith Garrett the better off she would be. She was too acutely aware of him when he was near. It was too potentially dangerous to foster this blossoming friendship. The prudent thing for her to do was to plead the press of school and forget about seeing Keith again, but for once she couldn't force herself to be prudent.

"I'd love to make some sketches of your house," she said.

"You know, Mona, I can't remember ever meeting anyone I'm so relaxed with. Do you know what I like best about you?"

She pretended to give it serious thought. "My incredible good looks, my sparkling wit and my delightful personality?" she teased.

"Besides those things, of course," he teased back.

"I can't imagine."

"I don't have to sit around and wonder what you're thinking. You just come right out and say what's on your mind."

If he only knew! There were plenty of thoughts churning in her mind at that moment, thoughts she preferred he knew nothing about. Striving to keep her voice casual, she asked, "May I give you a call at your office when my sketches are completed?"

"Of course—or better still, I'll be coming out here every weekend this summer, Mona. I'd like for you to come, too, if you'd like."

"Again?" she asked in surprise, and that crazy inner excitement welled up again. She had hoped she might see him again, but to come to River View? She certainly hadn't let her hopes stretch that far.

"Certainly," Keith said. "Every time, every weekend. I'll tend to ranch business, and you can use the time any way you choose."

"Are you serious?"

"Perfectly serious."

She shouldn't, of course. But then, they were friends. She did enjoy his company, and he must truly have enjoyed hers or he wouldn't have invited her again. And if the roles were reversed, Claire wouldn't bat an eye about accepting. "You've got yourself a deal, Mr. Garrett."

CHAPTER FOUR

THE TELEPHONE IN THE LIBRARY was ringing shrilly when Mona arrived home from school Monday afternoon. She reached the room's threshold just in time to see Lettie lifting the receiver.

"I'm home, Lettie, if it's for me."

Lettie nodded and spoke into the instrument. Then she held it out to Mona. "It's Alan Palmer."

Mona's hopes fell to earth, and she silently berated herself. There was no sound reason for her to think Keith might call. She took the phone from Lettie. "Hi, Alan."

The husky male voice on the other end of the line chuckled. "I'll swear, Mona, you really keep my feet on the ground. I'm used to much more enthusiasm when a young woman learns I'm on the phone."

"Your modesty is overwhelming, Alan," Mona said dryly. "What's on your mind?"

"Are you busy?"

"No. I just got home from school."

"Can you scoot over here? I want to show you something."

"Oh? What is it?"

"I'll show you when you get here. I need help."

"Okay," she said, interested in spite of herself, for she couldn't imagine why Alan, of all people, would need her help. "Give me a minute to change into shorts and grab a bite to eat. Then I'll be there."

"Thanks, Mona. Come around back."

Mona raced up the stairs, deposited her books on the drafting table and changed into shorts and a halter. Then on her way out of the house she stopped in the kitchen and rummaged through the refrigerator for something to eat. She was caught in the act by a frowning Lucille. The cook was very possessive of her private bailiwick and preferred that the family members steer clear of the kitchen. Kitty was only too happy to oblige. Mona thought her mother might actually be a woman who literally did not know how to boil water.

"What are you doing, Mona?" Lucille asked disapprovingly.

"Looking for something quick to eat."

"Young lady, sit down at that table and let me fix you a proper lunch."

Mona backed out of the refrigerator, triumphantly waving a piece of fried chicken and a can of Coke. "I don't have time, Lucille. I'm on a mission of mercy." She popped the top of the can. "I'm on my way over to the Palmers."

"Mona, do you know how long it's been since you've sat down at the table and eaten a whole meal? If your mother knew about this—"

"But she doesn't and she won't," Mona insisted firmly. "Now, Lucille, if I get a call be sure to—"

"We know, Mona. Get a name and number."

Mona took the path between the Lowery and Palmer houses and marched purposefully across the lush grounds of her neighbor's imposing Mediterranean-style mansion, entering the pool area by way of a clanging wrought-iron gate. She found Alan, clad in swimming trunks, sprawled out on a lounge beside the pool, a can of beer in his hand. The area surrounding the pool was a cluttered mess. All around Mona was evidence of some sort of recent construction. Boards, empty paint cans, spattered drop cloths, nails and sawdust littered the place.

"What's been going on over here?" she asked.

Alan grinned and got to his feet. He indicated the house with a jerk of his thumb. "Mother's parting gesture to me was to contract to have a sun room added onto the house." He raised his eyes and arms to the heavens. "Just what I needed! Fifteen rooms already and I get another one! Then mother and Jeff took off for Hawaii, and I'm stuck with this mess. Come on, I'll show you."

The new addition was a long, narrow, glass-enclosed room opening off the kitchen and overlooking the pool and cabanas. "Nice," Mona murmured appreciatively, but like Alan she wondered why his mother had felt compelled to build onto a house that was already much too large for their needs.

"Yeah, I suppose it is, but I sure don't need it. Mother could just never stand to leave anything alone. So now I have a sun room, and I don't have the first clue what to do with the thing. Mother suggested hiring a decorator, and that's when I thought about you. Would I be imposing if I asked you to lend a hand with it?"

Now Mona was interested. She began walking slowly up and down, her practiced eyes studying every detail of the room. "Since it looks out over the pool I suppose you want it light and airy and casual."

Alan shrugged. His manner suggested total disinterest. "*I* don't want anything, but obviously it has to have something done with it. If you're too busy to take this on, Mona, I can call someone else."

"Don't be ridiculous!" she quickly said. "This will be fabulous experience for me." She moved about the room, thinking. "It just cries out for plants, plants and more plants. You have great exposure for them. And I think wicker or rattan furniture. Admittedly it's expensive...but so popular. How does that sound? And no draperies. They would be too heavy. But you'll need something to block out the worst of the summer sun—vertical blinds perhaps. I'll have to think about that some. And since it's so close to the kitchen maybe one corner should be given over to a small glass-topped table with latticework chairs. It would be a wonderful place to have breakfast. Oh, this could be such a stunning room!"

Alan couldn't have been less concerned. "Well, do whatever you want with the thing. I'll give you my bank card."

"No, we'll go about this very professionally. I'll decorate the room for you and then present you with a whopping bill! Now, just let me study the rooms immediately around it. What's in here?" She tapped on a door opening off the room.

"A closet."

"And here?"

"The utility room."

Mona stepped up into the kitchen and glanced around. It was the predictable mammoth collection of gleaming stainless steel and wood, chock-full of every modern convenience. She stepped back into the sun room and went to a door at the opposite end.

"What's in here?" she asked, opening the door without waiting for an answer.

Quickly Alan moved to her side and reached for the doorknob as if to close it. "Oh, that's just my workshop."

Mona shot him an amused glance. "Workshop? What do *you* work at?" She stepped into the room and discovered to her amazement that she was in a studio, an artist's retreat. The room had a sloped skylight in the ceiling, and everything was bathed in a lucid light. The tools of the trade were everywhere. Shelves and tables were strewn with paints and brushes and cloths and several palettes. Paint-smeared smocks hung from pegs on the wall. Easels holding canvases in various stages of completion stood in front of the window and under the skylight. The stench of turpentine was overpowering.

Mesmerized, Mona moved from canvas to canvas. The majority of the paintings were landscapes and were, she thought, lovely. There wasn't one she wouldn't have enjoyed owning.

"Alan!" she cried breathlessly. "You did all this?"

He grinned sheepishly like a small boy caught in the process of committing some mischief. "Aw, this is just something I dabble in when I'm bored. It's nothing, not even much of a hobby. I'm thinking of giving it up and taking up something else—photography maybe."

That was a lie, Mona sensed. She had a feeling Alan loved painting. There was evidence of it all around her. "Dabble indeed! It takes a long time to complete so much work. How long have you been at this?"

"Oh, six or seven years, I guess."

Mona moved on to another canvas. "Have you ever had any real training?" she asked, squinting at the painting. "The brushwork and detail are marvelous."

"I took a few art courses at the university—when I was supposed to be studying petroleum engineering."

Alan's landscapes were the predictable Texas scenes: Padre Island, the brooding Davis Mountains, Guadalupe Peak and the wide-open spaces of cowboy country. But the painting that most captured Mona's attention was not a landscape at all but a city scene, a charming oil of Turtle Creek when the azaleas were in bloom. There was no great trick to finding loveliness in natural wonders, but to find it amid the steel-and-concrete jungle of the city took an artist's eye. Mona herself was not entirely without art experience, and though not exactly an expert she thought she recognized talent when she saw it. At least she knew what she liked, and she liked Alan's paintings very much.

With shining eyes she turned to her friend. Discovering this new facet of his personality was quite a revelation. "Alan, you're awfully good at this— awfully good!"

But Alan seemed anxious to make light of the whole thing. "Aw, Mona. I just play around with this."

"That's your problem. You play around with everything. I refuse to believe you want to spend your life as a tennis bum when you're capable of work like this. Why don't you do something serious with your painting?"

"Oh, come on! Don't make a big deal out of this."
He shook an admonishing finger at her. "And I
don't want you blabbing this all over town. It'll just
be our little secret, okay?"

Mona looked at him scornfully. "Are you afraid it
will spoil your macho image?"

"Well, it certainly wouldn't help it along."

But Mona persisted. "Alan, I have a friend who
has a gallery. You know her, too. Stephanie Means.
Please let me show her some of your work. My God,
you could turn out to amount to something after
all!"

Alan laughed. "No chance. I'm hopeless, haven't
you heard? Everybody knows that."

Mona had picked up the Turtle Creek scene and
was studying it intently. "This one I love!" she said
truthfully.

"Then it's yours. Take it."

"Oh, no, Alan. Let me buy it from you."

He burst out laughing. "Good grief, Mona! Buy it
from me? Come on."

"I mean it. Your work is worth something."

"All right. The price is ten dollars—and I'll have
to have it in cash."

Mona was thoroughly disgusted with him. "Alan,
what can I do to get you serious about this? Don't
you realize you have real talent?"

"No, I don't. Like I said, this is just something I
play around with. But take the painting if you like it.
Otherwise it will just lie around the studio gathering
dust. Now let's get back to the business at hand.
What do we do with the sun room?"

Reluctantly Mona allowed Alan to lead her out of
the studio, but she had no intention of dismissing the

matter as lightly as he had. She propped the painting
he had given her against the wall and forced her attention back to the decorating project. "Tomorrow
after school I'll make the rounds of some of my
favorite stores and I'll give you a call. First of all,
though, get me something to measure with—and pencil and paper."

SUMMER SUDDENLY BECAME a very busy time for
Mona, and the days slipped into a pleasant satisfying
routine. During the weekdays she was occupied with
her studies and the decoration project she had under-
taken for Alan. At night she usually labored over the
sketches she was doing of the house at River View.
And she made a point of taking the Turtle Creek
painting to Stephanie Means.

Stephanie was an elegant spectacled woman, a girl-
hood friend of Kitty's. The little gallery that bore her
name was like the woman herself—small, neat, proper. So many art galleries, it seemed to Mona, were
rather junky establishments where one had to sift
through the insignificant to find work of merit, but
not at Stephanie's. Her place was designed to show
off art to its best advantage, and Mona delighted in
dwelling on the possibility of one day seeing Alan's
landscapes adorning the walls of one of the gallery's
small rooms. She had no idea what Alan would think
of this somewhat bold move of hers, nor did she care.
There were some people who would rock along on
dead center all their lives if they weren't given a
shove, and Alan was one of them.

Stephanie greeted her warmly, inquired about her
family, then listened with interest as Mona explained
her reason for being there. The woman took Alan's

painting and studied it with knowledgeable eyes while Mona watched and waited with her hands clasped in her lap.

Finally Stephanie said, "I like it, and do you know what I like best about it? Whoever the artist is paints for the sheer joy of it. I'm so tired of these deadly serious types who have a message for mankind. They have their place, of course, but it's refreshing to see work like this for a change. Did you say the artist is a local one?"

Mona nodded.

"I'm featuring local artists next month, Mona, and I'd like to show a smattering of unknowns along with the names. Could you get in touch with him for me? Perhaps he has other things."

Mona tingled with excitement. "Why don't you get in touch with him yourself, Steph? You know him, I'm sure."

"Oh? Who is he? I thought I knew every artist in north Texas."

Mona smiled. "You're not going to believe it."

"Try me."

"Alan Palmer."

Stephanie stared at Mona in astonishment. "Surely you don't mean the late Jackson Palmer's son!"

"One and the same."

Stephanie's eyes flew back to the painting. "My word! Old Joy Boy himself! I wouldn't have thought Alan Palmer capable of doing anything more creative than mixing a martini."

"Oh, Steph," Mona said earnestly, "Alan has an entire studio full of things like this. I guess he's been painting all his adult life, but he refuses to be serious about it. And he has no idea I'm talking to you about this. When you contact him he's, one, going to be surprised and, two, going to try to make light of the whole thing, so you're going to have to be very persuasive. Please don't take no for an answer."

"Don't worry, Mona. I've spent my life dealing with the fragile egos of temperamental artists."

"That's the trouble, Steph. Alan doesn't know he's an artist. He refuses to look at this as anything more than a rich playboy's hobby."

Stephanie looked at her quizzically. "What's your interest in all this, Mona? Alan Palmer himself?"

Mona was taken aback. "Oh, no! Not at all. Alan and I have been friends since we were kids, and if I feel anything for him it's more often irritation and exasperation than anything. He's always been so... so frivolous. A week ago if you had asked me to define Alan's philosophy of life I would have had to say it was to swing a mean tennis racket, down the booze and bed the ladies. To suddenly discover him capable of such beautiful work...well, it's been a surprise—a nice surprise—and I do so wish I could get him to pursue it. I'm afraid I could plead with him until I'm blue in the face and it would do no good, but you...you might be able to convince him that his work has real merit. I hope so, Steph, and I don't know how to thank you."

Stephanie smiled. "It is I who should thank you, Mona. A new artist always excites me. I'll give Alan a call, and I'll let you know how things are going."

But the most special part of the summer were the weekends Mona spent with Keith at his ranch. Time passed quickly—too quickly, she thought. Summer would be over before she knew it, and she tried not to think too much about the very real loss Keith's absence from her life would be. Occasionally during the week the telephone would ring and his voice would come over the line. Mona wondered if she would ever get used to the warm flush that spread through her whenever she heard that rich resonant voice.

"I'm just checking up on you," he would say. "Just wanted to see how you're doing."

But he never came to the house, nor did he ever suggest going to a movie or having dinner. Mona thought she understood. He would not particularly want to be seen squiring his girl friend's little sister around. And in all truth, Mona did not especially want word of her friendship with Keith to reach Claire's ears, as it inevitably would if they were seen together in public. Moving about in their select social circle was much like living in a small town; gossip was quickly and effectively circulated.

And Keith never talked much about his life in the city. He didn't live with his father, that much she knew. He had an apartment, but she had no idea where it was. She didn't know, although she had wondered dozens of times, if there was a woman whom he saw on a regular basis now that Claire was away. Mona thought surely there must be—a man like Keith Garrett wouldn't live the life of a celibate for very long—and she tried to imagine the sort of woman who would capture his interest. Mature, intelligent, someone who liked good talk and good food and good wine. She would be pretty, of course. Not in Claire's league perhaps but lovely nonetheless. Mona envied her, as absurd as that was.

At least Keith's weekends belonged to her. They had not once missed spending the weekend together since that first time. Every Friday she waited for the sound of the Mustang's arrival, for the blast of its horn, and she would be off to River View with Keith. It had come to be the most important part of her life.

Keith was thoughtful and intelligent and good company, and one day she told him so.

"I'm glad you think so, Mona," he said with a smile, "because I think you're a helluva great gal, even with that sharp tongue of yours. I like having you for a friend. I like you period."

"That's good," she said with her customary lack of guile. "I like you, too, Keith. I really do."

Keith, after much careful consideration and many changes of mind, had singled out a particularly gentle chestnut mare for Mona to ride whenever she wished, and she had come to think of Mandy as hers.

"Mandy's sort of the dowager queen around here," Keith told her. "Bess over there is her daughter." Mona's eyes flew to a prancing, proud and haughty mare, buff colored in contrast to its mother's rich hue. "Mandy's getting along in years but she's still a good riding horse, and I won't worry about you if she's your mount."

Enlisting the aid of Sam, Mamie's husband, Mona had learned how to groom and feed Mandy, had learned all her behavior traits, and she talked to the mare as though Mandy were a person. "Mandy understands every single word I say," she solemnly told an amused Keith, and soon the dark-haired girl and the chestnut mare were a familiar sight around the ranch.

Keith had told Mona she could ride wherever she wanted, provided she never went out without telling someone she was leaving.

"Why?" she'd wanted to know.

"Because something might happen while you're riding. Mandy could go lame, or she could get spooked and throw you. But as long as someone knew you were out, not too much time would pass before we came looking for you. I want you to train yourself to use your eyes and ears and watch out for pitfalls."

"Such as?"

"Oh, holes in the ground, big rocks, squirrels, rabbits, snakes. It's like defensive driving."

So together Mona and Mandy had inspected most of the ranch. Much of Keith's property was still pristine and untouched, some of its remoter parts a little eerie and foreboding. At night the noises coming out of those woods sounded strange and frightening to a city girl's ears. Spooky, Mona had thought when she first began coming to River View. The sky was darker, the stars were brighter and the days less uncomfortably warm than they were in Dallas. Here it seemed to Mona that everything inside her shifted into low gear. For the first time she realized just how nerve whipping the cacophony of the city could be.

She had found something of a friend in Jim Browder, the foreman. He often rode with her on her outings and bouts of nature study, and it was from Jim that Mona learned more about Keith.

"I've known Keith about ten years, I guess," Jim said. "I was sixteen when I first hired on here. It was some sort of summer-school project. A bunch of us kids who thought we might be interested in farming or ranching got jobs in the area. Keith was getting out of college about then, ready to take over his daddy's business. But, hell, I knew from the start that he wasn't near as interested in the business as he was in this ranch. He's made a lot of improvements in ten years, and there'll be more. He's a good cowhand. I've learned a lot from him.''

"He loves this place, that's for sure," Mona said. "He told me he's going to live here all the time one of these days.''

Jim shifted in the saddle to look at her. "And how do you feel about that—you being a city girl and all?''

Mona frowned. "I beg your pardon?''

Jim grinned. "Well, if Keith intends living here all the time, I guess that means you'll be living here all the time one of these days. How do you feel about that?''

Comprehension dawned on her. "Oh, no! Keith and I are only friends.''

"Come on, Mona. Tell me another one! That's the favorite topic of conversation around the bunkhouse. Tops the weather any day. Nobody can ever remember Keith bringing a pretty gal out here—not once or twice but every weekend. We're all hearing wedding bells.''

"Then you're all going to be very disappointed. Jim, you must set everyone straight. It's my older sister who's Keith's love interest. He and I are nothing but friends.''

Jim gave a little hoot. "Sure, ma'am, whatever you say." But the look he gave her clearly indicated that he didn't believe a word of it.

That evening after dinner Mona told Keith about the conversation with Jim. "You'd best tell them the truth, Keith. Good heavens, no telling what kind of stories are floating around the bunkhouse. The men probably think we're...well, you know...."

He was half-reclining in the chaise next to hers. He rolled his head toward her, and his eyes glittered with amusement. It crossed Mona's mind that he often looked at her with amusement. She supposed he thought her a simple soul, terribly naive, and she thought that a terribly unfair assessment. She was merely inexperienced and therefore not a cynic.

"Sleeping together?" Keith asked.

Nonplussed, she looked at him fully. "Well. . . yes, they might."

"They probably do," he said without the slightest trace of concern.

"Keith, tell them. Please."

"No, Mona. Be sensible. If I go to great lengths to protest that you and I are nothing but friends, those boys are going to be damned sure we're much, much more. Besides—" his face broke into a grin "—if those boys out there in the bunkhouse think that a darling girl like you is madly in love with me, I'd be a fool to destroy that illusion."

But Mona had something else on her mind. "Keith, these rumors. . . if they persist, they might reach someone you would prefer did not hear them."

His facial muscles twitched. "You mean Claire."

"Of course."

"Small chance of that, I'd think. Claire has nothing to do with this ranch." He paused, then added, "Mona, people are going to think what they want to think. You and I know what our relationship is, and that's all that matters."

Ah, yes! She knew what their relationship was. They were good friends, nothing more.

KEITH LIKED HER SKETCHES of his house. "I can't believe it's the same place!" he exclaimed. "What would be involved in getting the house looking like this?"

"Not as much as you might think. If you'll notice, I've made no really major changes. Most of the effect has been achieved by rearranging the furniture, bringing in color and using the right accessories."

He studied the drawings a moment longer. Then he looked up. "Would you like to take on the job?"

Mona's eyes shone. "Of course I'd like to take on the job!"

"Then go to it!"

Now she had two jobs—no great problem since she was nearing completion on Alan's sun room. With the River View project she had the time of her life, since Keith gave her a free hand to do whatever she wanted with the house. If she asked for his opinion on one matter or another he invariably said, "I know nothing about this sort of thing, Mona, and I trust your judgment completely." He was a decorator's dream!

Now when Keith called for her on Fridays she would come laden with boxes and paintings and plants and pillows. Every spare minute of the week was spent shopping. By this time she had become quite a familiar sight in all the flea markets and antique shops, furniture stores and flooring establishments—not a bad thing since these were the people with whom she would be dealing when she was in business. She was constantly in a rush; there weren't enough hours in the day. A call from Alan one evening made her realize just how thoroughly preoccupied with River View she had become.

"Hey, where the hell have you been?" Alan admonished. "I thought you were coming over here to finish the sun room. I've expected you every night, but every time I call you're out gallivanting around somewhere."

"Oh, Alan, I'm sorry! I meant to stop by the greenhouse and pick out the plants for the room, and I've had the pillows here for days. I've just been so busy. Tomorrow night for sure."

"What in the world have you been up to? Other than meddling in my affairs, I mean."

At first Mona was puzzled, then she understood. "Stephanie called you!"

"Yeah."

"Well?"

"Well, nothing. I told you, Mona, you're making too big a deal out of this. It's a hobby, nothing more. Lay off!"

"Oh, Alan, you irritate me, honestly you do! I could—"

"Back to the original question," Alan interrupted. "What's been keeping you so busy?"

Briefly Mona explained about a friend with a house in the country that she had been asked to redecorate. Names and location were carefully omitted.

"Well, get over here when you can," Alan said.

"I'll call first."

"There's no need to call first, Mona."

"Oh, yes, there is!" she insisted. "I might come charging over there and find you with a woman."

Alan laughed. "Come to think of it, maybe you'd better call first."

Mona hung up, shaking her head and feeling very sorry for any woman who had the incredibly bad fortune to fall for Alan Palmer.

THAT WEEKEND, while Keith tended to ranch chores, Mona kept busy with the house. Her enthusiasm was boundless, and she had found a willing helper in Mamie.

"This house has needed a woman in it for so long," Mamie said. "I do what I can, but it's not the same. A house needs a mistress. When Keith's mother died I hoped Mr. Garrett would remarry, but it didn't happen. And, too, I thought Keith would be married long before now." Mamie loved to gossip about the family, for they had been such a big part of her life for so long. "Keith was always... well, special, I guess. My favorite. I don't think he ever gave us any trouble, although he was something of a pest when he was a youngster, always dogging the cowboys' footsteps and asking a million questions a minute. But it paid off handsomely. Ask any man on the ranch and he'll tell you Keith was born to do what he's doing now."

Mamie pointed out the window. Following her gesturing finger, Mona's gaze found and fastened on Keith. He was sitting on the corral fence, watching a pair of ranch hands halterbreaking a filly. Shirtless, his skin glistened with perspiration.

"He runs Garrett Instruments to please his father," Mamie said, "but I honestly can't picture Keith sitting in an office all day. Knowing him the way I do I don't see how he stands it."

The picture wouldn't form in Mona's mind, either. Nor would another—the picture of that handsome, outdoorsy, utterly masculine man married to Claire. It would be a shame, a crime, the mismatch of the century! Claire would make his life miserable from the first day, pulling him one way when he wanted to go another. Why couldn't Keith see that? Why?

"Were there other children?" Mona asked.

Mamie nodded. "A sister. She's married and lives in El Paso with three little ones, so we don't see much of her. A pity. I so want to see children in this house before long. But—" she gave Mona a knowing glance "—I'm having fresh hope."

"Don't hope," Mona said wistfully. "Keith and I are good friends, Mamie, nothing more. He...he's going with my sister, and she's out of town for the summer."

"Is she anything like you?"

"She's much much prettier."

"I didn't ask about her looks," Mamie said. "I asked if she's anything *like* you."

"Not at all. We're completely different."

"Then we'll see," Mamie said obscurely. "I see such changes in Keith, such changes. He seems... oh, happier, younger. And it's only happened this summer. That can't be entirely coincidence."

Again Mona's gaze went to the window, to the corral, to Keith. Merely looking at him made her heart pound. All this would end once the summer was over. Once Claire came home these trips to River View would stop, and the lovely summer would become only a memory. Thinking this, Mona was gripped by an overwhelming sense of sadness. It wasn't fair! She and Keith had developed such a warm close friendship, and they had discovered a curious and wonderful thing along the way: they could communicate without benefit of words. A nod of the head, a quick glance between them, and they understood each other perfectly.

"Do you believe in what the kids today call 'soul mates'?" he had once asked her.

"I do now," she had answered, and their eyes had met. Mona remembered with amazing clarity the crazy pulsating in her chest when she had looked into his eyes on that particular occasion.

Such an open, completely honest relationship. And Claire would put an end to it. Claire, who didn't deserve a man like Keith.

MONA LEANED BACK in the lounge and closed her eyes. From the speaker above her head came the soft strains of a love song. Apparently Keith had put a record on the stereo. The music soothed her mind. She felt limp, languid, glutted with satisfaction, yet strangely sad, too, and the sadness had a bittersweet tinge to it. The summer was almost over—the beautiful halcyon summer, the summer of her life. If only she could hold back the hands of time!

Gradually, without even realizing it was happening to her, she had become too fond of Keith. She hadn't meant to. It seemed like cheating, and Mona didn't want to be a cheat.

She should have seen it coming and nipped it in the bud; it was easy to see that now. She had been attracted to Keith from the beginning, so she should have known all this chummy togetherness would only heighten that attraction and make her grow fonder and fonder of him as time went by. And in all truth she feared that "fond" was only a euphemism for a word she dared not let enter her thoughts. "Fond" did not begin to describe the turbulence Keith sometimes stirred up inside her. She had been fond of a lot of people in her life, but she certainly hadn't felt for any of them what she felt for Keith.

It frightened Mona to death to think she might be falling in love with the man who was in love with her sister, for she knew only too well where that would lead. If she had a shred of common sense in her she would put a stop to these weekends. She was playing with fire, asking for trouble, leaving herself wide open to a good case of heartbreak. Once Claire returned it would all be over anyway, so she really ought to stop now.

Yet Mona knew she had no intention of doing any such thing. No amount of common sense could override her very real desire to spend all the time with Keith that he was willing to give her. If heartbreak was lurking just around the corner, she would deal with it when she rounded that corner.

Oh, Claire, damn you! It seemed to Mona that most of her life's troubles had somehow been associated with Claire. Forget that many of those troubles had been of her own making—like this one.

She heard Keith's footsteps behind her, then sensed he was standing beside the lounge. She felt his hand brush across her hair, and a fluttery feeling rushed over her skin. She opened her eyes and looked directly into his.

"You have moonlight in your hair," he said with a smile.

Her mouth curved. "How poetic of you."

Keith bent over her and extended his hand. "Would you like to dance under the stars?" he asked, pulling her to him without waiting for an answer. When she was against him, his hand curved around her waist and rested on her hip. Mona could feel the warmth of his palm through her clothing, and she distinctly heard the thump-thumping of her own heartbeat. "I can't think why we haven't done this before," Keith said softly.

The feel of those strong arms around her sent a dizzying sensation rippling through her. She was thankful he held her tightly; she didn't think she could have stood on her quaking legs if he hadn't. Her breasts were crushed against his hard chest, and the hand at her waist moved to mold her against his hard length. She rested her head on his shoulder, settling it into a niche that seemed made just for it.

All her senses had sprung to life, and she was sharply conscious of everything about him—his hand holding hers against his chest, his hard thighs brushing hers as they moved together, his warm breath on her forehead, his mouth against her hair. The musky aroma of his after-shave was heady and stimulating. Never before had she thought of dancing as a sensual exercise, but this was. She wouldn't have dreamed that breasts could actually throb, but hers were.

His nearness sent her mind stumbling, reeling. Within Mona was growing an unnerving need that cried out for assuagement. His warmth pervaded every fiber of her being. As his hand moved up her back, pressing, she shivered, and her head settled farther into the comfort of his shoulder, forcing her lips to lightly brush his neck. She wondered what he was feeling, if anything. Was he aware of her lips and breath against his skin?

She raised her eyes to his for a brief second, and she thought she read something in those deep gray pools. The smile he gave her was both sad and tender, and Mona felt so warm, so incredibly warm. It was like being submerged in a pool of silky fragrant water. She was floating...floating....

"You're a wonderful dancer, Mona," Keith said. "I might have known you would be. Is there anything you don't do superbly?"

Mona swallowed hard. *Control my emotions when you're near,* she might truthfully have said, but the question really didn't require an answer. She merely melted against him again, savoring the feel, the smell of him, desperately trying to emblazon on her brain the memory of this moment. She wanted to lock it away in a safe place where it could be recalled on demand.

When the music ended it was a moment before Keith released his hold on her and another moment before Mona could collect her wits enough to step away from him.

"Thank you," she said in a voice that didn't sound like her own. "That was lovely."

"Shall I start the music again?" Keith asked quietly. "Would you like to dance again?"

Would she like to? She wanted to dance with him all night. She would have liked nothing better than to collapse into his arms. She felt as though she were standing on the edge of a precipice. One more step and—

Mona's hand went to her temple. "I . . . I have a bit of a headache, Keith. It's been coming on all evening. I . . . think I'll just go on to bed, if you don't mind." It wasn't much of a lie; her head was swimming. It seemed prudent to put some distance between herself and this disturbing man.

"I'm sorry," Keith said with concern. "Would you like me to get you something for your head?"

"No, no. I'll be fine. I'll just go to bed."

"All right, Mona. Whatever you say. Good night."

"Good night, Keith."

The feel of those strong arms was still with her when she undressed for bed. She glanced at her reflection in the dressing-table mirror before climbing under the covers, and she was astonished to see she looked the same. She felt so changed. How could she look the same?

This, then, was how it felt—the sexual desire she had read so much about, heard so much about but had never before experienced. It wasn't what she had imagined it would be. She had expected something soft and satisfying. But the palms of her hands were wet, her fingertips itched, her loins ached, her head was spinning. Downstairs she had wanted to be kissed so badly, kissed in a way she had never been kissed before. It had been a feeling so hot and intense it could never have been explained, only wondered at.

Pulling the sheets tightly about her, hugging her pillow, Mona was swamped by dizziness, shaken to the core. If it had been anyone else, anyone else on earth, she could have coped. But it was Keith, her sister's man. So dangerous, so impossible. She had waited a long time to feel this way about a man. Why couldn't it have happened with anyone but Keith Garrett?

AT SOME POINT during the night Mona awakened with a startled cry. She had been having a dream, and in the dream Keith had been kissing her. No, more than merely kissing. He had been caressing her, fondling her, making love to her.

Mona thought she could feel his lips on hers, feel the places on her body where his hands had been. She shot straight up in bed. She was trembling all over, shaking as though she were freezing to death, yet she felt hot.

Dear God, she had to pull herself together! She

couldn't turn into a mindless trembling creature every time Keith got close to her. She would end up embarrassing both of them and destroying the friendship she had nurtured so carefully all summer.

At that moment the door to her room flew open, and Keith stood silhouetted at the threshold. "Mona?" he asked, his voice throbbing. "Mona? Are you all right? I thought I heard you cry out. Is something wrong?"

She sat paralyzed, her mouth slightly agape, her eyes wide with alarm. She couldn't find her voice. She simply stared at him in mute shock. Keith was wearing pajama bottoms, nothing else.

At the sight of Mona's shocked face, he instantly crossed the room, sat on the edge of the bed and gripped her hands in his. Mona's mind was fogged, but even so she was aware of the flimsy nightgown that scarcely covered her full breasts. With her hands imprisoned in his she could not cover herself, but she was not certain she could have done so had her hands been free. She seemed to be only half-conscious, incapable of movement or speech, still caught in the spell of that beautiful terrifying dream.

Keith searched her face anxiously. "Mona... Mona, what on earth...? You look as though you've seen a ghost. Are you all right? For God's sake, talk to me!"

"I—" She gulped and tried again. "I...had a dream."

Keith's shoulders sagged; relief engulfed him. He expelled his breath and uttered a little laugh. "Oh, thank God! A dream. From that look on your face I'd say it was more like a nightmare."

"Y-yes. A nightmare."

"Wow! You had me worried." Thus relaxed and reassured, he sat back and allowed his glance to roam over her, down the graceful curve of her neck to the creamy pink-tipped mounds straining at the thin fabric of her gown. A primitive response seemed to blaze from his eyes.

"Oh, Mona," he murmured, "you are so lovely!" One hand strayed up her arm and rested on her shoulder. "Your skin looks and feels like silk."

Mona had not moved, not a muscle, not a flicker. Even as she watched his dark head bend, saw his face coming near her, she did not move. Only when his warm mouth touched hers was she shaken free of her hypnotic state. She gasped, parting her lips, and his kiss deepened, sending a million wild sensations rushing through her already fevered and excited body.

Both his hands went to the sides of her breasts, then under and over, cupping and fondling. Mona's arms went around him to meet at his back. She rubbed the strong corded muscles of his shoulders, then moved down, feeling the satisfying warmth of his skin. Keith was soft and hard, tender and fierce all at the same time, and she began a tentative exploration of his body. This instinctive awakening of her sensuality disturbed and delighted, frightened and soothed her. She heard small, strange, guttural sounds emanating from deep in his throat, and she was startled to hear a moan escape from her own mouth.

At the sound, Keith lifted his head and stared down at her. Glittering sparks leaped from his eyes. "Sweet Mona...sweet Mona, how soft you are! Your body has such delectable curves." His hands began tracing them with tender petting motions.

Mona was too absorbed in the wonder of him to give any thought to protest. She wanted, in fact, more of him. She raised one hand to reach for his chest, then quickly withdrew it. Keith grabbed it. "No," he said. "No, there's nothing wrong with wanting to feel me." Gently he placed her palm against the fine mat of dark hair that covered his chest, and he covered her hand with his own. Her fingers teased at the curling hairs, and an involuntary shudder ripped through her. "Oh, Keith, kiss me again, please."

He did, giving her a long, drugging, breathless kiss. Mona felt herself slipping beyond rational thought. As Keith gathered her to him tightly, her hands began an even more reckless exploration of him. Never had she touched a man so intimately, and the experience was mind shattering. This was Keith...*Keith!* Unbelievable!

When at last their mouths parted, they were both gasping for breath. Mona rested her head in that comfortable niche in his shoulder. His hands continued their caressing movements, and she found herself drifting into a magical kind of enchantment. Her lips roamed over his shoulder, across his neck, down his chest, tasting the salty-sweet flavor of his skin. Then again she settled her head on his shoulder and delighted in the things his hands were doing to her.

Turning her head, smiling blissfully to herself, she opened her eyes and...saw Claire's face! It was as clear and distinct as if her sister had been in the room with them. Mona gasped, and the apparition moved closer. Claire's face wore a grim, pinched, accusing expression. Mona closed her eyes, opened them again, and Claire was gone.

Oh, damn her! For one wonderful glorious minute
Mona had forgotten her sister completely. Her body
slumped, and she grasped Keith's hands to remove
them from her breasts, suddenly ashamed and revolted. What was she doing? What in hell was she doing?
Behaving quite wantonly with her sister's boyfriend,
that's what! Whatever must Keith think of her?

"Keith, I'm sorry," she said in a choked whisper.
"I...I can't imagine what came over me. Forgive
me."

"Forgive you? Forgive you for what, Mona? For
being a woman? You're forgiven. Mona, I...."

His hand went to the nape of her neck and she
shivered. With the fingers of the other hand he tilted
her chin so that she was forced to look at him. A
warm restless yearning overtook her. It would be so
easy, so easy...if only it weren't for Claire. If only
Keith's lady friend had been some unknown faceless
creature whom Mona could dismiss from her mind.

Her eyes met Keith's, and that rare communion
took over. *I want you, and you want me,* they said.
So why not?

Mona shuddered. She had not entirely taken leave
of her senses. The summer would not last forever.
Claire would be back. She mustn't forget that.

"Keith," she whispered, "I can't. It's...Claire!"

Abruptly his hands stopped their sensuous wander-
ings. Mona heard his breathing become ragged and
felt his hold on her slacken. The lovely enchantment
had been shattered in an instant just by uttering
Claire's name. She pulled away from him slightly so
that she could look into his eyes, but a mask had
slipped over his face. For the first time she could not
fathom even a part of what he was thinking. Keith

stared down at her for a long wordless moment. Then his hands dropped to his sides, and he stood up with some difficulty. Only by exercising the greatest self-control did Mona prevent herself from reaching for him. She kept her eyes fastened intently on her trembling hands, but she could feel Keith's dark stare boring down on her bent head.

"Yes, I quite forgot that, didn't I?" Keith said. "I'm sorry, too, Mona. I'm going to have to keep my guard up. I almost loused up a rare and wonderful thing. Go back to sleep, my dear. Everything's going to be all right." And he turned and left the room.

Hot tears splashed out of Mona's eyes. All right? *All right?* Things would never be the same again.

THE FOLLOWING DAY, for the first time since she had begun coming to River View, Mona found herself wishing the weekend would pass more quickly. The charged air, the strained silence between them was new and distressing. Keith was preoccupied, vacant, distant, miles removed from her, and Mona felt tensely tired and regretful. They swam, rode horseback, ate meals, teased and talked, but it was different. Their warm and easy camaraderie had been replaced by something more like forced cheerfulness.

Tentatively, because they had always been able to talk so freely, Mona tried to reach him. "Keith, don't you want to talk to me? If it's about last night, I. . . ."

The tender smile he gave her made her heart ache. "No, no. I'll talk to you, Mona, when the time is right. I have to do some thinking."

It was Claire, of course; Mona knew that much. Claire was between them, and she would always be between them. Mona was convinced she had been right to call a halt to the lovemaking. She found herself almost longing for Claire's return. With Claire at home, Mona could end her journey to never-never land, Keith would be his usual self again and things would return to normal. And it seemed to Mona that was proof of her very real affection for him. She wanted his happiness above all.

When they left the ranch Sunday afternoon the western skies were darkening ominously, and there had been a noticeable shift in the direction of the wind. Keith put up the top on the Mustang, just in case a summer thundershower was in the offing.

Conversation inside the little car was strained. "I wasn't very good company this weekend, Mona," Keith apologized. "I know that, and I'm sorry. I have some things to sort out in my mind."

"I understand," Mona said simply. There was little use in pretending it had been the same. It had been awful. Her insides were a dull aching void.

"I think you really do understand most of the time. I'm not so sure you understood this time, but...next weekend is going to be different, I promise."

She looked at him. "Will there be a next weekend, Keith?"

"Of course there will! Surely you don't think I would give up our times together. Bear with me a bit, Mona. I have to do some thinking."

"About Claire?" she asked, studying the hard set to his jaw.

"Yes. That...and other things."

So enigmatic. Mona experienced a sense of hopeless frustration, and life suddenly seemed very complicated. She thought back on all those promising young men she had brought to the house, the ones who had fallen for Claire like a ton of bricks, and she tried to remember if she had pined for any of them for long. She honestly didn't think so. Some sort of inner defense mechanism had enabled her to dismiss them from her mind once she realized they were captivated by her sister. She sighed and stared out of the car window. Something told her it wasn't going to be so easy this time.

Dark clouds had heaped on the horizon when the Mustang pulled into the driveway of the Lowery house. Keith switched off the engine and settled back in the seat, but Mona's body was rigid. She wanted him to talk to her, yet she didn't. She supposed she was afraid of what he might say. Eventually, sometime before their summer ended, she supposed he would tell her about his true feelings for Claire. She waited, and still Keith said nothing.

Finally, desperate for something to say to break the awful silence, she spoke up. "Thanks for the weekend, as usual."

"I was a bore," Keith said firmly. "It wasn't intentional, but when I have something on my mind I tend to withdraw."

"I told you I understand."

Then he turned, and their eyes met. Those eyes of his! Would she ever be able to look into them without experiencing that crazy surge in the region of her heart? The expression on his face was inscrutable. A lot had changed between them, and somehow Mona felt it was all her fault. If only she had kept her stupid wayward emotions in check....

She was only dimly aware that Keith was leaning

toward her, that his head was bending, and she uttered an involuntary little cry when his mouth came down on hers. It was a warm, moist, gentle kiss. There had been no physical contact between them since that night in her room, and she needed that kiss. It was like a transfusion: she felt gentle warmth spreading from the top of her head to the tips of her toes.

"Wh-what was that for?" she asked in a tremulous voice.

"For being what you are."

"What am I?"

"A lot of things. A friend, a companion, a soul mate. An unusual and wonderful person. A darling girl. A feast for my eyes, balm for my soul. So many things. I could go on and on."

Awfully nice words. Too bad they weren't the ones she longed to hear.

"Thank you," she said simply.

"Next Friday? Same time, same place?"

"Are you sure you want me to go with you, Keith?"

"Very sure."

"All right. Next Friday it is," she said. Then, piecing together the fragments of her shattered composure as best she could, she opened the car door and got out just as the first drops of rain began to fall.

An hour later, in an elegant north Dallas condominium, Keith stood at the window and watched the rain pelt the curved walkways and lush green grounds of the fashionable and exclusive apartment complex, hoping that River View was getting a good soaking, too. There the rain would do some real good. Here in the city it would merely raise the humidity and turn tomorrow into an insufferably muggy experience that would spoil the sunniest of dispositions.

He lit a cigarette and stood smoking and thinking. Returning home to his empty apartment on Sunday evening always had a depressing effect on him, and tonight his depression was more marked than usual. It had not been a good weekend, not like the others, and for that he had only himself to blame. Damn his propensity for drawing up inside himself whenever he had something on his mind. It was a Garrett family trait. His dad was like that, too.

Thinking of his father brought a brief smile to Keith's lips. He and his parent shared a close relationship based on mutual affection and respect. It hadn't always been that way. Simon Garrett was a self-made man, a real wheeler-dealer of archtypical Texas style, and he thrived on the complexities of the world of business. His quieter, less flamboyant son had been something of a mystery to him in younger years. Simon had never been able to understand why Keith found greater joy in the birth of a calf than in the sealing of a million-dollar business deal.

Keith was aware of all this, and he knew there had been times when his father had feared he would forsake the family business altogether in favor of his first love—ranching. But time had brought acceptance, and now Keith was pretty sure his father loved him, pretty sure his father was proud of him. He was damned sure he would never hear anything of the kind from Simon's lips.

Keith chuckled to himself. If his father hadn't been on an extended vacation in the New Mexican mountains he might have given him a call. Just to chat. It

had been some time since they had done that, and
Simon loved to talk at length about anything and
everything. His conversation was so liberally spiced
with ribald Anglo-Saxon epithets that it took him
twice as long as necessary to say anything meaning-
ful, but Keith usually came away from their father-
son talks with a few pithy observations to ponder.

Peculiar, this sudden desire to have someone to
talk to, someone who would listen while he poured
out all the doubts that were beginning to plague him.
Three months ago he had been fairly confident that
he had his future all mapped out. The business was
running smoothly; he had no more than an average
amount of interoffice squabbling to contend with.
He had accomplished some of the things he had set
out to do at the ranch, and it, too, was a smooth-
running operation. And he had thought he had found
the woman he wanted to spend the rest of his life
with.

Claire Lowery had seemed to fit the bill perfectly.
She had the right background, she was beautiful and
socially poised, and he had imagined she would be a
notable hostess who would run their social life as ef-
ficiently as he ran Garrett Instruments. Together they
would be part of the country-club scene and would
participate in all the important civic and charity func-
tions. Their pictures would grace the society pages
frequently, they would travel and in time there would
be children who would go to all the "right" schools.

There was nothing really wrong with that kind of
life, Keith mused, but the very predictability of it all
left him feeling weary and empty. Sometimes he wondered if the fascination ranching held for him was in
some way tied to its inherent uncertainties. The never

ending cycle of ranch life! Knowing that never, ever would the people at River View be able to sit back and say, "There! It's all been done. Now everyone can rest."

That's what he really liked, what he would do full-time if there were no other obligations. And as lovely as Claire Lowery was, as delightful and charming as she could be at times, Keith was wise enough to know she didn't fit in with that sort of life.

He angrily stubbed out his cigarette in an ashtray and rubbed his eyes, while he willed his mind not to think of another dark-haired beauty who would.

CHAPTER FIVE

THE TEXAS SUMMER lay hot and heavy on the land. Dallas simmered under a heat wave. A record number of hundred-plus-degree days filled the newspapers with grim reports of heat-stroke cases and dermatologists' warnings of what this kind of heat could do to skin. Energies were sapped by midday. Mona lethargically crossed the college parking lot to her car. Lacking the inclination for worthwhile activity, she made a detour on her way home to stop by Stephanie Means's art gallery.

"Oh, Mona, I was going to call you this afternoon," Stephanie said by way of greeting. "I'm not having any luck with your friend at all. I've telephoned him twice with no results. He simply refuses to believe that I'm serious about seeing more of his work."

Mona sighed and threw up her hands. She was disappointed—and disgusted with Alan. "Oh, that man can be so exasperating!"

"It's really a pity. I'm excited about next month's showing, and I'd love to see some more of his work. This is a new experience for me. I'm accustomed to having unknown artists grovel at my feet in gratitude."

Mona knew she shouldn't care so much. If Alan preferred the idle life of a playboy to the creative one of an artist, she should just let it be. It was Alan's life after all and none of her business. Yet oddly enough she couldn't leave it alone. "Don't give up yet, Steph. I'm going to march over to that house and steal those other canvases if I have to. Alan might never get another chance like this."

"More than that, he might never have another friend who cares so much," Stephanie said with a smile.

"I'll see you in a little while. I'm going home to collar Alan Palmer and give him a piece of my mind!"

But Alan was not at home. Mona was so informed by Bentley, the Palmers' stone-faced butler. "And I don't expect him for the remainder of the day, Miss Lowery."

Mona stood at the front door of Alan's house and shifted uneasily. Bentley had always seemed a rather formidable old gentleman. She remembered giving him as wide a berth as possible as a youngster. An impudent plan was forming in her brain, however, and she couldn't let the butler be a stumbling block.

"Ah...Bentley...Alan must have forgotten, but I was supposed to pick up some paintings from his studio this afternoon. I'm sure it slipped his mind that today was the day. Would you be kind enough to let me get them?"

Bentley scowled while he, Mona assumed, tried to think of a reason to deny her request. Apparently finding none, he stepped back to allow her to enter the house, but he hovered suspiciously while Mona gathered up four canvases from Alan's studio, slipped them under her arm, then thanked the grim butler profusely before leaving the house. Chuckling under her breath, she put the paintings in her car and within a half hour was back at Stephanie's.

Mona moved soundlessly through the quiet splendor of the gallery rooms to find Stephanie in the workshop at the rear of the building. Here the clutter was in sharp contrast to the neat organization of the outer rooms. Paintings of all sorts were propped in disarray against the walls; objets d'art were clustered in confusion on tables and shelves. Mona surrendered Alan's canvases, then watched excitedly as Stephanie studied first one, then another and another.

"He's good, really good, Mona," the gallery owner said at last, sending Mona's spirits soaring. "How did you persuade him to give them to me?"

"I swiped them," Mona said impishly. "He has no idea I have them. But surely now that someone knowledgeable has shown appreciation for his work he'll approach it with more. . . more purpose."

"Well, obviously I can't display these things without his okay, but I'll stay after him." Stephanie continued to study the landscape she was holding. "If it hadn't been for you, Mona, this kind of work might have languished in a closet for years. It would be a shame for this artist to remain a Sunday painter. I sense some great things for him, if he's willing to work at it. Such harmony and balance! I get such a feeling of loneliness. There's a quiet pathos to his art."

Mona was amazed. Harmony, balance, loneliness? *Alan?* If Stephanie was right, and Mona had to believe she was, the real Alan was quite different from the character he presented to the world. Maybe she really didn't know him at all.

And then she thought of Keith, for no particular reason except that her thoughts were rarely far from him. She recalled his pensive withdrawal of the previous weekend, and she wondered if she really knew him as well as she thought she did.

Stephanie was speaking to her, so Mona shook herself out of her reverie. "Would you like some ice tea, Mona?"

"Thanks, Steph. That would be nice."

Stephanie led the way to a small table in a far corner of the workroom. Around it were four chairs, and behind it stood a small refrigerator. Stephanie filled two glasses with ice cubes and poured tea from a pitcher. "Lemon or sugar?" she asked.

"Nothing. Just straight."

The two women sat at the table and sipped their drinks. The conversation touched on Mona's fledgling career and quite naturally got around to the weather. It was all anyone seemed to talk about these days.

"Hasn't this heat been awful!" Stephanie said. "And miserable for business. Who wants to get out and browse when he can stay home in air-conditioned comfort?"

"I know. If we don't get some rain soon, mom is going to go into a decline when she sees the lawn and flower beds. Lettie says it's impossible to water enough to keep up the yard in such heat."

"I guess Kitty and Ben will be coming home soon."

"Three weeks," Mona said, and her heart turned over. Three weeks! Was it only three? It would be over so soon.

Stephanie turned to her with bright eyes. "Oh, that

reminds me. Guess who I ran into at Neiman's the other morning.''

"Who?"

"Your Aunt Beth."

Mona stared at her in uncomprehending surprise. "Who?"

"Beth. Kitty's sister."

"Good heavens! Are you sure, Steph?"

"Of course I'm sure. I knew both Kitty and Beth all the way through school. I couldn't believe my eyes. I hadn't seen Beth in twenty years or more. It took me several minutes of staring to be sure it was she, but it was Beth all right. She hasn't changed much. Older, of course, but aren't we all! You mean you didn't even know she was in Dallas?'' Stephanie asked, seeing the look on Mona's face.

"Steph, I didn't even know I had an aunt. Oh, I mean I knew mom had a sister, but I've never met her, and I didn't know where she was. Does, er, my aunt live here now?''

Stephanie nodded. "She said she moved back a month ago. My God...and she hasn't gotten in touch with her sister? That's incredible! Kitty and Beth never were what I would call close, but it wasn't surprising, given the difference in their ages and personalities. I must say, though, it wouldn't have occurred to me that they didn't even speak to each other."

"I know. It's always seemed so strange to me." Something stirred in Mona then, a peculiar longing to see her aunt, to catch a glimpse of a past that probably was none of her business. "What's her last name, Steph?''

Stephanie frowned in thought. "I think it's Sinclair. Yes...I'm sure it's Sinclair."

"I wonder how I could find her. I don't suppose you have any idea where she lives or what she's doing," Mona prodded.

"She's not doing anything to speak of. That much she told me. She's recently divorced, and of course she and Kitty have inherited money of their own. She asked me to give her a call sometime and we would have lunch. Maybe I can find her number. I'm sure I wrote it down." Stephanie got up and searched for her handbag, then rummaged through its contents until she produced a slip of paper. "Ah, here it is. The address, too."

Mona stared at the writing on the paper, copied out the number on another sheet, then carefully folded the sheet and slipped it into the pocket of her jeans. Common sense told her to drop it, but human curiosity filled her with a desire to meet this unknown aunt, and the desire stayed with her long after she had left Stephanie's gallery and returned home. She tried to shake it, but it persisted until she finally gave in to the urge and looked up the address on a city map.

AT FOUR O'CLOCK that afternoon Mona parked her car in front of the imposing high-rise apartment building, but it was several minutes before she mustered the courage to get out. Did she have the right to seek out this aunt whom her parents obviously preferred she know nothing about? And truthfully, if Beth Sinclair cared anything about seeing her family, wouldn't she have made the effort by now?

Perhaps she didn't dare, Mona thought, then wondered at the thought. She bit her lip and opened the car door. Without actually remembering entering the building, she found herself standing in its luxuriously appointed lobby, searching the register for her aunt's name. Then she was stepping into the elevator and pushing the button.

All the way to the eighth floor she debated the wisdom of her actions. She should have telephoned first. No, a note would have been better. Awfully formal for family, but then this wasn't family, not in the true sense. Oh, she shouldn't have come at all! Why had it seemed so important to meet her aunt? It had been an audacious move on her part—and there was that word again.

The elevator doors opened with a whoosh, and Mona stepped into a long, dimly lit, carpeted hallway. Arrows on the wall told her that apartment 8A was to her left. She stopped to inspect her appearance in the long mirrors flanking the elevator door. She smoothed the skirt of her simple green dress, then fidgeted with its neckline and patted her lustrous hair. Satisfied, she walked to the cream-colored door, hesitated momentarily, then rang the bell.

The slender dark-haired woman who answered her ring looked at her with open curiosity. Mona's immediate impression of her aunt was one of fragility. Time had not been as kind to Beth Sinclair as it had to Kitty Lowery. Tiny lines etched her too thin face. Ten additional pounds would have done wonders for her, Mona thought.

"Mrs.—Mrs. Sinclair?" she stammered, quivering inside. "Beth?"

"Yes."

"I'm Mona Lowery."

The woman's dark eyes widened, and her mouth made a little O of astonishment. "Mona," she murmured in awe, and for one awkward moment the two women stood at the threshold simply staring at each other. Then Beth stepped back and made a sweep with her arm. "Please come in."

The apartment was full of neat expensive furniture, but there were no adornments of any kind— no paintings or other wall hangings, no throw pillows, no knickknacks, no plants. It had probably been leased furnished, Mona decided. It looked rather like a hotel suite, just a transient's temporary quarters.

"How on earth did you find me, Mona?" Beth Sinclair asked.

"Stephanie Means told me she had seen you, and she gave me your address. I—I just decided to come. Foolish of me, I suppose."

"No," Beth said quickly. "Please sit down. Forgive me... I'm still reeling with surprise."

"I can imagine." Mona sat on the sofa and crossed her legs. But that felt uncomfortable, so she uncrossed them, planted her feet squarely on the floor and folded her hands in her lap.

"May I get you something?" Beth asked. "Coffee or tea or a Coke?"

"No, thank you."

Beth took a chair across from her, and her long slender fingers were occupied with the business of lighting a cigarette. Mona wished she had one, too, but she had none in her handbag and she wasn't about to ask for one. Besides, the long ashtray at Beth's elbow seemed to be the only one available.

Through a haze of exhaled smoke Beth smiled at her. "You have a sister named Claire, don't you? Are you the younger or older?"

"Younger."

"How...how is your family?" Beth asked with what appeared to be some difficulty.

"Fine. At least, I think they're fine. Mom, dad and Claire have been in Palm Springs all summer. They'll be home in a few weeks." She lowered her eyes, then lifted them and looked at her aunt fully. "So you see, no one knows anything about this."

Beth's smile faded, then returned; this time the smile was touched with sadness. "A pity. For a moment I was wishing they did. I was hoping Kitty knew and approved."

"I don't think she would."

"Why? Has she said something or...?"

Mona shook her head. "No one ever mentions you at all. The only reason Claire and I knew mom had a sister was because we saw some pictures in the old family album. We asked about you and were told a lot of vague nonsense about how you left home and didn't stay in touch. We were just kids, and it wasn't important to us. But I think I always knew the two of you didn't get along."

"It wasn't that," Beth said dully. She took a few nervous puffs on the cigarette, then stubbed it out. "Tell me about yourself, Mona."

"What do you want to know?"

"Anything. Everything."

Mona pursed her lips. "Oh...I'm twenty and in my final year of college. I'm going to summer school so that I can graduate in January. That's why I didn't go to Palm Springs. I'm studying interior decoration, and with luck I'll be in business for myself before next summer."

Beth looked appreciative. "How wonderful for

you! You're so young, yet you already know what you want to do with your life. I envy you. I suppose this place makes you cringe."

"No, not at all. It could be lovely."

"Well, perhaps if I decide to stay in Dallas I'll commission you to decorate it for me."

Mona's eyebrows arched. "Is there some doubt? About staying here, I mean. You might not?"

Beth shrugged. "I don't know. My plans rarely stretch beyond tomorrow. Now...your sister, er, Claire. What does she do?"

"Nothing," Mona said, not intending sarcasm, but there wasn't anything else for her to say. Claire honestly did nothing. "She takes after mom. Oh, I—I didn't mean that the way it came out. Actually, mom does a great deal."

Beth laughed a light lovely laugh. Like Claire's, Mona thought. "Don't apologize," Beth said. "I know what you meant. So tell me about Kitty."

"Mom's...just mom. Very busy, very active. There are several charitable organizations in this city that would fold if it weren't for Kitty Lowery."

Beth nodded. "Our mother was like that, and Kitty always took after mother. Is Kitty as pretty as ever?"

"She looks wonderful. At least, I think she does. Of course, dad's spoiled her horribly," Mona said with a smile.

Did the light in Beth's eyes dull a bit? Mona thought so, but it could have been her imagination. "Your father," Beth said quietly. "How is he?"

"Splendid."

"Has his business done well?"

"Oh, yes! It's grown by leaps and bounds. Dad's fantastic!"

"And he's a superb father, I suppose."

"The best," Mona said with conviction.

"I always knew he would be. Kitty's a very lucky woman. I hope she realizes it."

"Does anyone ever . . . really?"

Beth looked at her then, and Mona was startled to realize she was experiencing something of the same feeling she had for Keith in the early days of their friendship. Instant rapport. How she would have loved to have known this woman all these years. "Why don't you come to visit us?" she blurted out.

A faraway look came into her aunt's eyes. "Oh, Mona . . . for a lot of reasons. Foolish things that happened long before you were born."

"Was it a . . . family feud? Something like that?"

"Yes, something like that."

"But why let it go on so long? Can't it be water under the bridge? Time's supposed to heal. I'm surprised my father didn't put an end to all this years ago. Mom I can understand. She's . . . well, she's a bit on the dramatic side. But dad has no patience with nonsense, and he deeply believes in strong family ties."

"Mona, let's just say there are some wounds that time does not heal," Beth said with a tired sigh, and Mona felt obliged to let the matter drop.

"So . . . I've told you about us. What about you, Beth? Where have you been all these years?"

"A lot of places. Virginia mostly."

"Lovely place. Did you like it?"

"Oh, at times I liked it. At times I didn't. Usually I didn't think about it one way or another."

Mona hesitated, then said, "Stephanie told me you're recently divorced. Are you sad?"

Beth uttered a sharp laugh. "My, what a bold one you are, Mona!"

Mona felt her face flush. She had overstepped proper bounds again. "I'm sorry. You'd be surprised how many people have told me that."

Fortunately, Beth did not seem to take umbrage. "I'm not happy about the divorce certainly, but Steve and I got married for all the wrong reasons. I seem to have a penchant for getting married for the wrong reasons. You see, dear, this is my second divorce. When a first marriage fails, a woman can plead youth and inexperience. But when a second one fails—" Beth spread her hands "—it has to be my fault. I'm afraid I'm incapable of making marriage work. I don't intend trying again."

"How awful!" Mona said with real compassion. "So you see, you need family even more."

"It's impossible, Mona, and if I were you I wouldn't mention having seen me to either of your parents. It would do no good and might even do real harm." Beth's voice had a grating edge to it.

Mona frowned, acutely puzzled. "But I would so love to have an aunt. We're such a small family."

Now Beth smiled, broadly and with delight. "And I would love to have a niece. I see no reason why the two of us can't get together occasionally. I imagine that at your age you don't have to account for every moment."

"No. I've never given my mother and father any cause to worry about me, so I'm fairly free to come and go as I please. But. . .I don't like lying to my parents."

"And so you won't. Lunch in town with a friend.

What could be more natural? And I would like us to be friends, Mona. Good friends.''

"Oh, Aunt Beth!" she cried. "I'd like that, too. So much."

IT WAS FRIDAY AFTERNOON, and the hundred-degree temperatures had finally broken. The radio promised a high of only ninety-eight. "A regular cold wave, folks!" the jovial weather forecaster had said. Mona was once again sitting in the living room waiting for the sound of the Mustang's horn. She was ready earlier than usual, since Friday's classes at the college had been canceled due to a faculty meeting. The idle day had given her far too much time for thinking, and now she was edgy and restless.

The week had seemed unusually long and restive. Alan's success and the meeting with Aunt Beth had been brief bright moments in days that were otherwise filled with disquietude. Mona felt taut and under a strain, yet she knew the strain was of her own making.

She told herself that all was well between her and Keith. He had telephoned once during the week simply to ask how she was and to tell her how much he was looking forward to the weekend, as though he expected this particular one to be somehow special. But in her heart Mona knew that things were not the same for her. She had been sexually aroused for the first time in her life. A woman was never supposed to forget that. How could she be the same again?

She thought about Keith all the time. At school she would hear a throaty masculine laugh and she would think of Keith's laugh. Or ahead of her a man with a free loose gait would walk and she would see Keith striding across the grounds of River View. A silly television movie would bring tears to her eyes. Now when she read a novel the hero always looked like Keith.

Even Alan, whom Mona had never thought the most observant of men, had noticed her preoccupation. She had spent one evening that week at the Palmer house, putting the final touches on the sun room, and he had bluntly asked, "What in the hell is the matter with you, Mona?"

"What makes you think there's something the matter with me?"

"I'm not sure, but you're not yourself. At first I attributed it to enormous guilt over the way you've been manipulating my life. I still can't get over your gall, but—"

That reminded Mona of something. She turned to Alan expectantly. "Have you heard from Steph?"

"Not since she informed me you had taken matters into your own grubby little hands. I could probably have you arrested, you know."

Mona smiled. "You won't. And Steph says you have real talent."

"Humph!" Alan scoffed. "Mona, you've made way too much of the fact that I like to play around with paints and brushes. And you're evading the original question. What's wrong with you these days? You're a million miles away, and you've got a hangdog look about you."

"You're imagining things!" she protested, and forced herself to straighten up and put on a cheerful face. But she knew there was plenty wrong with her, and some of it was baffling.

From the beginning she had known Keith was smitten with Claire. So how in God's name had she let herself become so emotionally attached to him? She had never stood a ghost of a chance when Claire was the competition, and she thought she had long ago accepted that as a fact of life. Yet she had willfully made too much of this brief interlude with Keith. Mona rubbed her forehead and sighed a struggling sigh. She would have thought she was smarter than that.

Not surprisingly, that night in her room at River View often came to mind, and she was convinced she had no illusions about Keith's romantic overtures. He was a man, she was a woman. They had spent a lot of time together, and he no doubt was missing Claire very keenly by now. Mona assumed he would have assuaged his physical needs elsewhere during the past week and this weekend he would treat her as before—as a close and trusted friend.

But Mona had no such emotional outlet. Her longing for Keith had, if anything, heightened and intensified until it consumed her. What in the world was she going to do when the summer ended? Would Keith return to calling at this house for Claire and expect Mona to revert to being his girl friend's little sister? In all probability that was precisely what would happen. Well, Mona wouldn't. She couldn't! She would get an apartment of her own or something. She would do something.

Mona heard the heavy thud of footsteps across the front porch. It would be the postman. She got up and retrieved the mail from the box, glanced through it absently, then noticed a letter addressed to her in Kitty's neat script. Tossing the rest of the envelopes on the foyer table, she carried her mother's letter to the sofa, tore it open and read:

Dearest Mona,

I tried to call you night before last but was told you were staying late at school. I hope you haven't spent the entire summer with your nose stuck in a book. You need to get out and find a real interest in life, dear, something besides interior decoration. To be frank, you could do with a little romance in your life.

And Claire could do with a little less. Your father and I are a little disturbed by some of her new friends. They are a very affluent group and a little on the wild side. I wouldn't be surprised if some of them use drugs. Claire needs some settling down. I'll be glad when she gets back home and starts seeing that nice Keith Garrett again. He's a good stabilizing influence on her. I've never approved of matchmaking and vowed I would never involve myself in such nonsense, but parents can't be too careful these days. In Claire's case I just might try my hand at it. I desperately want Claire to marry Keith, and so does your father. Things were so different in my day. I think parents had an easier time of it. . . .

There was more to the letter, but Mona didn't bother finishing it. One line fairly leaped off the page to hit her between the eyes. "I desperately want Claire to marry Keith, and so does your father."

Dear God, it was going to be hard. So incredibly hard. Mona wasn't sure she could get through it. If Claire and Kitty and Ben all wanted a marriage to Keith, there was no doubt in Mona's mind that they would get it. And how on earth could she face life as Keith Garrett's sister-in-law?

EACH TIME MONA RETURNED to River View she felt a sense of coming home. It was such a serene little world, far removed from the confusion of the city. And how Keith loved it! When the wooden gate loomed into view he pressed the accelerator closer to the floor. Mona wondered if he was even aware he did it. Like a horse returning to the barn at the end of the day, the closer he got the faster he wanted to go.

The ranch house dozed in the afternoon heat; the grounds looked deserted. Small wonder. This was hardly the kind of weather for brisk outdoor activity. Mona stepped into the cool interior of the house and glanced around. It was so familiar now, and her hand was on everything. The changes she had wrought were dramatic. Gone was the cold, impersonal, uninspired decor. Now everything was softer, lighter, less confined. Pastel shades of green and yellow predominated, accented by lots of white and an occasional hot splash of orange. The profusion of plants she had insisted upon brought the outdoors in. Mamie confessed to having to devote an entire morning every week to nothing but plant care. "But it's worth it," the housekeeper was quick to add. "The house is so lovely now, Mona."

Mona turned to find Keith watching her. "Pleased with your handiwork, aren't you?" he said with a grin.

She tossed her head. "Well, shouldn't I be?"

"Yes, you should," he said seriously. "You've done wonders with the place, Mona. Yes, you should be very pleased."

Their weekend routine seldom varied. The moment they arrived at the ranch Keith went to find Jim Browder and get his weekly report, and Mona went to the barn to pay a call on Mandy. Then she returned to the house to change into her swimsuit in the large room she now thought of as hers. Certainly it had been hers all summer. Keith slept across the hall in his childhood room. The master bedroom that had once belonged to his parents was spacious and had a private bath. Mona now felt as much at home in it as she did in her own bedroom in Dallas. She had stocked the bathroom with her own personal toiletries to preclude the necessity of having to bring so many things with her every Friday. Soon, she supposed, she would be moving out, a dispiriting thought.

If there were no minor emergencies concerning the ranch's operations, Keith normally joined her at pool side. Then they changed for dinner. After a few cocktails and dinner they talked. A few times they had watched television, a few times they had spent the evening hours on the patio listening to music. But mostly they just talked.

Once Keith had commented, "You know, Mona, when we first began coming out here we talked so much I was afraid we'd run out of something to talk about in only a few weeks, but I haven't detected any noticeable lags in the conversation. Have you?"

It was true. They both had ideas, and their ideas more often than not coincided. It was as though they were destined to know each other. Only the previous weekend had there been any strain in their relationship. Now Mona searched his face for any lingering traces of that preoccupation and withdrawal, and she found none. Apparently he had completely forgotten that first hesitant approach to romance.

How she wished she could forget! It seemed to her

that the past week had lasted an eternity, that she had been waiting only for this time with Keith, praying that her ill-disguised emotions hadn't spoiled things for them forever.

He had arrived at the Lowery house that afternoon while Mona was still pondering the impact of her mother's letter. When she saw him she had felt a constricting band around her chest. He had been dressed in dark slacks and a white polo shirt, a departure from his customary jeans, and he smiled when she appeared, also not dressed in jeans but in a white sun dress that showed off her golden tan spectacularly.

"Two minds with but a single thought!" he exclaimed. "How lovely you look!"

Mona admitted she had wanted him to think her lovely. That was the reason for the dress. She couldn't remember if Keith had ever seen her in a dress. Around the ranch she wore jeans and boots like everyone else—and not the designer jeans and eel-skin boots she had shown up in on her second visit to the ranch, thereby inviting Keith's hooting derision. Now she wore tough Levi's and cowhide boots that were comfortable and practical.

But not this weekend, at least not exclusively. Mona wanted Keith to take notice of her, not as his good and trusted friend but as a desirable young woman. With that in mind, she had gone to a smart dress shop, one that her mother and Claire often patronized, for the express purpose of buying clothes for this weekend. All of her purchases had been appropriate, things that would be perfectly suitable for their activities at the ranch, but all were as feminine as possible, all were chosen to emphasize her figure, all were designed to make Keith take note of her.

It was the first time in her life that she had purchased clothes with anyone but herself in mind. And this was the first time she was giving more than offhand attention to her personal appearance. How she wished she were more adept at this sort of thing. She had always thought it hilarious that Claire could spend so much time in front of a mirror, but now Mona was wishing she had paid more attention to the things Claire did. Maybe a woman needed to know some tricks of the trade in order to get a man to notice her.

God help her! She had fallen in love with Keith—totally, helplessly in love with him—and she knew as well as she knew her own name that it was the most foolish thing she ever had done. What if she succeeded in making him want her for a little while? Where would that leave her when Claire returned? The sense of loss would be tremendous, her jealousy of her sister would be more overwhelming than ever, and Keith would doubtlessly feel uncomfortable around her, so there would go the friendship. It would be so much smarter to nurture their warm platonic relationship and forget all these seductive maneuvers, something she was hardly skilled at in the first place.

Yet her sensible inner arguments were sparring with something else entirely—the fact that every cell in her body ached for him in a way that was anything but platonic.

Keith already was at the pool when she came out. Apparently he had been in; his lean bronzed body, stretched out on the lounge, glistened with water. Mona had seen him this way dozens of times, yet today the sight of him made her flesh tingle. His eyes were closed, and he looked blissfully peaceful. Mona envied him that peace.

"The water feels good," he told her as she came to stand beside him. "Cools you off."

"Just what I need, then," she said, and left him to dive into the pool. She knifed through the water, swam the pool's length, then lifted herself out. Trailing water behind her, she went to lie next to him.

Keith had often told her he could read her thoughts, and indeed there were times when it seemed he could, but Mona hoped today was not one of those times. Today her thoughts were such a confused tangle, and they all were of him. What a strange thing the man-woman business was—so at odds with all normal rules of behavior. Guidelines formulated throughout a lifetime just had to be thrown out the window.

Mona wasn't at all sure of what her reaction would be if Keith were to make a move toward serious love-making. She had, of course, expected her first sexual experience would be with her husband. No man had ever come close to arousing passion in her, so she had thought remaining a virgin would be the easiest thing in the world.

Now she wasn't so sure. She was slowly abandoning her rather supercilious attitude toward women who slept with men to whom they were not married. She was not married to Keith, and there was nothing to give her hope she ever would be, but the thought of lying beside him throughout the night.... Oh, the thought!

She sighed so gustily that Keith turned to her and asked, "Is anything wrong, Mona?"

"No, no...nothing's wrong."

Her physical awareness of him sharpened with

each passing minute. Through veiled lashes she watched him. He made her skin hum, tingle, burn. By the time they went inside to change for dinner Mona felt like molten lava on the brink of eruption.

She wore another new dress to dinner, this one a clinging coral-colored creation with tiny spaghetti straps. The sales clerk had predicted that no man within sight of her would be able to resist her in that dress. Keith's eyes swept over her when she appeared in the living room for cocktails, but in no way did he appear to find her irresistible.

Little was said by either of them during Mamie's splendid meal. Keith, Mona noticed, drank several glasses of wine with dinner, and this after three cocktails. Normally he didn't drink much. Why the alcoholic fortification? It had been her experience that men drank more on one of two occasions—when they were gloriously happy or unbearably sad. Which was Keith? He looked contented enough, but she hardly would have described him as looking gloriously happy. So that left unbearably sad, and again Claire popped into her mind.

Mona had been heartened and encouraged by the fact that Claire's name was now seldom mentioned. Perhaps she shouldn't have been. It could be that Keith missed her so much he simply didn't want to talk about her. Mona knew that Claire had written him only twice; Keith had told her that much. Yes, he must be unbearably sad, Mona decided, and having Claire's sister around only intensified the sadness. Perhaps he was regretting his expansive gesture in inviting Mona to spend every weekend with him. She might have simply turned into a constant and painful reminder.

Mona thought she had known jealousy before. Now the green monster threatened to suffocate her.

After dinner Keith suggested television. All the regular shows sounded dreadful, but there was a movie that boasted an excellent cast and a story line that promised to be exciting. Unfortunately it wasn't. Only the television censors saved it from being out-and-out pornography. Mind-boggling violence and illicit sex. Mona was embarrassed to be watching it in Keith's company.

Apparently his reaction was the same. "Idiocy!" he said in disgust as he got up and switched off the set halfway through it. "I kept thinking it would get better, but it just got worse."

"They've certainly taken the romance out of love-making," Mona remarked.

"I agree. Nothing but trash! Sex was more exciting when it was shrouded in mystery and taboos. Don't you think so?"

Mona's head was resting on the back of the sofa. She rolled it toward him. "Keith...how would *I* know?"

He laughed. "You're not that inexperienced surely."

"About as inexperienced as you can get, I should think. I guess men don't have the time or patience to gently lead, to instruct. Not anymore, not when there are women of experience around. And God knows, from all I've read lately there seems to be an awful lot you have to know to please a man. The art of giving pleasure seems to be a complicated thing."

Keith was smiling at her, giving her his indulgent smile, the kind of smile one gives to a sister or young child. Mona was beginning to detest that smile.

"Oh, Mona, the so-called experts confuse and complicate something that's basically so simple. Love and instinct will guide you when the right time comes."

"But how do you know when the time is 'right'?"

"Lord, Mona, if I knew the answer to that one I'd write one of those self-help books and retire here at River View. Again I guess it all comes down to love and instinct. Surely there's been someone, if only briefly—someone who lit a fire in you."

She shook her head. "You've been closer to me than any other man ever has," she told him in all candor.

Keith sucked in his breath, and his eyes widened, but he said nothing. Mona decided she had spoken hastily, said too much...again. It was her worst failing. Suddenly, sitting and talking to Keith was not the comfort it normally was. She stood on shaking legs, placing her hand on the back of the sofa to steady herself.

"I'm tired, Keith. I think I'll be going to bed now." It wasn't much of a lie. She *was* tired, although not so much from physical exhaustion as from mental and emotional fatigue.

Keith's look was speculative, uncertain. "Get a good night's sleep," he said, watching her closely. "Tomorrow we'll go riding."

"No work?" she asked. Usually Keith spent every Saturday totally engrossed in ranch chores and book work. It was, he had told her, the only way he had of keeping up with what was going on.

"No, not tomorrow," he said. "This is a slow time around the ranch. I'll have Mamie pack a picnic lunch for us. How does that sound?"

"It sounds like fun. Good night, Keith."

"Good night, Mona."

She slept badly. Most of the night was spent lying on her back, staring at the ceiling and thinking wild, dangerous, wonderful thoughts. She remembered the night in this room when Keith had come because he had heard her cry out. He had wanted her that night, and there was no doubt in her mind that she had wanted him. Badly. She shouldn't have alluded to it tonight, no matter how obliquely. Keith's entire manner suggested that he wanted to forget all about that night.

Mona wondered if he felt any guilt over making a pass at his girl friend's sister. Not that it mattered if he did or didn't; she felt enough guilt for both of them. She was eaten alive with guilt over lusting after her sister's man, and that was a laugh! Why did she care? She should just seize the moment and tomorrow be damned!

Oh, God, if falling in love was as sweet and wonderful as all the books claimed it was, why was it making her sick to her stomach? The way she felt about Keith was so raw, so basic, almost primitive. And she suspected that with minimal effort she could make him want her, too. . . for a little while.

Wanting him, yet afraid of the wanting. Afraid of her ability to handle the situation should it arise. Afraid of losing his friendship, yet longing for something more than friendship. Afraid Keith might play with her until Claire returned, then toss her aside.

Just afraid. . . period.

AFTER BREAKFAST the following morning Keith saddled Mandy and his horse—the gear was much too cumbersome for Mona to handle—and they rode far up the banks of the Brazos. Although Keith often complimented her on her seat in the saddle, she could in no way compare with the way he sat as a man born to it. He rode with the easy motion of a man in a rocking chair. Lagging behind a little, Mona watched him—and absurdly thought of Zane Grey and Louis L'Amour and John Wayne.

It was as stupefyingly hot as only Texas in August can be, but at a spot along the riverbank a great stand of ancient oaks formed a protective arch and afforded badly needed shade. There they dismounted, spread a blanket on the ground and ate the picnic lunch that Mamie had prepared for them. The housekeeper had provided enough food for a crew of hungry lumberjacks, but surprisingly Mona and Keith did justice to it. Thus surfeited, they lay side by side on the blanket Keith had spread, tipping their big hats forward to protect their faces from the incandescent midday sun.

Their shoulders touched, and the back of his hand rested against hers. He shifted his position, and his leg brushed against hers. Mona's fingertips itched, and she dug them into the blanket to preclude the possibility that, of their own volition, they might reach for him. If only he would turn to her....

Minutes passed. Hesitantly Mona lifted the hat from her face and glanced in Keith's direction. He was lying perfectly still, limp, and his chest rose and fell in shallow even breathing. He was asleep. Inwardly Mona laughed wryly. Apparently her proximity wasn't bothering him a bit.

Since he didn't know he was being studied, she felt safe enough in allowing her eyes to travel the length of him. Everything came under her sharp observation—the angles and planes of that strong angular face, his hard masculine body, his large but gentle hands. A warm flush of sexual desire began at her toes and crept up, engulfing her.

I am obsessed with him, she thought.

Once again Mona covered her face with the hat and sighed. Dear God, she wanted him so, and she was acutely conscious of the need to hide that fact from Keith. If their relationship was to grow into something more profound and intimate, he would have to be the one to make the first move.

All this inner turmoil was exhausting, and coupled with the food and sun, it created a sluggish stupor in Mona. For the first time that weekend she felt a great loosening taking place within her.

SHE REALIZED WITH A START that she must have fallen asleep. She pushed back the hat and found Keith still lying beside her, propped on one elbow. He was looking down at her and smiling.

"Oh...."

"You've been asleep for hours," he told her. "But don't worry. I kept you shaded."

"Why did you let me sleep so long?" she asked groggily.

"I slept quite a while myself. And you looked so peaceful lying there. I figured you must have needed the rest."

"Well...I didn't sleep very well last night," she admitted.

"Did you have a headache or something?"

"Yes...or something."

"You should have asked me for an aspirin."

"I'm afraid an aspirin wouldn't have helped."

She lifted her eyes to his, and she found him looking at her with a very odd expression on his face. It was indecipherable. Something awful was happening between them. She rarely had any trouble knowing what he was thinking. Usually he just came right out and told her whatever was on his mind, but even when he hadn't she had been able to discern his feelings. Now she sensed that he was keeping something from her.

But then, she was doing the very same thing. "What time is it?" she asked.

He glanced at his watch. "Four-thirty."

"Good grief! We've been out here all day!"

"That we have," Keith agreed. "Isn't it nice just to do nothing for a change?"

Mona stared to rise, but the languor would not permit it. She lay back down and stretched her arms over her head. "Oh, this has been such a summer... and I have you to thank for it. I do so hate to see it end."

Keith's gaze beat down upon her. "Why does it have to end, Mona? Who says that when September comes everything stops? I had imagined that these weekends would continue for as long as you like. Years and years possibly, who knows? I had hoped we would stay close for the rest of our lives."

Years and years. Friends for life. Yet ultimately, Mona knew, if the relationship remained friendly and nothing more, they would drift apart. It was inevitable. There would be spouses. And Mona feared Claire would be Keith's. The thought of visiting Keith's house when Claire was his wife, of cluck-clucking over his children.... She shuddered. It was abhorrent. She couldn't do it.

"You're forgetting Claire," she said quietly, sensibly. "I have a mental picture of Claire's allowing you to devote your weekends to her sister."

Heavy silence lay between them like a third person. Then Keith's face was over hers, blocking out the sun. Her breath caught sharply in her throat, and her heart hammered frantically.

"Mona..." he began.

"Y-yes?" she said expectantly.

"Mona, I...."

"What is it, Keith?"

His mouth opened, then shut into a grim line. His eyes clouded. Abruptly he jumped to his feet, stood over her and held out his hand. "Nothing," he said. "Come, Mona. It's time we were going."

CHAPTER SIX

MONA BATHED SLOWLY and spent a long time deciding what to wear to dinner. The long white dress—a "patio dress," the sales clerk had called it—was tempting. On a hanger it looked shapeless, but on a body it was anything but that. The soft fabric molded, clung, draped itself to reveal breasts, waist, hips, thighs. There was an almost sensual feel to the dress as it swirled around her legs. The neckline plunged rather alarmingly, showing a distinct amount of cleavage, and was trimmed with wide lace bands that fell halfway across her full breasts. "The effect is what we call 'demurely sexy,'" the clerk had said. "And for goodness' sake, don't make the mistake of wearing a bra with it. The suggestion of skin under the lace is very provocative."

"Good Lord!" Mona muttered aloud as she slipped the dress over her head. A month ago she wouldn't have considered wearing a dress like this, but look at her now! She felt as wicked and sinful as if she had just posed for the centerfold of a men's magazine.

"You should wear white all the time," Keith said when she made her appearance in the living room. He was standing behind the wet bar, mixing two drinks. He handed her one, and the strong molded lines of his mouth curved upward into a kind of half-smile. His gray eyes narrowed, and Mona had the strangest feeling he knew the dress had been purchased and worn for his benefit. "The sun dress yesterday and now this," he said. "You're a vision!" And even as he sipped from his glass he did not take his eyes from her.

"Thank you," she almost whispered, averting her gaze to the glass she held in a trembling hand. The amber liquid undulated and sloshed precariously near the rim. Steeling herself, Mona raised the glass to her lips. Liquid courage.

But Keith's manner was normal, relaxed, and nothing he did or said indicated that he found her behavior unusual. He chatted amiably throughout dinner, mostly about his future plans for River View, and he appeared not to notice that Mona answered in monosyllables and could not look at him for long.

Shape up, Mona, her nagging inner voice commanded. *You're a nervous wreck and it shows. You've got to pull yourself together. He knows you too well. He's bound to notice sooner or later. You're running the risk of losing his friendship if you don't pull yourself together!*

"Brandy on the patio?" Keith suggested as they left the dining room. His hand was at her elbow, propelling her gently.

"That would be nice," she said.

A white gold moon shone through the branches of the oak trees, and a million stars glittered on a black lacquer sky. From somewhere in the quiet reaches of the woodlands a calf bawled for its mother and received a lowing reply. In the distance a coyote howled mournfully. Country sounds, now familiar. Everything was so stilled, so hushed. Mona leaned back in the chaise and closed her eyes.

How she had come to love this place! If she were to have to go away, never to see it again, she thought it likely that she would miss it every day of her life.

She and Keith drank their brandy in complete silence. They, who had spent countless hours talking, talking, talking, were saying nothing. Mona searched her brain for something, anything, to say, but her mind was blank. All she could think of was the masculine presence next to her.

Keith held out his empty glass. "Another?" he asked.

She shook her head.

"Music, then? Would you like to dance?"

To dance with Keith tonight? To be held in those strong arms again when her brain was already spinning? She shouldn't. It was much too dangerous. She was not in control of herself. Much too dangerous. But she heard herself saying, "Thank you. That would be lovely."

He disappeared into the house, and within moments Mona heard soft music drifting from the overhead speaker. She stood on decidedly unstable legs and watched as Keith walked toward her. Then he was so close all she could see were his eyes, those deep steely pools. And she was in his arms.

They moved together in perfect accord, each sensitive to the other's movements. Mona rested her head on his shoulder, settling it into that comfortable niche. Her palm moved over the corded muscles of his back. Oh, he felt good! Her body was infused with the force of his warmth. It was this she had remembered all week—how warm he was and how good it felt to be close to him.

His thighs brushed against hers, causing a little

shiver to race through her, and her veins were filled with liquid fire. Mona closed her eyes and drank in the intoxicating fragrance of him—the mingled aromas of shaving lotion, tobacco, soap and brandy. She wanted to memorize the unique smell that belonged to Keith and no one else.

She became a mindless creature, soft and pliant in his arms, strangely free of the inner unrest that had plagued her all day. Now a soft gentle peace washed over her, and she wished only that it never had to end. Keith's hand stirred in hers, then gripped firmly, and the arm around her waist pulled her more tightly to him.

When the music ended, their bodies stilled but he did not release her, and she made no attempt to move. They stood, locked together, not speaking. From the house came the sound of a grandfather clock chiming the hour and shattering the quiet. Then all was still once more, and they did not move.

Keith's hand released hers, and his arms slid around her to gather her into an all-encompassing embrace. All pretense of dancing was abandoned. Mona trembled, an involuntary response that she was powerless to check, and she knew Keith could not have avoided feeling her tremors. If only she could collect her wits. . . .

He stepped away from her slightly, and a hand moved to her chin. Gently he forced her to raise her head, and their eyes locked. "What's the matter, Mona?" he asked.

"I. . . I don't know what you mean."

"Come on. This is me, remember? You're trembling right now, and you've been tense and nerve whipped all weekend. I've unloaded on you often enough. Why don't you talk to me? Something's troubling you. Surely you didn't think you could hide it from me. I know you too well. That's what has always made us so special. Now talk to me, please.''

"Keith. . . .'' Her eyes flew to his in silent appeal. If that rare communion was still there between them, surely he would read the anguish in her eyes and drop the matter. "I. . . I can't. I just can't.''

"Can't what?''

"Can't. . . tell you.''

"I wouldn't have thought there was anything you couldn't tell me.''

Nor would she have thought so before this. His very nearness made her pulses throb. "If I could, Keith, I would, you know that, but. . . I can't.''

"You might try,'' he persisted. "Just start at the beginning.''

"I can't. I. . . I want to sit down.'' Numbly she withdrew from his sheltering embrace and stumbled back to the lounge, almost collapsing onto it. To her surprise and dismay he came over to share it with her. She was forced to move to make room for him.

She couldn't think with him so close. He was making a casserole out of her brains. Wearily she raised one hand and rubbed her eyes, succeeding only in calling attention to the tears welling there.

"Good Lord!'' Keith muttered under his breath. "You look miserable. I'm going to insist, Mona. Tell me what's wrong.''

"Nothing!'' she almost shouted.

"I don't believe you.''

"Well, I can't help that!''

"Is it something I've done? Something I've said? Have I hurt your feelings, offended you in some way? You haven't been yourself this weekend, and if I'm at fault I want to correct it. Have I done something, Mona?''

A wry laugh escaped her lips. What would he have thought had she said, *yes, you're alive. That's what hurts my feelings, offends me, bothers me*? She only said, ''No, Keith, you've done nothing.''

She heard him suck in his breath, and she thought she felt his body tense. ''Then it has to be...has to be,'' he said quietly, almost as though he were talking to himself. ''I've suspected...but I couldn't bring myself to come right out and ask.''

Mona's brows knitted. ''Wh-what?''

''The reason for the fashion show.''

Mona gasped. Keith's hand touched hers, held it. Then he raised it to his lips to kiss her fingertips. The burning tingling tips were laid on his cheek, and he pressed his face into her palm. When he lifted his eyes to her, Mona saw the gentle flame leaping in them.

''Mona, Mona, whatever happened to all that refreshing frankness? My dear, darling woman, is it so terribly difficult for you to tell me you want me?'' he asked in the tenderest voice she had ever heard.

A large obstruction blocked Mona's throat and would not go away. Wide-eyed, mouth agape, she sat frozen. My God! Had she been so blatant? In a sharp flash of total recall, her mind remembered all her actions of the weekend, and she shuddered with shame. Now she could see that a fifteen-year-old would have handled it with more finesse. It must have been hilariously obvious to Keith that she was trying to get him to notice her as a woman.

Keith was watching her, tense and still. Sympathy,

understanding, communion—all were there in those gray eyes and more. That wasn't what she wanted from him. "Wh-what?" she repeated dumbly. What could she say to him? She had been stripped naked. The worst kind of sick humiliation swept through her.

A soft smile curved his mouth. "There's nothing wrong with wanting me, Mona. It's natural and normal. I should think it would be the predictable result of our summer together."

"Keith, my God!"

"I can say it easily enough," Keith said. "No trouble at all. I want you, Mona."

Her chin trembled uncontrollably. "No, no, you don't. You. . . you just want someone—not me."

Both of his hands came up to cup her face. "You're very wrong, you know. If I only wanted someone, anyone, I wouldn't have to look very far. You're. . . well, you're very special to me. I really do want you. Furthermore, you want me, too. I've seen it all day, or at least I thought I saw it. I was afraid it might just have been wishful thinking on my part."

Mona didn't know what to say. She should have known she couldn't hide anything from him, particularly not when she had been wearing her emotions on her sleeve.

"I kept thinking," Keith was saying, "that you would blurt it out in your customary blunt fashion, but now I see that wanting me bothers you. Why, Mona? I can't think of anything more natural between a man and a woman."

Mona's eyes burned with embarrassed tears. She tried to utter a little laugh, but it came out with a hollow ring to it. She despised feeling uncomfortable with Keith. She wanted to bask in the quiet contentment his presence once brought her. But in all truth, she had not felt totally relaxed around him since she realized she had fallen in love with him.

Well, the womanly guiles were a thing of the past. From this moment on she intended being completely honest with him, even if it hurt. "Oh, Keith...I swear I don't know what's wrong with me. I've never been so...so brazen before."

He chuckled softly. "Oh, yes, you have! But about other things. Not about sex."

The word hung in the air. "Are you ashamed of me?" she asked quietly.

"Ashamed? No, of course not. Not at all," he said just as quietly. "To tell you the truth, Mona, I'm flattered as hell."

She was sexually attracted to him, and he knew it. Mona accepted that. "Keith, you must understand how difficult this is for me," she began haltingly. "I've never felt this way. I've never wanted a man before...and I don't want to want you, but it's there. It's more than a little frightening."

"It shouldn't frighten you, Mona," he said, and his voice was like velvet.

"I felt it happening, and I knew I should stop coming out here with you, but I just couldn't. I tried to put it out of my mind, to tell myself it was nothing but a girlish crush, but it just kept on building and building until I.... I'm completely without expertise in male-female relationships, and I...I let it get out of hand. Oh, God, sometimes it hurts so damned much!"

Keith gathered her into his arms then, forcing her to curve her body to his lest she fall off the lounge.

His fingers laced through her dark hair and he kissed the top of her head.

"I sensed something...some change," he said thoughtfully. "At first I was afraid I'd done something. I thought perhaps it was that night I came to your room. Maybe I came on too strong. You might have thought me the worst sort of philanderer, a man who tried to make it with every woman he met. But then, yesterday and last night, I thought I was getting some pretty smoldering looks from you, and again I was afraid it might be wishful thinking. I dealt with it in the time-honored way of men—by downing considerable quantities of booze to steady my nerves. Oh, Mona, you've always been so brutally honest. Why in hell didn't you just *tell* me?"

She slipped her arms around his waist and held on to him tightly, relieved that it was out in the open. Whatever the result, it was better not to have it festering inside. "I...I think my greatest fear was that I would frighten you off. Then I wouldn't have our friendship. I wouldn't have anything. Instead I went through this ridiculous charade this weekend, primping and posing, trying to get you to notice me."

He chuckled. "All those gorgeous clothes! I felt as though I had somehow stumbled onto the spring fashion show at Neiman-Marcus. As if you need special clothes to make me notice you. I'm aware of you every second you're near, and when you aren't near I think about you all the time."

"Really?"

"Really."

"Ah, Keith, I've been behaving so foolishly. Whatever must you have thought? I'm surprised you didn't burst out laughing."

She felt a rumble of laughter in his chest. "I think so many things when I'm with you, Mona...so many delightful things. But before I tell you what they are...this is something I should have done a long time ago."

He slid a forefinger under her chin and forced it up. Then his mouth sought and found hers. Their lips fused, clung, parted, came together again. Mona's body trembled, shaken by the feel of his warm moist mouth claiming hers again and again, each time with increasing hunger. The hotness had such a sweetness to it! As Keith's probing kisses deepened urgently, shudders racked her.

Then his hands were traveling over her, touching, teasing, fondling, cupping. Mona felt as if she were going to faint; it definitely hurt to breathe. His exploring fingers, his warm mouth, his probing tongue—all combined to awaken forces of rapture in her. She was caught up in a whirlpool of desire, driven by primitive instincts she could not control. His sensitive hands burned her flesh as she clung to him in exquisite agony.

She heard him groan. "Oh, Mona," he said against her throat, "all week I kept remembering the way you feel. Such soft deep curves. I couldn't stop thinking about them."

Her hands went to his hips to draw him against her, and nothing could disguise the needs of his body. Keith's hand traced the gentle curve of her throat down to the dress's plunging neckline, and it slipped inside. The first touch of his fingers on a taut nipple sent a hot dizzying sensation coursing through her veins. His head bent to pillow itself on the cushioned softness of her breasts. The dress fell from her shoulder, exposing a creamy-smooth mound to his exploring tongue. He teased and tantalized; Mona wound her fingers through his thick dark hair and held his head against her.

"Oh, Keith," she gasped, "I've spent weeks thinking about this. I even thought about trying to...to seduce you. Isn't that awful! I don't know the first thing about seduction."

"You're doing a helluva job right now. I would have been an easy conquest, darling."

"Now I'm just ashamed of myself."

"Don't be, sweetheart. I've been miserable this past week, trying to sort out and analyze all these crazy feelings for you, trying to decide how far and fast I should go. You see, love...I, too, was worried about losing your friendship, losing everything. I thought I was falling in love with you, and I wasn't at all certain how you felt about me."

"That's the one time we weren't completely honest with each other, and we should have been. I've been miserable, too, Keith—wanting you and hating the wanting."

He lifted his eyes to her, and she saw in them what she had been longing to see—pure, shining, overflowing love. "Mona, darling," he said in a voice thick with emotion, "haven't you felt it between us from the beginning? I have. That communion of minds. I can't explain it, but it stuns me when I think how finely attuned to you I seem to be. This hasn't been some wild impetuous thing, no falling in love at first sight and all that rot. It's been growing, slowly but surely."

Mona didn't think her mind could assimilate the wonder of it, not now, not right away. It would take time for it to sink in. *He loves me!* She thought she would burst with happiness. "Say it," she begged.

"Say what, darling?"

"If I have to tell you, we'll call this whole thing off."

He understood. "I love you, Mona. I love you, I love you."

"And I love you. I love you so much I think I'm going to explode."

"I want you to be my wife."

Her body stilled in his hands. Things were moving so fast, so fast. She wouldn't have dared to let herself hope.... Mona fastened her dark eyes on him, and her mouth parted in fascination and wonder.

A small frown creased Keith's forehead. "Mona, did you hear me?"

"Y-yes, I heard you. Keith...are you sure about what you're saying?"

"Completely sure. I never meant anything more."

"I wouldn't ever want you to be sorry."

He kissed the tip of her nose, then her chin, then her mouth. "I'll never be sorry, you can be sure of that. We'll live in my place in the city, and once you graduate you can work as much or as little as you like. But one of these days, not too far into the future I hope, this will be home."

"Oh...." She melted against him, radiant in her happiness. This man! This place! More than she ever dreamed of. Keith's hands had resumed their erotic maneuvers. With trembling fingers he teased the exposed breast that neither had thought to cover up. Then both his hands slipped around to meet between her shoulder blades. He arched her breast toward his waiting mouth, and he caught the hardened point between his lips. A soft moan of satisfaction escaped Mona's lips. Her head was spinning crazily, and every part of her ached with the need to be touched, petted, fondled. Hot waves of desire swamped them both.

"Keith!" Mona cried softly, a little frantically. "What are we doing? What if someone were to come out here?"

With some effort he lifted his head from the cushion of her breasts. "You're right. If I can walk I'm going to take you into the bedroom and make love to you all night long."

The slight loosening of his embrace was all that it took for warning bells to start ringing in Mona's fogged mind. Not about the physical act itself. There was no doubt or fear about Keith's lovemaking. She wanted it every bit as much as he did, and she thought her need must surely be as great as his. Nor was she afraid of losing her virginity. Keith was the man she loved, and she would follow him anywhere.

But there was something else, something old and ominous and very real, and she could not shake it. Cold reasoning was taking over, tensing her body, and Keith felt it.

"Darling, I know you're frightened, but don't be. I'll be so gentle with you. I'll make it good for you, you'll see."

"Keith... darling Keith. We can't... I can't...."

"Of course you can, Mona. You want it as badly as I do. Trust me, sweetheart. I'll never hurt you. I'm going to take care of you the rest of my life." His reassuring arms enveloped her, and for a brief moment Mona felt her defenses crumbling.

But there was the inescapable reality of the other

thing. "Oh, Keith, I do trust you, darling. I know you mean what you say, and I'm not afraid of being hurt or any one of the things you might be thinking of. I . . . Keith . . . it's *Claire*!"

Now Keith went rigid, and his embrace was no longer warm. He looked down at her with a dark expression that made her cringe inside. "Dammit to hell, Mona! Why do you persist in mentioning her every time I get close to you?"

Her eyes pleaded for understanding. "Don't you see, Keith? How can I make love to you until I'm sure about you and Claire?"

His face registered total disbelief. "Mona . . . Mona," he groaned. "I don't believe this is happening! For God's sake, I just asked you to *marry* me, and for your information, my love, you're the only woman I've ever asked to marry me."

Mona stroked his face lovingly. "Keith, darling, I know you mean it right now, but Claire has been gone a long time. It could be that you've simply forgotten what you once felt for her. But she's coming back soon. What if you and I make love and then she walks in and . . . it's all over between us? I'm not sure I could live with that."

Keith's face blazed with incredulity. "My God, what kind of monster do you think I am? Do you honestly believe I could go from your arms to your sister's without a backward glance?"

"No," she said quietly, carefully controlling her voice to encourage him to get some of the fury out of his. "No, I think it would hurt you terribly to have to hurt me. But . . . what if you find you can't help yourself? One more reason for us to be absolutely sure before we do anything rash."

He drew her closer and covered her face with light kisses. "That's the most absurd thing I ever heard of!"

Mona squirmed under the onslaught of his kisses. "Oh, Keith, stop doing this! I'm trying to discuss this with you sensibly."

"There's nothing sensible about love, Mona. It's madness, pure and simple. I'm mad about you!"

"Please listen to me, Keith. You haven't lived with it; *I* have. I've been watching from the sidelines all my life. Men just seem to lose all sense of reason when Claire's around."

"Love-struck schoolboys!" he said derisively. "I'm way beyond that stage. I've been around the track a few times, and I know what I want. I want you, only you. I'm aching to make love to you. Come with me, darling. You won't have any doubts afterward. I'll make sure you don't."

Mona expelled a soft laugh. "Keith, I love you so much. I'm tempted, believe me, for the memory if nothing else. And I hope you'll be the first one, the only one. But there's not going to be any lovemaking until. . . until you've seen Claire again."

Keith's grip on her loosened so abruptly that Mona fell back and bumped her head on the chaise. "You and that damned jealousy!" he fumed. "My God, I don't believe this! Are you telling me that I've got to take Claire out before you'll let me love you?"

Mona bit her lip to still the trembling. She couldn't lose control, even though the thought of Keith's being with Claire again made her insides churn with dread. But she had to be sure. She had to be absolutely certain, and not even Keith's glowering look—a

look that had never been directed her way before—
could sway her.

"I'm trying to look at this realistically, Keith. Stop
glaring at me! I'm doing this for your sake, too. If
you see Claire and decide it's really her you want, I'll
have spared you the painful task of having to break it
off with me. Please try to understand. To lose you to
her now would hurt, but to lose you to her after we
had made love. . .Keith, I don't think I could bear
it."

He moved away from her then to sit at the foot of
the lounge and bury his head in his hands. Mona
rearranged her disheveled clothing, then reached out
to touch him. She leaned forward to place a soft kiss
on the back of his neck, and she rubbed his shoulder.
"Keith, surely you know how difficult this is for me.
It's going to be so hard, damned hard to have you
come to that house and call for Claire."

He raised his eyes to her. "Then marry me now,
right away—the moment it can be arranged. I'll be
your husband when Claire comes home. You'd be
sure of me then, wouldn't you?"

She smiled sadly and shook her head. "I'm afraid
that would be worse. I'd always wonder. My way is
best, Keith. Please."

"Oh, Mona. . .Mona, darling, why don't you
exorcise that demon?"

She lowered her eyes. "If you come to me after
you've been with her, it'll be gone forever."

He laughed harshly, a grating sound. "Are there
any further instructions? How many times must I
take her out? After how many kisses will you be convinced of my love?"

"Don't, Keith. Don't."

"Shall I make love to her? Will you be absolutely sure of me if I come to you after I've made love to your sister?"

Mona clenched her teeth together tightly; no tears were going to fall if she could help it. "Does it please you to torture me?" she managed to ask.

"What in hell do you think you're doing to me? You want me to walk into that house, to call for your sister, knowing you're there even if I can't see you? Dammit, I'll be able to *smell* you! And what about this house here at River View? Your hand is on everything. I can't walk through the rooms without feeling you beside me. Does that please you?"

Mona held her chin high. She was doing the right thing; she was sure of it. "No, of course it doesn't please me. But if you'll give yourself time to think, you might agree that this is the smart thing to do. If. . .if everything works out as I hope it will, we'll start off with the slate wiped clean. No regrets for you, certainty for me and, I hope, no hard feelings on Claire's part. This. . .this thing with Claire goes back a long way, and I've been swamped with guilt for weeks over lusting after my sister's boyfriend."

"Oh, for God's sake!" Keith made a futile gesture with his hands. "I don't know how to deal with this sort of thing."

"Keith, bear with me, please. Just a little while."

He sighed heavily and then reached for her again. Mona slid into his arms and kissed his neck, snuggling against him. "So where does that leave us, Mona?" he asked. "The rest of the summer, the next few weeks? What about those? Do you want to stay away from me entirely, or do you want to spend those last days here?"

"I'd like to spend them here," she said quietly, "but I'll understand if you prefer I don't."

"Weekends of chaste hugs and kisses while I ache for you with a passion I didn't know I possessed?" He uttered a sharp laugh. "That's asking quite a lot of me, you know."

Mona settled her head into the comfort of his shoulder. She rubbed his broad chest sensitively, trying to emphasize the very real affection between them rather than the sexual desire. "It's up to you, darling. . .Keith, darling. I'll do whatever you wish."

"Anything but make love to me," he said in a dull voice.

"I have to be sure, Keith."

His mouth twisted grimly. "So you've said."

THE FOLLOWING WEEKS were an agonizing time for Mona, hating to see the summer end, yet knowing her own future would be in suspense until it did. She had taken to meeting Beth Sinclair for lunch after classes every Wednesday and found their meetings to be the nicest part of the weekdays. There was a poignant kind of sadness about her aunt, and Mona would have loved to probe her dark depths, but Beth was a master of steering the conversation away from personal matters, and so Mona merely enjoyed her company, marveled at the rapport they shared and did not pry.

But except for the Wednesday lunches, the days seemed unbearable long. She wasn't accustomed to having time on her hands; it had always seemed to her that there weren't enough hours in the day. Now she tried to recall just what had filled those hours, and the only thing that came to her was books—

schoolbooks, books for pleasure. How long had it been since she had curled up with a good book and let the rest of the world go by? Now when she tried to read she ended up daydreaming. It made for some long empty hours.

And the weekends weren't all that much better. She still longed for them, longed to be with Keith, but now there was tension between them. They both worked hard at avoiding sensuous situations, and their physical contact was pretty well limited to, as Keith had predicted, chaste hugs and kisses. That, too, made for some long and frustrating hours.

On the last Saturday before Mona's family was to return from Palm Springs, she walked to the barn and asked Sam to saddle Mandy for her.

"You'll take good care of her for me, won't you, Sam?" she asked, nuzzling and stroking Mandy's neck. "I might not be back for a while." Or forever, she thought glumly, then chastised herself. No, she wasn't going to think like that. She wasn't going to let her self-confidence crumble. Keith loved her. He did!

"Don't you worry, Mona," Sam promised. "Nothing's going to happen to this old gal while I'm around. Did Keith tell you she's going to be a grandma?"

"Yes, yes, he did." Keith was pleased as punch that he had finally succeeded in breeding Bess to Royal Blue, the ranch's palomino stallion. What Bess thought these days was something else, it seemed to Mona. The haughty aristocrat no longer pranced proudly around the corral now that she was entering the tenth month of her pregnancy.

"That should be *some* foal," Sam gloated.

Mona mounted, wheeled Mandy around and rode off down the riverbank, far from the house. How she loved the warm feel of Mandy's smooth sleek coat between her legs. There had been a thunderstorm during the night, ushering in a weak cool front that had brought a respite from the awful heat. Mona had lain in bed, listening while nature unleashed her fury, wishing she could lie in the comfort of Keith's strong arms. It would have been so easy—just to get up, walk across the hall, open his door, and he would have happily welcomed her. Small wonder she had spent half the night hugging her pillow and shedding tears of frustration.

The air and earth smelled so good! It was a sparkling afternoon. The temperature had plummeted several degrees, and the azure sky shone with a brilliant clarity that hurt the eyes. The grass seemed a several-shades-deeper green. It was amazing what one good rain could do to the land.

At a particular grouping of oak trees Mona reined in, slipped out of the saddle and tethered the mare. Then while Mandy cropped the sweet-smelling grass, Mona sank to the still-damp earth and rested her head on her knees. It was over! The idyllic summer was past history. One minute there had been all the time in the world, and the next it was over. Tomorrow, as he had done every Sunday for months, Keith would drive her back to her house in the city, and the following day her family would return.

"Shall I call on Claire Monday night?" Keith had asked only yesterday, rather caustically, Mona thought. He seemed to be taunting her lately, and that was something new.

"Keith," she said with a feeling of helplessness, "I

don't know. Just do whatever you think you must . . whatever you want.''

''No, sweet Mona, not what *I* want. This is your show, remember? Tell me . . . Claire always made me wait a dreadfully long time before putting in an appearance. Will you be there to entertain me while I wait for her?''

And she had given him a slight punch in the midsection. ''Not if I can help it!''

Now Mona raised her head and looked down at the water sloshing over the limestone rocks of the riverbed. The Brazos rolled through the pages of Texas history. The Comanches had lived on the very spot where she sat. Later, the first state capitol, Washington-on-the-Brazos, had been built on its southern banks. Paddlewheelers had plied its waters, and cotton plantations had flanked its shores.

It suddenly occurred to her that she might never see this spot again, and she experienced a sense of foreboding that was stifling. Dear God, she would miss it! Dear God, she would miss *him*!

The hammering of a horse's hooves interrupted her thoughts. She turned to see Keith riding toward her at a fast gallop. Quickly getting to her feet and brushing at the seat of her pants, she watched him approach, dismount, and then he was so close she could see the fine lines etched around the corners of his eyes and mouth.

''I've been looking all over the place for you,'' he admonished.

''I had to get out of the house for a while. I guess you're happy about the rain.''

Keith kicked the ground with the toe of his boot. ''Well, I'm grateful for anything I get, but one rain followed by a day of sunshine doesn't break a drought. What we need is days of rain followed by clouds and more rain." He gave her a serious look. "What have you been doing out here all by yourself?"

"Thinking."

"And I think I know the thoughts churning in that fertile brain of yours," he said with a knowing smile. He put out his arms to draw her to him. There had been so little touching lately. Mona had understood, of course; no sense flirting with too many temptations. But she needed to feel him, to smell him. She melted against him pliantly and slipped her arms around his waist. Her hands met at the small of his back, and she rubbed him lightly.

"Oh, you're so smart! What am I thinking?"

"You're thinking that this might be the last time—that you might never see River View again."

Numbly she nodded her head, stunned by his perception. "You amaze me. I'll never try to keep a secret from you. It would be useless."

"You're wrong, you know," he said gently. "But as you've pointed out to me at least eight dozen times, you have to be sure. I'll see to it that you're sure, Mona. When next I come to you, you won't have any doubts."

"Oh, Keith," she whispered, "I hope you're right. How I hope you're right! How I hope you'll come to me again!" And she lifted her mouth to receive his kiss.

CHAPTER SEVEN

THE LOWERYS' RETURN HOME was accompanied by almost as much fuss and ado as their departure had been. They returned with at least twice as much luggage as they had left with, and Ben was fuming because the airline had misplaced one of his bags. Kitty not so much entered the house as assaulted it and began issuing a barrage of orders to Lettie and Lucille, instantly resuming control of the household. Mona smiled, thinking that the poor women must surely have considered the summer a blissful respite.

She greeted her parents with heartfelt warmth, realizing that she had truly missed them. She was more tied to home and family than she had thought. "My, don't the two of you look marvelous!" she exclaimed. "All that sun and relaxation did wonders for you! Oh, but I'm glad to see you!"

"And we're glad to see you, dear," Kitty said. She was dressed in a smart linen suit, her hair had been cut in a becoming style and her figure was as firm and trim as a woman's of considerably fewer years than forty-seven. Her practiced motherish eyes took in her younger daughter. "You must have been spending some time at the pool, Mona. You look tanned and fit. I must say I'm relieved. I was certain we would come back to find you pale and wan from spending all your time with the books."

"Yes...I...I've got in some swimming, particularly on the weekends. It hasn't been all study."

"Good. I'm so glad to be home. I hate having the family separated like that. Now, tell me, Mona how have things been?"

"Hot!"

"Oh, we read about that heat wave in the papers. It must have been just awful! I'm sure you're glad that the summer is over."

Mona smiled ruefully. If only her mother knew. It was one summer she wished had never ended.

Ben spoke up. "I've got to call the office," he announced, and went into the library.

Claire called after him, "Tell me when you're finished with the phone, daddy. I want to call Keith. He must be on pins and needles." She turned to Mona. "Have you seen him at all this summer?"

Mona swallowed hard. "A...a few times." Claire looked as stunning and ravishing as ever. Mona's heart constricted sharply. *I must be out of my mind to deliberately throw Keith into this woman's company. No man would be able to resist her.*

"Well, I'll certainly be glad to see him," Claire said. "I didn't realize just how special he is until I was away from him so long."

"I told you, dear," Kitty said with a smile. "Don't let that young man get away. There aren't many like him around."

Claire laughed and a mischievous gleam danced in her eyes. "Don't worry, Mona. I intend to make very sure of him this time. No doubt he's found some little charmer to keep him company this summer, but I'll get rid of her fast!"

A decidedly sick feeling was churning in the pit of

Mona's stomach. She had been a prize fool! Keith was the one, the only one, and she was virtually handing him to Claire on a silver platter. If Claire deliberately set about to snare Keith.... Well, Mona's muddled mind couldn't even dwell on that possibility. She had to keep remembering how close she and Keith had become. They had shared something very special, and it just might have been special enough to override Claire's beauty and charm. She had to keep thinking that. If she lost Keith, there would never be anyone else.

Ben came out of the library to announce he was going to the office, waving aside Kitty's protests. Claire swept in after him; Mona heard her on the telephone. Within moments her sister emerged, her face wreathed in a satisfied smile.

"Oh, it was good to hear his voice again! Mama, I won't be here for dinner. Keith is taking me out."

"I don't think we'll have much for dinner tonight," Kitty mused. "It seems all we've done this summer is eat. I know I've gained weight. How does soup and a salad sound? Will that be all right with you, Mona?"

"Fine." Her voice had a hollow ring to it. "I'm not very hungry."

Claire's eyes were shining. "Mama," she said, "what do you think I should wear for my reunion with Keith? Something smashing! What about that green dress I bought last week?"

"Oh, that will be perfect, dear. You look so lovely in it. Keith won't be able to take his eyes off you."

There was a paralyzing numbness in Mona's chest. "I...I have some studying to do," she muttered, and fled upstairs to her room.

She didn't know how she was going to get through the evening. One would have thought Claire was dressing for the governor's ball, judging by all the attendant fuss and furor. Every time Mona looked up there was Claire, sweeping from her room to the bathroom and back again, humming a little tune, a radiant glow on her face. Mona couldn't ever remember seeing her sister so excited over a date.

"May I borrow those little pearl earrings of yours?" Claire asked.

"Sure. Help yourself," Mona said, pretending absorbed interest in the book in her hand.

"What about that French cologne? I'm fresh out."

Mona made a sweeping gesture in the direction of her dressing table. "Take whatever you want."

Claire shot her a quizzical look. "Something wrong?"

"No!" Mona said too quickly and too brightly. "Why?"

"You look like you just lost your best friend."

I have, Mona thought. *I'm afraid I have.*

THROUGHOUT DINNER THAT NIGHT Ben and Kitty chatted happily away, recalling the days in Palm Springs and bombarding Mona with anecdotes about the summer. She feigned rapt attention, and neither of her parents seemed to notice she was having difficulty eating. She toyed with her food, trying to eat enough to satisfy Lucille, but all the while her thoughts were elsewhere. She thought of Mamie's delicious meals, of those leisurely dinners at River View with dancing on the patio afterward. The food stuck in her throat.

The moment the table had been cleared Mona returned to her room, again pleading the necessity of study. "Goodness," Kitty exclaimed, "I can hardly wait to see your grades! They must be something! Study, study, study. There's more to life than that, dear."

Upstairs in the sanctity of her room Mona didn't even open a book. She suspected her grades were suffering; she had been so wrapped up in Keith and River View that she had neglected them shamefully. How was she going to explain *that* to her parents when they thought she spent virtually every waking minute with schoolwork? She threw herself down on the bed and stared morosely at the wall.

She deliberately avoided going downstairs for the remainder of the evening to preclude the possibility of seeing Keith when he arrived. But she heard the doorbell ring at precisely seven-thirty, and she heard her father's booming welcome. And nothing could drown out Claire's glad cry nor the sound of that familiar, beloved, resonant baritone voice—not even the frantic hammering of her heartbeat.

Mona's imagination ran rampant. She almost could see the embrace, could imagine the glint of approval in Keith's eyes when he beheld the lovely Claire for the first time in three months. An involuntary shudder swept through her. Yesterday they had shared a lingering goodbye kiss, one that had left Mona dizzy with desire, and tonight he was here for her sister. The entire thing was so ludicrous it would have been laughable had it not been so painful.

At the sound of the front door closing, Mona jumped off the bed and moved toward the window to lift the curtains. It was a form of self-torture, she realized, but a compelling force was urging her to the window.

Looking down, she saw the splendid little Mustang parked in front of the house. Keith was holding the car door open. Claire stepped forward, but before she slid inside she raised her face and placed a light kiss on Keith's mouth. He smiled down at her, and words were exchanged. Mona felt as if a blow had been delivered to her stomach. She gasped, and hot tears scalded her eyes.

Keith closed the door behind Claire. Then—incredibly—he raised his eyes to the window where Mona stood, as though he had known she was standing there. The slightest hint of a strange smile played at the corners of his mouth, and the look he gave her was one Mona had never seen on his face before. He raised his hand to her in a kind of salute.

Their gazes locked, and that rare communion took over. *Is this what you want,* Keith's look asked. *Is it?* Mona's anguish was too evident. It would be transmitted to him in an instant if she wasn't careful. She dropped the curtain and listened as the car drove away.

It was the longest night of her life. She spent it lying on her bed in the darkened room, staring at the ceiling, waiting for the glare of headlights to signal their return, listening for the sound of Claire's soft tread on the stairs.

Mona's eyes burned from unshed tears. *No tears, no tears,* she cautioned herself. *Tears have to be explained.* It wouldn't do to show up at breakfast with red swollen eyes and have to endure her mother's questions.

And she was reminded of just whose idea all this

was in the first place. Had Keith had his way they would have been married by now. But that would hardly have solved anything. It would have been a shock to her family, and she would have always wondered if Keith had any regrets. After all, he would still have had to face Claire again with all her beauty and sex appeal.

Perhaps tomorrow he would call. Yes, she felt sure he would. It was a comforting thought and the only thing that got Mona through a very bad night.

BUT HE DIDN'T CALL the next day, nor the next, nor the next, and suddenly merely existing had become intolerable. It seemed to Mona that every time she turned around Keith was expected at their house. She had managed to avoid seeing him, but that could not go on indefinitely. She had turned into something of a recluse, forever hiding in the safety of her room. When her parents commented on this she began staying late at school to work in the library. It was becoming more and more difficult to concentrate on her studies, and for the first time in her life her grades were not exemplary, a fact that several of her professors brought to her attention.

Keith had been at the Lowery house seven out of the past nine evenings. He must have known what it was doing to her. Perhaps he no longer cared. When a few more days passed without his contacting her, Mona began to experience real anger. Who the hell does he think he is? One crummy phone call! Is that asking so much? Then rage gave way to resentment, and it in turn became a black despondency.

The worst part of it all was that Claire fairly radiated happiness. "I think I've finally found the one, mama,'' Mona overheard her sister telling Kitty. ''Keith is so superior in every way.''

Mona wouldn't have dreamed that words could hurt so much. Did that mean in his lovemaking, too? Had Keith actually fallen under Claire's magic spell again? She was afraid that she had been right all along, that her worst fears had been realized. She discovered she wasn't prepared for it, and until she could come to grips with her aching yearning for him, her only defense seemed to be to stay as far away from him as possible.

And on top of everything else, Mona was forced to suffer Kitty's endless speculation on the progress of Claire's romance. ''I think Claire has finally found the one,'' she told Mona. ''I hope so, and so does your father. Keith Garrett is the kind of man that girl has always needed. He'll be so good for her. And I've seen that look in his eyes. Men think they can hide it, but they can't. He's a man in love, that's for sure.''

Mona could not keep quiet. ''He's too good for her,'' she said bitterly.

''What?'' Kitty was incredulous. ''Mona, what a monstrous thing to say!''

''Yes, I suppose it was,'' Mona admitted.

''Well, then, why did you say it?''

''Probably because I meant it,'' was Mona's frank but unkind retort. ''Can you honestly imagine a man like Keith Garrett with a wife whose heaviest thoughts are centered on what she's going to drape over her body?''

Kitty's shock was genuine. ''For heaven's sake, Mona, I don't understand you sometimes. You should be ecstatic for your sister. She's happy, and so is Keith. Anyone can see that.''

Was Keith happy? Mona would have known in an instant if she could have seen him. One look into those gray eyes would have told her all she needed to know. But she didn't dare.

And so it came to Mona with resolute finality that Keith had discovered it really was Claire he wanted. She tried to convince herself that it was better for him to have discovered it now than after he had mistakenly married her. She tried to be glad she had possessed the wisdom and foresight to insist that Keith see Claire before making any hasty commitments. She tried to congratulate herself on being such a sensible, levelheaded young woman.

Nothing worked. She missed him, she longed for him, she loved him. She felt as though she were drifting, floating, falling, with nothing to cling to. Surely Keith would tell her soon; he owed her that. It shouldn't be all that difficult to find a few minutes to be alone with her and tell her. He would be very apologetic, of course, and it wouldn't be easy for him, but surely he would do it. And she would be extremely poised and gracious, very magnanimous.

Who was she kidding? She would be dying inside, and it would show, making Keith uncomfortable. Perhaps he was dreading it even now and putting it off. People were inclined to procrastinate in such matters. Mona wondered if she should be the one to make the first move, to call him and ask outright. She could almost hear him now. "Mona, I'm sorry," he would say. "I can't tell you how sorry I am, but...." She shuddered.

And so she waited, half hoping, half dreading. She knew if the thing didn't get itself resolved soon she was going to be a physical as well as an emotional cripple. She was plagued with headaches and digestive upsets. She was smoking too much. She slept badly and had no appetite. She had lost pounds she couldn't afford to lose, and her face was becoming a bit haggard.

Kitty noticed and fretted. "Mona, if you don't snap out of these doldrums I'm taking you to a doctor. I think you're coming down with something."

"I'm all right, mom," she protested, wishing with all her heart that there was a pill that would cure what ailed her.

"Oh, Mona, dress for dinner tonight, please," Kitty said. "I've invited Keith. I might as well do my part to get this romance moving along. I do so hope something will come of it."

Horrified, Mona quickly said, "I won't be here for dinner tonight."

"Oh? You didn't mention having plans for the evening."

"Didn't I? I'm sorry. . . I just forgot. I'm having dinner with some friends," she lied.

Kitty's eyes swept over her attire. "You're not wearing those rather disreputable jeans, I hope. The next time I go shopping I want you to come along. You definitely need some new clothes. No wonder—" Kitty checked herself.

Mona smiled wryly. *No wonder the young men don't beat a path to your doorstep,* was what her mother had wanted to say. Kitty and Ben were much too kind and doting to say so, but Mona knew they were beginning to suspect they had a wallflower on their hands.

"No, I'll change," she said, and went upstairs to her room. She sprawled in the chair at her drafting table and stared vacantly into space. What would she change into, she wondered, and where would she spend the evening? She had absolutely no place to go, and there weren't all that many places a lone woman could, or should, go in the evening.

She thought of Aunt Beth and dialed her number but hung up after the third ring, remembering that Beth was visiting friends in Houston. Their Wednesday lunch date had had to be canceled because of that. Mona idly drummed on the drafting table with her fingers. Then on an impulse she reached for the phone and dialed Alan Palmer's number. Small chance that Alan, of all people, would have nothing to do, but....

"Mona!" he cried with obvious delight.

"Hi! I thought if by chance you aren't doing anything tonight we might try to find some of that trouble you mentioned a while ago."

"What a coincidence! I was just going to call you."

"A likely story!"

"Honest! I'm overflowing with news, and since all of it is happy stuff and since most of it is due to your meddling, I thought I'd make the grand gesture and treat you to the Mexican buffet at the club tonight."

Mona breathed a sigh of relief. Good old Alan! She was beginning to think of him as her only friend. "I'd be delighted to go. You truly are the answer to a maiden's prayer."

"Good! I'll pick you up at seven-thirty."

Seven-thirty? If Mona remembered correctly, that was the time Keith was due at the house. "No, Alan," she said firmly. "I'll come over to your place at seven-fifteen."

"God, I hate pushy women who want to run things! Okay, Mona. See you at seven-fifteen sharp."

Mona luxuriated in a long, hot, fragrant bath, then gave special attention to her hair, makeup and what to wear. Not to impress Alan, of course. He had seen her at her best, worst and all points in between, and he wouldn't give a damn what she was wearing. It was more to give her own spirits a lift. She hadn't gone out in the evening in a long time, and she thought tonight just might be the first step in her long climb out of this melancholy.

The country club's Mexican buffet always drew a huge crowd, mostly a young crowd, and Mona was determined to have some fun for a change. It was a casual evening, probably the most casual of the club's week, but the men were required to wear sport coats, so the women could get by with almost anything except really formal wear. A pantsuit would do, but somehow she felt like something a bit more feminine. Her eyes swept over the garments hanging in her closet and fell on a lovely rose-colored jacket dress she hadn't yet worn. September in Dallas was quite warm, but the club's air conditioning would make the light jacket feel good. She slipped it off the hanger and threw it across the bed.

After dressing, Mona went downstairs and said good-night to her parents. Then, not wanting to trudge through hedges and across lawns while wearing her lovely dress, hose and high heels, she got in her car and drove next door to the Palmer mansion. Alan met her at the door with a drink in his hand, grinning from ear to ear. He was dressed in dark tan trousers and a pale beige sport shirt open at the neck.

Casual but impeccable. Mona knew only one other man who wore clothes with more style and flair. It was almost impossible for her to judge Alan's good looks objectively; she had just known him too long. But she thought she caught a glimpse of whatever it was that made him so irresistible to women. He was a devilishly handsome man, utterly charming, with just the slightest bit of wickedness about him.

"How come you're answering the door?" she asked as she stepped into the foyer. "Where's Old Sourpuss?"

Alan chuckled as he closed the door behind her. "Bentley?" he asked, referring to the Palmers' so proper, stern-faced butler. "Don't mind Bentley. He takes his work *verrry* seriously, and to Bentley's notion a butler should never smile. This is the servants' night off. Come on in and I'll fix you a drink."

"Okay. Vodka and something. . . I don't care."

"Tonic all right?"

"Fine."

Alan's eyes looked her over from head to toe. "Hey, you look downright fetching tonight, Mona. I'm not even going to mind being seen with you."

"Mercy, you'll turn my head with all that flattery," she gushed sarcastically.

Alan led the way to the newly completed sun room, then went to the wet bar in the kitchen while Mona surveyed the room. It was the brightest spot in the Palmers' elegant but cold house. The tile floor gleamed, and Mona decided that the rattan furniture with its boldly bright printed cushions had been an inspiration. Plants were everywhere—hanging from hooks, standing in huge pots in the corners, sitting on tables. The vertical blinds gave complete privacy when closed, yet were barely discernible when open. The sweep of windows afforded a splendid view of the brightly lighted, meticulously landscaped swimming pool. It all had sort of a South Seas look about it—exactly what she had been striving for.

Alan returned with her drink, handed it to her, then motioned for her to have a seat.

"Well, I'm dying of curiosity," Mona told him. "Out with all your happy news."

He plopped down beside her, reached in his shirt pocket, withdrew something and handed it to her. It was a folded piece of paper. "First this," Alan said, and a satisfied smile spread across his face.

"What is it?" Mona unfolded it and saw that it was a check, drawn on Stephanie Means's gallery. She gasped, and her eyes grew bright. "Oh, Alan!" she breathed.

"Mona, I'll swear things have been moving so damned fast. I'm not sure it's all sunk in yet, but—" he tapped the check in her hand "—that, my dear, represents the sale of the Turtle Creek painting *and* the Padre Island seascape!"

Mona threw back her head and gave a little whoop. "Oh, Alan, that's fantastic! See, what did I tell you? You really do have a marketable talent. Are you convinced now?"

"Stunned is a better word." Suddenly he grew serious. "I'll tell you something else that check represents, Mona. It's the first money I've ever earned in my life, and I've discovered that earning money is more fun than just having it...if you know what I mean."

"I know what you mean, believe me I do."

"But I haven't told you the best part. The Turtle Creek thing was purchased by some society psychiatrist who's opening a fancy new clinic shortly after the first of the year. He asked Stephanie if she thought I'd be interested in doing some things for the reception room. Isn't that something, Mona? I've been commissioned!''

Mona was so delighted for her friend that words failed her. "Alan, it's...it's...just fantastic, that's the only word I can think of. I'm excited for you, I'm proud of you, I...I feel as though I've just given birth!''

"And so you should. It was all your doing, young lady. If it hadn't been for you, Turtle Creek would still be propped against the wall in my studio.''

Mona clasped her hands together and luxuriated in feeling just a bit pleased with herself. All Alan had needed was a shove in the right direction. "So what now, Alan? What comes next?''

Shrugging, he took a long swallow of his drink. "I don't know, Mona. I'm just enjoying the hell out of taking one day at a time. I'll pretty up the good doctor's waiting room, then see what comes up next. It's a damned good feeling to hop out of bed in the morning, anxious to see what the day holds in store.'' He turned to her with a thoughtful expression. "And if you'll permit me to get serious for a minute, I owe you one.''

"You owe me nothing, Alan,'' she said emphatically. "It's going to be payment enough to be able to sit back and watch your career just blossom and grow and grow!''

He shook his head. "No, I mean it. I owe you one. Anytime you need someone to fix a traffic ticket or cover a hot check or bribe a jury, you know where to come.''

Mona laughed. "I'll remember that.''

"Come on, finish your drink," Alan said, draining his glass in a gulp. "We can have another at the club. God, that Mexican food is going to taste good!"

Mona sat her glass down without finishing her drink, and she stood up, smoothing her dress. "My car is outside. Shall we take it?"

Alan pretended horror. "Me? Ride in that sensible little compact of yours? Not on your life! We'll take my Porsche."

As Alan roared out of the sweeping driveway with Mona clutching the armrest for dear life, she turned and glanced toward her house. The yellow Mustang was parked in front, and she felt the all too familiar lurch in the pit of her stomach. Did Keith ever wonder how she consistently managed to avoid him? Did he ever speculate on what she did, whom she saw? Did he ever think of her at all now that Claire was home? Unfortunately she feared Keith's thoughts of her would take the form of qualms about facing her again, and she silently vowed to screw up her own courage and approach him. It was better to get it over with, but merely thinking about it caused a large lump to lodge painfully in her throat.

Oh, dammit! She wasn't going to spoil the evening by dwelling on Keith. She was going to have a good time if it killed her!

THE COUNTRY CLUB was an elegant structure. Tonight it was ablaze with lights, and the parking lot was jammed with cars. Inside, the place teemed with activity and the bar was doing a land-office business, as usual. The line of people queueing up for the buffet seemed hopelessly long, so Alan suggested a drink first.

"Let's let the crowd thin out some. I hate to eat with people glaring at me, impatiently waiting for my table."

As Mona had guessed, the young crowd was out in full force for the popular buffet. She and Alan were immediately hailed by mutual friends, and room was made for them at one of the long tables. She noticed with some amusement that she was the object of many an envious feminine glance. Alan was definitely the star attraction. He fairly oozed charm and lavished it equally on every woman at the table. Yet Mona had to give him credit—he was able to do it without incurring the wrath of their escorts.

The alcoholic preamble to dinner lasted a bit longer than Mona would have preferred, but Alan was having a grand time. He was an entertaining raconteur and one of those people who genuinely loved social affairs. All the noise and smoke and shine and glitter apparently stimulated him, and he seemed to gain strength and vitality with each passing minute. Like Claire, Mona thought irrelevantly. Her sister, too, was at her best when at a party.

At long last Alan stood up and announced that he and Mona were going to the buffet line. A few others around the table joined them, but most seemed to have settled down to a long drinking bout. The few who were hungry trooped into the dining room.

"I positively am not going to gorge myself tonight," Mona said as they took their plates and started down the line. "One taco, one enchilada, and maybe one *chile relleno*. That's it!"

"That's no Mexican dinner," Alan admonished. "You've got to take some of the rice. And what about tamales and the Mexican stew? You've got to take a little bit of everything.''

Mona groaned, but the cocktails had given her an enormous appetite and everything looked irresistible. She ended up taking a tiny helping of just about everything at the buffet, then proceeded to polish if off with ease.

"You know, Alan," she mused over dinner, "it's occurred to me that when I have my shop, you and Stephanie and I might make quite a combination."

"How's that?"

"Well, you'll be showing your work in Stephanie's gallery, and whenever one of my clients needs just the right painting, whose work do you suppose I'll think of first? We'll all three benefit."

Alan tapped his temple with a forefinger. "Quite the little businesswoman, aren't you?"

"Is that demeaning to an artist? Do you dislike thinking of your work in terms of filthy lucre?"

"Hell, no!" he sputtered. "That check from Stephanie is the biggest thing that's ever happened to me."

"It's really nothing more than pocket change to a man with your money, Alan," she reminded him.

"But that's not the point. The point is that I got a bigger kick out of that little check than I ever got out of my cabin cruiser or sports cars or Cessna or thoroughbred horses. I used to have to work so damned hard at having fun. Now just living is fun. It's the greatest feeling in the world, Mona. It's like opening night on a brand-new way of life."

"That's nice," Mona said with a smile, but suddenly she was enormously saddened. A brand-new way of life! Soon she would have one, too, when the semester ended and she went into business, moved out of the house, got her own apartment. She hoped she was ready for it. Above all, she hoped by that time her memories of Keith and River View and that wonderful summer would have grown fuzzy, that the pain would have diminished somewhat.

She pushed her plate away. "I'm stuffed," she complained. "Why do I always do that? Why can't I resist Mexican food?"

Alan, too, had finished his meal. He glanced around and satisfied himself that there were no hungry diners waiting for their table. He settled back in his chair, lit two cigarettes and handed one to Mona.

"I'd like to ask a favor of you, Mona," he said quietly.

"Have at it."

"Would you sit for me?"

She frowned. "What?"

"Sit for me. Pose for your portrait. I haven't done a portrait in a long time, and I'd like to give it a try. What do you say?"

"Well, I . . . ." She was enormously flattered, of course. "I guess so, Alan . . . but why me? There must be hundreds of more beautiful subjects—Claire for one."

"No, I want you. And I'll work around your schedule."

Schedule? What schedule? She went to classes in the morning and had lunch with Beth on Wednesdays, but other than that she seemed to have more time than she had anything else these days. "I'd love to, Alan. Thank you."

"Good!" Alan got to his feet and moved around

the table to hold her chair for her. "Let's go downstairs. I think they have a combo on buffet night. Would you like to dance?"

She stood up and linked her arm through his. "Sounds like fun. Maybe it'll help me work off some of this food."

The downstairs bar was a dimly lit place with cozy circular booths lining the walls. In the center of the room was a minuscule dance floor, and on a platform nearby four musicians and a female vocalist were pouring out a plaintive ballad. Alan ordered brandy for himself and a crème de menthe for Mona, then led her out onto the dance floor, where they glided effortlessly through two numbers before sliding back into the booth to sip their drinks.

Mona leaned her head on the back of the padded booth, and as she listened to the blond pink-cheeked vocalist croon an incredibly sad love song she became caught up in the lyrics lamenting a lost love. Why were songs about unrequited love invariably so beautiful? And why did frustrated lovers derive so much pleasure from listening to them? She sighed so audibly that Alan gave her a puzzled look.

"Was that a sigh of contentment?" he asked.

She shrugged. "Just a sigh. The singer's good, isn't she?"

"Not bad. She's got a quavery quality to her voice, like she's going to break down and cry any minute."

Mona smiled. "That's called a tear in the voice. Judy Garland had it. My dad was nuts about her. We have dozens of old records, and I remember listening to them when I was a little girl and thinking, *oh, wow, if I could sing like that I'd have the world by the tail.* Yet . . . she didn't, did she?"

"Few people do, Mona. I should think celebrities least of all... with a few exceptions, of course."

Mona sighed another heavy sigh, and Alan frowned. Then he rapped his hand on the table, making a sharp sound. "Damned if you're not a ball of fire tonight!"

"Sorry," she apologized. "Too much food, I guess."

"Too much heavy thinking. I've been watching you all night. You've only been half here. What are you thinking about?"

"Everything... and nothing. The nature of life and love, the mysteries of the universe, the relationship between man and his Creator, how the Cowboys are going to do this year."

Alan laughed a lusty laugh. "Well, all that *would* require some heavy thought. Best concentrate on one thing at a time."

It was impossible to stay pensive for long with Alan around. Mona smiled and shook herself out of her mood. "All right, what shall we think about?"

"Oh... the nature of love, I guess."

Wonderful! That was just what she needed! "Have you ever been in love, Alan?"

He grimaced. "Dozens of times."

"I don't mean that kind of love. Not infatuation or a casual affair. I mean, have you ever really been in love?"

"I swear I don't know, Mona. I've sure thought I was in love a few times. What about you? Have you ever been in love?"

A faraway look came to her eyes. "Once," she said remotely. "Only once. And that's supposed to be so terribly, terribly romantic. Baloney!"

Alan frowned. "Boy, you're really in a blue funk. What's got you so down? I don't think I've ever seen you like this."

Mona ran the tip of her finger around the rim of her liqueur glass. "I guess I have a case of the general blahs."

"It must be a man."

"A man would think that."

"Well, am I right?"

She nodded. "I'm afraid so."

Alan watched her with renewed interest. "Was this your first time out?"

"Yes."

"There'll be others, Mona. I don't care who it is, he isn't the only one."

"I hope you're right. I always thought the ideal would be to fall in love once, only once. Now I'm beginning to wonder. I think maybe it would be better to be like Claire. Like you, she's been in love dozens of times."

Mona's back was to the bar's entrance, and she saw Alan glance over her shoulder, then his eyes widened as though he had seen a friend. "Speak of the devil. There's your sister now."

Mona almost choked on her drink, and her stomach lurched. Oh, no, they hadn't! They hadn't decided on a night on the town after dinner! But Claire loved to come to the club for drinking and dancing. Mona hesitantly peered around the back of the booth, and her worst fears were confirmed. Keith and Claire were standing in the doorway, and Claire's eyes were making a sweep of the room. Why here, Mona silently groaned. There are two hundred other places they could have gone!

Quickly she sat back and faced Alan, her eyes fierce. "Now don't do anything incredibly dumb. like ask them to join us."

Alan's brows knitted. "What in hell is the matter with you, Mona? Besides, you're too late. Claire just spotted us." He flashed a welcoming smile and raised his hand to wave.

Mona rubbed her forehead; suddenly she seemed to have developed a pounding headache. But she steeled herself and managed a credible smile just as Claire and Keith reached the table. She refused to look up at him, but she could feel his penetrating gaze beating down on the top of her head.

Alan had jumped to his feet, and Claire uttered a small squeal as she hugged him enthusiastically. "Alan, how are you? I haven't seen you in ages! Mona didn't mention she was going out with you to-night. I'd like you to meet Keith Garrett. Keith, this is Alan Palmer."

"Alan," Keith acknowledged as the two men shook hands. "I believe we met some years ago. It was at a luncheon at the Petroleum Club, as I recall."

"That's right," Alan said. "I remember now. Someone was retiring from something. Nice to see you again. Well, folks, why don't you join us?" He ignored Mona's reproachful glare and stepped aside to allow Claire to slide into the booth. Then he sat beside her, leaving Keith with no choice but to sit beside Mona.

Claire was bright eyed and animated, at her enchanting best. "Mona, I wish you had told me you had a date with Alan. The two of you could have had dinner at the house with us, and we could have made it a foursome for the evening."

Oh, God, Mona thought. She would have preferred being shot. This was bad enough. It was a tight fit with four people in the little booth. Mona bumped against Claire's hip, and Keith's thigh was hard and warm against hers. She refused to entertain the notion that he was deliberately pressing against her a little too insistently. Her throat was so tight she thought she was strangling. Her nerves were stretched to the snapping point, and all her senses flared in awareness of him. That damned after-shave lotion of his—it was like an aphrodisiac!

"Good evening, Mona," Keith said in a stilted voice.

"Hello, Keith."

Fortunately Alan and Claire had a lot of catching up to do, and they became so engrossed in their gossip that they noticed nothing peculiar or strained about the way Mona and Keith were behaving. Mona pasted on a smile and pretended rapt absorption in the conversation, but she heard not a word of it. All she could hear was her own heartbeat. To her ears it sounded like the beating of a hundred drums.

A waitress came to take their orders. "Brandy all the way around," Alan said. "Oh...I'm sorry, Mona, would you prefer something else?"

She stared at the after-dinner drink that had become a watery pool of unappetizing green. "Brandy's fine," she said in a small voice.

Alan and Claire continued chatting happily away until the drinks arrived. Then it was with the utmost dismay that Mona saw her friend jump to his feet and hold out his hand to her sister. "Come on, Claire, let's dance," Alan said amiably, and the two of them headed for the dance floor.

Mona thought surely there could be nothing more obvious than two people trying not to look at each other. Quickly she put some distance between herself and Keith, and the silence between them was like a wedge.

Finally Keith spoke. "Would you like to dance?"

"No!" Mona cried much too vehemently, horrified at the thought of being held in those strong arms again.

"Smile, Mona. Casual acquaintances usually try to make polite conversation in public. Look at me and don't glower."

Mona didn't know how she summoned the courage, considering the frazzled state of her nerves, but somehow she managed to turn to him and lift her eyes, and she was looking into those dark gray orbs that held such fascination for her. He was dressed in gray, too—a faultless gray gabardine business suit. Natty, she thought. His mouth was curved upward in a challenging smile, one that Mona tried to imitate, but she did not succeed. Looking into that face for the first time in weeks was a jarring shock.

"Is that the best smile you can summon up, Mona?" he asked quietly. "You look as though you're suffering from indigestion. In fact, you don't look good at all. You've lost weight."

"Thanks," she said caustically. "That's always nice to hear. You, on the hand, look fit as a fiddle."

One dark eyebrow arched. "I do? I'm surprised. What is Alan Palmer to you?"

"A friend."

"Obviously or you wouldn't be out with him. How good a friend?"

"How good a 'friend' is Claire to you?" she snapped viciously.

Now his eyes darkened. Mona didn't think she had ever seen him looking so ominous. "Dammit, where the hell have you been? How can you hide in that house so effectively?"

She was humiliated that he would think that, even though it was the truth. "I haven't been hiding! I've been very busy. I have hundreds of things clamoring for my time."

"Now, Mona, you listen to me—"

"Smile, Keith. Casual acquaintances don't snap at each other in public."

"I've got to talk to you!"

There was, of course, no need for her to ask what he wanted to talk about. Now she met his gaze steadfastly, with a lift of her chin. She had vowed she would make it easy for him, so he must never, ever know how deeply hurt she was. "Naturally," she said. "Talk away."

The music ended, and both Keith and Mona quickly glanced out over the dance floor. But Alan and Claire were not returning to the table. Instead they were talking and laughing, and when the music started up again Alan slipped his arm around Claire's waist and they began dancing once more.

Keith turned to Mona. "No, I don't mean here. I've got to see you, and I can't very well show up at your house asking for you. Can you get away for the weekend? Can you meet me at River View Friday afternoon?"

Mona swallowed hard. She did so want to see the ranch again, to see Mandy again. She had, in fact, planned to skip a day of school one day soon and drive out—sometime when she knew Keith wouldn't be there. But she didn't want to hear the bad news there. Wouldn't anyplace do? "Does. . . does it have to be at River View, Keith?"

"Yes, it does." The corners of his mouth lifted. "Mandy's been asking for you."

Mona sighed. "Oh. . . all right. Friday it is. I'll tell mom I'm spending the weekend with a friend, to study for exams or something. But what are you going to tell Claire?"

"Just leave that to me. I'll try to make it by four— five at the latest," he said under his breath. Then he put on a smile and got to his feet just as Alan and Claire returned to the table.

CHAPTER EIGHT

WHEN MONA LEFT THE RESTAURANT where she and Beth had met for lunch on Wednesday afternoon it was raining, and the rain continued throughout the night and the next day. As was typical in a land of weather extremes, the rain came in the form of steady, hard, driving sheets of water, not gentle soaking moisture. Mona, who rarely paid much attention to rain except to bemoan its presence on a weekend when outdoor activities were planned, now watched in fascination, knowing that what everyone was calling "lousy wet weather" was just what the people at River View needed.

But there had been no letup in the downpour by Thursday evening, and Mona sat worriedly in front of the television set, watching the weatherman's arrow-dotted map and satellite photos. A Canadian cold front had collided with warm moist air from the Gulf of Mexico, and as often happened, the collison took place smack over central Texas. The drought had broken with a bang!

Mona fervently hoped her mother wouldn't use the weather as an excuse for refusing to allow her to drive to her "friend's" place in the country. Kitty, the city dweller, however, did not seem to notice anything unusual about the rain, and she accepted without question Mona's explanation for her absence from home over the weekend. And Mona heard Claire telling Kitty that Keith was spending the weekend on his "smelly old ranch," and so their tracks were covered. She hoped that once this thing was resolved she would never again be forced to resort to such deception. It was a new role for her, and she was not comfortable with it.

She had two days to rehearse what she would say when Keith dropped the bombshell. She loved him enough to help him get through it as easily as possible. It was going to be awkward enough for them merely being in the same house together. She couldn't let him see her pain. They had once been good friends, and somehow she would call upon that former closeness to give her the strength to get through it.

"I understand, Keith," she would say with poise and dignity. "You don't have to explain or apologize. I hope we'll always be friends." And then she would retire to her room, and the next morning she would get in her car and drive back to the city.

She hadn't given much thought to what would come after that. She supposed she would try to find a small apartment near the campus, move out of the house in order to avoid seeing so much of Keith. It vaguely crossed her mind that if Keith married Claire, she might want to move to another city. It would be a tremendous upheaval in her life, and it would take her far longer to become established in a strange city. Furthermore, she wouldn't be around to watch Alan's blossoming career burst into full bloom, a career she had more than just a casual interest in.

But somehow none of that seemed as important as

putting distance between herself and Keith. His nearness was impossible to bear. She had discovered that
much the night in the club's bar. So if she found she
had to move, she would do it. It was as simple as
that.

Ben would hate it. Her father felt so strongly about
families staying close together. Mona knew his dream
was to have both of his daughters and their husbands
and children living nearby, getting together for Sunday dinners, Thanksgiving, Christmas and the like.
He would be appalled if Mona left. There might even
be what Kitty would call a "scene." But there was no
way on earth Mona was going to be available for
cozy little family gatherings if the family included
Keith Garrett.

The days of waiting while the gloomy rain fell
steadily had every muscle in Mona's body tense and
taut by Friday. She moved restlessly around her
room, gathering her things and stuffing them in her
small case. It seemed senseless to pack very much, for
she was convinced she would be returning home the
following day. A pair of jeans, a shirt and something
to sleep in. She wouldn't need a swimsuit—not in this
foul weather.

As her eyes roamed over the garments hanging in
her closet they fell on one in particular: the white
patio dress she had been wearing the night Keith told
her he loved her. He wouldn't remember, but she
did. There would be no dancing under the stars this
weekend, but it would be a stroke of drama, she foolishly thought, to be wearing the same dress when it
all ended. Impulsively she pulled it from the hanger
and tossed it in the case.

Road conditions were horrendous. Mona chose to

take the loop that skirted the Metroplex on the south, but immediately regretted her decision. Eighteen-wheelers apparently had scant regard for the weather, and the mammoth trucks constantly splashed her little car with muddy water and kept her hugging the right lane. The wipers swished frantically in an effort to keep the windshield clear. By the time she left the four-lane for the relatively traffic-free country road, Mona's entire body was a tight coil of tension.

She was only minutes away from Keith's ranch when she saw the roadblock. Highway patrolmen in slick black raincoats and hats were stopping every car. Mona braked behind a station wagon and watched as a patrolman approached the car and spoke to its driver. Then her heart fell in dismay as she saw the car make a U-turn to travel in the opposite direction.

The patrolman motioned Mona forward, then put his hand to halt her. Mona rolled down the window.

"How far down the road you travelin', ma'am?" the officer asked.

"Two miles maybe. Three at the most." They were having to shout at each other over the noise of the pelting rain.

"You sure about that?"

"I'm on my way to River View Ranch. I'm sure it's not more than three miles farther."

"Yeah, I know the place. This whole area is under a flash-flood watch. Ten miles from here the road's completely washed out. We're evacuating families right and left. But I can let you go through to River View if you're sure you're not going any farther than that."

"Honestly I'm not, officer. And it's either River

View or back to Dallas, and I don't think I could make the return trip now. I'm exhausted.''

"All right, but don't go beyond there. And once there, stay there. New travelers' advisories are being issued every minute, and none of them good.''

A great fear rose in Mona then. Keith! "Officer, from here back to Dallas seemed all right to me, except for the rain. I have a friend who'll be coming along pretty soon. Do you think...?''

He shrugged. "Can't tell, ma'am. The worst of it is west of us, but that could change any second. You just hurry on and get out of this stuff. I wish I could keep these roads clear of traffic until this rain stops.''

Mona rolled up the window and proceeded ahead cautiously. Less than half a mile from the ranch she thought she understood the patrolman's concern. The road was under water. Not more than an inch or so, but still.... The rain was falling at a steady clip, and her thoughts were all of Keith, who most likely was only now leaving the city.

River View's gate loomed ahead like a welcoming beacon. Mona immediately felt some of the tension drain out of her as she drove through it. As she moved slowly up the drive her headlights shone on a blue pickup that was parked in front of the house. It was not a familiar vehicle. All the ranch's trucks were tan and had River View Ranch painted on the doors. Mona parked behind the pickup, then slipped into the raincoat that was resting on the passenger seat. Gathering up her suitcase, she opened the door and sprinted for the front porch.

Mamie answered the doorbell. "Mona!" the housekeeper cried, astonished. "What in the world are you doing here? Come in, come in. Oh, it's good to see you again!''

Mona shrugged out of her raincoat, gave it a shake or two, then stepped into the house. "God, what a day! Have you ever seen so much rain? I ...." She paused, realizing they were not alone. To her left, the living room was full of people. There was a man seated on the sofa, staring vacantly into space. Two small towheaded boys were stretched out on the floor in front of the television set, and a thin sad-eyed young woman holding a baby paced up and down, vainly trying to silence the crying infant. Mona turned to Mamie and quizzed her with her eyes.

"The Campbells from down the road a piece," Mamie explained. "Such a shame. They've been washed clean out of their place. The sheriff stopped and asked if I could put them up. It seems all the shelters for miles around are full tonight. Lots of folks are going to have some mopping up to do." Then she thought of something. "Oh, dear! If you're here, I guess Keith is expected, too."

Mona nodded. "Didn't he call you?"

"I haven't heard from Keith in weeks."

"Strange. It's not like him not to call. He asked me to meet him here no later than five."

"Oh, dear," Mamie said again, making a helpless gesture with her hands. "Mr. and Mrs. Campbell are staying in the master bedroom, and the children have Keith's room. If only I had known.... Well, I'll just have to make other arrangements. I simply couldn't turn them away. They have enough troubles as it is."

"Of course you couldn't, Mamie," Mona said soothingly. "Don't worry about Keith and me.

There's the sofa, and no doubt we can find a cot or sleeping bag or something.''

"Well, let's not stand here. Come on in the kitchen where we can talk. Just set your bags down until I decide where everyone is to sleep. Oh, it really is good to see you, Mona. I've missed you.''

"I've missed you, too, Mamie.'' Mona followed the housekeeper into the big, homey, warm kitchen. Some indescribably delicious aromas were emanating from a huge kettle on the back of the stove. Trust Mamie to have food ready no matter what the exigency. "How on earth are you coping with the onslaught, Mamie?''

Mamie took the raincoat Mona was holding and hung it on a peg near the back door. "Thank heavens the freezer was full. I put fifteen quarts of chili in it last week, and most of the garden vegetables had been harvested and put up. Good thing, too. We had some hail the other night when this storm broke, and everything left in the ground was beaten to a pulp.''

"I guess that's the chili I smell. It's going to taste wonderful on a night like this.''

At that moment the two young boys whom Mona had seen in front of the television burst into the room, laughing delightedly, their spirits and energy obviously unhampered by the fact that they had just been washed out of their home. One bumped into Mona, then continued on without breaking stride. Mamie looked exasperated.

"I told you boys there would be no rowdiness in the house! Go watch television or something.''

"It's all fuzzy,'' one childish voice piped up. "'Sides, daddy wants to watch the news.''

The news? Mona's eyes flew to the clock on the

wall. Was it five o'clock already? A sick fright overtook her. Where was Keith? The steady downpour
had not lessened a bit. Outside the window, late
afternoon had become as dark as dusk. With the
flash-flood warnings in effect, sections of road could
be closed off without a moment's notice, and that
coupled with negotiating Dallas's rush-hour traffic in
this kind of weather.... Mona's stomach made a re-
volting turn, and although she tried not to, she kept
trailing her glance back to that clock. The minutes
ticked by with agonizing slowness.

Mamie had succeeded in getting the Campbell
boys out of the kitchen and into the living room,
where presumably their parents would take them in
hand. She turned to Mona and raised her eyes to the
ceiling.

Mona slipped onto a stool at the breakfast bar and
chuckled softly. "I thought you were the one who
wanted to see some children in this house before
long."

"Oh, it's hard, so hard when you aren't used to little ones."

"I can imagine. I'll bet it's hard when you *are* used
to them."

Just then the boys' harried and worried-looking
mother entered the kitchen, cradling the still-bawling
infant in her arms. "Mamie, I guess I'm going to
have to feed her. Will I be in your way if I do it in
here? Harry has a hammerlock on the boys, so they'll
stay put for a while."

"Of course not," Mamie said. "I put the baby's
bag over there on the table. Carol, I'd like you to
meet Mona Lowery. She's a friend of Keith's."

"Hello, Mona."

"Hello, Carol. It's nice to meet you. I'm sorry about your misfortune."

"Well, we aren't the only ones," Carol said wearily. "I just hope the house is salvageable. It took Sam five years to build it, and he only finished it last spring."

Mona's mind flashed to the vacant-eyed man she had seen sitting on the living-room sofa, resigned despair written all over his face. Small wonder! Five years of work washed away by one swift caprice of nature.

Carol Campbell was juggling the infant on her hip as she rummaged through the large canvas bag. Mona jumped to her rescue.

"Here, let me hold the baby for you while you get her food ready. It appears you could use two hands."

Carol gratefully relinquished the child. "It's been years since I was able to use two hands for anything."

While Carol opened jars of baby food and spooned their contents into a divided plastic dish, Mona cradled the infant in her arms, rocking her back and forth gently. The baby's tiny perfect fingers fascinated her, as did the rosebud mouth and luminous blue eyes.

"How old is she?" she asked Carol.

"Two months."

"What's her name?"

"Susannah."

Mona smiled down at the suddenly contented baby. "Well hello, Susannah. Pretty name for a pretty girl."

Carol was ready for her daughter, so Mona handed Susannah to her mother, and her eyes flew back to the clock. She walked to stand at the sink and stare morosely out the window at the steady rain. She rubbed her wet palms on her jeans, then clasped and unclasped her hands nervously.

"Worried about Keith?" Mamie asked knowingly.

"Yes."

"Keith will be all right. Pacing won't help, Mona. Neither will staring out the window. Come and sit down and let me get you a cup of coffee—or would you like something stronger?"

"I'll...wait for Keith." She went back to the breakfast bar and sat on the stool. "Keith once told me that what the land needed was a good rain, followed by cloudy days and more rain. This ought to make him happy."

Mamie set a cup of coffee before her anyway. "I don't think he was talking about anything like this. When it comes to rain, it always seems to be feast or famine. Six weeks ago the ground was powder dry. Now this!"

"Is the house in any danger, do you think?"

Mamie shrugged. "Who knows? We're high and away, but if this keeps up...."

"Aren't you worried?"

"Sure, but I just take it as it comes. We've been through floods before. We will again."

Mona marveled at the housekeeper's calm accepting attitude. Then her eyes moved to the stoic grim Carol quietly feeding her baby. Mona imagined that Carol had been very pretty once, but now she looked frail and weary and old before her time. She doubted Carol had seen her thirtieth birthday, yet a lifetime of worry was etched around her eyes and mouth. A hardy lot, these countrywomen. Did Keith honestly think he could turn Claire Lowery into something like these two?

No, of course not. Keith was too astute for that. So to Mona's mind that would only mean one thing: it was he who would change. He would abandon his dream of being a full-time rancher. River View would continue to be only a weekend diversion. And if that was what he wanted, so be it. But Mona found it hard to believe that was what Keith wanted. All those hopes and dreams he had confessed time and time again. Apparently Claire was more important.

What a shame! Like so many men before him, Keith had simply been blinded by Claire's radiant magic. And he had seemed so unusual, so exceptional. A feeling of loneliness and frustration and bitter hurt crushed down on Mona. She had been very wrong about him, and that knowledge hurt, too.

Once again she lifted her head to look at the clock, but she caught movement at the door out of the corner of her eye and she turned toward the shape with a jerk. Keith's tall lean frame, covered by a dripping poncho, filled the doorway. Mona uttered a relieved cry and slid off the stool. Her first impulse was to throw herself into his arms, but good sense checked her.

"Keith!"

"I see you made it."

"Yes, I made it."

The two Campbell boys raced into the kitchen just then, slipping under Keith's arms and making for their mother. Keith frowned and his eyes followed them, then settled for a moment on the sight of Carol Campbell and her baby, drifted past Mamie and focused squarely on Mona. "What in hell is going on here?" he sputtered.

"THIS ISN'T EXACTLY what I had in mind for this weekend," Keith growled at Mona when Mamie, Carol and her children had left the room and they were alone.

"Nor I," Mona said, knowing that it would be almost impossible for them to talk tonight and so the thing would drag on another day. "But I'm sure the Campbells didn't expect to get washed out of their house, either."

"True. Damned shame." His eyes were dark and cloudy, and his expression suggested anger and disappointment. Unaccountably Mona felt herself trembling inside. He was no doubt anxious to get this over with and was gauging the advisability of having their little talk while there were outsiders in the house. Perhaps he feared he would have a sobbing female on his hands. Well, he could rest his mind about that one. There would be no tears while she was here at River View. Afterward she couldn't promise there wouldn't be a torrent of them, but not here. Not for the world!

"Have you been here long?" he asked.

"No, not long."

"I guess Mamie was glad to see you."

"Yes, she seemed to be. But you should have called her, Keith."

"I just forgot. I've had a helluva lot of things on my mind."

Haven't we all, Mona thought. "Did you have any trouble on the way here?"

"Only with seeing," he said glumly. He crossed the kitchen to sit at a small desk in one corner. Overhead there was an intercom system that was, Mona knew, connected to the bunkhouse. Keith pressed a button.

"This is Keith," he said into the speaker. "Is Browder around?"

A minute passed, and then Mona heard the foreman's muffled voice. "Yeah, Keith, I'm here."

"Fill me in, Jim."

"I've had someone on patrol almost constantly. The low area of the west end is under water, but everything else is secure so far. We got the herd to high ground, and I don't think we lost any. But when that hail hit Wednesday night it beat hell out of the alfalfa crop. I got in touch with the twenty-four-hour weather service, and they tell me it looks like this thing might end before morning. If it does, I figure the river down at this end will crest below flood level, so we'd be in pretty good shape."

"Well, let's hope the weather boys don't bust their forecast. Keep me posted, Jim."

"I'll do that, Keith."

Keith switched off the intercom just as Mamie swept into the kitchen looking preoccupied. "Sometimes I think this is a big house," the housekeeper murmured, more to herself than to either Mona or Keith, "but then I've never had to find sleeping room for so many people. I suppose I could put the two boys on the living-room sofa bed and free a room for Mona, but where would you sleep, Keith?"

Keith rubbed his eyes tiredly. "Don't worry about it, Mamie. Leave things as they are. Those two kids are going to have to go to bed early. Mona can take the sleeper, if need be. And I...I can bunk with the hands tonight." Then he muttered something unintelligible under his breath.

Mona glanced at him quickly and found he was looking at her with one of those unfathomable expressions of his. Usually she could read him so well, but when he wanted he could slip to depths she was powerless to penetrate.

"Are you sure you don't mind?" Mamie was asking.

"Of course I don't mind." He was speaking to Mamie but looking at Mona, and this time she had no trouble knowing what he was thinking. He minded a great deal. "You can't very well throw people out in the rain. If I'm not mistaken, there are some sleeping bags around here somewhere. Just don't worry about it."

Mamie looked relieved that everything had been settled. "Well, then, that just leaves getting supper on the table. I think those young ones are getting hungry."

Mona swung around. "I'll help," she quickly offered.

"No!" The exclamation came from Keith. Mona turned to him with surprise. "No," he said more quietly. "I want a drink before dinner, and I want you to join me. We can eat later. It's much too early for me."

It was too early for Mona, too. She wasn't in the least hungry. "Do you mind, Mamie? I'll clean up any mess we make later."

"Oh, of course I don't mind. I imagine you and Keith want to be alone, and your weekend has been thoroughly spoiled as it is. Just go along and try to enjoy yourselves, and I'll take care of the others."

Keith stood up and walked to the back door. Flinging it open he scowled at the rain, then closed the door. He jerked his head in the direction of the raincoat hanging from the peg. "Is that yours?" he asked Mona.

She nodded.

"Put it on."

"Why? Where are we going?"

"To my office." He crossed the room and put on the poncho he had thrown across the breakfast bar earlier.

"In this rain?" she demanded.

"We won't melt."

Mona recalled that Keith's office was a small room at one end of the workshop building. Just beyond the corrals and barn, not far unless one was walking through a blinding downpour. Keith must have desperately needed some privacy, and there could only be one reason for that. Mona steeled herself for the inevitable and slipped on her raincoat.

"If we're not back in an hour, don't come looking for us," Keith threw over his shoulder to Mamie as he opened the back door and almost pushed Mona out onto the porch. She huddled deeper into her coat, recoiling at the wind-whipped rain and thinking of her sneaker-clad feet. The ground would be thoroughly waterlogged. Keith at least was wearing high boots. As if reading her thoughts, he effortlessly scooped her up into his arms and hunched over her to protect her as much as possible. Then he walked into the pelting rain, down the rise to the building behind the barn.

The interior of the workshop smelled of sawdust and grease and gasoline. It was pitch-dark inside, but Keith didn't bother with a light. He set Mona on her feet and silently led her through a maze of work-tables, past the medicinal-smelling emergency station, where wounded or sick animals who couldn't wait for the veterinarian were treated, to a door at the back. Opening it, he reached for the light switch and stood aside to allow Mona to enter.

She had been in the office only once before. It was an ugly utilitarian room, austerely furnished. A door to the left opened to a small lavatory. A wooden desk dominated the cubicle, and it was surrounded by battered filing cabinets. Stacks of outdated cattlemen's journals and government bulletins stood on every available flat surface. Shipping orders and market reports were nailed to a huge bulletin board in no apparent order. At one end of the room was an unmade bunk and near it was a small refrigerator. The room was musty and smelled of stale tobacco. Mona felt suffocated.

Keith must have noticed the stuffy air, too, for he went to the office's one tiny window and cracked it open slightly. Then he was beside her again. "Give me your coat," he said. Mona shrugged it off, and he hung it up along with his own on a hook on the workshop side of the door. Then he closed the door and, Mona noticed, locked it.

And they were alone. For the first time in weeks. Mona's body shivered involuntarily. "Cold?" Keith asked.

"A little."

"It's the dampness. The temperature isn't all that chilly." He motioned to the bunk. "Sit down and I'll get you something to warm you up."

Numbly Mona followed instructions and watched as he pulled open one of the desk's lower drawers and produced a bottle of Scotch and two glasses. "Emergency war rations," he said, and grinned. It was the first smile she had seen from him that afternoon.

From the refrigerator he produced an ice tray and

with a great deal of twisting and banging and cursing managed to dislodge the cubes. He plopped a few in each glass, then liberally—too liberally, Mona thought—doused the cubes with Scotch. A quick trip to the lavatory filled the glasses with water, and he returned to sit beside her. Handing her one of the drinks, he lifted his glass. "Cheers."

"Salud," she returned without enthusiasm. Scotch and water on a stomach as empty and nervous as hers did not seem a very good idea, but she took a hesitant sip and felt the liquid burning all the way down her throat. God, it was strong! She coughed lightly.

Keith was watching her over the rim of his glass, and his scrutiny was thorough and disturbing. Mona's eyes darted around, searching for a safe place to rest, but there was little in the drab room to inspire interest. Once Keith had told her that he often slept in the tiny office when paperwork required him to burn the midnight oil. The narrow little bunk was hard and uncomfortable, but she had learned that he required little in the way of creature comforts, especially when he was at the ranch. In the city he seemed such an urbane and sophisticated man, but once he got to River View he was instantly transformed into a rustic man of the soil. There were actually two Keith Garretts, and the one she knew so well, this one, would never have been interested in a woman like Claire.

So perhaps it was the other one, the Keith who was president of a multimillion-dollar corporation and moved in the uppermost reaches of society, who was the real Keith Garrett. If so, he and Claire would make a good pair. Claire would be in her element as that Keith's wife. It didn't lessen the hurt or sense of loss, but at least Mona felt she was beginning to come to grips with the thing.

The liquor had begun to loosen him, and he grew relaxed and amiable. He was making small talk about local politics, a book he had read, a television show he had seen. He reached in his shirt pocket and withdrew a package of cigarettes and a lighter.

"Cigarette?" he offered.

"Yes, thank you."

He lit one and handed it to her, and immediately Mona was sorry she had asked for it. Her fingers were trembling so badly she could hardly hold it. Keith pretended not to notice, but she was sure he had. He smoked lazily and kept up his cheerful banter. After a time he got up and mixed another drink, then came back to sit beside her.

Oh, why didn't he just go on and get it over with? Why all the stalling? Perhaps he hoped his attitude and casual conversation would have a tranquilizing effect on her. Perhaps he had braved the elements to bring her to this secluded office in order to spare her the humiliation of an emotional outburst in front of strangers. Well, he was in for a surprise. Her emotions were completely under control. She was prepared for it—she hoped.

Viciously Mona crushed out her cigarette in the ashtray they were sharing, then leaned over to set her glass on the desk. Then she sat back and waited, carefully avoiding contact with his eyes. Keith slowly ground out his cigarette and set both the ashtray and his glass on the desk beside Mona's. She felt him turn toward her, and her heart fluttered with dread.

"Had enough?" he asked quietly.

Mona frowned, having anticipated anything but that. "Wh-what?"

"I want to know if you've had enough," he repeated, as if he were speaking to a dim-witted child. "Can we stop this ridiculous charade?"

Nothing was making sense to her. "K-Keith. . . I don't understand."

"I've had it up to here, Mona!" Suddenly he sounded very irritated, and his hand made a slicing motion across his throat. "And what's more, I feel like eight kinds of a fraud. Are you convinced? Have I proved it to you to your satisfaction? I've done what you asked of me, but how much is enough? I kept thinking you would call, but apparently you can hold out longer than I can. I love you, Mona, darling, and I'm about to go out of my mind from needing you."

Mona simply stared at him for one long disbelieving moment, unable to accept what he was saying to her. Then her body sagged. "Oh, God!" With a great cry she threw herself into his arms. "Oh, Keith—" she was sobbing and laughing all at the same time "—I thought you were bringing me out here to break it to me gently, to tell me it was Claire you wanted after all. I. . . I spent days rehearsing the most magnificent speech. . . ."

Keith wound his strong arms around her, and she thought she had never known such warmth. He began nuzzling her neck. "Mona, Mona. . . how could you have doubted me? I'm so damned much in love with you, and if you hadn't hidden from me you would have known it. If you'd even once come downstairs when I was at your house and looked at me, you'd have known. You were right to make me see

Claire again. It only made me want you more. I think you knew what you were doing.''

The wonder of it all was slowly taking root, and Mona was staggered by the intensity of her feelings for this man. "No, darling, no. I thought I had done the worst possible thing. I've been through hell, knowing you were with her, frightened to death at first, then being so certain I had lost you. If you only knew! I had reached the point where I was planning to move away so I would never have to see you again. I think I went a little crazy.''

"Sweetheart, how could you not have known?'' He shifted his weight and gently forced her down onto the bunk. She moved to make room for him, and he fitted himself against her as his lips descended to claim hers.

Their mouths moved together hungrily, almost brutally at first, but then the wild desperation went out of the kiss, and slowly it evolved into something so sensually sweet it consumed Mona. All of her passion for him surged, rose, spilled over. Her hands traveled over him on a journey of rediscovery. She had needed him before, but what she was feeling for him tonight was a wild new sensation. A churning eagerness boiled inside her, leaving her unafraid of anything that was to come.

When their mouths finally parted, Keith looked down at her with adoration-filled eyes. His hand moved up to settle on her breast, and it swelled to fill his hand. With deft fingers he freed the buttons of her blouse from their holes, then undid the front-hooking brassiere. He bent his head and his tongue traced a lazy pattern around one hardened nipple. Mona curled her fingers through his thick dark hair and pushed his face into the cushioned mound. She moaned and called his name.

"This is positively the last time I'm going to ask you," he said, his breath fluttering warmly against her breast. "Are you going to marry me? Are you sure of my love now?"

"Yes...yes...yes!"

"Oh, Mona...." His hands began an exquisite torture of her inflamed body. "This was what almost drove me crazy, remembering the way you feel. I've thought about nothing but holding you again. I damned near died in that booth at the club the other night. It was all I could do to keep my hands off you. That's when I knew this thing had to end."

"But so long, Keith...such a long time. When you kept on seeing Claire I was so sure...so sure."

"Ah, Mona, perhaps I handled that badly, but I wanted to prove to you that I had given the other every chance. I didn't want you to have the slightest trace of doubt. And, too, since the whole business was your idea, love, I think I was hoping you would call me. Silly nonsense. I'm glad it's over." His mouth found the pulse point at the base of her throat. "Did I ever tell you that you smell better than other people? And it's not a smell that comes out of a bottle. It's you! You smell like...like roses."

Mona could have told him a thing or two about unique smells. The musky male scent that was Keith was driving her wild, filling her with an urgent and compelling need for assuagement. Her fingers inexpertly but lovingly began unbuttoning his shirt, for she longed to feel his flesh against hers. He raised himself slightly to give her better access, and when his shirt was thrown open she caressed the broad satisfying warmth of his chest.

"How long do I have to wait, Mona?" he asked huskily.

"You don't have to wait at all."

"For the wedding?"

"For anything. I told you, all I wanted was to be sure you would never have any regrets."

"Are you sure about what you're saying?"

"Completely sure. Keith, I love you. I want to belong to you."

She heard the quick intake of his breath, then a choking sound. "I'm going to get a blanket for us, darling. There's one in the cabinet in the bathroom." He started to get up, then stopped and looked down at her lovingly. "You know, I've had visions of how it would be for us the first time, and those visions always involved candlelight and champagne, satin sheets and you in some flimsy thing I could rip off you—not on an unmade bunk in a dingy room while a storm raged overhead."

Deep emotions shone from Mona's eyes. "Nature's on a rampage. . . but then, so am I." It was true. She was only dimly aware of the sound of the driving rain, of the lightning and thunder. The storm's fury could not match the tumult building inside her. "What do trappings matter, Keith? All that matters is you and me."

"You're right. Man and woman in love. That's all that's ever mattered. And lovers seize any opportunity. Now, for that blanket."

First he bent to give her a long, thorough, competent kiss. Then he straightened, swung his long legs off the bunk and stood up.

And abruptly, startlingly, the eloquent sweet mood of the moment was shattered. Keith uttered the foulest oath Mona had ever heard him use.

She bolted upright, instinctively pulling her blouse together as she did. "Keith, what's the matter?"

He looked down at her and his eyes were wide. "Mona, I'm standing in about an inch of water!"

Mona, still caught in the grips of a searing passion, did not respond immediately. She wasn't sure she had heard him correctly. But as his words sunk in and their implication became clear, she leaned forward and peered over the edge of the bunk. "Oh, my God!" she gasped. The floor definitely was under water, and the water was not still. It was moving . . . and therefore rising.

Keith walked to the window, and the water splashed around the heels of his boots. He looked out, uttered another oath, then closed the window and locked it. His face was dark and disbelieving as he quickly buttoned his shirt. Turning, he looked at Mona with apologetic eyes.

"I'm sorry, baby. But we've got to get out of here."

CHAPTER NINE

THERE WAS NO QUESTION they had to get out of there. In the time it took them to put on their raincoats and walk through the dark workshop the water seemed to have risen another inch. Outside the rain was coming down with renewed force. It poured off the roofs of the buildings in silvery sheets and was now accompanied by strong winds and a great deal of lightning and thunder, bringing to Mona's mind the memory of the only tornado she had witnessed in her life. That just-right combination of wind and rain and electricity always created a fear-induced nausea in her, and instinctively she moved closer to Keith.

All around them was water—black swirling water. The barn and corrals stood in the center of a miniature lake that was fast becoming a much larger lake. Ahead of them the lighted ranch house stood on its rise like a fortress surrounded by a moat. If only there were a drawbridge, Mona thought absurdly.

Keith bent and shouted so that she could hear him. "Mona, I want you to take my hand, and no matter what happens, hold on to it. That water and wind are going to be pushing against us, so don't let go of me for an instant!"

"Don't worry, I won't!"

"We're going to walk alongside the corral fence. Hold on to it with one hand and on to me with the other. There are going to be rocks and debris out there—no telling what has washed in from the river. The footing is going to be treacherous, so be careful, honey. Just don't let go of me.''

Numbly she nodded. He grasped her hand tightly, and they moved into the storm. Holding on wasn't as easy as it sounded: the rain made their skin slippery. Mona locked her fingers into his so tightly her nails bit into his flesh, and gingerly they inched along the fence.

Water lapped her legs at mid-calf level, and there seemed to be nothing solid under her feet, just a soft oozing mess that sucked like quicksand. Dear God, how had it happened so quickly? But then, she supposed that was why they were called flash floods. What was so surprising was the force of the water, swirling like a whirlpool and making them fight for every step. The storm's winds hit them head-on, and it seemed to Mona they were making no headway at all.

This was a new storm and no ordinary one. A vicious one. A jagged scar of lightning split open the black sky, followed by an earsplitting burst of thunder that was like an explosion. The storm was right overhead, and they were taking the full brunt of it. Mona didn't think she had ever felt so vulnerable or been so frightened in her life.

Keith held on to the fence railing with one hand and clutched her with the other, so her first fall was not a bad one. A rock slipped beneath her feet and she started down into the black water, but Keith's reflexes were excellent. He quickly halted, let go of the fence and grabbed her until she could right herself. Her ankle throbbed painfully—she'd twisted it, she guessed—but there was no real harm done.

Once Keith was satisfied that she had regained her footing he started ahead, and somehow Mona found the strength in her legs to move along with him. The second fall was worse. The pounding force of the rising water and the roaring winds buffeted them, staggering Keith momentarily, and Mona lost her grip on him altogether. She fell sideways, cracking her head on the fence railing. Not even her raincoat's hood could soften the blow. Temporarily stunned, she felt herself slipping, falling, and the water came higher and higher. Her head reeled from the blow, and she was only vaguely aware of Keith's hands under her arms, of being lifted, lifted. Desperately Mona tried to clear her fogged mind and get a grip on reality. God, how could she be so clumsy? She was soaked to the waist as a result of the fall, and she tasted blood in her mouth. She realized she must have bitten her lip. There was a burning sensation in her head, and her ankle was killing her, but miraculously it would still support her weight.

Keith had hold of her again, and they moved forward. The wind-driven rain felt like tiny hammers pounding through her clothing, and the floodwaters were now well above Mona's knees. A tree trunk, torn from its bed by the rampaging water, crashed into her thigh, then lodged against the fence. Suddenly Keith stopped, and Mona knew they had reached the end of the corral. He pulled her close to him, bent his head and shouted.

"We'll be starting uphill in a minute, darling, and it's going to be tough sledding. But we'll soon be out of the water and I can carry you. Put your arm around my waist and hang on. You're doing fine."

The swirl of dirty water and debris was moving

with amazing speed. Each step required a herculean effort, and for every two forward they made, the water forced them back one. The gentle rise on which the house stood might as well have been Mount Everest. Mona felt as though she weighed three hundred pounds and that the journey from the workshop to this spot had taken hours. She fastened her eyes on the lights shining from the windows of the house, drew in strength from the sight of their goal and, clinging to Keith, pushed on.

And somehow they were out of the water—had crawled out of it, Mona thought—and she was being lifted into Keith's arms. An odd light-headed sensation washed over her. She slumped into the cradle his arms made and limply allowed him to carry her to the high dry safety of the house, although how long it would stay safely dry only God knew.

Mamie gave a cry of horror when she saw them, and indeed Mona knew they must look a fright— filthy, covered with mud and leaves and soaked in the bargain. Dazed, she was aware that Mamie was helping her out of her raincoat, tsk-tsking all the while.

"Oh, you're drenched—absolutely drenched! You've got to get out of those clothes and let me get you something warm to drink."

Mona tried to put her weight on her throbbing ankle and uttered a muffled cry. The pounding pain in her head blinded her. From far off in the distance she heard Keith's voice. "To be honest, I was more worried about snakes than anything. They'll be leaving their dens and scrambling for higher ground.... Mona? Mona, darling, what's wrong? You look...."

Mona couldn't understand why he sounded so far away, why nothing was coming into focus. She reached for something, anything to hold on to. Then she felt herself going over the edge, and she sank into black nothingness.

WHEN SHE AWOKE she was lying down. Someone was sponging the painful spot on her head and holding an ice cube against her lip. Images swam before her eyes. She blinked once, then twice, and her vision cleared. Her first conscious awareness was of pain: her ankle hurt, her thigh hurt, her mouth hurt, her head hurt. She tried to move, but it required more effort than she could expend.

She turned her head and saw that someone had made up the sofa bed in the living room, and she was lying on it. She felt warm and dry, and her head was resting on a pillow. Keith's anxious face was hovering over her. She tried to smile at him, but her lips felt swollen.

"How many fingers am I holding up, Mona?" Keith asked in a voice that throbbed with concern.

"Two. Oh, God, my head hurts!"

"I shouldn't wonder, from the looks of that goose egg. You don't feel sick to your stomach or anything like that, do you?"

She shook her head, and once again the pain stabbed at her.

"Good. Now once more, darling. . . how many fingers am I holding up?"

She squinted. "Three."

"And now?"

"One."

"Thank God! I don't think you have a concussion, just a nasty bump. You gave me a helluva scare when you keeled over."

"I can't imagine what happened to me. I've never fainted before. Oh, my ankle hurts! In fact, I hurt all over. Not much of an outdoors type, am I?"

He smiled at her affectionately, then bent and lightly brushed her mouth with his lips. His tongue gently licked her wound, and its saltiness stung a bit. "Dear God, Keith, what all is wrong with me?"

He chuckled. "A bump on the head, a swollen lip and an angry bruise on your thigh, plus—" his gaze traveled to her foot "—that!"

Mona propped herself up on one elbow. Her right foot had been elevated by three pillows, and an ice bag wrapped in a towel had been laid on her ankle. Carefully Keith moved the bag aside to let her see the damage. Mona gasped. A sickly purplish green lump the size of a baseball was where her ankle should have been. She groaned and lay back down. "Stupid clumsiness!"

Keith replaced the ice bag and Mona winced. "You couldn't help it, darling, but you're going to have to stay off that foot."

Something occurred to her then. "Keith...the storm...the water. Is the house all right? What about the animals...about Mandy?"

"Shh. Listen. What do you hear?"

She cocked her head to one side and listened. "Nothing."

"Exactly. The rain stopped shortly after you zonked. You and I, love, were out in its last hurrah. The water's high, but the house was never in any real danger. I won't know until tomorrow if we lost any livestock or buildings—"

Mona's eyes widened. "Mandy!" she cried.

"Relax, Mona. Jim and the boys got all the animals out of the barn. Mandy's fine."

Relieved, Mona sank back on the pillow. "Where is everyone?"

"The Campbells have gone to bed and Mamie's in the kitchen waiting to hear that you're ready for something to eat. A couple of the hands have crashed in the sun room because the bunkhouse took some water, but most of them were out in the camp close to the herd."

Mona took his hand and laid it against her cheek. Then she turned her head and kissed his palm. "I'll bet I look a fright."

"You look pretty good to me, sweetheart—even with a puffy lip." His other hand strayed to her shoulder, then to the nape of her neck. "Now I'm going to get you a cup of tea. And if that stays down all right, you can have some soup. No chili for you tonight."

She watched him depart, then struggled to sit up. Glancing down, she saw that she was wearing her nightgown. When Keith returned with the tea she asked him if he had undressed her.

He grinned. "I was going to, but Mamie looked so thoroughly shocked that I made myself scarce and let her do it. She's laundering our clothes now. Yours were a mess."

Mona sipped at the tepid tea while Keith watched her anxiously. "Is it settling in your stomach okay?" he asked.

She nodded. "It seems to be."

"Then I'll get the soup, and it'll be off to dreamland for you. If anyone ever needed a good night's sleep, you do."

"Keith. . . where are you going to sleep?"

He pointed to the empty half of the sofa bed. "Right there."

Mona's eyebrows arched. "That ought to give Mamie a start!"

He laughed. "Mona, I would hardly try to ravish you in the middle of the living room with a house full of people wandering about—and with you in your present condition yet! I have much more delicate circumstances in mind for our first time together. Tonight I'll sleep on top of the covers with my clothes on. I think you're all right but I want to be sure, so I'm staying close."

Mamie's homemade soup was wonderful, shared with Keith from a tray. It was quite late when they finished eating, and after Mamie had carried the tray to the kitchen and bid them good-night, Keith held out his arms to Mona.

"Come, darling, I'll carry you to the bathroom."

"Oh, dear, what a nuisance I am!"

"Not at all. A damsel in distress, maybe, but not a nuisance." He scooped her up and carried her down the hall. Pushing open the door to the bathroom he carefully set her on her feet. "Now don't put any weight on that ankle. Can you make out all right?"

Mona clutched the tile counter for support and hobbled inside. "Yes, I'm fine."

"I'll wait out here. Call when you're finished."

The first thing that caught Mona's eye was the sight of herself in the bathroom mirror. She groaned in dismay. Her hair was a fright, there was a purple knot the size of an egg on her temple and her bitten swollen lip gave her a demoniacal look. Oh, God, that Keith had seen her like this! Awkwardly but hurriedly she hobbled through bedtime preparations, and then she was opening the door. Instantly Keith was there to scoop her back into his arms.

"That was quick," he said approvingly.

"I had to hurry. I couldn't wait to get out of sight of that mirror. Keith, I look like something out of a horror movie!"

"One does not emerge from a flood with not a hair out of place, Mona."

"You look all right."

He carried her back to the sofa bed and gently put her down. "Up with the foot. Are you comfortable...or at least as comfortable as possible?"

"Yes, darling. Thank you."

"I'll be right back."

Minutes passed and he was back, smelling of soap and water and carrying a pillow and blanket. He whipped off his belt, then sat on the edge of the bed and took off his shoes. Mona heard the thud as they hit the floor. A flick of the lamp, and the room was dark. The bed sagged as his body settled next to her. She reached for him and was gently gathered into his arms. She sighed contentedly as the sheltering cocoon enveloped her.

"I'd kiss you, darling," his husky voice said in her ear, "but I'll hurt your mouth."

"Kiss me anyway."

He gave her a quick kiss, as light as the brush of a butterfly's wings, artfully keeping it to one side of her mouth.

"Our lovely romantic evening...thoroughly spoiled," she said ruefully.

"There'll be other evenings, Mona. Thousands of them. We're together, and that's what I've been waiting for. Sleep, darling."

Her eyelids felt like lead. "Good night, Keith."

"Good night, Mona."

She forced herself to stay awake long enough to watch him fall asleep. It was a most intimate experience. As his breathing became shallow and even, she studied his lean face, amazed at how little boyish he looked when completely relaxed. He possessed the power to raise her to the heights of frenzied passion, but she felt so much tenderness for him, too. She placed her hand on his chest; he stirred but did not awaken. Smiling against his shoulder, Mona at last gave in to her exhaustion and slipped into a deep slumber.

THE WORLD THEY AWAKENED TO was a gluey mud-soaked mess, and the sparkling bright sun only illuminated and magnified the storm's destruction. The water had receded during the night, leaving behind only isolated puddles and piles of debris and trash. Everyone was galvanized into action soon after daybreak to begin the monumental task of cleaning up after the flood. By midday word reached them that all roads throughout the area were now passable, and the Campbells hurriedly piled into their truck, anxious to get to their own place to assess the damage.

The day passed slowly for Mona, sidelined as she was by her ankle injury, but by late afternoon she and Mamie both agreed that the swelling had gone down considerably. Certainly the worst of the pain was gone. Feeling stiff and bedsore, Mona pleaded to be allowed to get up for a bit. Mamie fussed and fluttered but finally relented and even produced a cane.

"Can't think how we came to still have this thing," the housekeeper said. "It must have been a holdover from one of Keith's father's periodic attacks of gout. I guess it's true you should never throw away anything but the garbage.''

Mona leaned on her newfound support. ''Is there something I can do around here, Mamie? I feel so useless.''

''Oh, heavens, no! You're not that fully recovered. Just wander around and get your sea legs, and . . . you might want to fix yourself up some.''

Mona laughed. ''That bad, huh?''

''Well. . . .''

''How's the lip?''

Mamie gave her a thorough inspection. ''Honestly, Mona, it's barely noticeable. A little lipstick and it won't show at all. Go on now, get yourself all prettied up for Keith. Tonight I'm going to fix the two of you a dinner to remember.''

Mona couldn't deny that the prospect of getting ''prettied up'' was irresistible. Mamie had put her things in her old room, the one she had slept in all summer, once the Campbells had vacated it. Though Mona moved rather awkwardly and with some pain, she managed to take a shower and shampoo her hair, then to pay careful attention to her makeup and clothing. She wore the white patio dress, loving the luxurious feel of the silky fabric as it slid over her skin and swirled around her legs. Her reflection in the mirror told her that she really looked none the worse for wear. The nasty bump on her head was artfully concealed by makeup, and Mamie had been right about the lipstick. Feeling renewed and refreshed, she leaned on the cane and carefully walked back to the living room. She was sitting demurely on the sofa, leafing through a magazine, when Keith came into the house at five o'clock.

"Wow!" He gave a low whistle. "What a transformation!" Quickly he crossed the room and bent to give her a kiss. "Feeling better?"

"Much!"

"You look fantastic."

"And you look exhausted."

"Well, I'm not. But I'll bet I smell like hay and manure," he said with that charming grin.

Mona wrinkled her nose and laughed.

"Give me fifteen minutes for a shower and a change, and I'll be much nicer to be near."

True to his word, when he reappeared in less than half an hour he crackled with potent vitality. His slim-cut tan trousers hugged his hips and thighs. His cream-colored shirt was opened three buttons down, exposing coarse dark chest hairs. His face was wreathed in a smile and he was full of the day's news. The barn had taken a lot of water, so they were forced to spend much of the day spreading hay to dry before it soured. And they had lost two calves to the swollen river, but all in all they had weathered the storm in good shape.

Mona listened and hoped she was making appropriate comments, but she actually heard very little of what he was saying. Her concentration was all on Keith, on the way he looked and what his presence did to her, and her mind kept wandering to the previous evening, to the time before the storm had forced them out of the office. And to the delicious sense of peace that lying beside him all night had brought her. She remembered waking time and time again to the realization of him and remembered how warm and secure she had felt each time. And to-night.... A tingling sensation began at her toes and crept up. Her fingers longed to reach for him.

Mamie announced dinner, and Keith solicitously helped her to the dining room. The meal was a culinary masterpiece—tender beef bathed in a buttery rich mushroom sauce, soufflé potatoes, baby carrots, a tart green salad, flaky rolls. Mamie, without question, was a magician in the kitchen, and Mona was ravenous. It was good to enjoy, really enjoy, food again. She had been so torn up over Keith for so long that her appetite had been nonexistent. But now, thank God, that was all behind them.

When Mamie appeared to begin clearing the table after the meal Keith suggested finishing their wine out on the patio. "You're going to find this hard to believe, darling, but it's a true Indian summer out there tonight."

"My word, it is!" Mona exclaimed as she stepped onto the patio and felt the soft night air on her face. "Last night might never have happened...except I have my ankle to remind me."

Keith placed two lounges side by side, helped her to seat herself in one and propped her cane next to it. "Well, you know what they say about Texas weather—if you don't like it, just wait a minute!"

They drank their wine in companionable silence and listened to the night sounds coming out of the woods. Tonight the green black woods were warm and fragrant, and Mona pondered with wonder what a temperamental female Mother Nature was. To lash you on one hand with last night's storm, then to turn around and beguile you with a night like this.

Keith turned to her. "Happy?"

"Deliriously."

"That's good, because so am I. And we should be

making plans, Mona. How long do you suppose it takes to get married?"

"I don't know. I've never got married before."

"I don't want this thing to drag on any longer than it has to."

"Nor do I." Mona paused. A nagging worry had begun to plague her. "But we have a problem, Keith—one that we've carefully avoided mentioning."

"Claire?"

"Of course."

His mouth set grimly. "I'm sorry for the way I handled that. I don't think I encouraged her in any way, but the fact remains that she thinks our relationship is more than it is. I'm going to have to tell her immediately, and it's not going to be easy."

"I know," Mona said quietly. "She talks about you all the time. That's what made me think you were going to tell me you were in love with her."

"I don't understand how you could have doubted my love for you, Mona. I think I knew from that first weekend we spent here together—I knew I was destined to spend the rest of my life with you."

Mona reached across the space between the two lounges and took his hand. "Keith, if it were anyone else but my sister...anyone else. I have this terrible feeling inside. I don't want to be the cause of bad feelings in my family, and mom practically has you and Claire standing at the altar."

"You know Claire, sweetheart. She'll have someone else before the week is out. I'm sure she'll never mention my name again once I tell her."

"I hope so," Mona said, but was not encouraged. If Claire had been running true to form, she would

have lost interest in Keith by now. The nagging worry
persisted.

Keith saw it. "Mona, you have a right to think of
yourself, too."

"But...my sister!" was all she could think of to
say.

Keith set his wineglass down, stood up and moved
around to Mona's chaise. "Scoot over," he ordered.

There was not much "scooting" room; they merely wound their bodies around each other and held on.
Keith's mouth made a slow journey down the side of
her face until it found, fastened over and held her lips
in a deep probing kiss. Then he lifted his head. "Did
that hurt?" he asked.

"Not a bit," Mona said dreamily. "Feel free to
continue."

He did. His warm mouth possessed hers, and his
hands knew all the right things to do. Their expert
gentle movements were designed to arouse desire,
and they made her ache with a familiar longing.
Claire was forgotten. Mona wound her arms around
him, stroked his broad back and arched her body to
fit against his. His hand moved up to her shoulder
and clutched the lace neckline of the white dress.

"This damned dress!" he said in a choked voice.
"You wore it on purpose."

"Keith, don't tell me you remember this dress!"

"How could I forget?" His hand pushed aside the
fabric to expose one creamy breast to his touch. "I
did this once before, I think."

A tremor raced through Mona. She covered his
hand with hers and pressed it deeper into her flesh.
His thumb teased the nipple to erectness, then his
descending mouth caught and held the hardened

point, eliciting a low moan from somewhere deep inside Mona's throat. A burgeoning passion was building in her, gaining force and strength, and she buried her face in his thick hair to muffle her cries of desire.

Then his head lifted, and his gray eyes bore into hers, seeing through to her very soul and reading her desperate need. His voice was a throbbing sound. "Do you want to go into the house now?"

Mona hesitated, but only for a second. "You know I do," she whispered.

With some difficulty Keith got to his feet and pulled her with him. Mona clung to him, hobbling precariously. He scooped her up into his arms and carried her into the house and down the hall to her bedroom. Inside the room he kicked the door closed with the heel of his boot, then in three long strides crossed to the bed. He gently set her on her feet and with sure swift movements had her free of her dress and the few remaining items of her clothing. Jerking the bedspread back he eased her onto the bed, into the deep comfort of the sweet-smelling sheets. Elated, Mona watched him standing over her, drinking in the sight of her satin-smooth young body, and a powerful surge of love and desire swept through her.

"Oh, Mona, you are the loveliest creature on earth...pure perfection." His voice was thick and strained; his eyes blazed with emotion. He knelt beside the bed, and his hands performed their love ritual. They swept down the length of her, then moved up to cup and fondle her breasts. His mouth wandered from her ear to her lips, down her throat to the valley between her breasts. Mona sighed and trembled from the onslaught.

"There can't be any turning back, darling," Keith said against her skin. "You have to want this as much as I do."

"I do...oh, I do!"

"After tonight we'll be changed forever."

He stood up and began undressing. His broad tanned chest was exposed to her, then he was free of his slacks. She had seen this much of him before, but now it was different, so different. Tonight he seemed taller, broader, stronger. Her face flushed hotly at her first glimpse of his naked male body, so vital and powerful. He was beautiful!

Then he was with her, and the feel of his warm flesh against hers was a startling incredible sensation. "I love you," she whispered, never meaning it more. "I love you...."

"Oh, Mona, Mona...it seems I've been waiting for you half my life...."

Her fingers curled into the dark hair on his chest, moving up to his shoulders to feel the sinewy corded muscles. Then her tongue traced the same fevered path. Kneading, her hands traveled down his arms and slipped around his waist to draw him closer, but still he was not close enough. "Darling, I want you so..." she choked agonizingly.

Keith clung to her, to her face, her hair, her body. With his tongue he parted her lips and slipped inside. His hands were never still—cupping, fondling, inciting, lifting her to new heights of pleasure and desire, until she thought she would scream for consummation. Mona turned to him and arched her hips, delighting in the low groan she elicited from him, and she closed her eyes to shut out everything, everything but the astounding joy of belonging to him completely.

At last he was over her, and his slow litany of love reverberated in her ears. Instructing her gently, he expertly guided their lovemaking and soon inspired in Mona instinctive responses that were as old as time itself. At the ultimate possession of her body she was only dimly aware of a sharp stab of pain, for she was caught in the grips of another kind of pain, the ache of passionate longing.

His tender concern was a wonder to her, and it seemed to Mona that they moved together for hours in that most intimate coupling, lost in a mysterious enchantment in which nothing had reality but this act that made them one. They were man and woman in love, feeding their hungry bodies to each other in a tumult of golden rapture.

Then suddenly the union that had begun so tenderly changed to one of driving urgency. Strange incoherent sounds were coming from Keith's throat. Mona heard her name being called over and over in a voice that did not sound like his. She felt deep shudders racking his body. Stunned by the power of the pleasure she was giving him, she silenced his cries with her mouth, then held and stroked him, soothed him until he at last collapsed against her and lay in her clinging arms.

Afterward they lay together in quiet happiness with Keith's possessive arms around her and her body dovetailed into his. Mona drifted into and out of sleep, then stirred and carefully turned in his arms to face him. Burying her head on the pillow they shared, she watched him sleep. But soon she was unable to resist the lure of that relaxed male mouth. Leaning forward, she gently captured his lips between her own.

His eyelids fluttered, and the arms that held her tightened. "Don't go," he muttered sleepily.

Smiling, Mona brushed at a stray lock of his hair. "I'm not going anywhere. Where would I go?"

He opened his eyes. "I prayed I wasn't dreaming."

"You weren't dreaming," she assured him.

"You're actually here with me!"

"I'm actually here with you."

He sighed against her. "It was beautiful, sweetheart."

"I wasn't clumsy...or awkward?"

"Surely you know you weren't. Mona, you are my life...my life!"

She sighed and snuggled closer to him. And he was hers. She was overcome by the intensity of her love for this man.

Nothing must ever happen to what they had together. Nothing!

CHAPTER TEN

ON MONDAY EVENING Mona escaped the house immediately after dinner and stayed at the school library until it closed. She had not wanted to be at the house when Keith came to see Claire, as they had agreed he would. A burdensome twinge of guilt persisted; Mona could not shake it. And it didn't help a bit to know that, had the situation been reversed, Claire wouldn't have felt the slightest guilt. Claire was Claire, and Mona was a woman of an entirely different bent.

Cloistered in the library's hushed halls, Mona desperately tried to concentrate on her studies, for they badly needed heavy concentration. Her grades had suffered mightily during that awful period of depression, and she had a lot of catching up to do. But nothing could prevent her mind from wandering back to the wonderful weekend.

Saturday night had been so love filled it still stunned Mona when she thought about it. And before leaving the ranch Sunday they had made tentative plans. They would live in Keith's apartment, and it would be up to Mona to decide if she wanted to work out of there or buy the small shop she had been coveting for so long. A great deal would depend upon how much she wanted to work. That was something else Keith insisted she decide.

And River View, of course, would be home on the weekends and during vacations. More than anyplace else in the world, the ranch house seemed to Mona to be "her" house. Someday it would be their permanent home, but that was a long way down the road. Right now was important, and there was so much to think about.

Neither Mona nor Keith wanted a big wedding—only a simple ceremony with family present, then a few quiet weeks alone at the ranch. Kitty, who feasted on grandiose social affairs, probably would go into a dramatic decline over missing the chance to throw a grand wedding with all the trimmings, Mona knew. Her mother was one of the few people whom she could envision as a Jane Austen heroine having an attack of the vapors.

Mona hadn't given much thought to how her parents were going to react to her marriage to Keith. She simply hadn't wanted to dwell on it. It was difficult enough to think of Claire's reaction. But her sister was highly sophisticated and experienced where men were concerned. Surely she would understand. Mona even allowed herself the faint hope that Claire would merely shrug it off and set about finding a new suitor.

The lights in the library flashed on and off several times, signaling the imminent closing. Mona gathered up her books and papers, realizing with a sigh that she had done far more daydreaming than studying. She left the building and crossed the parking lot to her car. Once away from the campus she drove home slowly, apprehensive about what she would find there. With luck everyone would be in bed and she could simply go to her room and push all this out of her mind until she could talk to Keith in the morning. She hoped tonight hadn't been too difficult for him.

She parked her car in the driveway and entered the house by way of the side porch, praying that all would be normal. But she hadn't gone more than a few steps before she realized her prayer had not been answered. There were voices coming from the living room, and one of the voices—a feminine one—sounded as though it was choked with sobs. Mona's heart caught in her throat. She moved soundlessly through the dining room, crossed the foyer and with some trepidation peered into the living room.

Claire was seated on the sofa, flanked by her parents, and she was sobbing deep racking sobs. The sound tore through Mona's heart like a knife. Both Ben and Kitty wore expressions of sympathy and grave concern. Mona stood at the threshold staring at them, and the obstruction in her throat grew to gigantic proportions. She would have given anything to flee upstairs but was seemingly rooted in place. Finally it was Kitty who looked toward the doorway.

"Oh, Mona," Kitty said, her normally placid face twisted with worry. "We've had quite a shock. It seems...it seems that Keith has called it off...." Kitty spread her arms in a gesture of helplessness as though unable to believe it.

Claire raised her head from her hands, and her eyes, too, showed disbelief. "Another woman!" she cried to Mona. "Can you believe it? Another woman! He wants to *marry* her!"

Mona's hand flew to her breast. Of course Claire couldn't believe this was happening. She had never been on the losing end before. It must have been a staggering blow. *I can't be causing all this,* she thought irrationally. *I can't!*

Claire had got to her feet and was pacing up and down the room. "Another woman! Oh, I begged him to tell me who she was, but he wouldn't! It would do no good for me to know in my present 'distraught' state, he said. Well, I'm distraught, all right. That *bastard*!"

"Yes, dear," Ben agreed too heartily. "This is probably some last-minute sowing of wild oats before Keith settles down for good. You know there's not another woman alive who can compete with you, Claire."

But Claire paid no attention to him. The stalking up and down continued, and Mona could see the wheels churning in her sister's head. She could see something else, too—Claire's disbelieving heartache was turning into cold fury. And when Claire was furious, anything could happen.

"I'll find out who she is," Claire muttered. "He won't be able to hide it from me forever. She might even be living with him, who knows? But I'll find out."

"Oh, Claire," Kitty began agitatedly, "what good would that—" She stopped when she realized her words were falling on deaf ears.

Claire whirled to face her father. "Daddy! How much does it cost to hire a private detective?"

Mona thought she was going to faint.

Ben frowned. "Oh, Claire, surely you wouldn't—"

"How much? *How much?*"

"Why. . . I have no idea, dear, but I suppose I could—"

"Find out, daddy. Find out!" Claire's voice now

had an ominous pitch to it. Mona thought this was worse than the frantic sobbing. "I'll have him followed. I'll know every damned move he makes, and if there's some woman right off the streets who's giving him—"

"Claire!" cried Kitty, shocked.

Claire spun around, hands on her hips, an ugly look in her eyes. Two bright red spots diffused on her cheeks. *Why, she's not even pretty right now,* Mona thought, then instantly regretted her unkindness.

"Well, what else could it be, mama?" Claire demanded. "It's bound to be sex! Someone's sleeping with him and has got his mind so muddled he can't think straight. How else could another woman take him away from me?"

"I suppose it's not beyond the realm of possibility," Kitty said. "Men will be men, and they can get their heads turned by some very unlikely women. But never mind, dear. Nothing can be done about this tonight. Whatever happens the family will support you. We're all in this together, and we're all thoroughly disgusted with Keith. Right, Mona?"

Fortunately Kitty did not require an answer. Mona was numb.

Ben rubbed his chin thoughtfully. "I must say I'm more than a little disappointed in Keith. He seemed such a mature, dependable young man. Perhaps we're being too hard on him. I can't believe he would allow himself to be taken in by a cheap—" Two pairs of feminine eyes, Claire's and Kitty's, glared him into silence. Neither was in the mood to be reasonable.

Mona's head throbbed painfully, and she thought if she didn't get out of that room and into the privacy of her own she was going to pass out. Muttering some-

wrong, try to remember that. And remember something else—how much I love you. Keep thinking about it. I'll see you first thing in the morning, my love.''

Rest. Sleep. They sounded simple when Keith said them, but they proved to be elusive things. Over and over the enormity of past actions assaulted her. She had thought she was being so wise to insist that Keith see Claire again, but it was the worst thing she could possibly have done. It had only served to make Claire think Keith was still interested in her. How easy it was to see that now. What a pity that perfect hindsight was so worthless!

From below came the sound of Claire's voice, brokenly sobbing one minute, coldly bitter the next. There was nothing whispery or little girlish about that voice tonight. Mona preferred the tears. Broken hearts mended, but hell hath no fury....

She shuddered. And she had thought her troubles were over. She suspected they had only just begun.

AT BREAKFAST THE NEXT MORNING Kitty persisted in dwelling on the family "crisis." It appealed to her sense of drama.

"Claire had a miserable night, poor dear," she announced to Ben and Mona. "I don't think I've ever seen her so agitated. Ah, the perfidy of men! Remember this, Mona, and be very sure of a man's trustworthiness before you give your heart to him."

Mona stared at the eggs on her plate.

Ben coughed lightly and looked distinctly uncomfortable. "That's rather severe, isn't it, dear?" he admonished his wife. "To indict all men because of the actions of one? I'm usually a pretty good judge of character, and I don't think Keith's a scoundrel or womanizer. You have to remember that we're very prejudiced in this matter.''

Kitty shot her husband a withering glance that Mona was at a loss to interpret. "I'll tell you one thing," Kitty said. "Keith Garrett better not ever show his face around this house again! At least Claire is fortunate that she has the three of us. It must afford her a measure of comfort to know that we will stick by her through this mess. That's something else you would do well to remember, Mona—you can always count on family. Others might desert you, but your family never will.''

Abruptly Mona stood up, unable to endure another moment. The crushing weight of the guilt was making her sick, actually physically ill. "I've got to be going.''

"But, Mona," her mother protested, "you've scarcely touched your breakfast.''

"I'm not hungry," she said truthfully, gathered up her books and fled the house.

She found Keith's apartment without trouble, and when he opened the door she all but collapsed into his arms. He held her as though he hadn't seen her in a month, and when they finally broke their frantic embrace he gave her a long thorough kiss.

"I've often thought," Mona told him when his mouth left hers, "that your kisses are something of a life-support system. I don't think I could live without them.''

He smiled down at her. "Pray God you'll never have to try. Sit down and let me get you a coffee. How's the ankle?''

"Fine." Mona took a seat on the sofa and studied Keith's apartment. It reflected the personality of the man who lived there. Elegant without being ostentatious, completely masculine without being austere or somber. It was a rich man's retreat, there could be no mistaking that. Everything was done in exquisite taste, and she found herself wondering if he had sought help with the decorating.

Keith emerged from the kitchen carrying a steaming cup of coffee, and he noticed her scrutiny. "Are you thinking what you could do with this place?" he asked. "Shall I give you a free hand with this, too?"

"Oh, no! Actually I was thinking what an absolutely charming place it is. I don't think I would change a thing about it."

"Coming from you that's a real compliment."

He handed her the cup and then sat beside her. Appreciatively his gray eyes raked over her. She was dressed in simple but becoming green slacks with a matching blazer and a sheer creamy blouse. A few gold chains hung around her neck; two sparkling gold studs shone from her earlobes. Her long dark hair glistened. "You're a vision, Mona," he said quietly, his eyes glowing with love. "I could spend hours just looking at you."

She sipped from her cup, then set it down. The coffee was an excellent brew, but Mona's taste buds seemed to have stopped functioning altogether. "I'm glad I look all right," she replied with a wan smile. "I feel terrible."

"Sweetheart, get that worried look off your face. It pains me to see you so cloudy."

She rubbed her forehead. "I spent a tormenting night. If there had been any way I could have done so, I would have come to you in the middle of it. I never needed the comfort of your arms so badly."

He opened them. "Well, here they are."

Gratefully she slid into his embrace and nestled her head on his shoulder. He smelled marvelous. Apparently he had just showered before she arrived. Her fingers curled through the still-damp hair at the back of his neck. His freshly shaven face was smooth and fragrant with soap and after-shave lotion. "Keith, this whole thing has turned terrible. Not only is Claire disappointed and heartsick, she's furious, and ever since I can remember I've been wary of Claire when she was mad. I've seen her go to some pretty ridiculous lengths to get back at someone she had a grievance against."

Keith's hands soothed her, rubbed and petted. "I must say she surprised me. I don't think I've ever had a woman speak to me in such colorful terms. She called me a miserable deceitful bastard—and that was the only part I care to repeat."

Mona's anguished eyes came up to meet his. "How can I tell them, Keith? Think about it realistically and tell me how I can do it. Mom and dad are completely upset and have convinced themselves you've taken up with some woman who's using sex to hold you." She managed a small smile. "They're not far wrong, are they?"

"Hush, Mona...don't! You and I are in love, so we made love. There's a world of difference between that and what your parents are suggesting."

She lowered her eyes. "Oh, I know. That was a dumb thing to say, and I'm sorry. Damn, damn! I expected today to be one of the most glorious of my life. I thought everything would be resolved and you and I would be deep in plans. Now I can see I was being very naive. I should have known it wouldn't be so simple."

"Listen, Mona, we should be deep in plans. We

need to get busy and get the license and the blood tests. I could call my doctor and we could go in for the tests this afternoon.''

"Oh, Keith, I'm not getting through to you at all! I can't tell my family, not today.''

"Yes, you can, Mona,'' Keith said firmly. "You'll find a way. We'll go to your house and tell them together.''

Mona's eyes widened. "Oh, God! Not in the mood mom's in. She's furious with you, doesn't want you ever darkening our door again! Dad might be a little more understanding, but not mom. She forgives slowly, if ever.''

Keith did not seem disturbed. "I can handle myself, honey. I've been doing it for years.''

Mona clenched her hands into fists and shook them. "Oh, I was so wrong to insist you see Claire again. It was my stupid jealousy that got us into this. We should have been waiting for them when they returned and told them right then and there. It's all my fault.''

Keith pulled her back into his arms. "No, it's mine. I shouldn't have let it go on so long. I should have told Claire that first night, but I was afraid one night wouldn't convince you. However, dwelling on what should have been done is a useless pursuit.''

"Good, what a mess!''

"Mona, you have to tell them. You have to.''

She took one of his hands and began idly playing with his fingers. "Keith, you must understand something about my father. He's a man with a *thing* about family. He is absolutely convinced that we, like the Three Musketeers, are all for one and one for all, united against the world. He has no idea of the animosity I often felt for Claire. Neither does my mother. I doubt that Claire even suspects it. If I go to them now and tell them I am marrying the man who has Claire so upset. . . .'' Mona shuddered. ''Traitorous is the only word I can think of, and I'm not sure that adequately describes the way they would feel about me.''

Keith's hold on her tightened. ''Mona, Mona, I know how awful this must be for you. You think I don't understand, but I do. I can imagine what these warring loyalties are doing to you, but the fact remains—you and I are going to get married soon. They have to know. You realize that, I hope.''

''I know, Keith, but—''

''You must tell them, and the quicker you do it the better it will be for everyone. Claire isn't going to let this cramp her style for long. Hell, she wasn't all that crazy about me. She's just sore about being a loser.''

''You and I know that, darling, but the rest of them. . . .'' Mona let the words trail off. Her mind was such a confused jumble she couldn't put her sentences together. There had to be a way, there had to be. . . .

The comforting shelter of Keith's arms briefly supplied her with courage. She would just go home and tell them, that was all. Just come right out with it and be done. What could they do—beat her?

But as quickly as the courage had come, it vanished. Mona knew that feeling courageous while enveloped in Keith's arms was one thing; the courage to face her family alone was something else entirely. It would help her if Keith were with her when she told them, but she wasn't going to put him through that. Kitty could be very, very frosty, and Claire. . . no telling what Claire would do.

Mona's hands trembled on his chest, then began rubbing him. "I don't want to go to school," she moaned.

"Then don't go," Keith said. "Just stay here with me, where you belong."

His mouth began moving over her face and came to rest on her parted lips. He gave her a warm melting kiss, almost unbearable in its sweetness. She responded, desperately needing the disburdening effect his kisses had on her. Close to Keith she could almost believe that all was right with the world. She returned the kiss hungrily, and suddenly it was no longer sweet. It deepened to become raw and explosive. His tongue probed, unleashing the now familiar passion, and his hands practiced that exquisite torture, touching her with increasing intimacy. Sharing his urgency, Mona moved her body eagerly against his.

Throwing back her head she looked at him with eyes ablaze with desire. Could it possibly have been less than two days since they had lain together? She ached for him as though it had been months. "Keith, I'm positively wanton where you're concerned. All you have to do is touch me. . . ."

He spoke against her mouth. "That's the way it should be between husband and wife, darling."

"I'm not your wife. . . not yet."

He lifted his head, and his eyes registered all his emotional turbulence. "Yes, you are, Mona, my love. I married you on Saturday night. All that's left are the legalities. You belong to me; I belong to you."

"Oh, Keith, making love solves a lot of problems, but it won't solve this one."

"Want to bet?" he muttered thickly and pushed her deeper into the comfort of the sofa's cushions.

Drawing strength from the force of his vitality, Mona eased herself along his hard length, and they clung to each other in a fierce sort of desperation. All doubts and worries were swept aside. Nothing was going to happen to keep them apart, nothing! What they had was too special. She wrapped her arms around him as his hands guided her hips against his. Totally alive, filled with the fire of longing, she reveled in the wondrous things he was doing to her and gave him intense pleasure in return. She knew that never again would they be able to deny themselves these feelings. Keith was everything, everything!

Suddenly she realized she was being lifted and carried in the cradle of his arms, then set on her feet. One quick glance around and she saw they were in his bedroom, that the big bed was still unmade. With deft nimble fingers they stripped each other and slipped between the sheets. A wave of hedonistic delight swept over her as she noted that everything smelled of him.

When he leaned over her she reached for him hungrily. In his arms she was a burning flame. Her body pulsated, throbbed. Until that moment Mona thought she had known sexual desire. She thought their weekend at River View had taught her all about it. She knew nothing! From the first touch of his warm flesh she knew this was to be different. This union of their bodies was at once agonizing in its sweetness, joyous in its ferocity. Spirals of heat radiated from the core of her body. Keith was unearthing the very taproot of her being.

His hands beneath her arched her to him, and she gasped. Over and over he carried her to the peak, held her in suspension, then gently eased her down, until easement no longer was possible. Mindless with wonder at their bodies' perfect harmony, Mona thought she heard her voice crying his name, but she couldn't be sure. Nothing existed but Keith, Keith and the white-hot flames of the explosion beginning inside her.

They stunned her—shock wave after shock wave of pure ecstasy! Mona's eyes widened, and as she heard her name being groaned again and again in her ear, felt his body tense, then shudder for long seconds in her hands, she knew Keith was experiencing his own version of her tumult.

"My God!" she cried, then as the raging fire slowly ebbed, her voice became a breathless whimper. "My God!"

He rocked her, cuddled her, soothed her. "I know...I know...I know..." he crooned.

IT WAS WELL into the afternoon when Mona returned home, determined to do what had to be done. She and Keith could not wait any longer. They were no longer able to be alone without making love, and she agreed with Keith that a prolonged affair was not for them. His parting words rang in her ears. "Go home and tell your mother, darling. I don't care what you tell her, but remember—the bottom line is that you and I are going to be married before another week passes. Then meet me back here at five for our celebration. What would you like to do? Dinner atop Reunion Tower? Or the chateaubriand at that little French place on McKinney Avenue? Maybe you feel like Mexican food. We could drive over to Fort Worth and eat at Joe T's. What would you like?"

In the end they decided that Keith would cook steaks for them and they would have a cozy dinner for two at his apartment. Mona's palms were wet and her mouth was dry as she entered the house. She explored all the rooms and finally found Kitty upstairs in the small cubicle off the master bedroom that her mother liked to refer to as her "office," although Mona thought there surely could be no soul on the face of the earth who less needed an office.

Had Mona had her way she would have gone to her father first. She had always been able to talk to Ben more easily than to Kitty, but it was difficult to find her father alone, and both parents would have to be told anyway. She might as well get the hardest part over first.

She noticed that her mother looked tired and worried. Worried about Claire, of course. The torment sliced through Mona, ripping and tearing. Kitty Lowery was a woman who liked to sail along on untroubled waters without so much as a surface ripple to disturb the calm. How could she tell this sad-faced woman that it was she who was rocking the boat?

Kitty was seated at her small desk, and she looked up as Mona entered the room. "How was school today, dear?" she asked idly.

"I . . . I didn't go. I just didn't feel up to it."

"I know," Kitty said, thinking she understood. "We're all taking this business about Claire very badly. Poor dear. She was actually at the plan-making stage. Then to have it end so abruptly. . . ."

"By the way, where is Claire?"

"She's spending the afternoon with Becky Thornton. It'll do her good to be with an old friend, someone who will commiserate with her. Oh, if I could get my hands on Keith Garrett, I . . . well, it frightens me to think what I might do to him," Kitty said in the angriest tone Mona had ever heard her use. Then she turned back to her desk. "I've been trying to get some letters written, but I just can't seem to think at the moment."

Mona opened her mouth to speak, but nothing came out. She moved to the small window across the room, pushed aside the curtains and looked out. Below her a team of yardmen were working industriously, sowing, clipping, raking. The rains, for all their destruction, had been good for the earth. Everything was so fresh and green and lovely and would be for weeks. Normally they could not expect first frost until late October, often much later. Unaccountably she thought of River View and summertime, of the Brazos at its most peaceful and of limestone hills rolling up behind. She thought of green black woods, of lark sparrows and wrens and the far-off lonely cry of a coyote. And she was surprised to realize she was experiencing a feeling akin to homesickness.

Mona let the curtain drop back into place. This was accomplishing nothing. Desperately she searched for the right words, words that would clearly convey not only her very real love for Keith but her equally real sorrow at having been the cause of so much worry and trouble in the family. Something her mother would understand and, she hoped, sympathize with. But what? *What?*

She supposed there was only thing she could say— the truth—and that would take very few words. Her gaze went to the back of Kitty's head. "Mom," she said with the greatest difficulty, "I'm the other woman."

She saw her mother's head come up and her back stiffen. Then slowly Kitty turned to her, and she pushed the reading glasses farther down on her nose and peered over them. "I beg your pardon, Mona? What did you say?"

Mona swallowed hard and fastened her eyes on a spot just above Kitty's head. "The other woman in Keith's life...the one he wants to marry. It's...me."

Kitty stared at her with incredulity for what seemed forever. Then, with great deliberateness, her mother took off her glasses, laid them on the desk and folded her hands in her lap. "When did all this happen?" she asked coolly.

"This past summer."

"Why didn't Keith tell Claire the moment we got home?"

Now Mona stared at the floor. "Because I insisted he see her again. I wanted him to be sure it was truly me he wanted. He had been away from Claire for months, and...I've lost men to her before. This was just too important for me to take a chance. I...I thought I was doing the smart thing. I know now that it was a mistake."

Kitty did not speak for a moment. She merely sat perfectly still and seemed to be trying to collect her wits, to analyze what her younger daughter had just told her. Then, very quietly and evenly she said, "Mona, why don't you sit down and tell me everything from the beginning."

In the corner of the little room there was an old wicker rocker. Mona pulled it away from the wall and wearily sank into it, relieved in spite of everything. At least someone in the family now knew the truth. With luck perhaps her mother would come up with a solution to the nagging dilemma, although the look on Kitty's face made her doubt it.

Mona began speaking slowly, as though she were

telling Kitty about a story she had read or a movie she had seen, something that had nothing to do with any of them. She went through it all—the weekends at River View, falling in love, her doubts, the reasons behind her wanting Keith to see Claire again, and the past weekend when he had asked her to marry him. It all came out, and when she had finished speaking she felt as though a great weight had been lifted from her. It reminded her of the time she had finally admitted to Keith her love for him. An emotional draining that was agonizing yet relieving.

Kitty had not uttered a word, not a sound, but her eyes never left her daughter, and when Mona raised her head to meet her mother's gaze she was astonished at the expression on Kitty's face. There was something so unreadable, almost frightening, about that expression. Kitty looked as though she had been slapped and was still reeling from the shock.

Mona couldn't have been more startled. She had expected Kitty to be surprised, of course, but she certainly hadn't expected her to react as though she had received a stunning blow. Puzzled, she watched as her mother raised one hand and began rubbing her forehead. Then very slowly, as though she were struggling for control, Kitty straightened in the chair and began to speak. Even then Mona thought she knew what was going to be asked of her.

"Mona, dear, it's impossible," Kitty said quietly. "Absolutely impossible. We can't even entertain the notion of this marriage. It's unthinkable! How could you do it to your sister? And could you actually go to your father and ask his permission to marry the man who has Claire so upset? I don't think so. I would be terribly disappointed in you if you could."

Now a bit of defiance welled up in Mona. "What

about all those nice young men I brought home only to have Claire turn on the charm and woo them away from me? No one seemed to notice or take umbrage then.''

Kitty's eyes softened somewhat. ''I noticed more than you thought I did, Mona. If you had been truly upset I'm sure I would have found a way to intervene, but you never seemed to mind all that much. You were always more, er, adaptable, better able to handle life's little disappointments. I rather admired the way you dealt with them. Claire is not your emotional equal.''

Mona looked at her mother in distressed appeal. ''Mom, I'm not talking about some silly schoolgirl crush now. I love Keith, and he loves me. He is the only man I've ever loved, the only one I ever will love.''

''Mona, dear, don't be melodramatic.''

''*Me?* What about Claire? A private detective yet! My God, the way she's carrying on one would think she had lost the only love of her life! She can't even remember how many times she's been in love. For me Keith is the one, the only one, and if that sounds melodramatic, so be it. My love for him is real, so real. I was quite prepared to hand him over to Claire if that was what he wanted. I love him enough to want him to be happy. But he loves *me*, and I want to be with him.''

Kitty's mouth twisted unpleasantly. ''Most men don't know whom they love. They're after the thrill of the moment, and the devil take the consequences.'' Then, as though ashamed of being caught behaving ungraciously, she composed herself but remained unyielding. ''It's impossible! And I don't want a word of this to get to Claire or to your father, is that clear?

If this thing between you and Keith is real, it will be real in several months. You have to give Claire time to get over this. If you don't, this family will be torn apart and the damage will be irreparable. Your father would never forgive you. You young people think only of the moment. Think of the rest of your lives. Do you want to spend those years totally estranged from your family?''

A feeling of desperation swamped Mona. She was losing control. ''But, mom, you don't understand. There's . . . so much between us. Keith and I—''

Kitty raised her hand to interrupt. ''Mona, I really don't want to know how far this thing between the two of you has gone. Wait . . . just wait. Tell Keith you must wait. And I think it only fair to warn you that your father and Claire intend to persist in this matter of hiring a private investigator to follow Keith.''

''Oh, that's so absurd!''

''I agree. I don't approve, of course, but Claire is absolutely obsessed with finding out the identity of the other woman, and as long as Claire wants it your father will do it. That's the way he is so far as you two girls are concerned. He would do anything for either one of you. I'm sure I don't have to tell you how dreadful it would be for Claire to learn from that detective that her sister is Keith's, er, friend.''

Mona realized what her mother was trying to tell her, and she didn't like it one bit. ''You're telling me that not only can I not marry Keith now, I can't see him at all! That's not fair, mom!''

''Fair, Mona? Would it be 'fair' of you to tear this family apart?''

Mona's chest heaved with futility. ''All to satisfy

one of Claire's stupid whims! I can't stay away from him. I can't!''

But Kitty was not moved. Implacably she looked at her daughter. Whatever she was feeling she kept carefully hidden. "Of course you can. Mature people can do anything they have to do. Both your father and I have made personal sacrifices in the name of family, and I don't think either of us has ever regretted it.''

Mona raised her hands as if to plead further, then let her arms drop to her sides. Never had she felt so impotent. As far as she could see there were only two courses of action for her—open defiance, which might lead to years of estrangement from her family, or asking Keith to wait until Claire simmered down so that they could be married with everyone's blessing. Not much of a choice.

"Mona—" Kitty's voice had mellowed somewhat "—I'm going to trust you to do the right thing. I'm sure when you've had time to think about this you'll realize what you have to do. Now please don't discuss this with me again. I don't want to hear another word about it. It's thoroughly spoiled my day as it is. And remember, not one word of this is to reach your father's ears. Is that understood?''

Wearily Mona nodded her head.

"Good." Kitty picked up her glasses, the sign that Mona was being dismissed. "Now if you'll excuse me, dear, I'm going to try to get these letters written.''

Mona turned on her heel and left the room. With leaden feet and an aching heart she went into her own room, closed and locked the door, then slumped dejectedly in the chair at her drafting table and put her head in her hands.

Part of what her mother had said had been predictable. The rest was a mystery. Why was Kitty so adamant about keeping this from Ben? He was a man; he might understand. It might be a good thing to look at this from a man's point of view. Ben might have a solution.

She tried to view the whole problem. Right now it was a choice between Keith and her family. And as much as she needed Keith she also, in different ways, needed her family. Perhaps she even needed Claire, who could tell?

It was going to be hard, so hard to stay away from him. But that was what she had to force herself to do because of her deeply ingrained loyalty to her family. Oh, she had known from the first word her mother had uttered that it would come to this, a temporary separation. And Mona wasn't sure how she was going to get through it. Before last weekend perhaps it wouldn't have been so difficult, but now.... Sex was talked to death these days, but once it was experienced with the one, the right one....

A feeling of total emptiness came over her and she dwelled on the fact that life had become damnably hard to live. It was so full of the things she wanted to do at war with the things she knew she had to do.

Sighing deeply, Mona rose from her chair, left her room and returned to her mother's office. From the threshold she said, "Mom, I'm having dinner with Keith tonight. I'll...I'll tell him then."

"Thank you, dear," Kitty said without lifting her head or turning around.

CHAPTER ELEVEN

MONA DRESSED CAREFULLY for dinner at Keith's that night, choosing a blue crepe dress that clung seductively to her bosom and midriff, then fell in graceful drapes and folds about her legs. Blue to suit the mood. She was screwing pearl drop earrings into her lobes when she glanced in the morror and was surprised to see Claire's reflection. Her sister was standing in the doorway behind her, looking very downcast and forlorn.

"Nice dress," Claire said without interest. "Heavy date?"

Mona shrugged and affected nonchalance. "Not really. Just dinner with a friend."

"Have fun," Claire said, and walked away.

The guilt. The awful guilt. It weighed down. Mona's spirits had hit rock bottom.

She fought her way through the oppressive rush-hour traffic, and at exactly five o'clock she was ringing the doorbell to Keith's apartment. He greeted her with a welcoming smile, a warm embrace and an enthusiastic kiss. Then he stepped back to hold her at arm's length.

"I don't think I've ever seen you in blue," he commented.

"You're amazing...and very observant," Mona remarked admiringly. "I don't often wear it."

"You should. You look beautiful. Make yourself at home, darling. There are steaks waiting to be grilled, and the champagne is chilling. If I can impose on you to make a salad later, we should have a superb meal. Not like Mamie's, of course, but this is not River View. First, though, I'll get us a drink."

There was a certain lighthearted cheerfulness to his manner this evening. Mona didn't think she had ever seen him looking happier or more relaxed. He thought everything had been resolved. If he only knew!

"Keith," she began hesitantly, "I've got to talk to you."

"I know, but first let's have a drink." He stepped back to look at her, seeming to notice her worry for the first time. "Was it a bad afternoon?"

"It wasn't good."

He bent to kiss her solicitously. "I'm sorry. Get comfortable, honey, and I'll be right back."

Mona sat down on the sofa and listened to Keith's movements in the kitchen. He was whistling! Dear God! And she had thought it difficult to talk to her mother. This was going to be torment.

Keith returned with two drinks, handed one to her, then sat down beside her and leaned over to give her another warm melting kiss. "I can tell from the look on your face that you told you mother," he said softly and with sympathy. "I'm sorry you had to go through it alone, Mona."

Mona sipped at her drink, then set it down on the coffee table and clasped her hands in front of her. Keith was waiting anxiously, but somehow the words wouldn't form.

"Mona...Mona," Keith said with concern, "it can't have been that bad."

She shot him a rueful look. "You weren't there. Mom was hardly thrilled over the whole business. As a matter of fact she acted quite peculiarly. I still haven't figured it out."

"Well, for God's sake, don't keep me in suspense. What did your mother say?"

Mona inhaled deeply. "Just exactly what I knew she was going to say. She said that right now our marriage is impossible. She said we are going to have to wait."

The hand holding his drink was on its way to his mouth; it paused in midair. "Wait? I hope you told her we have no intention of waiting."

Mona said nothing. "Mona," Keith persisted, "you did tell her we aren't going to wait, didn't you?"

She turned her head and looked at him levelly. "No. No, I didn't, Keith. I couldn't." Then she looked away.

He set his glass beside hers on the table and took her shoulders in his hands, roughly turning her to face him. His fingers clutched her so tightly she wanted to cry out. How she hated that dark menacing look! He had directed it at her only once before— the night she told him she wouldn't marry him until he had seen Claire again. Inwardly Mona winced under the onslaught of those piercing eyes, but on the surface she managed to present him a calm face.

"Dammit, Mona, I thought I told you...."

"I'm sorry, Keith," she said quietly. "I wish I could have done as you wanted, but I couldn't. I got an earful, believe me, and what it all boiled down to was either we wait...or I will be doing irreparable damage to the family unit and my father will never forgive me."

"Well, Mona, I guess you're just going to have to decide what you want the most—to be my wife or your father's little girl."

Mona was disappointed in him. He wasn't even trying to understand. "That, my love, was a cheap shot!"

He sighed wearily. "Yes, I suppose it was. But that's the way it is."

She laid her hand on his arm, feeling that familiar overwhelming combination of love and compassion and communion she always had felt for him, from the first day, she now thought. "Please, Keith, I'm depending on you to be my rock, to shore me up with a little moral support. These past few weeks haven't been easy for me. Don't make me fight you, too. I need you. I need to lean on you a little."

"And what am *I* supposed to lean on?" he demanded bitterly.

"I...I guess I didn't think you needed anything or anyone, not even me for strength. You've always seemed so strong."

"Well, you're wrong. I do need you. I don't feel strong at all without you." He slumped against the back of the sofa. "Dammit to hell!" he muttered, then slammed one fist into the palm of the other hand. "I must say you're taking this very calmly."

"If that's what you think then you don't read me nearly as well as you think you do," Mona shot at him sharply. Then she immediately softened her tone. "Keith, I know you're disappointed. I'm disappointed. And I know you're thinking I probably didn't try hard enough, but you weren't there. Mom had me over a barrel from the start. She made some rather oblique references to personal sacrifices that both she and my father have made in order to hold the family together, and she let me know in no uncertain terms that our marriage right now would lead to a total estrangement from my family. I simply couldn't tell her that I didn't care. Surely you can see that.''

Keith looked at her and scowled. ''How long am I supposed to wait this time?''

Mona spread her hands in a gesture of uncertainty. ''I don't know, darling. Just until Claire can handle this better. She truly is upset, more so than I would have imagined. She seems to vacillate between unhappiness and blind fury, and she has mom and dad so upset. I don't know....''

Keith stood up and began pacing the room. ''Then we might not be talking about days? We might be talking about weeks...or even months?''

''I don't know,'' Mona repeated tiredly. ''Surely not months.''

Keith stopped his stalking and looked down at her for several wordless seconds. Then he asked a question that jolted her. ''What if you're pregnant, Mona?''

Mona's eyes widened, and she stared up at him in disbelief. ''But I couldn't be.... We made sure of that.''

Keith shrugged. ''There's always a chance. Now I wish I hadn't been so careful, though,'' Keith grumbled. ''A baby on the way might get this thing resolved in a hurry.''

Mona smiled for the first time that evening. ''I know you're only joking.''

''I'm not so sure. Oh, Mona, I'm no prude, God knows, and the thought of our having to settle for an affair for the time being isn't the worst thing in the world. As long as we're together I don't suppose it matters how, but...oh, honey, we're so special, and I wanted more for us. I want you to be my wife! Somehow the 'love-nest' thing doesn't sit well with me—having you come to this apartment only to have to leave to go home. Hiding in dark places...although in this day and age there seems to be damned little hiding going on. I guess I'm the old-fashioned sort. I wouldn't have thought so, but it appears I am.''

A lump was forming in Mona's throat that no amount of swallowing would dislodge. This was going to be the worst part, the hardest part. She steeled herself for the explosion she was sure was coming. ''Keith...I'm afraid there's not going to be an affair...or anything for a while. I'm going to have to stay away from you altogether until this thing is resolved.''

He gripped her hands so tightly they hurt. His body grew rigid and the dark volcanic look came back to his eyes. ''What did you say?'' he demanded harshly.

''I said...oh, you heard what I said!'' She leaned toward him, her enormous eyes pleading for understanding. ''Keith, listen to me. As absurd as it is, Claire is hiring a private detective to have you followed. She has become obsessed with finding out who the other woman is. I can't risk coming here or going to River View or meeting you anywhere unless it's in a public place where it would look like a coincidence. It would be so much worse for her to find out that way.''

Now Keith was on his feet again, stalking the room

like a caged animal. His eyes blazed with fury, his face flushed with rage. "Oh, she is, is she! What the hell is this? Who the devil does she think she is? Since when can Claire Lowery run my life? There's such a thing as invasion of privacy, you know. I'll have her arrested—her and that detective and your father, too, if he's in on this! They can all go to hell! Your whole damned family can go to hell!"

"Oh, Keith, come on . . . you don't mean that."

"The hell I don't!" he thundered, and marched out of the room.

"Where are you going?" Mona called after him, shaken by his fury and despising the fact that she had to be a part of it.

"To fix another drink! A strong one!"

Mona leaped up from the sofa and followed him into the kitchen. From the doorway she watched as he angrily poured at least three ounces of Scotch into a glass, threw in a couple of ice cubes and drank the entire thing in two gulps.

"Are you planning to get drunk?" she asked wearily.

"I might."

"Keith, please. What good would that do?"

"It might help me forget, if only temporarily, that I ever met anyone named Lowery."

Mona took a deep breath. "Including me, I suppose."

Keith slammed the glass down on the counter, then faced her with arms akimbo. "Listen, Mona, I'm so damned sick of this I could throw up! All I want to do is marry the girl I love. You'd think I wanted the moon with a red ribbon tied around it. First there was all that rubbish about your wanting me to see

Claire again so that you would be sure. Now Claire is upset, so we have to wait. Next it will be your mother or father who has to be placated. Well, I'm sick of it!''

Mona let him rant and rave for a few minutes. Then, as only a few steps separated them, she closed the gap very quickly, slipped her arms around his waist and hugged him. It was like embracing a marble statue. ''Hush, darling,'' she said softly. ''You know I hate this as much as you do, probably more. This will be the last delay, I promise. And I won't let it last one second longer than necessary. I love you so much, you know I do.''

But his mood was a foul one and not easily soothed. ''Oh, no, you don't, Mona! You can't come on wiggling that appealing little body of yours and expect to get your way every time. It won't work!''

She settled her head on his chest and sensitively rubbed and massaged his tense muscles. Pressing herself against him, she kissed him and murmured his name over and over, as though calming a stormy child. Her ministrations were slow and deliberate, as tender as they were sensuous. She knew very well what she meant to him. He could storm and rage all night, but she knew he loved her. He wouldn't be so furiously disappointed if he didn't love her with the same intensity she felt for him.

At first he responded to her in no way, only stood immobile with his hands at his sides, but gradually she felt the taut muscles loosen, felt some of the tension go out of him. Her hand moved up his chest, and she felt the rapid beating of his heart slow, to pound rhythmically against her palm. Almost reluctantly his arms moved up to encircle her, and a small satisfied smile lifted the corners of Mona's mouth.

"Oh, hell!" Keith groaned. "I guess it will work."

Now Mona raised her face to him. "I told you, you are my life-support system. I can't live without you."

His warm moist mouth came down to drink from her lips. Then his tongue flicked away a lone salty tear that had escaped from her emotion-filled eyes. "Come away with me, Mona. Tonight. We'll elope. To hell with everything else. Tell your family you have your own life to live, that you're sorry if you've brought them any unhappiness but you have to seize the moment. They'll come around in time."

"And if they don't? What then, darling?"

"We'll learn to live with it."

She rubbed her face on the soft cotton of his shirt. The warmth of his body seeped into her, bringing a sweet solace. Oh, it was tempting! All she wanted was to be with Keith. Why did something so basically simple have to be so complex?

But it was, it was. "Keith, what if we wait a week or two and everything turns out to be all right again? Wouldn't that be so much nicer? How would you like it if your father disapproved of me, if he wouldn't have anything to do with us after we're married?"

Keith did not reply immediately. Then Mona heard him sigh deep within his chest. "Ah, I suppose it would distress me horribly. I owe my father a great deal, and I can't imagine our being on the outs. I'd probably never stop trying to get back in his good graces, and I can see how something like that would put a strain on a new marriage."

"Exactly."

He held her away from him, and the look he gave her was so warm it made her heart pound. "So where does that leave us tonight, love?" he asked softly.

"Oh, Keith, let's just make it wonderful! I want tonight to be perfect. Then I'll try to pretend you're simply out of town on a business trip or—"

"Only I won't be, and you'll know it. You'll know I'm right here in town, longing for you. I'm wondering if you actually will be able to stay away from me."

"I'll have to," Mona said with regret. "Please help me, darling. You're not the only one suffering, you know."

"All right, Mona, all right. I give up. But I'm warning you, this is the last delay. Do whatever will make you feel right about soothing your family, but it had better not take long. I'll go along with you, but only to a point. Then *we* come first. If I have to march up to that house and drag you away by the hair of your head, I'll do it. Understood?"

"Yes, Keith. Thank you. You've been wonderful."

"Wonderful, hell!" he fumed. "It's just that I know when I'm whipped. Being up against your family is like trying to fight the Mafia single-handed." He drew her to him again, kissed her soundly, then released her. "Now, love, I'll see to the fire. Then we'll have another drink and I'll cook dinner. And after dinner...." He grinned and winked at her. "You be thinking of something we can do after dinner."

DURING THE DAYS that followed, Mona had plenty of time to ponder Keith's warning. She knew his patience was not limitless, so it was imperative that their separation be brief. But the first few days away from him passed with agonizing slowness. Her thoughts kept drifting back to that last night in his apartment, to his sure, gentle, intense lovemaking. She was totally committed to him and could never endure a prolonged separation from him. Keith was as necessary as air to breathe and just as vital to her well-being, for she was no longer ignorant of all the wondrous things his body could do to her. At times the yearning was unbearable.

However, no matter how great the emotional turmoil, a human being usually manages to function in all the normal ways—walking, talking, eating, sleeping—and so did Mona. Her mother, at least, was valiantly trying to spare her. Mona noticed that Kitty never mentioned the Keith-Claire business in front of her, and if Ben or Claire happened to, Kitty quickly tried to divert the conversation into another channel. And in deference to Mona's feelings, her mother had tempered her harsh criticism of Keith. For all of this Mona was grateful, although she somehow suspected Kitty's motives. Her mother was behaving oddly. She seemed rather skittish, as though she were living in dread that Mona's involvement with Keith would become common knowledge. And there was that absolute insistence that Ben must never, ever hear about it. None of it made much sense.

But the worst part of it all was that Claire, for reasons that escaped Mona completely, had suddenly decided to make her younger sister her confidante.

"I just don't understand it, Mona," Claire said. "I'll swear I don't. That detective has been on Keith's trail for days, and he's found nothing. He says there can't be another woman, yet you and I know damned well there is. Why would Keith lie about something like that? No one comes to his apartment or to the office. Keith leaves promptly at nine every morning, lunches at his desk or in the company cafeteria with his vice-presidents. He goes home at five and doesn't leave again until the following morning. The detective even questioned the cleaning woman, and she said there's no sign of a woman's ever having been in the apartment. It doesn't make sense. Keith Garrett is no celibate, of that I'm sure.''

Poor darling, Mona thought. Not much of a life for him.

Claire continued her ruminating. ''I suspected his secretary, whom I've never met, but then I found out she's fifty-five and was his father's secretary before him. I'm beginning to think Keith's lady friend lives in another town.''

Mona sighed exasperatedly. ''Why don't you just let it be, Claire? If you ask me, this is the dumbest thing you've ever done! Just drop it and get on with your life. That Roger What's-his-name has been hanging around again, practically panting over you. Why don't you give him a much deserved thrill and leave this other thing alone?''

Claire's eyes grew bright with savagery. ''Not on your life! I'll find out who she is if it's the last thing I do. If she's from out of town, Keith will go to her sooner or later.''

Mona twirled and faced her sister, hands on hips. ''And what will you do if you find out who she is?''

''Something. I'm not sure. I have to know who she is first. But I'll make her life miserable, make no mistake about that. And Keith's, too.''

Mona threw up her hands in despair. ''Good God, Claire! Surely you don't think that making Keith's life miserable will bring him back to you.''

''I'll get him back, Mona,'' Claire hissed.

''No, you won't!'' Mona exploded impulsively.

Claire's eyes narrowed. "What makes you think I won't?"

Quickly Mona averted her gaze from Claire's quizzing eyes. "I. . .I just don't think you will, that's all. He's been gone for some time now. He has someone else, so accept it. Why in hell don't you just drop it?"

Claire drew herself up haughtily. "What do you know about such things? You never go out with anyone. You've never been in love. Anything you know about love must have come from those novels you're always reading."

Suddenly Mona had another of her crushing headaches, and this exchange with Claire was only serving to intensify it. "And you've been in love more times than I can remember," she said, trying hard for patience. "You will again, Claire, I promise. You didn't even care about Keith until you knew you couldn't have him. Why don't you leave the poor man alone and let him be happy?"

Claire frowned darkly. "What in hell do you care about Keith Garrett's happiness?"

As usual, Mona knew when she had said too much. She only wished she thought about such things before she said too much. "Drop it, Claire. Let it be!"

But Claire had no intention of letting it be. If anything, she appeared determined to drag it out. In a sharp flash of insight Mona realized that Claire was enjoying all of it. She was actually having a good time. She liked the sympathy and attention her parents were lavishing upon her, and she liked being the center of attention. My God, Mona thought, this could go on forever!

At least she and Keith had the telephone, although Mona couldn't decide if the instrument was a lifeline or a torment. Mona had to do the calling, and she tried to do it when there was no one else in the house, but still she was forever listening for the telltale click that would tell her someone else wanted the phone. She felt deceitful and frustrated. What could be said over the telephone? Often Keith merely sounded angry—the way he did tonight.

"I'm not going to wait much longer, Mona! I'm going to show up at that house one of these nights, and—"

"I wouldn't if I were you, Keith. I don't think you'd care for the reception waiting for you."

"Well, what's going on over there? Is this thing any nearer being resolved?"

"Oh, God!" Mona groaned. "If anything, Claire is being more dramatic than she was a week ago. She is a woman possessed. And the worst part of it all is that she's decided I'm her best friend. I can't tell you how wretched I feel when she starts confiding in me."

"Mona, darling, love of my life, how can I make you understand? None of that matters compared to us! I'm warning you—"

"Patience, love, please. You've been magnificent so far. I'm going to a party with Claire tomorrow night. She won't go alone, so I'm going with her in hopes she'll meet someone who will take her mind off you."

"Party? What sort of party?" he snapped. "I don't want you going places where other men can ogle you."

Oh, he was in a foul mood. Quickly Mona explained. "It's a party Becky Thornton's parents are giving. Becky's grandparents are celebrating their golden wedding anniversary, and hundreds of people have been invited. Surely Claire will meet someone there. She draws men the way honey draws flies. And don't worry, darling. Let the men ogle all they please. I have the only one I want.''

''You'd damned well better come over here and claim him soon, or . . . .''

Mona's heart lurched. She was sure he didn't mean it, but she hated it when he terminated their conversations with that ominous ''or else.''

''Or what?'' she asked.

There was a slight pause, then a weary expelling of his breath. ''Or nothing,'' he said with resignation. ''I wish to hell I thought another woman would solve my problem.''

''What problem, Keith?''

''The fact that where you're concerned I seem to exist in a permanent state of erotic arousal, and with other women I'd be hopelessly impotent. Unfortunately I seem to be the total monogamist. There's only one I want.''

''Soon, darling, soon, I promise.''

IF THERE WAS ANYTHING Mona did not want to do it was attend the party at the Thornton home. She detested huge social gatherings of any kind, but this promised to be the sort of affair that Claire had always reveled in. Mona would have gone anywhere, done anything if she thought it would help get Claire's mind off Keith and occupied with someone else. She forced some enthusiasm into her voice and spoke of the evening's party with glowing anticipation.

Unfortunately Claire was not cooperating the way Mona had hoped. ''I'm not sure I want to go tonight,'' she told Mona pettishly. This had been one of her bad days. Mona noticed that her sister spent most of the afternoon in her room, listening to "somebody-done-somebody-wrong" songs. Mona struggled with her own temper and patience. Was it never going to end?

"Of course you want to go!" she told Claire brightly. "You'll see a lot of old friends and meet some new people, and Becky's feelings would be hurt if we didn't show up. You've got to stop this moping around the house, Claire. There's still a great big world out there, and it's full of interesting things. This party is just what you need. You always shine at parties."

"I'm not in the mood," Claire said sourly.

"Well, get in the mood because we're going!"

The Thorntons moved in the topmost level of the upper class, the cream of Texas-style society, and their Highland Park mansion made the Lowery home seem like a cottage by comparison. Everyone who was anyone would be at the party, so Mona was convinced it was the perfect way to get Claire back in the social swim. At the very least it might whet her sister's appetite for a more active social life, and that would be a plus.

The festivities were well under way when Mona and Claire arrived. The enormous house was ablaze with lights and jammed with people. Loud music and raucous laughter rocked the walls. Mona wondered what a seventy-odd-year-old couple would think of all the hilarity, but upon being introduced to Becky's grandparents she saw that they were having more fun than anyone there.

"Stay with me," Claire commanded rather pitifully.

Mona looked at her sister and shook her head in bewilderment, amazed at Claire's transformation from belle of the ball to an Alice-sit-by-the-fire. "No, dammit! I'm not going to stay with you. How are you going to meet anyone if your kid sister is tagging along? Go out there and mix and mingle. Use the old razzle-dazzle and have a good time! And, for God's sake, if some stunning Greek god wants to give you a lift home tonight, let him!"

It wouldn't be too difficult for her, Mona thought. Every male head in the place turned the moment Claire came into view. And not a few female ones glowered jealously. Mona smiled and sent up a prayer: *Please, God, let Prince Charming show his face tonight!*

In her customary fashion Mona slipped quietly into the background and stayed there. She accepted a drink from a white-coated waiter, nibbled on some hors d'oeuvres, greeted and chatted with a few friends from school. The guests ranged in age from seven to seventy, as was to be expected at an anniversary party, but Mona was acquainted with few of them. For the most part she was content to pass the time strolling through the rooms, admiring the grand house and mentally deciding what she would do with such a place given the opportunity. But she did, however, make it a point to speak to her host and hostess, and she sought out Becky.

Becky Thornton had been Claire's best friend for as long as Mona could remember. She was a round dimpled blonde who seemed to exist in a constant state of bubbly good humor, and her face was never in repose. She shrieked gaily when she saw Mona.

"Oh, I'm so glad you could come, Mona!"

"I wouldn't have missed it," Mona lied. "It's a

fantastic party. Your grandparents are darling. So young acting."

"Aren't they a couple of dolls! I have tons more fun with them than I do with my own folks. But can you imagine living with one man for fifty years?"

Strangely enough, Mona could imagine it. "Amazing!" she said.

"But, God, Mona, I hope we don't have another fiftieth anniversary in this family anytime soon!" Becky clasped her head theatrically. "I've never seen so many relatives! And the worst part of it is that half of them aren't speaking to the other half, and I can't remember which is which. Poor mother's been on pins and needles all day, trying to keep them apart and not spoil the party."

Mona laughed. "Families!"

"Ain't it the truth!" Becky cried. "And not just families. Is Claire here?"

"Somewhere, yes. Why?"

"Oh, God, I almost died when I found out mother had invited Keith Garrett to this wingding. I'm just hoping and praying he won't come."

He wouldn't; Mona was sure of it. "I hope so, too," she said weakly.

"The rat!" Becky said with menacing eyes. "Claire has been so torn up over all this. I keep telling her he isn't worth it."

Mona bristled slightly, then reminded herself that Becky was very partisan in the matter. "She'll get over it," was all she could think to say.

"Yeah, we always do, in spite of what we think." Becky's good humor returned. "Well, Mona, it was good seeing you. I guess I'd better go and mingle. Have a good time."

"Thanks, Becky."

By the time an hour had passed, Mona was wondering how on earth she was going to get through the interminable evening. Her eyes searched the crowd, looking for Claire. She spotted her standing in the center of a circle of people, all of them male. Claire was talking animatedly, and her eyes sparkled merrily. Mona breathed a sigh of relief. Satisfied that her mission was at least partially accomplished, she slipped unobtrusively through the crowd and made her way to a side terrace.

The soft night air had turned a bit chilly, so the terrace was almost deserted. At a table in the corner a few couples sat talking quietly. Mona stepped off the terrace and walked to a secluded spot in the garden where she sank onto a bench to enjoy some much needed solitude.

Not far from where she sat a pair of lovers were reclining under a tree, wrapped in an uninhibited embrace, oblivious to anything but each other. Mona's heart constricted sharply. They were unbearable to watch, and she turned so that her back was to them. She thought, not surprisingly, of Keith's strong arms, and a tremulous sigh escaped her lips.

It shouldn't have to be this way for us, she mused. *We deserve more. Certainly Keith deserves more. It should be as free and easy for us as it apparently is for those two out there on the grass.* And suddenly she felt a great wave of sympathy for poor lovers everywhere who could not be together.

Mona did not hear approaching footsteps on the soft ground and so was startled when a very familiar baritone voice spoke from behind. "I do believe it's Miss Lowery," the resonant voice said. "Aren't you enjoying the party, Miss Lowery?"

She leaped to her feet, her pulses throbbing, but Keith smoothly took her by the arms and pushed her back down, sitting with her. His gray eyes flashed like steel, but they were warm with love.

"Oh, Keith," she whispered breathlessly. "Darling...I...."

"After I talked to you yesterday I checked with my secretary and discovered that I had indeed been invited to the Thorntons' party."

Mona leaned toward him, but he put a restraining hand on her arm. "Careful, my sweet. One never knows who's watching, and you're not supposed to be looking at me like that." His mouth curved upward in a charming smile, exposing all those white teeth.

"How am I looking at you?" she asked, unable to take her eyes off him.

"As if you're starving and I'm a porterhouse steak."

"That's the way I feel," she said softly. Then a fresh thought came to her mind. "Keith, Claire is in there. Did...?"

"I saw her but she didn't see me. I made sure of it. But it took me a devil of a time to find you. I had to see you." His eyes raked over her, and a look came to his face that Mona knew only too well. Pure, perfect desire. Warm languorous sensations spread through her body, and Keith read them in her face. "Maybe I shouldn't have come," he said softly. "You're too lovely. God, Mona! I've missed you so much!"

"I know, darling, I know. Can't you kiss me?"

His face took on a grim look, and with a barely perceptible jerk of the head he indicated the terrace. "I'm afraid not, my love. My bloodhound is here. No...don't turn around. I'm not supposed to know he's there, remember? He's so damned obvious. I think I would know I was being watched even if you hadn't warned me. And he's got a fair share of gall, I'll grant him that. He questioned my housekeeper! Of course, she couldn't wait to tell me. Your father is wasting an awful lot of money on that inept clod.''

"Oh, Keith, you're being so good about this!''

"Dammit, Mona, how much longer is it going to go on?''

She was trembling, more from the excitement of having Keith near than from any fear of their being discovered together. "Not long,'' she said with grim determination. "I'm hoping tonight's party will make Claire feel she's missing something. She might even meet someone interesting. But whatever the outcome of tonight is, Keith, I'm going to tell my father. He's out of town on a business trip, but he'll be back in a couple of days. I'll tell him then. I really don't care anymore. I've got to be with you!''

"It's about time!'' Keith's eyes traveled over her shoulder to the couple lying beneath the tree. "How I envy them!'' he exclaimed. "If it were up to me I would throw you down on the ground this minute and ravish you. But for your sake, no touching. I just wanted to see you. I'll slip out as quietly and unnoticed as I arrived.''

Now his eyes grew mellow, and his strong mouth trembled. "I want you to remember how much I love you, how I'm longing for you, and if you can stay away from me remembering that, you're in better control of your emotions than I am.''

She shook her head. "I'm an emotional wreck, Keith. I need my...transfusion.''

"Then resolve this once and for all. I want you to be my wife before another week goes by.'' He stood up, and Mona tried to reach for him, to cling to him for just one more minute, but his steady hand restrained her. "Good night, my love. Sweet dreams," he said, and was gone.

WHEN MONA RETURNED HOME from school the following day she was filled with steady determination. The moment Ben returned home she was going to tell him. It would mean openly defying her mother and taking the coward's way out with Claire, but she was going to do it. She wasn't being fair to Keith, and all her loyalties should be to him, the man who was going to be her husband. Keith had shown remarkable patience throughout, but it was only a matter of time before he became really angry over all this. He might even turn to another woman for solace. It couldn't happen. . . it mustn't!

As she crossed the foyer she was met at the bottom of the stairs by a frowning Claire. "Guess who was at that party last night," her sister said.

"Who?"

"Keith."

"Oh?" Mona steadied herself. "How did you know that?"

"My detective. I called him this morning and he told me. But Keith didn't stay long. The detective told me that the only person Keith talked to was. . . my sister. Why didn't you tell me, Mona?"

Mona forced herself to meet Claire's eyes. "I didn't see any point. We only talked a few minutes."

Claire was watching her intently, making her acutely uncomfortable. "I know. The detective told me that, too. Did. . . did Keith mention me at all?"

"He only said that he had seen you." Mona now

thought she knew what Keith had meant when he had said he felt like eight kinds of a fraud.

Claire's expression was frankly suspicious. "The detective said it seemed to him that Keith went to the party... for the sole purpose of finding you."

"That's ridiculous!" Mona blurted out much too quickly and vehemently. "Your detective friend is clutching at straws. He's making a lot of money off this family, and he isn't earning his keep!"

"Good heavens! Why so angry, Mona?"

"I'm not angry!"

"You're giving a good imitation of it."

"Oh, this is so stupid, Claire. Why don't you send that detective packing and stop this nonsense?"

Claire folded her arms across her chest and stared at her sister. "I still think it's damned funny that you didn't tell me you had talked to Keith. What did you talk about?"

"Nothing! Small talk. 'How've you been,' and stuff like that. Now, if you don't mind, I'm going to my room."

Mona fled up the stairs, feeling Claire's eyes on her all the way to the top. Would that have been a good time, she wondered, a good time to tell Claire and get it over with? It had happened so quickly and surprisingly, making Mona feel like a child caught with her hand in the cookie jar, that there had been no time to think. Perhaps she should have told Claire.

But if it had sent her sister off on another emotional tangent, Kitty would have been furious. No, Mona decided it was better to speak to her father first. Let Ben's cool calm common sense prevail. He would know what to do, she was sure of it. She wished she had gone to him in the first place.

CHAPTER TWELVE

SINCE THE DAY Mona had taken a personal interest in Alan Palmer's artistic career she had begun reading the arts section of the newspaper, particularly the column by the art critic Jeffrey Gallagher, and this morning the Gallagher column was of special interest to her:

> On the list of events not to be missed will be this week's showing at the Stephanie Means Gallery. Opening Thursday evening and continuing until the end of the month, the showing will be featuring the works of local artists, some of whom will be familiar names to enthusiasts, but many others are new to the Dallas art scene. Long an ardent supporter of our area's artists, Ms. Means told this column that she is particularly excited about the work of Dallas artist Alan Palmer, and indeed Mr. Palmer's haunting landscapes add depth and interest to the exhibit, the most ambitious yet undertaken by the Means Gallery....

Quite forgetting the early hour, Mona jumped from her chair at the dining table and ran into the library, where she dialed Alan's number. The phone rang five times before it was answered, and then not by one of the servants but by Alan himself. His sleep-drugged voice rasped in her ear.

"Hello."

"Good morning," Mona trilled brightly. "Have you seen the paper?"

"Paper?" he cried incredulously. "Oh, God! Mona, is that you? What the hell time is it?"

"Oh, dear, it's only seven-thirty," she said, looking at her watch for the first time. "I didn't realize it was so early. But you really should rise and shine, artist. You've just got your first review."

A long agonizing groan came over the line, followed by a lusty yawn. "Seven-thirty! I haven't been up at seven-thirty since I was in high school. Ah... what's this about the paper?"

"You've made the newspapers, Alan. Section D, page two."

"Well, I'll be damned!"

"Say, I truly am sorry about the early hour. You sound absolutely dreadful. Bad night?"

"Just a late one."

"You're really going to have to do something about your life-style now that you're going to be famous."

Alan chuckled. "Don't be ridiculous, Mona. Artists are supposed to be debauched."

At that moment a muffled, sleepy, feminine voice cooed, "Who is it, Alan?" and Mona was swamped with chagrin.

Another muffled sound followed. Mona guessed Alan had covered the mouthpiece with his hand while he explained to his companion just who was calling at this ungodly hour. Then he spoke again to Mona.

"Thanks for telling me, Mona. I'll pad down and

get the paper. Oh, by the way, you will be at the showing Thursday night, won't you?''

''With flags unfurled and cymbals clashing!'' Mona promised. ''I wouldn't miss it for the world. And, Alan, I really am sorry about calling. I just didn't think. Why on earth didn't one of the servants answer the phone?''

''Last night was their night off. They don't come in until noon today.'' Another unstifled yawn. ''Don't worry about it, Mona. I'll see you Thursday night.''

Mona hung up and left the library. While she was gathering up her books from the foyer table, Lettie accosted her. ''Your mother and Claire are going to a luncheon today,'' the housekeeper announced. ''Lucille wants to know if she can expect you.''

''Nope. This is Wednesday. I'll be having lunch in town.''

''I wondered why the dress instead of jeans.''

''The restaurant is very quaint and very French. Jeans just wouldn't do at all.''

THE QUIET, ATMOSPHERIC and very expensive restaurant, with its cloth-covered tables, blue-and-white-checked wallpaper and pots of geraniums in the windows, had become a favorite place for Mona and Beth Sinclair to meet for lunch every Wednesday. Mona arrived early, and Beth was late—something Mona had learned was the norm for her aunt. A waiter led her to a table in the rear of the dining room, where she waited patiently while studying the familiar menu.

It occurred to her that between Keith and Beth her life had become a series of clandestine meetings,

cover-ups and out-and-out lies. The duplicity bothered Mona enormously, but she was quite human
enough to be glad that Kitty had not asked many
questions. Had her mother been a more inquisitive
type of person, Mona wasn't sure what she would
have told her about these Wednesdays. As it was, the
subject had only come up once, when her mother had
asked, "Lunch in town again? This is becoming an
every-week habit. Is your friend someone I know?"

"I...I only met her this past summer," Mona had
evaded.

"Well, you must invite her to dinner here at the
house sometime," Kitty had said absently and
dropped the matter.

At least she hadn't had to lie that time. How Mona
wished the estrangement between the two sisters
wasn't so firmly entrenched, for she had grown very
fond of her aunt. In the beginning of her friendship
with Beth she had harbored hopes of being the go-
between who would bring them back together, but
those hopes had quickly been dashed by Beth herself.

"It's impossible, Mona, and I'm going to ask you
not to attempt a reconciliation. Believe me, my dear,
it would do more harm than good for you to tell
either of your parents that I'm in town."

"But aren't you worried that you might accidental-
ly run into one or both of them somewhere?" Mona
had asked sensibly.

Beth had smiled then, a very poignant smile, Mona
now recalled, and had said, "It's very easy to get lost
in a city this size, Mona. And your parents and I no
longer move in the same social circles. Too, a lot of
years have passed, and I've changed, probably much
more so than Kitty or Ben have. Were I to see either

of them, I could make myself scarce before I was recognized.''

Mona remembered being astonished. ''Do you mean to say that if you saw one of them you wouldn't even say hello?''

''That is precisely what I mean,'' Beth had said decisively. ''I know that sounds odd, but it's for the best, my dear.''

What, Mona wondered for the dozenth time, could keep two sisters so irrevocably separated for so long? But it puzzled more than bothered her, and she had not brought up the subject again. It had to be enough that she and her aunt had established a warm relationship, friendly but totally free of personal confidences. Beth did not like to talk about herself. Mona hadn't the slightest idea what Beth's private life was like. She didn't know who her aunt's friends were or how she spent her time. And Beth, Mona now realized with some surprise, knew absolutely nothing of Keith Garrett.

At that moment Beth approached the table, breathlessly as usual. ''Been waiting long?'' she asked, as she invariably did.

''No,'' Mona said. ''Just a minute or two.''

Beth slid into the chair across from Mona and opened the menu. Her face was flushed, which did wonders for a complexion that was normally much too wan. The pearl-gray suit she wore was stylish and flattering, and Mona thought her aunt looked lovelier than she had ever seen her. She had gained some weight since coming to Dallas, which helped, and there was an animated sparkle to her dark eyes that had been completely missing in those earlier days.

In spite of what Beth kept insisting, Mona knew her

aunt was much too young to have given up all hope of having love in her life again, so she couldn't avoid speculating on the woman's new radiance. Perhaps there was a man. Mona hoped so, but she wouldn't ask. If Beth wanted her to know, she would tell her in due time.

"What sounds good today?" Beth asked, her eyes sweeping over the menu.

"I thought the spinach salad and the quiche," Mona said.

Beth closed the menu. "Me, too. Wine?"

Mona shook her head. "Drinking wine in the middle of the day always makes me sleepy."

Beth laughed. "Wine never makes me sleepy, but a glass usually makes me want another...and another. And I have some shopping to do this afternoon, so no wine."

Conversation throughout the meal was minimal. The restaurant did a considerable lunchtime business and so was crowded and noisy, but since most of its patrons had jobs to get back to, the place pretty well emptied out by one o'clock. No one hurried them, so Mona and Beth settled back over coffee for their weekly chat. The talk usually was not personal or intimate, but today Beth had news.

"Well, Mona, for better or worse I think I've finally decided to stay in Dallas."

Mona clapped her hands together in delight. "Oh, Beth, I'm so glad. I've got used to having an aunt."

"Yes, I don't think I can do better...and I've made a few good friends whom I would miss were I to leave. None of the old crowd, of course. I'm much too far removed from them now, but...I'm managing to forge a bit of a life for myself, and I don't think I want to pull up stakes again."

"I think that's wonderful, naturally, but...." Mona hesitated, uncertain if she should ask what she wanted to ask.

A knowing smile came to Beth's face. "But aren't I afraid it will increase my chances of seeing Kitty again?"

"Well...yes."

"Possibly. But as I once told you, my sister and I don't move in the same circles, and I'm a rather solitary person. I don't flit around to luncheons and teas and the like. However, if it happens, it happens. It no longer seems so important to me."

Mona's eyebrows shot up. "Oh?" This was a change.

"I've met someone who's made me see that dwelling on the past is one of mankind's most foolish pursuits."

A bright smile lit Mona's face. "A man?"

"Yes, a man. He asked me a very pithy question once. 'Would armies march, would governments topple if you and your sister chanced to meet again?' Suddenly I had it in the right perspective. So, it wouldn't distress me in the least to see Kitty again. How she would feel, however, might be a different matter."

Breathlessly Mona waited. She felt that Beth was on the verge of divulging some confidence. A faraway look had come to her aunt's eyes. Her mind seemed to be drifting back in time to whatever ancient hurts and grievances had stood as a wedge between the two sisters for so long. Incredible, Mona thought. It was said that time heals, yet twenty-odd years had not healed those old wounds. And inevitably she thought of Claire. Would it be that way between herself and Claire, too, if she married Keith before Claire had got over him? She watched as Beth sat absorbed in her private thoughts.

Then, as quickly as the pensiveness had come, it vanished, and Beth was crisp and alert once more. "So, Mona, since I'm going to be staying and since my tentative forays into apartment hunting haven't turned up a more desirable place than the one I now have, I've simply got to do something with it. Am I striking a responsive chord?"

Mona's eyes brightened. "You know you are!"

"You'd like to help me?"

"Of course I would. When would you want to start?"

"Immediately," Beth said. "Now that I've decided to do this, I can't stand those dreary plain rooms a moment longer. I don't know how I've tolerated them until now. As a matter of fact—" she glanced at her watch "—I don't really have to go shopping this afternoon. It can wait. If you have the time, why don't we go to my place right now and you can start getting some ideas?"

"I have all the time in the world," Mona said, excited as always by the thought of a new project. "Mom and Claire have gone to a luncheon, so that means bridge afterward, and since dad is out of town mom will be in no hurry to get home. Did you drive?"

"No, I came by cab."

"Good. My car is parked in the lot in back. Let's go!"

MONA MADE AN UNHURRIED INSPECTION of her aunt's apartment. She would be working with a living-dining room with a vaulted ceiling, a kitchen and a breakfast nook, two bedrooms and two baths. The carpeting throughout was an unusual color, something of a taupe, but it was neutral enough to blend in with a variety of color schemes. She measured and took notes, while Beth watched and gave her some idea about her personal tastes.

"White," Beth said. "I wants lots of white. I want a feeling of light and cheerfulness. I've had enough of solemnity. My home in Virginia was old, very elegant but so full of heaviness. It had been in my husband's family for generations, and I think they were still living with the original furniture. Heavy draperies, heavy rugs, heavy furniture. And all so dark." She grimaced. "It had all the warmth of a mausoleum."

Mona scribbled in her pad. "White is very contemporary. You can do anything with white."

"Oh, Mona, suddenly I'm very excited about having a place that's mine, all mine. When can we get started?"

"Well, I don't see why I . . . ." Mona paused. She had started to say "tomorrow," but tomorrow would be impossible. She had promised Stephanie she would go to the gallery early. There simply wouldn't be enough time between school and the showing to get any serious shopping done.

And the following day was Friday. Ben would be home Friday, and no matter what else happened, Mona was determined to find time alone with her father Friday to tell him about Keith. There was no predicting what would happen after that. Mona was sure she wouldn't be in any mood for shopping on Friday.

Beth was anxious and excited; Mona sympathized and wanted to help her aunt, but her own future was so clouded with uncertainty. Even if her father was indeed the miracle worker Mona hoped he was and came up with a solution to her dilemma, she would then immediately be involved with Keith and their wedding, then their honeymoon. She hadn't given this enough thought. It probably hadn't been wise to take on another time-consuming decorating project until her own plans were clearer.

"Mona?" Beth's voice broke into her thoughts.

"Hmm? Oh! Well, Beth. . . certainly I want to get to this right away, but. . . there are some things coming up. . . ."

"Of course, dear. I didn't mean to rush you."

Mona heard the disappointment in her aunt's voice. "You're not rushing me, Beth. It's just that I. . . I don't know how free I'll be for the next two weeks. I might be completely tied up, or. . . I might have all the time in the world." The last was said with such a feeling of frustrated despair that Beth couldn't avoid hearing it.

Beth nibbled on a fingernail and studied her niece with some concern. "Mona, is something troubling you?"

"Wh-what?" she asked, dismayed that she had let her inner unrest show.

Beth smiled a small smile. "Forgive me. I don't want to pry. I think you know me well enough by now to know I'd never do that. I don't like others questioning me about my personal affairs, and I try to return the favor. But. . . lately it has seemed to me that you've had something on your mind, something that's bothering you. I've sensed it before but never quite like today. I thought perhaps you might like to talk to someone about it. It never helps to keep things bottled up inside, dear. It only serves to magnify them. So if you'd like to talk to me, I'd be happy to listen.''

Mona sighed and closed her note pad. Dear God, it would be nice to spit it all out. And Beth was far enough removed from the principals involved; she might be able to see things that had escaped Mona completely. Certainly she ought to understand sibling rivalries and jealousies. It might be a good thing to talk to someone about it.

''Oh, Beth...it's so damned complicated!'' she groaned.

''That's because you've been brooding about it for so long. I suppose there's a man in the picture. There almost always is.''

Mona nodded ruefully.

''Is it that artist friend you've been telling me about?''

''No, no. It's not Alan. I wish to goodness it were. Then all I'd have to worry about was being in love with a womanizing playboy!''

''Goodness!'' Beth exclaimed softly. ''Mona, you must tell me about it.''

The words spilled out, slowly at first, then in a rush. The account was a trifle disoriented at times, but it all came out. It took a long time to tell it, and it did sound complicated to Mona's ears. She had hoped a telling of the story would somehow simplify it. When she finished speaking she felt emotionally drained, and she slumped dejectedly in her chair.

For several long moments Beth sat across from her, absolutely stilled. The most amazing thing to Mona was the look on her aunt's face. Stricken, that was it. Where had she seen such a look before? Then it came to her: it was the same look Mona had seen

on Kitty's face the day she had told her mother exactly the same story! Trepidation shook her. Why did
she suddenly have the feeling she had begun something that was going to be damned difficult to end?

"Beth, what is it?" she cried fearfully.

Beth was rubbing her forehead and slowly shaking
her head. "Oh, Mona...if you only knew, if you
only knew!"

"Knew what?"

"What a Pandora's box you've opened!"

"What? Beth, you're talking in riddles. Please tell
me...." For the first time Mona was beginning to
suspect that she, in some inexorable way, was caught
up in whatever had transpired between her mother
and her aunt all those many years ago. But that was
ridiculous! What could that possibly have to do with
her? And yet she feared something. "Tell me," she
repeated.

"I'm not sure you want to hear it, Mona."

"Of course I do! I want to hear anything that will
help me understand."

Beth reached for a cigarette and lit it with visibly
trembling fingers. Exhaled smoke spiraled into the
air. "I'm afraid you've unwittingly taken your
mother and me back to a time neither of us is anxious
to relive."

"Please, Beth, you *must* tell me!"

Beth's face was again wan, almost ashen. Her
earlier radiance had vanished. She sighed deeply, as
though caught in the grips of a powerful sadness, and
she struggled with her words. "It...happened a long
time ago, Mona. Twenty-five years to be exact. I was
the same age you are now, and Kitty was three years
older. She brought this charming young man home

and announced to one and all that they were going to be married. I didn't blame her. Twenty-five years ago Ben Lowery was the handsomest man in north Texas. I wouldn't be surprised if he still is." She looked to Mona for confirmation.

Mona stammered, "I...yes...dad looks wonderful, I think. He's kept his trim figure, and the slight gray in his hair makes him look...distinguished, I guess."

"I thought so. I knew he would age gracefully."

Mona was impatient. "Beth, go on. My mother and father were engaged...."

"Yes, but there was a problem. Our parents were strictly upper upper-class. So proper. And Ben's father owned a small machine shop. Middle-class, hardworking...and that didn't sit well with my parents, especially not with my father, who expected 'great things' from Kitty. Me he had given up on—I was a nonconformist in an age when conformity was everything—but Kitty was the apple of his eye."

For a moment Beth's tone became bitter and harsh, but she quickly recovered and spoke almost dispassionately. "However, Kitty had a mind of her own and had a way with dad, so eventually the union received everyone's blessing, and preparations began for the society wedding of the year. I've never seen so much fuss and ado made over anything in my life. There had to be a six-month engagement, not a day less, and I don't think that during those six months Kitty and mother missed one day attending some grand event or another. Poor Ben. He was so out of his element, so stunned and bewildered by the whole thing."

Beth paused, and a haunting smile crossed her face.

Mona waited silently, letting her aunt savor whatever fond remembrance had captured her attention. Then Beth continued. "Our family was a pretty formidable bunch and must have seemed especially so to a man like Ben. And since I was the black sheep of the family, the one everybody despaired of ever amounting to anything, I guess it was only natural that Ben and I should become...friendly."

Mona felt an unpleasant tightening in her chest. She had a pretty good idea what was coming next.

"In those days Kitty was so busy she had little time for Ben, so he and I began taking long drives together, and he would talk to me, sometimes for hours. He was absolutely enchanted with Kitty, I could tell that. He couldn't believe that such a creature would cast favorable eyes in his direction. But he was lonely, too, and grateful for my company. Sometimes we would drive far out into the country, park the car and run through open fields like a couple of kids. One thing led to another and...." Beth spread out her hands, unable to further embellish her story, but such embellishment was unnecessary. Mona knew.

Beth sighed again. "We talked about going away together, but I don't think either of us ever thought it was anything but talk. The scandal would have devastated Kitty, and Ben really did care for her. He had made a commitment and wanted to keep it. I knew that, accepted it and was determined to enjoy whatever time we had together, then to fade out of the picture. I'm not sure I would define what Ben and I had together as love. We just happened to be thrown together at a time when both of us needed something." Beth faltered and winced from some inner pain.

"We...thought we were being so discreet, but—"

"But mom found out," Mona concluded for her.

Her aunt nodded. "A mutual 'friend' decided it was her duty to tell Kitty. Oh, it was ugly. Ugly and bitter. But I felt far sorrier for Ben than I did for myself. My family put him through hell for a while, but gradually he wooed Kitty back. It wasn't difficult since she was insane about him, and I think our affair threw a real scare into her. The wedding took place as scheduled."

"And you, Beth? What about you?"

"I was persona non grata around that house, let me tell you! I stood it as long as I could, and then I left. I had some money in the bank and a trust fund, but a few months later my father withdrew my trust. I, who had grown up in the lap of luxury, was reduced to working as a waitress. I swallowed my pride once and wrote to my mother, but all I got in return was a terse note telling me that my father had forbidden her to send me so much as a nickel, so of course she wouldn't dream of disobeying him. It's probably difficult for a modern young woman to believe, but people actually operated like that in those days!"

Beth took a deep breath and continued. Now that the soul-purging had begun, she seemed anxious to get it all out. "About six months after I left home I got a letter. It was from Ben, and it contained a thousand dollars. I have no idea how he got my address. He might have come upon the letter I wrote to my mother. I'm not too sure that thousand dollars didn't save my life. A person could live a long time on a thousand dollars twenty-five years ago. In the letter Ben asked me to take care of myself, but I'm afraid I didn't do a very good job of it. My first marriage was a disaster, and I flirted with pills and booze for too many years. Then my father died, and mother reinstated my trust. She made it clear she didn't actually want to see me, but she didn't want me hurting for money, either. I filed for divorce the day my first check arrived. I waited a number of years before trying marriage again, but the second one failed, too. And so here I am.''

So stunned by the revelations she could hardly think, Mona nevertheless ached for Beth...and for her father...and for Kitty, too. In a flash she felt more pity for them than she had ever felt for anyone. As many children do, she had molded her parents into straitlaced stereotypes. It came as a shock to get a glimpse of them as ordinary people, muddling along like everybody else, making mistakes and trying to do the best they could with the only life they would ever have. She was shaken to the core.

"Well," Mona said, lifting her arms in a gesture of utter futility, "that explains a lot. I always wondered why dad spoiled mom so. Now I guess he's still trying to atone for his, er, indiscretion. And it especially explains mom's insistence that dad must never, ever know anything about Keith and me...not while Claire is still mooning around over him. I think that part of it puzzled me more than anything.''

"It hit too close to home, Mona.''

"I know. It's almost uncanny.'' Mona rubbed her forehead wearily. "Beth, I had planned to tell dad about Keith when he comes home Friday. I just can't let this thing drag on any longer.''

Beth frowned thoughtfully. "I'd think twice about that if I were you, Mona. This thing is touchy. I'm sure Ben doesn't want to be reminded of it, and I don't see how he could give you permission to go with your young man without incurring Kitty's displeasure. I'm sure her sympathies are with Claire.''

"Completely." Mona was experiencing a sinking sensation in the pit of her stomach. So many obstacles, so damned many obstacles! It wasn't fair! "Beth, are you telling me to tread softly or I might cause friction in my parents' marriage?''

"You might," Beth said softly. "Kitty hates unpleasantness. Everyone does, I suppose, but Kitty expects perfection out of life. She wants no hills or valleys. She was always like that. And she never forgets a wrong...or forgives one. If anyone knows that, I do.''

Mona nodded. "Claire's like that, too.''

"The younger sister who has taken Claire's young man...oh, God, Mona, it's like a bad dream! It can't be happening again, not in the same family!''

Mona stood up and walked to the window, stared out for a moment at the sun-dappled city street full of busy people hurrying places, then went back to her chair. These warring loyalties were crushing down on her. "It was bad enough when I thought Claire's feelings were my primary worry. But to be the cause of trouble between my parents...I don't think I could live with that. But, Beth, I'll admit I'm scared. I have the most terrible feeling that I'm going to lose Keith if I don't do something right away. He's been good about this so far, but I'm beginning to sense an impatience in him when we talk over the telephone. If only Claire would send that stupid detective packing. This wouldn't be so unbearable if Keith and I could at least be together.''

"Have an affair, you mean." It was a statement of fact, not a question.

Mona glanced down at her hands. "Well...yes, I guess so. There are worse things. I know he loves me."

Beth's eyes were warm and sympathetic. "I wish I could help you, dear, truly I do. But when I think of how miserably I've botched my own private life, I should think my advice would be the most worthless thing in the world. But I can tell you one thing—and this is straight from the horse's mouth. It hasn't been worth it."

"Wh-what?"

"The estrangement from family. It hasn't been worth it. If there was something I could do to make amends, I would do it, but...there's nothing. My father died hating me, and when my mother died I couldn't even attend the funeral. It would have upset Kitty too much. So I haven't seen or spoken to my only sister in twenty-five years. It hasn't been worth it. If I were you, I'd try talking to that young man of yours. Try to make him realize you are dealing with more than hurt feelings and pettish jealousies. If he's the kind of man you think he is, he'll understand and help you."

Burning tears welled in Mona's eyes. Angrily she brushed them away, and a grief-stricken expression crossed her face. How could she explain this premonition that her love for Keith was doomed? Too many things were getting in the way, too many things over which they had no control.

"Keith is not going to wait forever," she said dully, knowing only too well the truth of that statement.

"He might. Wouldn't you wait for him?"

"Yes, but... men are different. I'm not even sure I have the right to ask him to wait indefinitely."

"Try him, Mona. Tell him and see what his reaction is. At the very least don't do anything rash or hasty. Give this plenty of thought. Quite a lot can change, almost overnight. And, dear... let's put aside the decorating for the time being. I think you have far too much on your mind as it is."

Mona certainly agreed with that. She gathered her notes together and stood up. "I guess I'll go on home now, Beth. I'll call you in a few days. And... thanks for everything."

"I'm afraid I wasn't much help."

"You listened," Mona said simply.

"Things have a way of working out, Mona, given a little time."

Mona looked down at her seriously "That sounds almost funny coming from you."

Beth's mouth set grimly. "Well... let's just say that most things have a way of working out."

All the way home Mona mulled over in her mind the things Beth had told her. Knowing now about those old grievances had cast a new light on her quandary. She had been hoping her father would be able to look at the problem more dispassionately than Kitty had, but now she could see it would be impossible. It would hit him close to home, too. Could she, in all good conscience, dredge up those ancient hurts, bring them to the surface where her parents would be forced to look at them?

But there was Keith, and, dear God, she couldn't lose him! She was quite prepared to believe there would never be anyone else. And Mona was not foolish enough to think a man like Keith would wait around indefinitely, dancing to her parents' tune. It was only a matter of time before he became lonely and discouraged and therefore receptive to more satisfying companionship.

Disconsolately Mona swung her little automobile into the driveway of the Lowery house, her mind groping for solutions. Her biggest problem, she decided, was that she had coasted through life, unbothered by life's vexing troubles. Now that her secure placid existence had been disturbed by a very real predicament, she simply did not know how to deal with it.

She entered the house by way of the side porch and crossed through the dining room, where Lettie was running the vacuum cleaner. When the housekeeper saw her, she switched off the machine.

"Have mom and Claire got home yet?" Mona asked.

Lettie shook her head. "The missus called an hour ago and said she and Claire had run into some friends and were going to have dinner with them. So Lucille wants to know what you'd like."

"Don't worry about me. A sandwich, some soup. Anything. I really don't care. I'll be in my room if anyone calls, Lettie."

Lettie frowned. "You okay? You look kinda sickly to me."

"Yes...I'm fine," Mona said dispiritedly. She passed through the room and up the stairs, hearing the whir of the vacuum start up again.

In her room she tossed her books on the drafting table, sank into the chair and reached for the telephone. After going through the switchboard, then Keith's secretary, she had him on the line.

"Keith, I want to talk to you," she said without preamble.

"Go ahead. What's wrong, Mona? You sound awful."

"I'm all right. Keith, I mean I want to see you and talk to you."

"Hell, I want to see you, too, and I don't want to talk. But I'm afraid that gumshoe is still on your father's payroll."

"Right now I'm not very concerned about him."

Something in her tone must have warned him. There was a long pause and when Keith spoke again his voice was icy. "I don't want to hear any more bad news, Mona."

She ignored that. "Listen, darling. Do you know Stephanie Means's art gallery? It's near the Quadrangle."

"No, but I can find it."

"Tomorrow night she's opening a new show. There'll be hundreds of people there, so that detective won't think a thing about your attending it. The showing starts at seven-thirty. I'll tell Steph I'm expecting you, and I'll wait for you in her office."

He uttered a foul oath, then said, "If this isn't the most patently stupid thing—"

"I agree, Keith," Mona said tiredly, "but I've got to talk to you. Will you be there?"

"Of course. . . if it means seeing you."

"There's a workroom in back, and Steph's office is beyond that. It will be private."

"I'll see you at seven-thirty. Mona, are you sure you're all right?"

"I'm not sick, if that's what you mean. Tomorrow night, Keith."

"Tomorrow night."

"I love you," she said without a trace of joy in her voice.

"I love you, too, Mona," Keith said, and his tone matched hers.

CHAPTER THIRTEEN

THURSDAY SEEMED to drag on interminably. Mona's gaze strayed to her bedside clock. She had been home from school for three hours, and during that time she had bathed, shampooed her hair, given herself a manicure and tried on half the dresses in her closet, and still she had time on her hands.

Standing in her slip and stocking feet in the middle of her room, she stared at the garments piled on her bed and thought again of the black dress she had earlier dismissed as being too provocative to wear to a gallery showing. Now she was having second thoughts about it. She returned to her closet, removed the dress, hung it on the door and stepped back to study it.

The dress's very simplicity appealed to her, and she did look good in black. True, its neckline plunged a bit dramatically front and back, making Mona wonder what on earth had prompted her to buy the thing in the first place, but a stole around her shoulders would take care of that. She could wear the pearls her father had given her last Christmas and those ridiculous shoes that were little more than a sole, a heel and a strap. Moreover, the dress was a perfect foil for her flawless creamy-smooth skin. A few more moments of indecision followed, then her mind made itself up. The black dress it would be.

Satisfied, Mona returned to her dressing table, sat down and stared at her reflection in the mirror. A pair of solemn brown eyes stared back at her. She was as nervous as a sixteen-year-old getting ready for her first date with the captain of the football team. Her stomach was churning. It seemed of paramount importance to look her very best tonight, as though a good appearance would somehow shore up her confidence and help her cope with whatever Keith's reaction to this new family problem turned out to be. She silently rehearsed what she would tell him, and when she had finished she tried to imagine what he would say. Unfortunately, nothing clear-cut came to her. She honestly didn't know whether to expect warm understanding or blind rage. And she had once thought she knew him so well, back in the early innocence of their friendship, when their relationship had been a simple one of trust and accord.

There was nothing simple about it now, and with the simplicity gone, some of that rare communion had been lost, too. Now Mona was beginning to believe it was impossible for one human being to fully understand and anticipate the actions of another, no matter how finely attuned they were.

Lost in her thoughts, she was unaware of Claire standing in the doorway, and she jumped at the sound of her sister's voice.

"Where are you off to tonight?" Claire asked with a discernible lack of genuine interest.

"To the opening of the new showing at Stephanie Means's gallery, remember?"

"Oh, yeah, that's right. I've never been to anything like that. Are they fun?"

A flash of alarm raced through Mona. What

would she do if Claire asked to come along? Claire wouldn't know Picasso from Pinocchio, but she had been restless and edgy for days and might seize any opportunity to get out of the house. "Fun? I wouldn't say a showing is fun, Claire. Interesting, perhaps. . . if you're into art."

Claire appeared to be giving it serious thought. Mona pulled a hairbrush through her hair and watched her sister, fervently hoping. There would be no way she could refuse to let Claire come along if she wanted.

However, Claire finally wrinkled her nose and said, "Oh, it doesn't sound like something I'd be interested in. And I certainly didn't know *you* were 'into art.' "

"Well, I try to stay a little interested in a lot of things," Mona said, relieved. "Is mom home yet?"

Claire shook her head.

"Then will you tell her I don't know what time I'll be home? I might stay and help Stephanie clean up."

"Will do," Claire said.

"What are you going to do tonight?" Mona asked.

Claire smiled pathetically. "Stay home. . . what else?"

Mona barely suppressed an irritated sigh. Claire wasn't even trying. Mona couldn't count the number of young men who had besieged her sister with invitations to this and that, but Claire kept turning them down, wallowing in self-pity and sopping up the attention she was receiving from Ben and Kitty—especially Kitty.

"Well, have fun," Mona said, her tone implying, *if that's the way you want it, so be it.*

"Yeah, sure," Claire said, and she walked away.

Mona stood up, slipped the black dress over her head, stuffed her feet into the shoes and clasped the rope of pearls around her neck. Then she studied herself in the mirror, trying to be completely objective. Was the neckline's plunge alarming? No, she decided firmly. She had seen far more revealing dresses in public, and no one paid them the slightest attention. Besides, the dress did marvelous things for her. It clung to the contours of her breasts, her waist, her hips, and the fabric swung seductively when she moved. She almost could see Keith's admiring eyes now. Surely he wouldn't fume and snort and accuse her of being "daddy's little girl," not when she was wearing this dress. She gathered the stole around her, slinging one end across her breasts and over her shoulder, artfully concealing any cleavage. Picking up her handbag she left the room, and by a quarter to seven she was driving away from the house.

Stephanie's gallery was ablaze with lights. A sign in front announced tonight's showing. Inside the building Mona found only a trickle of people, mostly the artists whose work was being shown and a few local critics. They were helping themselves to champagne and hors d'oeuvres, milling around and conversing with their colleagues. A quick search of the place did not reveal Alan, but Mona found Stephanie alone in one of the back rooms.

"Steph, I'm going to ask a big favor of you," she said in a confidential manner.

"Sure, Mona, what is it?"

"I'd like to borrow your office for a little while tonight."

"Help yourself. It isn't locked."

Mona smiled. "And don't call out the police if you happen to see a tall, dark, incredibly gorgeous man lurking around in back. He'll be looking for me."

Stephanie's eyes twinkled merrily. "How exciting! I wish he would be looking for me."

"And don't tell anyone, *anyone,* you've seen either of us," Mona cautioned, thinking of the detective. "I don't suppose you let just anyone wander around in the workroom. . . ."

"Absolutely not! The door will be closed and the No Admittance signs posted. Oh, I'll bet if I knew what was going on I would be intrigued to death!" Stephanie exclaimed.

"I really appreciate this, Steph. It's awfully important to me."

At that moment a masculine voice spoke from behind Mona. "Now what are you two whispering about?" Mona turned to see Alan, holding a glass of champagne and grinning from ear to ear. He executed a courtly half-bow. "How are my lovely benefactoresses. . . is that a proper word? Anyway, how are you two lovely ladies this evening? Your beauty illuminates these rooms. Perhaps we should put the two of you on display."

Stephanie winked at Mona. "Doesn't this man simply fill up a room!"

Alan, ever the charmer and diplomat, was careful to address his flattering remarks to both Mona and Stephanie, but his eyes were all on Mona. She thought how odd it was that a man's scrutiny could be so thorough and blatant yet contain not a speck of lust. Alan was simply studying her much as a horse fancier would appraise the merits of a particularly handsome animal. She slipped her arm around his waist and gave him a quick hug. "Are you bursting with excitement?"

"Well...not exactly bursting."

"You must be," Mona insisted. "Come with me. Let's go and look at your paintings. We'll see you later, Steph."

"Right," the gallery owner said. "But make yourself available tonight, Alan. I want everyone to meet you."

There were six of Alan's landscapes on display. Five of them Mona had seen in his studio, but there was a new one, one that Alan had worked at feverishly to have ready in time for this exhibit. *El Capitan at Sunset* took Mona's breath away. Its muted shadings of yellows and rust and browns and mauves captured the essence of the lonely Trans-Pecos region of far west Texas. Looking at it and the others, Mona felt an enormous sense of pride in what she considered her small part in her friend's success. She even experienced an absurd urge to cry. She flicked at a tear that threatened to fall, thereby calling Alan's attention to her emotional state.

"Hey—" he moved closer and looked down at her with astonished eyes "—you're really all choked up over all this, aren't you!"

Mona smiled sheepishly and looked away. "Oh, don't mind me. I cry at supermarket openings."

He wasn't fooled. "Mona, I don't think anyone has ever taken such an interest in anything I've done. My parents never did, that's for sure. Mother thought my paintings were 'cute.' I wish I were better with words. I might wax damned eloquent about now. I'm touched. Really touched."

"You're also really talented," Mona said, recovering her composure, "and I'm tickled to death that you're finally going to get some recognition."

"I owe it all to you. . . and to Steph, of course, but primarily to you. And I'm not a man who forgets. I still owe you one."

"Nonsense!"

"And you owe me something, too."

Mona frowned. "Oh?"

"The portrait," Alan reminded her. "I thought you were going to sit for me."

"Oh, Alan, I forgot!" Mona was genuinely dismayed. She supposed it was quite an honor that an artist wanted to paint her portrait. But she was no more prepared to take that on than she was Beth's apartment. She simply wanted no definite commitments of any kind until the Keith-Claire business was resolved. And the way things were going, that might take some time. "We'll get around to it one of these days, Alan, I promise. I'm just. . . just too busy with other things right now."

Just then Stephanie appeared to command Alan's attention. "Alan, I want you to come with me to meet Beatrice McIlhenney. She is an art lover without equal, and she's very influential."

Alan's face broke into that charming smile. This sort of thing was right up his alley. He turned and touched Mona on the arm. "I'll talk to you later," he said, and followed Stephanie. Mona watched as they approached an elegant dowager who was dressed in yards and yards of silver blue. She saw Stephanie make the introductions, then fade into the background and let Alan take over. Within moments he had the McIlhenney woman positively simpering. Mona smiled. From seventeen to seventy, the ladies simply couldn't resist Alan.

Her gaze wandered back to *El Capitan at Sunset*. The painting fascinated her. The scrubby grasslands in the foreground washed in the golden glow of the dying sun, with the majestic mountain rising behind, was a masterpiece of detail and brushwork. It was far superior to Alan's earlier works, and that could only mean one thing—he was growing as an artist, becoming deeply committed to his craft. He would never revert to his former life, and for that Mona could only send up a prayer of thanks, blessing whatever unknown force had prompted her to bring Alan's work to Stephanie's attention in the first place.

"Breathtaking, isn't it?" a masculine voice said, and Mona turned to see a tall, spectacled, dapper man staring at the painting over her shoulder.

"Yes. . . yes, it is," she agreed enthusiastically.

"Bold brushwork, great attention to detail. . . and such colors!" the man said. "Much more mature work than the earlier ones." He spoke with authority, with the air of someone knowledgeable about art.

"That's very discerning of you," she said, trying to sound knowledgeable herself. "Actually, *El Capitan* is Mr. Palmer's most recent work. The others are from years ago."

The man smiled down at her. "Are you with the gallery?"

"No, I'm only a friend. . . of both the artist and the gallery's owner."

"Oh? You know Stephanie?"

"Very well," Mona assured him.

"She certainly has a way of ferreting out new

talent," the man commented. "I'm constantly amazed at what I find here."

"You must be a frequent patron," Mona said, making polite small talk.

"I have to be. It's my business. Allow me to introduce myself, my dear. My name is Jeffrey Gallagher."

Mona gasped. "The columnist?"

"Yes."

Recovering quickly, she introduced herself, and they shook hands before he resumed his study of *El Capitan*. "I previewed some of these works earlier in the week, and I was impressed with Mr. Palmer's landscapes, but this... this was not here then. I must say I consider it the highlight of the exhibit."

Excitement bubbled inside Mona. She propelled Jeffrey Gallagher around and pointed. "Mr. Gallagher, the tall blond man over there...."

"The one talking to Beatrice McIlhenney?"

"Yes. That's Alan Palmer. Please... sometime this evening will you introduce yourself to him and tell him exactly what you've just told me?"

"I certainly will, young lady. I most certainly will," Jeffrey Gallagher promised, and he moved on to study other exhibits.

Mona glanced around. The gallery was beginning to fill up. It was time to make herself scarce. First she picked up two glasses of champagne from the refreshment table. Then she threaded her way through the crowd and left the main gallery, walked through the dark deserted workroom and entered Stephanie's office. She kicked the door closed behind her, then surveyed the room. It was pin neat and decorated in a cozy ultrafeminine manner. The antique white walls were, not surprisingly, lined with paintings, mostly soft pastels and watercolors. A glass-topped desk dominated, but at the opposite end of the office was a fireplace flanked by shelves displaying porcelains, miniatures and sculptures. On either side of the hearth, print love seats stood facing each other, and between them on the floor was a thick furry white rug. Mona's educated eyes approved of what they saw. The room was like Stephanie herself—quite, private, feminine and tasteful.

She carried the glasses of champagne across the room and set them on the desk. Then her eyes swept around until they found a clock. It was twenty minutes until eight. Now her earlier nervousness returned. The exciting prospect of seeing Keith again coupled with the trepidation she felt over revealing her latest bad news to him was playing havoc with her nerves.

She crossed the room to sit on one of the love seats, hugging the stole closer around her shoulders, for she suddenly felt chilled. She waited a few long silent moments, then stood up and began restlessly pacing the floor and rubbing her hands together.

Her back was to the door when it opened. She whirled around to see Keith stepping into the room. In the time it took him to close and lock the door she was across the room and into his arms. Her shoes' high heels gave her some advantage, but still Keith had to lift her off the floor to bring her up to meet his searching mouth. Mona hugged him to her in desperation, parting her lips under his hungry ones. The stole she had been primly clutching about her shoulders all evening fell to the floor in a heap.

When Keith at last released her he uttered a shaky

hoarse laugh. "God, do you know how long it's been?"

Mona nodded numbly. "To the minute."

He let her slide to her feet along the length of his body. Then, when her feet touched the floor, he held her away from him slightly, his arms gripping her shoulders tightly. "Let me look at you."

For a long moment he stared only at her face, seeming to be mesmerized by it. His eyes were wide with wonder, and his mouth had crooked into a small smile. Mona returned his study, drinking in the sight of that angular face, of those deep gray eyes. He was wearing gray trousers, a white shirt open at the neck and a navy blue sport coat. She knew no other man who dressed with such faultless savoir faire, whether he was wearing a business suit or faded jeans. He was so potently virile he made her pulses pound.

Very slowly his gaze moved down, and the gray eyes narrowed and darkened. The smile faded. One hand moved from her shoulder to her throat, then down the ivory-smooth V of skin to the gentle swell of her breasts. It slipped into the valley between them, and a tremor shuddered through Mona's body.

"Lord, Mona!" he groaned. "Has everyone out there seen you like this?"

His warm hand resting on her chest felt as though it belonged there. She covered it with her own hand and pressed. "No one has," she whispered. "I've been wearing that." With a toe she indicated the stole on the floor. "There's nothing indecent about this dress, Keith. I wouldn't wear it if there were."

His eyes, which had wandered briefly to the heap of fabric on the floor, returned to her face. "Perhaps... perhaps then it's only my own thoughts that are indecent.''

"Nothing we think about each other could ever be indecent,'' she said simply. Again she melted against him, warm and pliant, and again his mouth claimed hers. The first kiss had been urgent, born of longing; this one was more tender, filled with devotion. His tongue slipped inside to explore the moist sweetness of her mouth. Mona accepted its probing, savoring its flavor. When he dragged his mouth from hers, she asked with a small smile, "What have you been drinking?''

"Scotch. I had one before I left the apartment.''

She slipped free of his arms and walked to the desk, lifting the two glasses of champagne and extending one to him. "Will you share this with me?''

He took the glass and raised it to her. "Anything. I'll share anything with you, my love.''

She hoped he meant it. She hoped he meant he would share more disappointment with her, another setback. But Mona didn't want to talk about it just yet. She wanted to feast her eyes on him, drink champagne with him, kiss him and feel his hands on her again. She smiled at him over the rim of her wineglass. "In celebration,'' she said, and took a sip of the champagne.

His eyes widened. "Celebration? Mona. . . .''

Unfortunate choice of words, she now realized. She had raised his hopes. Quickly she said, "In celebration of our being together for a little while tonight. In celebration of . . . of my birthday next week.''

The hopeful expression vanished. "You have a birthday next week? The twenty-first one! I had no idea when your birthday was.''

"Next Thursday."

"Dammit, Mona, there's too much I don't know about you, and I'll never learn if we have to keep playing this stupid game of wait-and-see!"

She couldn't let him begin the evening angry. She set down her glass, took him by the hand and led him to one of the love seats. He followed her lead, watching her very carefully as she sat down. He placed his empty glass on the mantel, shrugged out of his sport coat and threw it onto the love seat opposite; then he sank beside her on the cushions. Mona slid into the warm comfort of his arms, and they clung together for wordless moments, content simply to bask in the pleasure they obtained from each other's nearness. Mona pressed her lips to his neck and tasted the salty musky flavor of his skin. Her nostrils flared at the remembered fragrance of him. It had been too long, much too long!

As if reading her thoughts Keith began nuzzling her neck, nipping and kissing. "Rose-scented skin," he said huskily. "It's been too long since I've smelled it."

Slowly his hands began practicing that familiar exquisite torture, fondling and caressing, rubbing and petting until Mona reeled from the intoxicating pleasure he brought her. Her breasts swelled to fill his hands. His seductiveness, his sensual power would never cease to amaze her. When Keith touched her, her body seemed to lose all its bones. With trembling fingers she fumbled with the buttons of his shirt, freeing them from their confining holes, and she pushed back the garment. Her hands roamed over his hard chest, fingers curling through the dark chest hairs. She heard him gasp, and his kiss deepened. His hands left her breasts. One slid around her waist, and the other cupped her small round bottom. Gently she was being lifted, and together they slipped off the love seat and onto the thick rug.

The furlike pile brushed against Mona's back; the hem of her dress inched up her thighs. She felt Keith's hand sliding up, hot against her stockinged leg. She moaned and struggled to come to her senses. "Oh, my God, Keith! What are we doing, tumbling on the floor like this? This is madness!"

His mouth was blazing a fiery trail down her throat to settle on the swell of her breasts. One leg was slung across her, imprisoning her and making her only too aware of his own arousal. "I told you," he muttered thickly against her skin, "love *is* madness."

"Keith, we can't! Don't you realize where we are?"

He raised his head, and his eyes were wild with desire. "Then let's get out of here! We can leave in your car. That detective will still be milling around out front wondering where the hell I am. We can go somewhere. . .to my apartment, to a motel—"

"Oh. . . ." Mona bit her lip to still her trembling chin. "You. . .you said that wasn't the sort of thing you wanted for us."

"It isn't," he hissed. "But I want *something* for us. I'll take anything I can get."

"Keith, I want to talk to you—"

"I told you I don't want to talk. I want to take you to bed. I want to make love to you. That's what I want. . .not talk!"

"And I can't very well talk to you if you're wound around me like this."

In answer to that, he tightened his hold on her and

he pressed himself against her even more insistently. "Does this bother you, Mona? Does it disturb you to know how much I need you?"

"Oh, God!" she groaned. "Of course it bothers me! That's why I want you to get off me so I can talk to you."

He expelled his breath slowly. "If I listen to what you have to say, will you go somewhere with me afterward?"

"I . . . we'll see, darling," was all she could think of to say, fearing he might not want her to go somewhere with him after he had heard her story.

Gradually his body relaxed. He rolled off her and sat up, resting his back against the love seat. "Okay, Mona, talk away. But it seems that every time you want to 'talk' to me, all I get is a catalog of problems."

Mona struggled to a sitting position, close to him and facing him. She curled her legs beneath her, then took one of his hands and began absently stroking it. If ever in her life she was going to be capable of eloquence, she prayed it would be right now.

"Keith, I have an aunt," she began. "An aunt whom I had never met until this past summer. And yesterday she told me. . . ."

Slowly and deliberately Mona recounted the tale she had heard from Beth the day before. During the beginning of the story, when she told him of the impulse that had prompted her to seek out her unknown aunt, he listened with polite interest. But when she got to the crux of the matter, she saw the light go out of his eyes and was aware that the hand she was holding was no longer responding to her caress. When she finished speaking, Keith didn't move a muscle and didn't speak for a long time. The quiet in the little room was so absolute that Mona could clearly hear the tick-ticking of the antique clock on the mantel. She sighed from weariness and waited for him to speak.

When he did, his voice carried no anger, but it carried no gentle understanding, either. His tone was flat and monotonous, and that alarmed Mona more than anger would have. "So," he said, "am I to understand that you're asking for another delay?"

"Y-yes."

He placed his hands on her shoulders, gripping, and pulled her face closer to his. "Are you honestly telling me that you and I can't get married because your father and your aunt were caught fooling around twenty-five years ago?"

"Keith, it's more complicated than that, and you know it! What you refer to as 'fooling around' has kept two sisters apart for two and a half decades!"

"I don't believe it! I honest to God don't believe it! I'm beginning to think you're afraid of marriage. That's why you keep coming up with these ridiculous stories—"

"That's preposterous!" Mona cried. "It's terribly unfair and terribly unlike you."

"Fair? What's fair about any of this, Mona? Is it fair to make me stay away from you?"

Mona decided to try a different approach. "All right, then *you* tell me what to do. I'll do whatever you say. You've heard the story, you know my family, you know all the circumstances. If you think it would be all right for us to get married now, then we'll do it. You tell me, Keith."

His eyes were as cold as granite. "That, my love, is what is known as passing the buck."

Mona removed his hands from her shoulders and held them tightly. "No, no. But you always seem so sure I'm handling things badly, so how about coming up with a little advice? I feel as though it's me against the rest of my family, and I could use a little moral support, but all you ever do is tell me to resolve it quickly. How about telling how I'm to do it? I'm open to all suggestions. God, am I! I'm tired of worrying about this alone."

At this, she thought his expression softened somewhat. His eyes became less remote and his body less rigid. Encouraged, she continued earnestly, "Darling, I don't see any point in telling my father about us, not now, not while Claire is still carrying a torch for you. What can he do? He can't give us his blessing without incurring mom's wrath. Her sympathies are all with Claire. Now I wish I hadn't even told mom. All I've done is open some old wounds—not meaning to, Lord knows, but I've done it just the same. And I sure don't like messing around with twenty-five-year-old marriages. They seem to be an endangered species."

She paused to see if he had any response, but he simply stared at her without speaking. His quiet manner and silence were disturbing, yet Mona sensed she was beginning to get through to him. She released one of his hands, and her fingers crawled up inside his unbuttoned shirt to rub sensitively while she spoke to him in her softest voice. "You've told me to reassess my priorities, to decide where my loyalties lie, but, Keith, I don't think it's that simple. For a complete life, I think I need marriage to you *and* the love and support of my family, and with a little time and patience I'm convinced I can have both. I'm not thinking only of myself, darling. I'm thinking of you, too. I want my parents to welcome you with open arms, to make you one of the family."

"Oh, Mona...they would come around in time," Keith said in a last-ditch stand.

She looked at him solemnly. "My mother hasn't spoken to her sister in twenty-five years. Does that sound like a woman who comes around in time?"

For what seemed forever he did not move, and Mona waited with suspended breath and pleading eyes. Then his breath came out in a long sigh of resignation, and she knew he understood and sympathized. He didn't like it, he was disappointed, but he saw her side of it. She sagged with relief.

Slowly Keith gathered her into his arms and pulled her forward to sit on his lap. One of Mona's arms stole around his broad back, and she kissed the top of his head, then his temple. Turning his head, Keith raised his eyes to her. She looked down at his somber thoughtful face with gratitude and shining emotion, then bent her head and placed her mouth on his. He responded warmly, thoroughly, but without passion. Mona lifted her head. "Thank you, darling," she said quietly.

"You're a witch!" Keith muttered. "A sorceress! I swear I think you have the power to hypnotize me. I came over here tonight filled with determination. We were going to set the wedding date and spend tonight together. Instead, I've let you worm your way into my sympathies and have agreed to another delay. Why don't you just put a ring through my nose or lead me around on a leash?" His eyes flashed, and a hint of warning crept into his voice. "But I won't wait forever, Mona."

"It won't be forever, Keith."

"Love is a living growing thing, and every living growing thing needs nourishment. I want the solace of a warm wife in my arms at night. I want to start a family. I don't want an affair. I don't want sex without the commitment of marriage. Maybe I'm old-fashioned. Maybe. . .maybe I'm just getting old."

Mona didn't know what to say to him. The weariness in his voice was something new and distressing. He had been surprisingly acquiescent, and she had been relieved, but perhaps she shouldn't have been. He did sound older, resigned—like a man giving up. She laced her fingers through his thick black hair and drew his head to her breast.

"Old!" she scoffed gently. "You'll never be old."

"I feel about sixty right now."

Desperately searching for a way to draw him out of his pensive mood, Mona said, "Keith, my father may be foolish about his family, but he's no fool. He's not going to continue paying that detective for nothing. We can be together. . . ."

"I told you, I don't want an affair. I can't think of one single affair I've ever known of that ended happily. You would hate it."

"I wouldn't hate anything that enabled us to be together," she said decisively. "And I'll go with you now if you want."

His body tensed again, and she heard him draw in a ragged breath. "No, Mona," he said quietly.

She frowned and stared at him. "No?"

"No, not tonight."

"You. . .don't want me?"

"Of course I want you!" Keith said furiously.

"I'm afraid I'll always want you. But I want you the right way."

Mona felt her face grow hot. "You didn't seem to mind having me before. As I recall—"

"That was different." His voice was harsh and brusque. "I expected us to be married right away. And tonight...tonight if I could see the light at the end of the tunnel I would take you somewhere and make love to you until dawn. But from what I can see, we seem to be back to square one."

With this he abruptly lifted her off his lap and stood up, leaving Mona to kneel on the floor and stare up at him in disbelief. He buttoned his shirt and jerked up his jacket, pushing his arms into the sleeves and shrugging the coat around his shoulders. His dark gaze bore down on her upturned face. "Whether or not you believe this, Mona, I do recognize that you have a problem and I sympathize with you. But don't wait too long. Don't wait until it's too late for us. I'm lonely."

A kind of panic washed over Mona at the sound of those words. She jumped to her feet and reached for him, only to have him grab her arms and hold them firmly at her sides. "No more touching tonight, my love. Making love to you tonight would only make our situation seem more frustrating. And please do me a favor—no more phone calls, no more meetings, not until this thing is resolved. Seeing you, hearing you—it just takes too damned much out of me. I can't take it anymore."

What strange creatures men were, Mona thought. Seeing him if even for a moment, hearing his voice if only over the telephone were comforting moments to her. Apparently it didn't work the same for him.

Eyes wide, mouth slightly agape, Mona could only stand mutely and watch as he turned his back on her and walked to the door. She fought back a powerful urge to cry out to him, to beg him to stay. Even if he complied, it would accomplish nothing. She stifled the words and blinked back tears.

At the door Keith paused and turned to her. He looked tired, so tired, but there was an odd twist to his mouth that suggested he was trying to smile and was simply not doing a very good job of it. "Mona, tell me something," he said. "Do you have any more relatives?"

In spite of herself Mona uttered a rueful laugh. "No, darling. No more."

"Thank God!" he muttered. Then he raised an index finger and shook it toward her. "It might be a good thing for you to remember something, Mona; your father turned to your aunt all those years ago because your mother was neglecting him. Think about it." Then he opened the door and was gone.

A large lump lodged in Mona's throat. She sank to the love seat, heartsick and forlorn and left with the frightening feeling that something very precious was in danger of slipping through her fingers. Keith couldn't have left her with a more torturous parting shot, and a part of her resented that. A light kiss, a reassuring hug, a few sympathetic words—that would have been more like Keith, not that monstrous remark about being neglected.

Edgy, nervous and sick with dread, Mona paced the little office. Her mind was such a confused tangle, and no amount of effort would clear it. She couldn't lose Keith, she couldn't! But she was putting his patience to the acid test.

Damn Claire, she thought irrationally, all the while admitting that so much of her dilemma had been of her own making. Mona knew her only hope lay with Claire. If her sister found a new interest—meaning a man, since men were all that ever interested Claire—then she could let her romance with Keith become common knowledge. True, they might have to go through a charade of a brief courtship, as though they were only now discovering each other, but that could be of short duration. She and Keith could at least see each other, could be together.

Yes, that was the only solution. Claire had to have a new love interest. Until she did, there was nothing Mona could do. An empty feeling of impotence settled on her. That was the worst of it—there was nothing she could do.

Mona heard a light tapping on the office door. She glanced at the clock on the mantel, startled to see how much time had elapsed. Stephanie, no doubt, wanted to use her office. Smoothing her hair with trembling fingers, Mona blinked back tears and struggled for control. "Come in," she said in a small voice.

The door opened, but it was not Stephanie who entered. It was Alan, and he was smiling broadly. "So this is where you've been. I've been looking all over...." His smile faded when he saw his friend's obvious distress. "Mona? What's wrong?"

Mona opened her mouth, but nothing came out. Words wouldn't form. She knew she must look terrible, absolutely miserable, but she didn't seem to be able to do anything about that, either. She simply shook her head and let it go at that.

Alan crossed the room and came to sit beside her.

Grave concern creased his features. Mona looked at him and thought what an amazingly open face he had, completely free of guile. Most people thought him a first-class dispenser of blarney, but Mona had come to think of him as the genuine article. Whatever he was, he was nice to have as a friend.

"Mona, you look as though someone just died. What's wrong?"

She lifted her shoulders and let them fall. "Nothing, Alan. At least nothing you can help me with."

"You might try spilling it. Sometimes it helps."

"Oh, I've spilled it! How I've spilled it! It didn't help. If anything, I only feel more wretched."

"A man?"

"What else?"

"The same guy you were pining over at the club that night?"

Mona smiled ruefully. "Yes. The same one."

"Doesn't he love you back?"

"Oh, he loves me all right."

Alan frowned. "Then I don't see that you have a problem."

"There's a problem," she assured him.

Alan nodded sagely, sure he understood. "Ah. Married, huh?"

"Oh, no!" Mona gasped. "No, Alan, I would never get involved with a married man. It's nothing like that."

Alan stared at her seriously. "Then I really am confused. If he loves you and you love him and neither of you is married, I don't see the problem. It's not religion...or the fact that you're first cousins or something like that, is it?"

"No, no. Nothing like that. It's...it's just

so...crazy and mixed-up that I...." Mona sat back, rested her head on the back of the love seat and, surprisingly, heard herself begin to relate the story again. Only this time the telling took forever. She went back to Keith and Claire, to herself and Keith and River View, ending with Beth's startling revelation. When she finished speaking, she turned to gauge Alan's reaction. He was pulling on his chin thoughtfully, sorting it out in his mind. Mona did not interrupt his thoughts. It was enough that he, like Beth, had listened with sympathy and interest. She supposed that was all that could be expected from any good friend—sympathy and interest.

"Well," Alan said at last, "I agree you have a problem."

"Thanks," she said dryly.

"All the time you were talking I was waiting for you to get to the part where I could come up with a solution for you. You never did."

"That's because there is no solution."

"You know, Mona, when we were kids I envied you that family of yours. Almost everyone we knew were just poor little rich kids whose parents shunted them off to one private school after another, left them for the servants to raise and that kind of thing. But not you and Claire. Ben and Kitty were always there, tending the home fires, worrying about your schoolwork, checking up on your boyfriends."

"You're not making me feel a bit better, Alan," Mona said sadly.

"I know, I know. And I know a family can be a stumbling block as well as a comfort. But I never had that family togetherness. Hell, I'd go months on end without so much as seeing my father. I can still remember going to his funeral and trying to cry, but I couldn't because I didn't even know him. And after his death mother started the marriage-go-round. Oh, she and I get along fine, but that's because we stay out of each other's way.''

Mona looked at her friend then with new interest. So that was the reason for the devil-may-care exterior, that frantic pursuit of female companionship. Alan was lonely! *And Keith's lonely. I'm lonely. The world's full of lonely people.*

Alan continued. ''I think. . . I think if I had a family like yours, I'd do whatever was necessary to keep things on an even keel. I admire your making personal sacrifices for them.''

Mona squeezed her eyes tightly shut, and then the tears did start to fall. Choking back sobs she got to her feet, then bent and retrieved her stole from the floor. ''Thanks for listening, Alan, and thanks for being a friend. As I said, there's no solution.'' She wrapped the stole around her shoulders in an attempt to warm the chill that had crept into her veins. ''My only hope is that some dashing Lochinvar will ride off into the sunset with Claire, making her forget all about Keith Garrett.''

Alan watched intently as she fished in her bag for a tissue, then dabbed it around her eyes and nose. She tried to force a small smile. ''Is my mascara running?''

''Not a bit.''

''Well, what do you know? It really is waterproof!'' She stuffed the tissue back in her bag. ''I'm going home now, Alan. I know tonight is going to be the beginning of a wonderful career for you, and I couldn't. . . be h-happier.'' She left the room before the torrent could start.

Outside in the workroom she met Stephanie. The gallery owner's face was flushed with excitement. "What a night!" she cried delightedly.

"Steph, would you mind terribly if I left now? I'm really not feeling well."

"Of course I don't mind. You've been a big help, Mona. Oh, by the way, I saw that divine young man of yours. Take my advice and don't let him get away. Somehow I just know he's the kind of man who would never give his wife a Crock-Pot for her birthday."

Mona burst into tears and fled the building.

Worriedly, Stephanie watched Mona's hasty departure. Then she ventured into her office in search of Alan. She found him seated on one of the love seats, head in hands. Stephanie momentarily wondered if Alan were responsible for Mona's anguish, then dismissed the thought as highly unlikely. If there was one thing she had learned during her association with these two young people it was that Mona Lowery and Alan Palmer were friends, real friends.

"Alan," Stephanie said, and he looked up.

"Yes, Steph, what is it?"

"There's a gentleman out front who is very interested in *El Capitan at Sunset*—so interested, in fact, that we're at the negotiating stage. I wondered if you wanted to sit in on it."

Alan smiled. "Steph, do you mind if I leave all that up to you? If the gentleman buys, call me and I'll shake his hand."

"Whatever you say, Alan. And Jeffrey Gallagher, the columnist, is asking for you. It seems Mona spoke to him earlier about you. She certainly looks after your best interests."

"Yeah. Oh, Steph, do you mind if I use your telephone?"

"Of course not. Help yourself. I'll close the door."

When Stephanie had gone, Alan got to his feet and crossed the room to the telephone on the desk. A foolish thought had occurred to him. It was absurd—and grossly conceited in the bargain—but worth a try.

Okay, hotshot, he thought. *You're supposed to be so damned irresistible to women. Let's put it to the test. You just might be able to do Mona a favor... and you sure owe her one.*

His hand reached for the instrument, and he dialed a familiar number. There were three rings and a click, and a voice said, "Lowery residence."

"Ah, Lettie, my love! This is Alan Palmer."

"Oh, Alan, how are you?" Lettie purred.

"Great, just great. Is Claire home by any chance?"

"Yes, I think so. Just a minute, Alan."

There was a rather lengthy wait before the lovely feminine voice came on the line. "Hello."

"Claire, this is Alan Palmer."

"Alan? My goodness, what a nice surprise. How are you?"

"I'm fine. Listen, I was just thinking that football season is well under way, and I haven't graced our box at Texas Stadium yet. How does this sound? The Cowboys and the Eagles, kickoff at three on Sunday. And I'm warning you, I don't like to take no for an answer...."

CHAPTER FOURTEEN

IT WAS THURSDAY AFTERNOON, shortly before one
o'clock. Mona crossed the parking lot to her car,
threw her books into the back seat and slid behind
the wheel. Within moments she was maneuvering
through the madness of Dallas traffic, her mind on a
hundred different things.

The past week had been a wet one—nothing pro-
tracted enough to cause a repeat of the flooding, just
frequent spates that kept area lakes and rivers flowing swift and deep. The first faint tinge of autumn
freshened the air, and Mona's heart ached to be at
River View, where a day like this one could be an experience!

It was her twenty-first birthday! One of life's
milestones. She would have thought today would
somehow be different, but it wasn't. Oh, there had
been the customary hoopla at the breakfast table that
morning, with cards from everyone, even one from
Alan, who, Mona now realized, had remembered her
birthday every year since she was six. And there had
been the ridiculously expensive gifts: a gold watch
from her father, a Bill Blass dress from her mother
and an opal pendant from Claire. All very nice and
thoughtful, of course, but....

But nothing from Keith—not a phone call, not a
card, nothing. And it hurt. Perhaps he had simply

forgotten. It crossed her mind that she had no idea whether or not he was a man who remembered birthdays and anniversaries, that she had no idea when his birthday was, and his words of a week ago came back to her: "Dammit, Mona, there's too much I don't know about you, and I'll never learn if we have to keep playing this stupid game of wait-and-see!"

One entire week without hearing the sound of his voice! Once or twice she had considered ignoring his request and telephoning him anyway, but then she had thought better of it. It would do no good and would only serve to remind Keith of their separation. Her greatest hope was that he was staying so busy with business that he hadn't noticed the passage of time.

Mona couldn't imagine why she raised her eyes when she did, why her gaze fell on the gigantic old red-brick building that she had seen thousands of times in her life. It stood squat and ugly among all the steel and concrete and glass, the four-foot-high letters on its side now badly in need of paint. Lowery Industries. She had forgotten how long it had been since she been in that building. There had been a time in her life when visiting her father in his office had been a really grand event. She wondered if Ben had had lunch yet. On an impulse she swung off the expressway at the next exit.

Her father greeted her with such delighted surprise that Mona berated herself for not having done this more often. "How's the birthday girl?" Ben cried, throwing his arms around her. "This is by far the brightest spot in my entire day!"

"I wondered if you had eaten lunch yet, dad. Is that little barbecue place still around the corner?"

"No and yes. No, I haven't had lunch, and yes, Pete's is still there, still doing a land-office business. But it's well after one now; the place will be almost empty. Darn, Mona! I'm glad you thought of this. I haven't had one of Pete's sandwiches in ages. And suddenly I'm starving!"

The dark little café known as Pete's was practically deserted. Three men in khaki work clothes sat at a table by the window, but otherwise there was no one around except the woman working behind the counter. She quickly came to take their order, disappeared into the kitchen and within moments returned with two gigantic sandwiches composed of homemade buns filled to overflowing with thick slabs of hickory-smoked beef brisket. The aroma was irresistible, and both Mona and her father devoured the sandwiches down to the last bite.

"Oh, that was so good!" Mona exclaimed.

"Wasn't it, though!" Ben agreed heartily, settling back in his chair. "And to think I was going to have a cup of yogurt for lunch."

For the first time Mona noticed the slight thickening around his middle. And he had always been so slim and trim and hard. He was a long way from fat, but the slight bulge over his belt surprised her. She reached across the table to pat it affectionately.

Ben grinned a bit sheepishly. "Yeah, I know. Once past forty it sure comes on easy and goes off hard. But I'll have to start working on it. Too much high living and good food over the summer. You should have come to Palm Springs with us, Mona. We had a great time."

"So did I," she said without thinking.

"Oh? What *did* you do all summer?"

Mona inhaled deeply. What she wouldn't have given to tell him exactly what she had done all summer. What a relief it would have been just to spit it all out. But first Kitty's warning popped into her head, then Beth's. Mona didn't want to upset her father. "Oh. . . nothing special," she said. "I. . . I just had a good time. School and all, you know."

Ben smiled. "I can't believe that in a few short months you're going to be graduating from college. And that reminds me of something I've been meaning to talk to you about. You know that little shop you've had your eye on?"

"Of course."

"Well, it's no longer for sale."

Disappointment swelled in Mona. "Oh, no!"

"It's for lease. Property owners are getting darned smart about holding onto real estate. So I started looking around and came upon something else. Do you remember. . . ?"

Ben mentioned an old residential section of the city, one that had once been a fashionable middle-class neighborhood but had fallen into disrepair over the years. "Yes," Mona said. "I remember it."

"Well, Mona, I wish you could see it now. People have started moving in and renovating those old houses and turning them into specialty restaurants and antique shops and. . . what are those places called that carry all that feminine frippery?"

"Boutiques."

"Boutiques." He fumbled in his shirt pocket for something. "There aren't many of those houses left, but this one is." He handed Mona a snapshot of a modest frame house that was badly in need of paint and general repair. "I know it doesn't look like much, but none of the others did, either, and you should see them now. It just seems to make good sense to own instead of lease. In this day and age I don't see how you can go wrong owning real estate, any kind of real estate.''

Mona studied the snapshot. Ben was right. The house didn't look like much, but she had a good imagination and she could see the possibilities.

"Gray," she mused. "I'm thinking it should be painted gray...with white shutters...and maybe a bright yellow front door. I might even call the place The Yellow Door!"

"No!" Ben protested. "No cutesy names. I want there to be a sign out front that says: Mona Lowery, Interiors. How does that sound?"

"Great!" Mona smiled at him fondly, but she was thinking, Mona L. Garrett, Interiors. "Oh, dad, this is fantastic! I don't know how to thank you. You're too good to all of us."

"Nonsense. It's the least I can do for this family's only college graduate. That's always been a dream of mine, to have a college graduate in the family, and Claire wasn't in the least interested. She's like her mother. College was out of the question for me, but Kitty could have gone. She and her sister could have had the finest education. Why they elected not to go is beyond me." Ben paused thoughtfully. "Oh, I suppose it was only natural that Beth wouldn't want to go; she was a headstrong little cuss. But Kitty should have gone."

Mona stared at him with astonished eyes. He had said Beth's name! Just like that! Without the slightest trace of qualm or guilt or wistfulness. Kitty and Beth had both led her to believe the mention of that name would be a trauma for Ben.

"You never met your aunt, did you, Mona?" Ben continued casually. "That's a real shame. Families shouldn't drift apart. I tried to keep up with her, but she faded from sight years ago."

Months later Mona would try to recall just what impelled her to say what followed. The words simply seemed to tumble out of their own volition. "Beth's in town, dad."

Ben stared at her blankly, totally without comprehension. "What, Mona? What did you say?"

She swallowed hard. "Aunt Beth...she's in town. She lives here."

Her father looked at her incredulously. "In Dallas? But, Mona, how did you find out? Come to think of it, how did you even know who she was?"

"A mutual friend happened to mention seeing her. It was someone who knew mom and Beth in school. I guess my curiosity got the best of me. I looked her up. We have lunch together every Wednesday."

The moment the words were out, Mona knew she had done the right thing. She sensed that this one impulsive act on her part might be the beginning of the end of her problems. Ben wasn't shocked or aghast or repentant or any of the things Mona had imagined he might be. If the mention of Beth's name had aroused anything, it was curiosity and interest.

"Well, I'll be.... How is she?" Ben asked.

"Fine."

"And you say the two of you get together every week? Do you like her?"

"Yes, very much."

Ben shook his head and chuckled. "I must say this has been something of a bombshell. I can't believe that Beth's actually here in Dallas. But...why on earth hasn't she got in touch with us?"

Puzzled, Mona said, "Surely you know the answer to that one, dad. It's mom, of course."

"Your mother?"

"Yes. Beth knows mom doesn't want to see her again."

Ben looked at her in disbelief, then exploded. "Oh, hell and damnation!" he sputtered, forgetting that he never cursed in front of his daughters. "You can't be serious!"

"I'm very serious, dad. Beth wouldn't come near our house, not in a million years. And frankly, she warned me not to tell either of you she's here. Naturally I haven't told mom, and to tell you the truth I don't know why I told you."

Ben raised his eyes to the ceiling. "Women!" Then apparently something occurred to him, for he became serious and his voice was wary. "Mona...just how much do you know, anyway?"

Mona glanced down at her hands. Absently she began drawing circles on the table with her fingernail. "Everything," she told him quietly. "All about you and Beth...and mom. Beth told me the whole story."

Ben studied his younger daughter for a moment, stunned to be seeing her as a mature young woman. Then he managed a small smile, something of a contrite smile, Mona thought. "Well, Mona, as hard as it is for me to believe, you're no longer a child. I'm sure by now you've learned something of human foibles and frailties. None of us is perfect. I committed an indiscretion. I'm not proud of it, but I'd like you to remember that it was before I was married... and I apologized to your mother profusely, then proceeded to give her twenty-five faithful years. Poor

Beth has endured a persecution that can only be described as vicious and relentless. I think we've both done our penance, and I'll be damned if I'm going to spend my life wallowing in self-reproach.''

"Dad, you don't have to explain anything to me.''

"I know that. You're a sensible young woman, and you've apparently known about this some time, yet I've noticed no discernible deterioration in our relationship. You know, Mona, I've always hated the fact that those two sisters have been estranged all these years, but I honestly thought it was Beth who had chosen to remain aloof. My God, I certainly thought Kitty had forgotten it long ago.''

"Believe me, mom has not forgotten, and Beth knows it.''

Ben frowned, then he shot his daughter a concerned look as something else came to mind. "Mona, what on earth got into Beth? Why would she tell you that story in the first place?''

It was so easy to talk to him. Mona wondered why she hadn't done it in the first place. Because of Kitty and Beth, of course. They had led her to believe Ben was still upset over those old events, but he had it all in the right perspective—a youthful indiscretion, long forgotten. "Because of something I told her,'' Mona said, taking a deep breath. "Because I'm in love with Keith Garrett and he's in love with me and we want to get married.''

At first Ben simply looked startled. Then he rubbed his hand across his mouth and an amused flicker danced in his eyes. "I must say, Mona, you're just chock-full of surprises today. When did all this happen?''

"In the summer, while all of you were in Palm

Springs.'' The story tumbled out once more, in a rush, and Mona concluded it with, ''When I told mom, I thought she was going to faint. She said I must never, ever tell you about it, not a word. Naturally I thought it was all because of Claire, but after I had that talk with Beth I realized it was because mom doesn't want you to start remembering all those old grievances.''

''Dammit to hell!'' Ben exclaimed in the most potent display of swearing Mona had ever heard from him. ''What does a man have to do to prove his devotion? I've given your mother everything it was in my power to give, and I've done it willingly, gladly, because I love her! Kitty's problem is that she overdramatizes everything.''

''She and Claire are so much alike,'' Mona said. ''I thought surely Claire would be over Keith by now, but I'm afraid if she learns about us she'll go into another decline and mom will be furious. I'm at my wit's end. Keith was so good and patient about this at first, but the last time I talked to him he just sounded tired. I would have preferred blind rage to that calm resignation. I'm afraid it's only a matter of time before he...finds someone else.'' Merely saying those words made Mona's heart ache with emptiness.

''Well then, *go* to him!'' Ben sputtered.

Mona's eyes widened. ''You can't mean that! Not with mom feeling the way she does. Not with Claire dragging around like a lost puppy.''

''Of course you can,'' Ben insisted. ''Mona, it's a wonderful thing to consider others. I'm glad you're that way. But you have to think of yourself, too, dear—and of Keith. I always liked that young man, and I'll bet he's had it up to here with this family.''

"I'm afraid so," Mona admitted.

"Then go to him. I'll take care of your mother and sister. And there's something else I'm going to take care of, Mona. If it's the last thing I do, I'm going to get Kitty and Beth back together."

Mona reached across the table to squeeze his hand. "It won't be difficult with Beth. She wants to see mom again, I know she does. Oh, dad...do you really mean it? May I go to Keith? Mom said you would never forgive me...."

Ben's eyes narrowed. "I can see it's time your mother and I sat down and had a heart-to-heart talk. It's easy to forget to do that when you've been married a number of years. You'd do well to remember that."

"Oh, you've given me the best birthday present I could have had!" Tears glistened in her eyes. A lone one splashed out and ran down her cheek.

"Good Lord, don't cry!" Ben moaned. "I never could stand it when one of my girls cried. I guess that's what had me so upset about Claire. She's shed buckets, but I suspect it was more over being a loser than it was over losing Keith himself. There'll no doubt be dozens of young men before Claire settles down, if indeed she ever does. But you, Mona... you're different. I think I know the guilt you must have suffered. You're the guilt-suffering type. But, dear, if you love Keith you should be with him. It should be the most compelling force in your life. You don't want to while away your dotage remembering 'the saddest words of tongue and pen,' do you?"

"'What might have been...'" she finished. "Dear God, no!" She was instantly on her feet, determined and anxious. "You're right, dad. I'm go-

ing home to call Keith, and if he asks me to come to
him, I'm going to. I hope I'm not rushing you, but
I'll take you back to the office now, if that's all
right."

Ben had risen also. "No, Mona, you just run
along. I think I'll walk back to work." He patted his
full stomach. "It'll do me good. And don't worry
about anything, especially not about your mother
and sister. What those two don't know about life
would fill volumes."

He grinned happily then, and Mona threw her
arms around his waist to hug him ferociously.

MONA LEAPED up the front steps of the house, pushed
open the front door, and the first sight that greeted
her was a vase of long-stemmed red roses displayed
on the foyer table. Crossing to it, she saw her name
scrawled on the small envelope that was tucked into
the flowers. Keith's handwriting. She would know it
anywhere. She opened the envelope and read the
message on the card: "To the woman with rose-
scented skin." That, also, was in Keith's handwriting, meaning he had not simply telephoned in his
order. He had gone to the florist and signed the card
personally. He hadn't forgotten!

Mona bolted up the stairs to her bedroom, went to
the telephone and dialed the number of Garrett Instruments. Within seconds Keith's secretary answered.

"No, Mr. Garrett is not in," the cool efficient
voice said. "He won't be back in the office until the
middle of next week."

Quickly Mona searched her brain for the secretary's name; it came to her. "Mrs. Jacobs, this is

Mona Lowery. Could you please tell me where Keith is? It's very important.''

There was a slight pause while, Mona assumed, the secretary gauged the familiarity of the name. Apparently satisfied, Mrs. Jacobs said, ''Miss Lowery, Mr. Garrett left the office some time ago, and I believe he said he was spending most of the week at his ranch. If it's that important I can give you the number there.''

''No, no, that's not necessary,'' Mona said. ''I have the number. Thank you.'' She hung up and stood indecisively with her hand on the instrument. Why had he gone on Thursday and why for a week? She wondered if there were some problems at River View. He might have asked her to meet him there, she thought petulantly. It was, after all, her birthday. But then she shook free of the pettishness. That detective might still be lurking around, and she had to remember that Keith wanted no more meetings until her family affairs were in order.

Well, as far as Mona was concerned, they were in as good order as they were apt to get. She *had* to go to him! She couldn't risk making the mistake her mother had made so many years ago. She had done all she could for the sake of family. Now she belonged to Keith.

Suddenly time seemed of the essence. Hastily she brushed her hair, freshened her makeup and took stock of herself in the mirror. She wouldn't win any beauty prizes, that was for sure. In fact, in jeans, boots and a long-sleeved Western-cut shirt she looked all of sixteen—young, fresh faced and healthy. Not precisely the image she wanted to project, but there simply wasn't time to do anything about that. She threw her small suitcase on the bed, opened it and began moving from bed to closet to dresser and back to bed, packing hurriedly.

It was then that she heard an unfamiliar sound. It was Claire, and she was humming! Humming an upbeat little tune. It had been so long since Mona had seen her sister in anything but the darkest of moods that the sound of that happy voice startled her. Come to think of it, she hadn't seen Claire at all for days. Curious, she left her packing and crossed the hall to peer into Claire's room.

Her sister was trying on clothes. The evidence was everywhere. Garments were lying all over the bed, shoes were scattered on the floor. The dress Claire was trying on was a stunning tomato-red creation that Mona hadn't seen before. She leaned in the doorway and watched until her sister spotted her.

"Oh, hi!" Claire chimed, twirling around as she inspected her reflection in a full-length mirror. Mona noticed that her eyes sparkled with a radiance that had been missing for a very long time.

"Hi. Heavy date?"

"Very heavy," Claire said emphatically, and smiled.

Mona's heart fluttered with hope. "Oh? What's the occasion?"

Claire fussed with the dress's bodice. "No occasion. Alan and I are just having dinner, then going dancing, and I'm trying to decide what to wear. What do you think of this little number?"

"Spiffy!" Mona said truthfully. "Alan?"

"Yes...Alan Palmer."

"That Alan?" Mona cried incredulously. "My word! When...when did all this happen?"

"He took me to the Cowboys game Sunday afternoon, and afterward we went to a country-music nightclub. I don't know when I've had a better time. He has one of those glass-enclosed, air-conditioned things at the stadium. If you have to watch football, that's not a bad way to watch it. Actually, we didn't do a whole lot of watching. Mostly we drank champagne, nibbled on goodies and reminisced. I had a ball!"

Mona couldn't have been more stunned. "Well, I'll be. I had no idea.... I'm...I'm so surprised, Claire. Alan Palmer, of all people!"

"Isn't that the truth!" Claire cried, and giggled happily. "The boy next door, yet! When I think of all I've been missing. Did you know he has his own plane, that he pilots it himself?"

"Yes...yes, I did."

"Oh, that's right. The two of you were always chummy, weren't you? I might have to get you to fill me in about him. Anyway, I don't know how this is going to sit with mama, but Alan wants the two of us to fly down to the Gulf this weekend because—"

Mona put up a hand to interrupt. "Don't tell me...because he knows this little place that serves great shrimp gumbo, right?"

"Right. And he has a condominium on Padre Island. I suppose mama will go into her best mid-Victorian routine over that, but good grief, I'm almost twenty-five! I know Alan has a terrible reputation, but he's not like that at all, Mona. I find him a complete gentleman."

"I know," Mona said quietly. Everything was slipping neatly into the cubbyholes of her mind: this was Alan's way of paying back what he imagined to be his debt to her. And it was working! Claire was happy again. She was interested and excited about a man again. And what a twosome they would make! A strikingly handsome couple with many interests in common. It had been a stroke of genius on Alan's part, and had he been there Mona thought she might have hugged him to death.

"Claire, do you really like Alan?"

Claire stopped fidgeting with the dress and turned to look at Mona. "Yes, I think I do. Strange isn't it? He's been right next door all these years, and I never noticed. I honestly thought he was nothing but a born-to-raise-hell playboy type, but he's really rather quiet and thoughtful. Perhaps he's one of those men who need some time before they start settling down. Did you know he's an artist? A real artist who sells his paintings?"

"Yes," Mona said simply.

Claire preened in front of the mirror. "He wants to paint my portrait," she announced grandly, and Mona forced herself to keep a bland expression.

So, she thought with some amusement, *it would appear I've scotched my one chance to have my own portrait painted.*

"I'll tell you one thing, Mona—Alan Palmer is the first man I've ever met who really knows how to live! He's mentioned taking me to the Mardi Gras and to the Indianapolis 500 and to the Kentucky Derby, the Super Bowl and—"

"Good heavens! Such plans!" Mona exclaimed.

Claire abruptly grew serious. "Mona, I'm dreading approaching mama with this, but. . . I'm thinking about getting an apartment of my own. I'm way too old to be still living at home."

"Alan's idea, I take it."

"Well. . .all right, I'll admit he was the first one who planted the idea in my head, but—"

"Never mind, Claire. I think it's a splendid idea. You'll like having a place of your own. I'd be happy to lend a hand with the decorating, if you'd like."

"Hey, that would be great!"

Mona could clearly feel the tenuous beginnings of a new kind of relationship with the sister who had seemed such a stranger to her for most of her life. She was warmly pleased and would have been even more so had it not been for the nagging guilt that persisted. She had planned to leave it up to her father to explain her absence from home, and she knew Ben would handle things admirably. But that was a coward's way. If she and Claire were ever to establish a warm relationship, they would have to learn to talk to each other.

Breathing in deeply, Mona said, "Claire. . .there's something I want to tell you."

Now Claire fixed her eyes on Mona, and she grew absolutely still. Her expression was speculative, expectant. "Oh?" she said. "What is it?"

Mona moved into the room and looked around for a place to sit. Finding only the stool at the dressing table, she sank down onto it and looked at Claire. She could hear the thundering of her own heartbeats. Nervously she said, "It's something I should have told you a long time ago. I hope. . .you'll try to understand—not only what happened but why it's taken me so long to tell you about it."

A strange sort of smile spread across Claire's face then. She clasped her hands behind her back. "Are you by chance finally going to tell me about you and Keith?"

Mona's eyes widened in total astonishment. For a moment she couldn't seem to find her voice, and even when the initial shock had passed she could only sit, numbed, and nod her head. A dozen questions came to mind, but one above all.

"Claire...h-how did you know?" she finally managed to ask.

"To tell you the truth, Mona, I didn't know until right now, the moment I saw the look on your face. But I've suspected for some time. I started putting two and two together and kept coming up with four. In all those weeks that the detective was following Keith, he didn't come into contact with even one woman outside the office—except you, that night at Becky's party. I didn't place too much stock in that at first, but then I did some serious thinking about it. I seemed to remember that whenever Keith came to the house, you disappeared. And you've been so withdrawn, which isn't like you at all.

"And the more I thought, the more I remembered. The weekend you supposedly spent with a friend from school was the weekend Keith spent at his ranch. And the very next night is when he told me there was someone else. Oh, I don't know...so many things. For one, the detective suspected Keith knew he was being followed. If so, who could have warned him? No one knew we had hired the man except the four of us, and I knew damned well neither mama nor daddy would have told Keith." Claire paused for dramatic emphasis, then said, "But last week put the frosting on the cake."

Mona frowned. "Last...last week?"

Claire nodded. "According to that detective, Keith had been living practically like a hermit, but he did go out one night last week. Guess where he went."

Mona rubbed her eyes. "To the showing at Stephanie's gallery," she said tiredly.

"Exactly! It was just too much of a coincidence. When I heard that, I told the detective his services were no longer needed."

For a moment it seemed to Mona that the room was spinning. "If you only knew how wretched I've felt, Claire."

"I can imagine. You're the type."

"It began as friendship, nothing more."

Claire shrugged. "Don't explain, Mona. I can imagine the whole thing. You kept him company during the summer, and one thing led to another, right? I can see how Keith would be attracted to you. The two of you are a lot alike. I was mad as hell when he told me there was another woman. No man had ever told me that before. Then when I began to have reason to suspect the other woman was my sister, I.... Well, I guess I wouldn't have cared so much if I hadn't been so damned jealous of you all my life."

Mona gasped. Surely Claire hadn't said what Mona thought she had said! "You?" she cried. "You...jealous of me?"

Claire glanced at her abjectly, almost humbly. "Not much of a sister, am I? Oh, I could tell you some pretty nasty things if I wanted to, which I don't. It was...it was just that you had your act so together. All those fantastic grades, all that ambition, while I had nothing but my looks, and I certainly couldn't take much credit for those. It's a good thing mama likes me as I am. I don't think I could have survived being compared to you otherwise."

Mona's hand went to her head. She experienced a

wild desire to laugh. "Oh, God! Claire, talk about ugly memories! I could keep you here for hours exorcising what Keith has called 'that demon.' Good Lord, what a couple of dummies we've been! What a criminal waste of time!"

"I guess I'll always remember Keith as the first one who rejected me," Claire said wistfully.

"Oh, Claire, don't! I have a feeling you and Alan have the beginnings of something wonderful and exciting. I can't imagine why I didn't think of getting the two of you together before this. You're perfect for each other!"

At this, Claire's eyes grew bright and she laughed lightly. "You know, I think you might be right. I don't know if anything permanent will come of all this, but in the meantime I intend having a wonderful time. Alan spends money as though they were going to stop printing the stuff tomorrow...and I've always adored that in a man."

"One thing is for sure," Mona predicted. "You're not going to have time to give Keith and me a thought." She jumped up, again aware of the time. "Well, I've got to be going. Have a wonderful time tonight."

"Oh, I will. I will."

"And Claire, let me give you a word of advice. About Padre Island, the apartment, everything...go to dad first." She winked and left the room.

CHAPTER FIFTEEN

MONA RACED ACROSS THE HALL, hastily finished packing, then scurried down the stairs. But halfway across the foyer she paused. She was overcome by the unmistakable feeling that she was running away, and that was ridiculous! She wasn't running away at all. She was going to Keith, and her father knew all about it.

But her mother didn't, and until she had spoken to Kitty, Mona knew she would never feel right about leaving the house. She wanted the slate wiped clean. She reminded herself that there was no sound reason for Kitty to object, not now that Claire's feelings were no threat to family harmony. Still, it was with an extraordinary sense of trepidation that Mona searched those rooms, looking for her mother. It seemed that nothing with Kitty Lowery ever came easily.

Kitty was seated on the leather sofa in the library, deeply engrossed in one of those mammoth "rape-and-take" sagas she swore she never read. When she heard Mona enter the room she glanced up, then quickly closed the book and placed it facedown on the coffee table.

"Hello, dear," she greeted her. "You were awfully late getting home from school today. Busy day?" Then she noticed the suitcase in her daughter's hand.

Mona had forgotten she was carrying it. Kitty frowned darkly. "Where are you going?"

"I'm going to Keith's ranch," Mona said with careful control.

A pinched grim look came to Kitty's face. "Now listen to me, Mona. I don't—"

"It's all right, mom. Claire knows about Keith and me, and she doesn't care. She has. . .other interests now."

Kitty's relief was evident. Once again she had been spared unpleasantness. "Well, thank goodness that's over! But I don't think I approve of your running off to spend—"

"Mom, please," Mona interrupted with extreme patience. "Keith and I are going to be married. If you should need to get in touch with me, there are three numbers listed under Keith's name in my address book next to my telephone. You'll recognize the ranch's number because it has a different area code."

"Well, I. . . ." Kitty hesitated, then shrugged, giving up. "You young people of today certainly don't operate the way we did in my time. Why, if my mother had thought for one minute—"

"I'll call you tomorrow," Mona promised, interrupting again, not wanting to be rude but not wanting to give Kitty time to dwell on it further. "I. . .I don't know what my plans will be."

Kitty looked away. Mona pivoted, wanting to leave quickly, but something held her firmly in place. The urge was strong, so strong to tell her mother about Beth. Why? She wasn't sure. Perhaps she felt it would be better if her mother heard about it first from her rather than from her father. Whatever the reason, the impulse was overtaking her. Turning again, Mona faced her mother.

"Mom...Beth's here...in Dallas."

It saddened and astonished Mona to see how ghastly her mother looked at that moment. All of the color drained out of Kitty's face; she was shocked. *I've gone too far,* Mona thought. *I had no right!* Appalled, she wished with all her heart she could have recalled those words.

But then, curiously, when Kitty recovered her composure, which she did almost instantly, it seemed to Mona that a mellowness had crept into her expression. "Beth?" Kitty whispered. "Beth is here?"

Mona nodded.

"But, Mona, I don't understand. How did...?"

"Last summer Stephanie Means happened to mention she had seen my Aunt Beth. I was intrigued, so I...I found her. Mom, Beth is the friend I have lunch with every Wednesday." To Mona it seemed that she was shedding life's burdens one by one, plucking them from her shoulders like petals from a daisy—and it felt good.

"How like you," Kitty mused. "You were always such a curious one." She glanced about helplessly. "Well, my goodness...I must say this is a surprise. How...how is she?"

"She's fine. Mom...she would like to see you." Mona wasn't naive enough to think her mother's stiff unyielding enmity could be swept aside in an instant, but she was encouraged by Kitty's reaction, by the absence of bitterness in her eyes and voice.

"I don't know, Mona," Kitty said quietly. "It's been a long time. There were circumstances—" She checked herself, and Mona saw no need to tell her mother that she knew what those circumstances were. Instead she set her suitcase at her feet, then walked to the desk, picked up a pen and began writing on a note pad. "I'm going to write down her name, address and phone number. If you decide you want to call her, I'm sure she'll be delighted."

She ripped the page off the pad and handed it to her mother, who stared at it as though spellbound. "Sinclair," Kitty said quietly. "Her name is Sinclair? Is her husband with her?"

Mona shook her head. "She's divorced—twice. I think she's badly in need of family. She hasn't had the greatest sort of life. Please call her, mom."

Kitty stared at the slip of paper a moment longer, then slipped it inside her book. "I'll think about it, Mona. That's the best I can promise."

"That's all I can ask." Impulsively, Mona leaned across the width of the coffee table and kissed her mother's smooth cheek. "And I'll call you tomorrow."

MONA REMEMBERED that her car's gas gauge was almost on empty, and the station the Lowerys had patronized for years was busier than she ever had seen it. She was forced to wait in a long line before filling her tank, then to negotiate the horror known as Central Expressway before she was, at long last, moving smoothly down the highway, heading for River View.

She thought it nothing short of a miracle that she reached the ranch road without an accident or a terse summons from the department of public safety. She was certain she had broken every traffic law on their books. She remembered nothing of the actual drive.

Her body felt strangely light and buoyant, whether from being relieved of emotional burdens or from excitement at the prospect of being with Keith again she didn't know. A combination of the two, she supposed.

River View's gate loomed into view. Mona drove through it and up the driveway's gentle rise toward the house. Keith's Mustang was parked in front, and behind it was a blue station wagon that was definitely not one of the ranch's vehicles. Someone was visiting Mamie, no doubt. Mona pulled alongside the Mustang, switched off the engine and got out, almost at a dead run.

That was when she spotted Mandy, saddled and tethered to the hitching post at the left side of the front porch. Mona's heart surged at the sight of her beloved animal. She ran to the mare, slipped her arms around her neck and nuzzled gently. She was rewarded by a welcoming neigh. "Hello, girl. Are you glad to see me? I'm sure glad to see you."

Mona rubbed at Mandy's coat, and her hands stilled. Then they moved under the saddle blanket. The mare felt warm and moist, suggesting she had been ridden recently. Mona smiled her approval. "Who's been riding you, girl? I'm glad someone takes the time to give you a workout. Can't have you getting soft and fat in your middle age. Maybe you and I can go for a ride later." She gave the mare one last affectionate pat before climbing the front steps. She knocked loudly on the door and stepped back to wait.

When no one answered her knock she tried again. Still no one came to the door. Mona glanced back at the Mustang and frowned. Obviously Keith was here.

He could have been in the barn or out riding the pastures, of course, but Mamie or Sam or someone should have been in the house. She knocked again, but still no one came.

She was considering opening the door and going on in when she heard music and laughter coming, she thought, from the rear of the house. She stood and listened for a moment. Yes, the sounds were definitely coming from either the patio or the pool. Mona leaped off the porch and walked around the side of the house, marching in the direction of all the racket.

It sounded as though some sort of party was in progress. Damn! Why hadn't she considered the possibility that Keith might not be alone? She should have called first. If he had company, a phone call would have given him the opportunity to get rid of them.

A latticework trellis covered with thick clematis vines swept around the patio, shielding Mona from view, and she stopped to take in the scene of merriment, wondering all the while what the occasion was. A dozen or so of the ranch hands were clustered around a man who was exuberantly plunking away on a banjo. Mamie and Sam were in the group. Everyone was clapping in time to the music, laughing and watching a couple engaged in a high-spirited dance.

Mona's stomach lurched as her gaze locked on the dancers. Keith and an exquisitely beautiful brunette were cavorting around like a couple of schoolchildren. They danced together like experts. The dance was some sort of folk number that required a great deal of twirling and kicking, and Keith and his partner executed the steps perfectly. Mona could tell this was not the first time they had danced together. When the music ended, both Keith and the brunette laughed merrily and threw their arms around each other.

"Oh, you're both so wonderful at that!" Mamie cried, and Mona pettishly thought that the house-keeper's obvious acceptance of the other woman bordered on the traitorous.

"One more time, Keith!" Jim Browder yelled. "I could watch the two of you dance all night long!"

"Then we might just do it!" Keith yelled back, grabbed the woman around the waist again and began twirling her around the patio as the banjo player struck up another tune.

Mona stood in a hypnotized state, despising the sight of them yet seemingly unable to tear her gaze away. Keith was dressed the way Mona liked best—tight-fitting jeans, checkered shirt open at the neck, those disreputable boots that he insisted on wearing even though he had a closet full of expensive ones. The woman, too, was wearing jeans, but they were the fancy designer type that Keith scoffed at. Her boots were "urban cowboy," her shirt silk. All dressed up for the occasion, Mona thought tartly, sensing that such attire was not the woman's cus-tomary mode of dress.

Burning tears welled in her eyes, and she com-pressed her lips in an attempt to hold them in check. Keith looked wonderfully happy, and seeing him that way made her ache with fear. There was no doubt about it—he was having a marvelous time. And she tried to remember the last time she herself had in-spired such happiness in that handsome angular face. Too long ago.

The second tune had ended, and Keith grabbed his partner's hand. "Now let's have a drink!"

A portable bar had been set up at the edge of the patio, just on the other side of the trellis, not far from the spot where Mona stood. Keith and the brunette moved toward it. Had the trellis not been there Mona could have reached out and touched them. The woman had a gay lilting laugh, and up close she was even lovelier than she had seemed from a distance. The sick feeling of dread churned in Mona's stomach alarmingly. She was actually feeling nauseated.

"Oh, Keith, I'm so glad I could come!" the brunette gushed.

"So am I," Keith said, placing ice cubes in two glasses. "It's been too long. Did you get a chance to take Mandy out?"

"Yes. We had a nice long ride. She's a wonderful mount. But you know, I've been so busy and excited since I got here that I forgot that other suitcase. It's still in the car."

Keith had mixed two drinks, and he handed one to the brunette. "I'll have one of the boys take it to my room," he said, and Mona's hand flew to her mouth.

Keith raised his glass. "Here's to what I hope will be a wonderful week for you."

The woman's eyes shone. "Oh, it will be, it will be!" And, arm in arm, the two of them rejoined the others on the patio.

Mona turned from the sight of them, stunned, strangled by bitter hurt. So this was why Keith would be out of the office until the middle of next week! The woman was staying a week. Sleeping in Keith's bed, riding Mona's mare, completely accepted by everyone, from the looks of things. Oh, that he could do this to her! She had loved him beyond good reason, had made love with him because she had believed he was totally committed to her.

Her mind was flooded with questions. How long had he known her? Where had she come from? Had she been to River View before? She and Keith were not newly acquainted, of that Mona was certain. Doubtless she was someone from the city, perhaps someone he had known before Claire, someone he had turned to again when his loneliness had become unendurable.

So she had done it after all! She had stalled him until he had had enough. She had put her family before him, not wanting to, not meaning to, but to Keith it would seem that way. She had finally driven him to find solace with another woman, and she couldn't even allow herself the luxury of being outraged. She was to blame for every bit of it.

Slowly she dragged her eyes up and back to the sight of Keith with his arms around the brunette. Both of them were laughing uproariously over something. Sadly Mona noticed that the woman was precisely the sort of dazzling beauty she had imagined Keith would be interested in back in the early days of their friendship—tall, beautiful, sophisticated. Far nearer his age than Mona was. No doubt she was successful in some career, modeling perhaps. She looked like a model. Never had Mona felt so hopelessly inadequate. Even in her anguished state, she had to admit that Keith and the woman made a striking couple.

Oh, God! What was she doing standing around like a simpleton? Someone could come along at any second. She had to get out of here, had to get away before someone discovered her presence. That would be the height of embarrassment, for both her and Keith.

Mona turned and fled, the tears now coming in a rush, blinding her. She rounded the corner of the house, heading for her car, when she again spotted Mandy, saddled and tethered, dancing sideways, growing restive. Mona paused in her flight, staring at the beloved animal through swimming eyes. Roughly she brushed away the tears. She was quite aware of the muddled state of her mind, but an odd longing swept through her just then, and it was too insistent to be ignored. It was a longing to ride Mandy once again through the green black woods down to the river. Who could predict if there would ever be another time?

One last ride. What harm would it do? And she was dressed for it. No one would know Mandy was gone. Everyone was having too much fun, and the party looked as though it would last for hours. She wouldn't go far or stay long.

Without waiting to give it further thought, she ran to Mandy's side, grabbed the reins and holding onto the saddle horn swung herself up in the saddle. Mandy stepped backward a bit, whisking her tail and tossing her head at the feel of the familiar burden.

"How's that, girl? Feel familiar, comfortable?" Mona straightened and cocked her head. Banjo music and laughter rang in her ears, Keith's booming baritone rising above the rest. Stinging with hurt, smarting from frustration, Mona pivoted the mare, nudging her flank and setting her in a westwardly direction. With daylight saving time still in effect, there were hours of sun left. She would have plenty of time to ride, return to the house, tie Mandy up and be on her way without anyone ever knowing she had been there. Returning home tonight with her tail tucked between her legs was a blow she wasn't sure her badly battered pride could take, but she would worry about that when the time came.

Mona rode at a fast gallop, the hammering of Mandy's hooves evoking fond memories. The wind rumpling her long hair gave her the sensation of flying. When she was completely out of sight of the ranch house she slowed the mare and pointed her north, skirting the cedar brakes that ringed the open pastures. Once she had passed through the north pasture gate and had closed it behind her, she was riding through the most untamed part of Keith's property. It was an area he referred to as Goat's End, where the land was so rocky and hilly that goats were turned out to forage among the limestone crags and crevices. It was here that Mona most liked to ride, where the wildlife population was most dense, where the river ran at its swiftest and clearest, where the countryside showed the least signs of human habitation. Carefully selecting her path, she rode until she reached the riverbank.

The autumn rains had done wonders. The river was flowing deep and strong, a far cry from the trickle it had become during summer's awful heat but not the terror it had been during the September flood. Mona reined in, slipped out of the saddle and tethered Mandy to a gnarled live oak. While the mare cropped at the prairie grass, Mona sank to the soft ground and gave in to her thoughts and miseries.

The early October afternoon was quite warm, yet

Mona knew the thin beads of perspiration on her forehead and above her mouth were not caused by heat. She was shaking all over, heartsick. Her eyes burned like fire, her heart felt like lead and the lump in her throat made swallowing difficult. She was sick, physically ill.

So where did she go from here? A rueful laugh escaped her lips. Well, back home for starters. Back home to the humiliation of facing her family after she had announced to one and all that she was going to get married. Back to school, back to concentrating on her fledgling career. Back to all the things that had seemed so important to her in June.

But all that could be borne and would—she fervently hoped—keep her mind occupied. The unbearable part was going back to the emptiness of being without Keith, for she was convinced it was over between them. He would never have gone to another woman if he still loved her.

She supposed she could try to win him back. They had once shared something rare and wonderful, and that was not easily dismissed. She had a powerful weapon in that special rapport that existed between them. It was highly unlikely he would ever feel that with someone else, so Mona suspected that with some effort on her part she could make him remember why he had fallen in love with her in the first place. It might well be that the brunette now dancing with him on the patio was only a casual flirtation.

Mona rested her head on her upraised knees and sighed. Damn him! Why couldn't he have been a little more patient? Why couldn't he have waited one more day? Some birthday this had turned out to be!

She sat there by the riverbank, oblivious to the

passing of time, swallowed up by her personal misery and the sense of loss. Over and over in her mind she tried to pinpoint some exact time when a different course of action on her part would have allowed them to be together. This was all her fault, wasn't it? Surely she could have done something differently.

No, dammit! There was nothing. She had done what she thought was right at the moment. She had been grappling with a dilemma, and she thought Keith had understood. All she had ever asked of him was a little patience and trust and fidelity. Fidelity above all!

And the moment that word popped into her head Mona felt some of the hurt quit her, to be replaced first by resentment, then by anger. Why was she sitting here on the riverbank weeping for a man who obviously wasn't the man she had thought him to be? It hadn't been that long, for heaven's sake! Not even a month. Couldn't a man remain faithful to one woman for a month? Had the situation been reversed, she would have stayed faithful to him. Love, indeed! And she had thought him so special. He wasn't special at all in that respect. One woman was as good as another once the lights were out!

The fire of her spirit flashed and flared, and the more Mona thought about Keith and his houseguest, the more she worked herself into a state of cold fury. She seethed inside. *How dare he!* He had once told her they were already married, that all that was left were the legalities. Well, if that was true then Keith Garrett was an adulterer! And furthermore she intended telling him just that.

With anger came a pumping of adrenaline. Mona jumped to her feet, hauled herself up into the saddle and wheeled Mandy around. "Come on, girl. You and I are going back to that house, and I'm going to give Mr. Garrett a piece of my mind! What do I care if he's embarrassed? If you want to know the truth, I can hardly wait to see the look on his face when I come riding up. Let's arrive at the house from the rear so we can sail right up to the patio. That ought to throw a wet blanket on his little tea party. And when I get through telling him what an unprincipled scoundrel I think he is, I'm going to ask him what the hell right he had to let that...that *woman* ride my mare!''

There were no open pasturelands between the riverbank and the rear of the ranch's headquarters. The going was tough and rocky, but Mandy was sure-footed and knew every inch of her limited universe. Completely caught up in her anger, Mona forgot all the carefully taught lessons of country life. She looked neither up nor down, left nor right, only stared ahead for the sight of the ranch house. Faced with an absence of orders from her rider, Mandy obeyed her instincts and took the most direct route home, following the rough riverbank for a time, then climbing a steep incline.

They had reached level ground when it happened. Mona's only warning was the sound—that dreaded spine-chilling sound made by the interlocking series of rings at the end of a rattlesnake's tail. Curled into a tight coil, the snake was dozing in the late after-noon sun. The chestnut mare and the dark-haired woman had disturbed it, and it was displeased.

There was no time to react, and though it all must have happened in a split second, for a moment Mona had the impression that everything was moving in slow motion. First Mandy's head bolted high in the air and she uttered a loud frantic whinny. Caught off guard, Mona fell backward, out of the saddle, down Mandy's rump, then down, down. Her buttocks hit first, a stunning jolt to her system. Then her back was scraping ground, and her head struck something that felt like rock. The world spun crazily. There was an enormously violent thrashing noise, and words flashed through Mona's mind: "As long as someone knew you were out, not too much time would pass before we came looking for you."

But no one even knows I'm here, she thought, and slipped into black nothingness.

WHEN SHE CAME TO she was aware of warm sun on her face. Then she felt the pain in her head. She struggled to open her eyes, but it was some minutes before she could do so. The sunshine blinded her, so she quickly shut them again. She waited a moment longer, then tried again. This time it was better. Slowly, because it hurt to breathe, it hurt to move, she turned her head. The branches of an ancient oak stretched above her. Mona's eyes traveled down the trunk, and she saw Mandy. The mare neighed, stomped the ground, tossed her head, flopping the loose reins about. *Good girl, good girl. You didn't leave me.*

Mona tried to rise but her weakness wouldn't allow it. She took several deep breaths, trying to muster some strength. It hurt so much to move that at first she was sure she had broken something. Gingerly she wriggled her fingers, moved her arms, bent her knees and satisfied herself that all was in working order. Apparently she was only stunned.

For a moment she had difficulty remembering what had happened, but then it came to her. The snake! That brought Mona to a sitting position quickly, causing a brief flurry of dizziness before her head cleared. Had she been bitten? How would she know? What did a snakebite feel like? She hurt all over, so how could she tell if she had been bitten? Dear God, she wasn't schooled enough in the great outdoors to go out riding alone, especially when no one knew she was around. And wasn't this a fine time to be thinking about that!

Glancing around a bit frantically, her eyes fell on the snake, and she retched. It was the most grotesque sight she had ever seen. The snake's head had been twisted at a forty-five-degree angle, its neck broken. It's mouth was wide open, exposing the whitish interior, and the fangs were bared. Its fat midsection had been crushed to a pulp. ''Agggh!'' Mona cried, shuddered and turned away, revolted. Mandy had stomped the snake to death.

Her only thought was to get herself somehow back up on Mandy, but she was so weak, so laced with pain, she decided to lie back down, simply to lie very still for another moment or two in order to regain her wind and strength. Her head was pounding sickeningly, and the ground beneath her was grassless, just bare earth strewn with shards and slabs of limestone that poked and scraped. There was no telling how many cuts and bruises she had suffered, and she should probably be seen to right away. If the knowledge of that didn't get her on her feet fast, nothing would.

Just then she distinctly felt the ground beneath her vibrate; horses were approaching at a fast gallop.

Again she struggled to get up, but before she could do so running feet reached her and she was being helped. Keith's strong arms were around her shoulders, holding her tightly. Now she was sitting with her face pressed against the smooth cotton of his shirt. She smelled the stimulating fragrance of his after-shave, and for a moment she forgot everything else. He was there and that was all that mattered.

"Mona, my God! What happened? What are you doing here? When I saw you lying on the ground I thought I was going to pass out." His voice throbbed with alarm.

Mona melted against him, momentarily lost in the comfort of his protective arms. It was amazing, the strength she drew from his presence. "The snake...." She pointed but could not look at it again. "It spooked Mandy, and she threw me. I...I guess she stomped it. I don't know. I was out cold. Oh, Keith, do you suppose she's all right?"

Keith's head moved sideways. "Check Mandy, Jim." Only then did Mona realize Jim Browder was there, too.

A few seconds passed. Then Jim said, "I don't see anything, Keith. She got it before it could get her—or Mona. If she's been bitten it must have been on her hooves, and that won't give her any trouble."

"She...she stayed with me," Mona said with wonder. "She just waited until I came to."

"Of course," Keith's voice soothed. "A good riding horse's first instinct is to stay with the rider." Again his head moved to one side, this time in the direction of the smashed snake. "God, he's a mean one! Five feet long if he's an inch. These rains have driven a bunch of those fellows out of their dens, and for your information, Mona, rattlers are just loaded with venom during denning-up season.''

She shuddered. Her mind was slowly becoming clearer, making her more aware of all the pain. "Oh, my head!''

Keith's hand made a gentle inspection of her skull. "You've got a nasty bash on your crown. You must have taken quite a spill. Just a minute.'' He stood up, pulled a handkerchief out of his hip pocket and walked to his horse. Removing a canteen from his saddlebag he moistened the cloth with water and came back to kneel beside Mona. Dabbing gently, he said with a chuckle, "You're going to be flaky by the time you're forty if you keep taking these lumps.''

"How did you know to come looking for me?'' Mona asked, wincing with pain at his ministrations.

"I sent Jim to get Mandy and take her back to the barn, but he came back to tell me she was gone. I went around in front, and lo and behold, there was your car. Jim and I went down to the barn to see if you'd possibly taken Mandy there, but when we couldn't find either of you we decided we'd best come looking for you. Jim remembered how much you liked riding to Goat's End, so. . . . Damned good thing we did, too. What the devil do you mean riding off like that without telling anyone? I thought I taught you better than that.''

Abruptly Mona was brought back to reality, remembering what had sent her riding off in the first place. Angrily she shoved his hand aside. "I'm all right now. You can stop it. And no lectures please. I don't think I could endure it.''

Puzzled by the tone of her voice, Keith sat back on his haunches and stared at her thoughtfully. Her

mouth was compressed in a taut angry line. Her eyes
were dull and cloudy. At a loss to understand her
sudden shift into this black mood, he quietly asked,
"What's the matter, Mona?"

"Nothing!" she snapped. "Not a thing."

"I don't believe you."

"Tough!"

"I think that bump scrambled your brains. Look
at me, Mona!"

Steeling herself, she turned to him and tried to
feign indifference. It took all the control she could
summon up. Looking into those questioning gray
eyes Mona felt a magnetic pull drawing her to him.
Body rigid, eyes challenging, she said, "Well, I'm
looking at you."

Sensing that something very complicated was
whirling around in Mona's head, Keith spoke sharply
to Jim Browder. "Jim, lead Mandy back to the
barn."

Instantly Jim was mounted. "Yes, sir!"

"No!" Mona cried, struggling to rise to her feet.
"Wait! I'll take her back."

But Jim had orders from the boss. He rode off,
leading Mandy, and Keith pulled Mona back to the
ground. He was on his knees, grabbing her by the
shoulders. "Now, by God, you're going to tell
me what this is all about! What are you doing here in
the first place?"

Mona shrugged out of his grasp. "Strangely
enough, I wanted to see you. Also strangely enough,
I didn't think I needed to give you any warning. I can
see I was wrong."

His bewilderment was genuine, she could tell that
much. He wasn't faking it. But of course he had no

idea she'd seen him with the brunette. "Mona...
Mona," Keith said, spreading out his hands in a
gesture of confusion. "Why are we behaving like
this? Why aren't you in my arms?"

Mona's mouth dropped open, and her eyes widened. "Oh, I don't believe you! And to think that
people say *I'm* audacious! You have all the nerve in
the world, I must say. Now just leave me alone and
get back to your party."

Keith rocked back on his heels and stared at her
blankly. "My what? Mona, you're not making any
sense."

"Just leave me alone!"

"Surely you don't think I'm going to ride off and
leave you out here in the middle of nowhere without
a mount. Come on, we'll ride back together on my
horse."

"Oh, that ought to thrill your lady friend to
death!" Mona's voice dripped with sarcasm.

"Who?"

"Come off it, Keith! I saw you dancing with her!"

She refused to look at him, so she could not see the
expression on his face, but she heard the quick intake
of his breath, and when he spoke she detected a hint
of mocking amusement in his tone. "So...you saw
me with Katie."

"Is that her name? Yes, I saw you," she said tiredly, sore and hurting both physically and emotionally.
"You looked as though you were having a marvelous
time."

"Oh, I was, I was. Katie's a great gal, a barrel of
fun!"

"You've obviously danced with her before. You
were great."

"Yeah, that's what everyone tells us. Katie and I have danced together hundreds of times."

Hundreds? My God, how long had he known her? "Good," she said, her calm voice not betraying the churning sickness inside her. "So you must be anxious to get back. Now please. . .go!"

"But, Mona, as I pointed out to you, you don't have a mount. It's an awfully long walk."

She couldn't argue with that. Sighing deeply, she relented. "All right, Keith, all right. Take me back to the ranch. But let's go by way of the west pasture. Then you can drop me off at my car, and then I'm going home."

"But I'd like for you to join the, er, party. I'd like for you to meet Katie. I think you would like her a lot."

Mona clenched her teeth together tightly. How could he say such a thing to her? He was needling her, getting an enormous kick out of all this, damn him! Still, she exercised self-control. "I don't think I'm up to meeting Katie this afternoon, thanks just the same. Now if you don't mind I'd like you to take me to my car and let me go home."

"Not on your life, Mona. You're not going anywhere until I say you can."

She swung at him blindly then, but he anticipated it. One arm shot out and captured her wrist, and he pulled her to him. Caught completely by surprise Mona fell against him with a thud, and the impact sent them both sprawling. In one swift easy maneuver Keith pulled her under him and slung one leg across her stomach, successfully imprisoning her with his body. She struggled valiantly but in vain, for she was powerless against his strength, and the spill she had taken earlier had left her weaker than usual. Acquiescing because there was nothing else she could do, Mona stopped fighting and gulped in air in an effort to bring her labored breathing back to normal.

Feeling the relaxation of her body, Keith raised his head to look down at her. Glints like steel danced in his eyes; their corners were crinkled. To Mona's utter astonishment she saw that he was grinning from ear to ear like the Cheshire cat.

"What's so damned funny?" she demanded, fuming, suddenly aware how much better she had felt in the past few minutes, how Keith's vibrancy had made her forget the pain in her head and muscles, how he had actually made it barely noticeable.

"You," Keith said. "You're funny...and adorable...and beautiful. And jealous! *Especially* jealous."

Hot with anger, frustrated and shamed because her emotions had been so transparent, Mona twisted beneath him. "And you're crazy!"

"Yes. Crazy about you." The rumble of laughter began deep in his chest and exploded from his mouth in a whoop. "Oh, Mona, I'm a lousy actor. I can't keep this up. Darling, I'm so damned glad to see you."

His mouth came down hard on hers, and to her dismay Mona found herself responding to his kiss. It had been a week, only a week since she had kissed him last, but it seemed years. His warmth seeped into her veins. She smelled the wonderful male aroma of him. His very nearness made her heartbeat quicken. What was this strange power he had over her? She was furious with him, heartsick over his infidelity, yet all he had to do was touch her and she grew all fluttery inside, perfectly willing to lie under him, to part her mouth and accept his probing tongue. Despite her abrasions, her traitorous body was wantonly begging his hands to plunder, which they did with delighted abandon. She made no attempt to halt the fingers that were fumbling with the buttons of her blouse, and when the hand that slipped inside encountered the confining brassiere, she heard a choked groan.

"Oh, God! Why do you bother with this damned thing?" he muttered, then pushed the strap off her shoulder to allow his fingers access to her soft breast. His thumb paused on the telltale hardened nipple. "We can't hide our emotions, can we, Mona? Our bodies give us away."

A tremor raced through her. How far did he intend to go? Surely he wasn't going to make love to her here on the ground. Someone might come along at any minute looking for them. And what about the raven-haired beauty back at the house? What on earth was he going to do about her? Wondering about this cleared her fogged senses. She wrenched her mouth free and turned her head. "You'd... you'd best be getting back to your...your friend, Keith."

"Only if you come with me," he drawled lazily.

Mona bit her lip. "I can't...and I don't know why you would ask me to do such a thing."

Keith's searching mouth found her earlobe. His lips closed over it and he nibbled gently. His warm breath in her ear made Mona shiver. "Because," he said, "I thought you might like to meet your future sister-in-law."

Mona's breath caught in her throat. She turned her

head to stare at him wide-eyed. His mouth was curved into a crooked smile, and she could hear another rumble of laughter in his chest. "Wh-who?"

"You little idiot! Katie is my sister! She and Ted and the kids are visiting from El Paso. How could you have thought for a minute there would be another woman?"

"I . . . well, I . . . ." Mona felt her face flush. Complete comprehension had not yet dawned on her. "When I heard . . . I mean, her suitcase in . . . in your room, I thought . . . ."

"Hmm. Eavesdroppers often hear more than they bargained for. Kate and Ted have my room, and I'm going to stay in the master bedroom, in *your* room. I told you, Mona—you are the one, the only one. I was prepared to wait for you forever. Nobody has what we do, honey. Nobody."

"Oh, Keith!" Her body went limp, absolutely limp. Her hands crept up his chest to lock behind his neck, and a feeling of complacent well-being swept through her. Keith's hands began stroking her, bringing her both a soft peace and a wild yearning. It was like coming out of a cold night into a warm room. This time when his urgent mouth descended she rose halfway to meet it.

"Oh, Mona," Keith groaned as he pulled his mouth away, "I've been so damned miserable without you."

"Same here," she said shakily. "I've robbed us of a lot of precious hours, Keith. I'm sure I don't deserve you."

"Probably not," he teased. "But you're the only one I want, so it appears I'm stuck with you."

"I'll make it up to you," she promised. "Every single minute."

"I'll hold you to that. And you can start tonight."
Then his face sobered as something occurred to him.
"Dammit!" he muttered. "I finally have you here
with me, and that house is crawling with kinfolk."

Mona laughed softly. "It doesn't matter, just as
long as we're in the same house together again. I'll
sleep on the sofa."

"Like hell! You'll sleep with me, where you belong, where you've belonged for a very long time."

"But, Keith...your sister and her husband. What
will they think?"

"Who cares? And speaking of kinfolk, you're
here, so that must mean that your family...."

Mona nodded. "They know. They all know now."

"Thank God!" His forefinger traced the gentle
curve of her mouth. "Was it bad, darling?"

"No. Dad was quite wonderful, and Claire..,
well, Claire was surprising. As a matter of fact, I accomplished quite a bit of fencemending today. I'll
tell you all about it, but first...kiss me again."

He complied expertly, giving her a long thorough
kiss that seemed to melt her bones. Mona clung to
him, wondering how she had lived without this for so
long. Keith was everything. The fear and emptiness
were gone forever. Such a contrast between this calm
serenity and her earlier agitation.

With his arms Keith levered himself up and away
from her. He jumped to his feet, pulling her with
him. Then he pulled her into his arms again and held
her with consummate tenderness.

"I almost forgot—happy birthday."

"The roses were lovely, darling."

"Any woman who can manage to smell like roses
even when she's just been thrown from a horse de-

serves to be surrounded by them. Now, come on, sweetheart,'' Keith urged, rebuttoning her blouse, ''let me take you to the house, where you can clean up and we can assess any damage. How do you feel?''

''Dirty, bruised and tired.''

''Well, then, we'll just have to retire early tonight.''

MONA WAS IMMEDIATELY TAKEN with Katie, who resembled Keith to a startling degree. Had she taken the time earlier she might have noticed the remarkable resemblance. How was it possible for two people to look so much alike and one be so undeniably masculine while the other was so softly feminine? Ted Harding, Katie's husband, was a quiet self-effacing man, the complete opposite of his vivacious wife. Katie definitely had Keith's forceful personality, and there was a closeness between brother and sister that was heartwarming to see. Mona could only devoutly hope that she and Claire might develop something of that in time. At least they had taken the first positive steps.

The first order of business, everyone agreed, was to determine if Mona had suffered anything in her fall from Mandy that would require a doctor's attention. But save for a cut on her arm, the bump on her head and some dreadfully sore places that would probably turn into bruises, she seemed none the worse for wear. She reveled in the luxury of a hot bath, shampooed her hair and dressed in a cranberry-red jump suit that hugged her slim figure in all the right places. By the time she joined the others for predinner cocktails, she could almost forget that the afternoon's accident had happened.

Her appearance in the living room elicited a low whistle from Keith, and all evening long Mona could feel his eyes on her. They shone with love...and lust, too, but that could never be offensive. Mona was itching with a bit of lust herself. And even though both of them joined in the sparkling animated conversation around the dinner table, their absorption in each other was total.

Mona politely inquired about Katie's and Ted's children and was told they were with their grandfather in the city.

"Furthermore," Katie said, astutely sizing up the situation between Mona and Keith, "I think we're going to have to change our plans for this evening, Keith. Dad swears he enjoys having the kids around, but I know what a nuisance they can be after a few hours. I think Ted and I will drive on back to the city tonight and give dad a break."

Ted opened his mouth to protest but was quickly and effectively silenced by his wife's warning glance. So shortly after dinner Katie and Ted gathered up their belongings and left, promising to see both Keith and Mona in the city the following week.

"Thank God for Katie!" Keith exclaimed when they departed.

"I feel rather guilty about ruining their plans," Mona said with chagrin.

"I don't," Keith said without a qualm. "Besides, we haven't ruined anything for them. Katie much prefers the city. She only comes out here to River View to please me...and to feast on Mamie's cooking."

By the time Mamie came to say good-night, Mona's heart was thudding with excitement, thinking of the long lovely night ahead. The blood throbbed in her temples. She watched mutely as Keith moved about the house, turning off lights, checking door locks. Then he came to her and without a word scooped her up into his arms and carried her down the hall to the bedroom where she had slept all summer.

Setting her on her feet, Keith closed and locked the door, then led her by the hand across the room to the bed. He jerked down the spread with one swift motion, then the top sheet, and he looked down at her with heavy-lidded eyes that were dark with passion. Mona returned his look with uncontained joy. Her arms slid up around his neck as his mouth descended masterfully. She parted her soft lips to receive his assaulting kiss, and there was the familiar eruption of passion in her loins. A wild rushing sensation swirled through her as Keith's big gentle hands began their sensitive explorations. Her shoulders, arms, breasts, thighs burned as he stroked her through her clothing.

"How do you get this thing off?" he asked in a choked whisper.

"The belt first. . . then the zipper. That's all."

He unzipped to her navel, then his hands slipped inside to cup and fondle, caress the soft mounds that were unhampered by a bra. The nipples leaped to his touch, eliciting a low moan and a smile from him. Her body's response told him how much she wanted him. He pushed the jump suit down her hips, catching her flimsy panties at the same time. Mona wiggled in an effort to help him, and the garments fell in a heap on the floor. She stepped out of them and stood before him, proud of the look on his face, pleased that the sight of her body could inspire such wonder and awe, such adoration.

Quickly he eased her onto the bed. Mona's head sank into the pillow, and she watched as he tugged impatiently at his own clothing. She drank in the sight of his vital splendid masculinity. It fascinated her to see the corded muscles of his shoulders as his arms moved to rid himself of the hindrances. When he sat on the edge of the bed, shirtless, to remove his boots, she gently stroked his broad back with trembling fingers, loosening his belt for him. Then he stood up and pulled off his jeans, and at last he stood over her, powerful and urgent.

"You're beautiful...beautiful!" Keith murmured, his eyes wild with passion.

"So are you," she said and pulled him to her. The bed sagged with his weight as he sank beside her. His hands reached, found, then raked her gently, performing their sacred love ritual.

"I'm not going to let you out of my sight until you finally belong to me—you realize that, I hope," Keith said softly.

"I belong to you now, Keith. I have from the very first day I spent with you."

He gathered her to him tightly. His coarse chest hair brushed against her straining breasts, he drank from her lips like a man dying of thirst and their previous lovemaking paled by comparison. His flesh was warm and hard under her hands, all rippling muscles and taut smooth skin. His body claimed hers; his potency devoured her. Mona's stomach cramped into a tight coil of desperate desire, a desire he assuaged perfectly. They moved together in complete accord, each sensitive to the other's needs. It would always amaze Mona that even at the height of his own frenzied passion he could think of her, of her satisfaction.

With the blood coursing hotly through her veins, Mona responded to his sensuous maneuvers, reveled in them. Expertly, with his hands and mouth, with his body, he carried her along on a voyage of rediscovery. Dear God, how had she lived without him so long? Her hands explored every inch of him, loving, remembering. She brushed her lips tantalizingly across her taut stomach and felt him tremble at the contact. She was discovering untapped depths of her own sexuality that staggered her. Was there no end to the kaleidoscope of emotions he could arouse in her? Her mind reeled and stumbled from new sensation heaped upon new sensation.

Suddenly her fingernails bit into the flesh of his shoulders. ''Please, Keith....''

Her words seemed to galvanize him into action. They both could stand it no longer. With an agonized groan he brought her to the ultimate peak of fulfillment before seeking his own release, and their mingled cries were smothered in a kiss that consumed them both.

THEIR DESCENT from the mountaintop was a gradual thing. They lay in bed side by side, sharing soft kisses. Mona was submerged in contentment. Her limbs had no feeling, and a wondrous peace had settled over her. In all the world there was only one man, this one! And all the talk, all the books, all the probing and analyzing and discussing—all of it came down to this: a man and a woman, together in love.

Mona sighed deeply and stirred in his arms. Then she snuggled closer, and a self-satisfied smile played on her lips. ''What a birthday this has been! I know it's one I won't soon forget. And when I think how awful I felt this morning! But the worst part of it, the absolutely worst moment of my whole life was when I saw you twirling that gorgeous creature around out there on the patio. I thought I really had done it—lost you because of my sense of loyalty to my family."

His fingers played with the long dark tendrils of her hair. "Ah, Mona...I handled that pretty badly. I should have given you more support instead of dwelling on my own disappointment so much. It's really quite a wonderful thing to have such a deep attachment to family. I hope our children will feel as strongly about us. Men tend to get too caught up in their own desires and needs and don't like to be thwarted. I've been a man with a problem for weeks, but under no circumstances would there have been another woman, sweetheart—not while there was any chance for us."

Mona rubbed her face in his mat of chest hair and pressed herself closer to him. "You're really a wonderful man, did you know that?"

"Of course," he said with affected seriousness. "I've known that for years."

"Do you want to hear what Stephanie Means said about you?"

"What did Stephanie Means say about me?"

"She said you're the kind of man who never would give his wife a Crock-Pot for her birthday."

Keith laughed and hugged her. "Well," Mona prodded, "was she right?"

"Probably. Red roses are more my style. And that reminds me...." He kissed the tip of her nose, then released her and threw back the covers. Mona watched as he crossed the room to the dresser, opened a drawer and removed something. Moonlight filtering in through the partially closed blinds fell on his naked body, illuminating its rippling contours, and Mona thrilled at the sight of the male body that belonged to her, only to her. She was filled with a warm lazy languor, a wondrous serenity. She stretched and purred like a kitten, then held up the sheet to allow him to slip in beside her once more.

He propped himself up on one elbow. "And this, too, is my style," he said, and handed her a small box, a jeweler's box. Quickly Mona sat up and took it. Opening it with trembling fingers, she stared down at the matched pair of diamond rings nestled against black velvet. Her eyes glistened, and she felt the tears come. "Oh, Keith...they're beautiful! Such rings! I've never seen such rings!"

He removed the engagement ring from the box. "When you told me when your birthday was, I bought them, hoping I would be able to present them to you on your twenty-first. The other one will have to wait until next week when we get married, but this one is for now." He slipped it on her finger. "Hmm...a bit loose."

"Just a little," Mona whispered, mesmerized by the sparkling gems.

Keith encased her small hand in his and lifted it to his lips. "Such slender fingers. I...good grief, Mona...are you crying?"

She gulped. "I...I always cry...when I'm h-h-happy."

Keith chuckled. "I hate to say this, but I hope you cry your eyes out for the next fifty years or so years."

He placed the box containing the wedding ring on the bedside table, then turned to her. Mona wrapped her arms around him and together they sank back onto the pillows. As his mouth closed over hers, as their bodies once again became one, she thought, *even after living with him for half a century I'll never, ever get enough of him.*

MONA WAS AWAKENED by the sound of Keith's voice. "Wake up, wake up. I want to show you something." His warm lips were brushing her forehead.

Slowly Mona opened her eyes. The room was pitch-black, and the moonlight streaming into the room told her it was nowhere near morning. With her hand she felt for Keith, but he wasn't lying beside her. She turned in bed and saw that he was standing over her, a wide grin on his face. She bolted upright, clutching the sheets around her bare breasts.

"Ah, you're lovely like this," Keith said softly. "All tousled and sleepy eyed."

"Wh-what time is it?"

"Two o'clock."

"A.M.?" she cried incredulously.

"Yes."

"Why are you dressed at two o'clock in the morning?" she asked, eyeing the jeans and shirt he had been wearing the previous evening.

"I want to show you something. Hurry up. Get dressed. Where is that red thing you were wearing earlier?"

Mona yawned, completely puzzled by all this. "Probably still on the floor where we left it."

Keith looked around, spied the garment and picked it up. Holding it, he said, "Hop out of bed, sweetheart, and slip this on."

"What in the world...?" But she slid out from under the sheets, turned her back to him and stepped into the jump suit, then thrust her arms into the sleeves. Turning, she zipped up the suit and fastened the belt. "Will I need shoes?"

"Yep. Where are they?"

"There are some sneakers in the closet."

Keith got them for her, and Mona sat on the edge of the bed and put them on. "Why so mysterious, Keith? Where are we going?"

"You'll see. Ready?"

She nodded and got to her feet, then took his hand and followed him through the hushed darkened house. Keith led the way through the patio doors, past the pool area and down the gentle rise toward the barn. Soft light shone through the open door. At the barn they paused. "Bess foaled tonight," Keith explained. "If you've never seen a new foal, you're in for a treat."

Inside the barn, Mona's nostrils were assailed by the aromas of sweet hay and pungent manure and kerosene from the overhead lanterns. The door to Bess's stall was open, and the two cowboys who had served as midwives leaned solicitously over the mare resting on her birth bed of clean straw. But at center stage was a bandy-legged foal who was valiantly trying to find its sea legs. One spindle leg shot out and down it went, only to struggle to its feet again. In a short time all four legs would be moving in synchronization, but now they were still completely uncoordinated.

"Oh!" Mona let out a gasp of delight. "It's all head and legs!"

"We've got us a fine new filly, Mona," Keith said, pleased.

"Mandy's granddaughter!" Mona murmured in awe.

"And I want you to have her. I want you to raise her from foal to mare. She'll be weaned in six months, and I'll teach you how to halterbreak her. Then when Mandy's too old and has to be put out to pasture, you'll have this one trained as your mount."

"Oh, Keith, I think I'm going to cry again!"

Born ravenously hungry, the little filly wanted its mother, and Bess, now on her feet, was giving her new foal ready access to food. The filly instinctively turned its head under its mother's soft underbelly and suckled noisily.

"She's not as light as Bess or Royal Blue. Some of Mandy's coloring has come out in this little lady. She's a sorrel, for sure."

"Oh, she's. . . beautiful!"

Keith chuckled. "Well, not now. But she soon will be. And I guess since she's going to be yours, Mona, you should have the privilege of naming her."

Mona stared at the little foal with a swelling heart. The offspring of Queen Bess and Royal Blue. Royalty all the way. "I think she should be named Princess. Yes, it has to be Princess."

"Then Princess it is. And just think, darling. . . when we have a child old enough for a horse, we'll be breeding Princess."

The never ending cycle of ranch life. It was a wonder to Mona, and right then and there she vowed to begin reading up on the complexities of horse breeding. Perhaps Bess and Royal Blue would found a splendid new line.

She slipped her arms around Keith's waist. And she and Keith would be responsible for bringing the fourth generation of Garretts to River View. Merely thinking about it made Mona's heart swell with pride. And why not? Was there anything wrong with dreaming of founding a dynasty?

Keith was looking down at her, no doubt wondering at the thoughts churning inside her head. Mona smiled a smug smile. The wide sweep of Keith's shoulder made a comfortable place for her to rest her very contented head.

CHAPTER SIXTEEN

"WHAT?" CLAIRE SCREECHED. "You're not coming to the Fourth of July barbecue? Mona, you and Keith have to come! It won't be the same without you."

The two sisters were having coffee on the terrace of the Garrett apartment. Already the morning sun was becoming quite warm, and Mona pushed her chair deeper into the shade. "Oh, Claire, I'm afraid I won't be up to it. Look at me! I feel like a baby elephant. I'll swear this blessed event is going to turn out to be triplets."

Claire giggled. "You really don't look all that big to me. And, my God, you aren't just going to sit around this apartment like a hermit for the next two weeks, are you? Time will pass faster if you're moving around, staying busy."

"I'll be more inclined to listen to all your marvelous advice, Claire, when you've been through a pregnancy of your own," Mona said dryly. She shifted her weight and rubbed at the small of her back. She had been plagued with a nagging backache for two days now, and she was acutely uncomfortable. But she couldn't complain. Her pregnancy had been a marvelously easy one. She supposed she could put up with a little discomfort during these remaining few weeks. "To tell you the truth, there are days when I feel as though I could lick tigers with my bare hands...and others when it's all I can do to get out of bed. I'd hate to promise to come to the barbecue and then have it turn out to be one of my bad days."

"But the barbecue on the fourth is so special, and we're having such a mild summer. I don't think we've hit ninety degrees yet, have we? Usually the fourth is a scorcher! If you don't attend the barbecue, won't Keith be disappointed?"

Mona laughed. "Claire, Keith Garrett is so caught up in this expected baby that if I asked to be carried around on satin pillows and spood-fed, he'd do it."

Claire nodded absently. "Everyone's excited. That's the reason we didn't go to Palm Springs this summer. None of us could stand the thought of not being around when the first grandchild appears on the scene."

"Baloney!" Mona retorted. "That might be the reason mom and dad didn't go, but the reason you didn't go is Alan Palmer. How is the dear boy, by the way? I haven't seen him in a month or more."

"Busy, busy, busy. He's in New York now, making arrangements for an exhibit there. He wanted me to go with him, but it was such a hurry-up trip. Hardly worth the trouble of getting ready for it."

"I noticed that the old Palmer mansion is up for sale. Is Alan getting a new place?"

"Sort of. He's got a studio with a bed and a kitchenette. I've discovered he needs very little when he's working—just great stretches of uninterrupted time. When he's not working he stays at my place."

Mona arched an eyebrow. "Oh? Does mom know about this?"

Claire looked at her sister and shot her a lopsided grin. "She knows, I think. She just doesn't say anything about it. And you know mama. . . if she doesn't acknowledge it, it doesn't exist.''

Mona lifted the coffee cup to her lips and peered over its rim. ''I keep expecting you to show up one of these days to announce wedding bells are to be rung.''

Claire grimaced uncertainly. ''Oh, Mona. . . I don't know. Alan's mentioned it, more in a 'wonder-if-you-and-I-should' way than anything. I think we're both afraid.''

''Afraid?''

''Yes. We're just having such a damned good time together. I think we're both afraid that getting married would spoil it.''

''Oh, Claire, you couldn't be more wrong!'' Mona cried. ''It's better when you're married. . . so much better!''

Claire leaned forward and propped her elbows on the table. ''But not everyone has what you and Keith have, Mona. Hardly anyone does, as a matter of fact. My God, you're both so insane about each other it's embarrassing to watch. Tell me the truth, have the two of you ever had an argument? I mean a real argument where one of you stalked out of the room in a huff?''

Mona thought about it. ''Oh, a few animated discussions, maybe. And he made me cry once. It was over something so trivial, but I was in the early months of this pregnancy, so the tears had more to do with my condition than anything Keith said or did. No, I guess Keith and I have never had a major argument—certainly nothing that made either of us stalk out of room.''

''See what I mean?'' Claire said knowingly. ''Tell me, is his father as thrilled over the baby as mama and daddy are?''

"Simon? Oh, he's a dear, very solicitous. But you have to remember that this isn't a first for him. Keith's sister has three children. If you want to know someone who is thrilled, it's Aunt Beth. She stops by about twice a week and clucks over me like a mother hen."

Claire sighed. "Dear Aunt Beth. It sure was a surprise to find out I had an aunt at this late date. She's so different from mama. I'll bet Beth was something of a scamp when she was younger. I can't imagine those two springing from the same family tree."

Mona smiled but said nothing. She took another sip of coffee, then asked, "Tell me, Claire, do she and mom see much of each other?"

"Not a lot. I get the distinct impression that mama has to work very hard to warm to her sister. They were apart for so many years, you know, and they seem to have nothing in common. But it's definitely cozier now than it was when Beth first started coming to see us. In those days mama was very correct, and when mama's being correct she's oh so frosty." Claire paused and pursed her lips. "You know, there's one thing that puzzles me: daddy seems to fade into the woodwork whenever Beth comes to visit, and he's usually right in the center of things. But then, I guess he wants to give the two sisters every chance to become reacquainted. I do sense that he's enormously relieved that they're at least trying to get closer. You know how he is about family."

"Do I ever!" Mona exclaimed. "He bought that little house for me, had it completely renovated, and now it's just sitting there, waiting until I can go to work. I would have forgiven dad a remark or two about all the money he's invested in turning me into an interior decorator, only to have me 'get with child.'

Aside from Madeline Porter's town house, I've done very little about my career, but there hasn't been a word from dad. Actually, I'll be eager to get busy within a year—at least part-time.''

"Well, you really haven't *had* time. Good heavens, you were already pregnant when you graduated. You and Keith sure didn't waste any time." Claire stood up. "I'm going to get another cup of coffee. Want some?"

Mona shook her head. "No thanks. One's my limit until Junior shows up."

Claire went inside the apartment, and Mona watched her retreating figure, reflecting on her sister's amazing metamorphosis. Claire was so much more serious, so much more serene. Alan had been good for her, and that would have to be one for the books—those two jet-setters settling each other down. Mona was almost certain that a psychologist could write an award-winning paper on the relationship between Claire Lowery and Alan Palmer.

Mona leaned back in her chair and let the warm morning breeze rumple her hair. Her hands rested on her swollen belly, and she felt her baby's violent kicking. The baby seemed as eager for the birth as Mona was. She churned with restless anticipation. She could hardly wait to see her baby, to hold it, feed it, kiss it. She had a feeling she was going to be a foolish mother who loved doing all the silly things people were inclined to do around babies. This baby was going to be inundated, surrounded, overwhelmed with love. Keith was almost simpleminded with gloating expectation. He had purchased enough baby paraphernalia for three sets of twins, and if the baby was a boy, Mona was sure he would be presented with a regulation football and helmet on his first birthday. And if it was a girl...oh, God! Keith would go mad over a daughter! A little girl would turn him into her slave in no time at all.

Mona smiled. She was happier than anyone had a right to be, she thought. These past ten months had been the nearest thing to pure bliss that anyone could expect to find on earth. Keith was thoughtful, considerate, a stimulating companion and a superlative lover. Once her body had begun to swell with their child he had begun pampering her outrageously. If he'd had his way, Mona feared he would have locked her in a sterile vault until the baby was born.

Now she sighed and stretched her arms high above her head. A few days earlier she had been bustling around, trying to find something to do, seemingly imbued with the strength and energy of ten people; today she was caught up in a listless lassitude. Her glance kept straying to her watch, and she realized she was timing all the peculiar twitches and twinges she had been experiencing since the evening before. The last one had been quite sharp. But the baby wasn't due for two weeks, and first babies tended to be late rather than early, didn't they? Surely all these funny little sensations weren't heralding the onset of labor.

At that moment it happened again, and she gasped. Looking at her watch she saw that only ten minutes had elapsed since the last one. They were definitely occurring at more frequent intervals. If this continued....

Claire returned, carrying a steaming cup of coffee. She sat down and began filling Mona in on local gossip. It often amazed Mona that her sister could be privy to so much intimate information. The young people with whom Claire and Alan associated were apparently very frank about their love lives. Claire knew who was going with whom, who was splitting up and for what reason, even who was sleeping with whom. It was the one Kitty-like aspect of Claire's personality that had not changed one iota. Her sister loved nothing better than speculating on the actions and motives of all her friends.

Mona listened with polite interest, but her thoughts were all on her own physical condition. Two more of the peculiar twinges gripped her, again ten minutes apart. This couldn't be it, she thought. She had expected something much more dramatic. She had had cramps that hurt worse than this did.

When the next one occurred seven minutes later, she conceded that the possibility of labor definitely existed. She interrupted her sister's monologue. "Excuse me, Claire. I have a phone call to make."

Inside the apartment she put in a call to her doctor, recited her symptoms, and he agreed that she should go to the hospital. Mona returned to the terrace. "Claire, I'm going to put some things in a suitcase. I think I might be going into labor, and the doctor agrees. You're going to have to take me to the hospital."

Claire's eyes widened, and she jumped to her feet. "Oh, no, Mona! You can't! Mama and daddy are at the lake for the weekend...and Alan is out of town...."

Mona marched to the bedroom with Claire hard on her heels. "I don't need mama or daddy or Alan, thank you."

"Then where's Keith? Let me call him."

Mona took out the suitcase she had purchased for

the occasion and began packing. "Keith's at a meeting in Forth Worth this morning. And it's very important...has to do with a multimillion-dollar government contract. The company has been working on it for months. So I don't want him notified until after one o'clock."

Claire was frantic. "Mona, you can't mean that! Please let me get in touch with Keith!"

"No," Mona said firmly. "Not until one o'clock. Then you'll have to call his secretary. I don't have the slightest idea where the meeting is, but Mrs. Jacobs could track Keith down if he were on an Arctic expedition. Now don't call her before one, Claire. Promise me. There's absolutely nothing Keith can do but wait and worry. Dr. Peters is very much against fathers cluttering up the labor rooms and delivery rooms. Oh, get that look off your face! No doubt Keith will get to the hospital before the baby is born anyway." She snapped the suitcase shut.

"Oh, Mona, this is terrible! How can you do this to me? I don't know the first thing about having a baby!"

Mona smiled. "Neither do I...but all you have to do is drive me to the hospital, Claire. The baby and the doctor will do the rest. Now pull yourself together and let's go!"

IT WAS NOT a difficult birth, but in the way of first babies, Emily Anne Garrett was in no great hurry to present herself to the waiting world. Even so, she was almost an hour old when a harried and anxious Keith entered Mona's room. He approached her bed with some apprehension, but when she raised her exultant eyes to him he relaxed immediately.

He bent over to place a light kiss on her damp forehead. "Oh, Mona, as usual you performed superbly. God, I'm sorry I wasn't here! Claire told Mrs. Jacobs you insisted I not be informed until after one o'clock. You're as audacious as ever!"

"Claire talks too much," Mona said, smiling and taking his hand. "Did you get the contract?"

"Yes."

"Then I did the right thing," she said with a note of satisfaction.

"Was it very bad, darling?"

"No, no. But 'labor' is a good word for it. I'm so tired. Keith, have you seen her?"

"Yes. . . and she's gorgeous, like her mother. I wonder if she's going to smell like roses when she grows up."

"Kiss me," Mona commanded.

He complied, warmly and tenderly. Then Mona clutched at his arm. "Now lie down beside me and hold me."

Keith glanced anxiously toward the door. "I'm not sure if I should, darling. There's a head nurse out there who would intimidate Attila the Hun."

"Oh, to hell with her!" Mona said. With great effort she moved her weary body aside to make room for him.

Keith eased himself onto the bed, stretched full-length beside her and carefully, as though he were handling the finest crystal, gathered her to him. They lay together for several long silent moments while Mona drew on his strength and warmth. His steady heartbeat under her palm was soothing and comforting. A tranquillity of a sort she could never have imagined washed over her.

Keith kissed her temple. "Your mother and father should be here in a couple of hours, sweetheart. Claire called them. And she called Beth, and I called Mamie. You're quite the center of attention today."

"I am so full of love for you that I think I could cry," she whispered.

"I know the feeling."

Suddenly the door to the room flew open, and a bulk of starched white marched in. Horrified eyes regarded the two figures on the bed. "Good heavens, Mr. Garrett!" the nurse cried. "Visitors are not even allowed to sit on the beds. What are you doing?"

"I'm holding my wife," Keith said, not moving.

"This is strictly against rules. You must get up!"

"But she wants me here with her," Keith insisted.

"Mr. Garrett, your wife needs her rest."

"She is resting. She was almost asleep."

"Please let him stay," Mona pleaded groggily.

"No, no, not now. Mrs. Garrett, I want you to sleep for a while, and then you're going to get up and take a shower. Mr. Garrett, you may return and have dinner with your wife at five, if you wish, but right now you must leave! Those are the rules!"

Resigned, Keith rolled off the bed and stood up. "Well, we don't want to tamper with the rules, do we?" He bent to kiss Mona. "All right, my love. Five o'clock it is. Sleep now. Rest on your laurels. Can I bring you anything from home?"

Mona opened her eyes and gave him her most shining and triumphant smile. "No, darling. I have everything. Simply everything." And she sighed happily at the truth of those words.

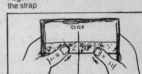